THE AVON

Four years old and better than ever!

We're celebrating our fourth anniversary...and thanks to you, our loyal readers, "The Avon Romance" is stronger and more exciting than ever! You've been telling us what you're looking for in top-quality historical romance—and we've been delivering it, month after wonderful month.

Since 1982, Avon has been launching new writers of exceptional promise—writers to follow in the matchless tradition of such Avon superstars as Kathleen E. Woodiwiss, Johanna Lindsey, Shirlee Busbee and Laurie McBain. Distinguished by a ribbon motif on the front cover, these books were quickly discovered by romance readers everywhere and dubbed "the ribbon books."

Every month "The Avon Romance" has continued to deliver the best in historical romance. Sensual, fast-paced stories by new writers (and some favorite repeats like Linda Ladd!) guarantee reading *without* the predictable characters and plots of formula romances.

"The Avon Romance"—our promise of superior, unforgettable historical romance. Thanks for making us such a dazzling success!

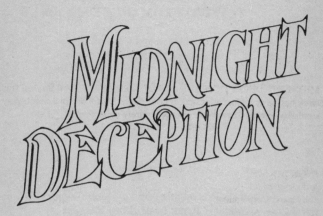

MIDNIGHT DECEPTION

LINDSEY HANKS

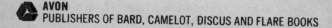

AVON
PUBLISHERS OF BARD, CAMELOT, DISCUS AND FLARE BOOKS

MIDNIGHT DECEPTION is an original publication of Avon Books. This work has never before appeared in book form. This work is a novel. Any similarity to actual persons or events is purely coincidental.

AVON BOOKS
A division of
The Hearst Corporation
105 Madison Avenue
New York, New York 10016

Copyright © 1987 by Georgia Pierce and Linda Chesnutt
Published by arrangement with the authors
Library of Congress Catalog Card Number: 86-92049
ISBN: 0-380-75273-5

First Avon Printing: June 1987

AVON TRADEMARK REG. U.S. PAT. OFF. AND IN OTHER COUNTRIES, MARCA REGISTRADA, HECHO EN U.S.A.

Printed in the U.S.A.

K–R   10 9 8 7 6 5 4 3 2 1

To Jeanne Womac . . . because we care.

Special thanks . . .
To Sonny, because he cared enough to give
his support from Day 1.

—G.P.

To Bill, for his love and understanding.

—L.C.

Chapter 1

New Orleans, 1836

A warm, jasmine-scented breeze drifted through the open doors of the second-story room. Sunlight splashed across the plush red carpet, its warm fingers caressing the lace netting that draped the large tester bed.

The cries of a woman in the deep heat of passion were muffled by the street sounds of bustling New Orleans.

"Now, Court, now!" she cried out, her hips arching as her mate plunged deeper, bringing their coupling to an ardent climax.

Exhausted, Court Sinclair collapsed on top of her voluptuous breasts. "Ah, Della, you're a witch with a magic touch. What a magnificent cure for a headache."

Della's long fingernails raked lightly over the wide expanse of his back. "You too, Court, have magic."

He cocked a wayward brow, a hint of amusement etching his face. "I'd think in your profession you would experience that touch of magic every night."

"I'm here only to please, not to be pleased," she murmured suggestively, trailing her hands over his back and buttocks, and wiggling seductively beneath him.

Court groaned as he removed his lean, hard

1

weight from her and rolled to the side. "No more, woman. I have business to attend to."

Della watched as he pushed aside the mosquito netting, rose from the bed, and with a fluid movement, pulled on well-cut trousers. His eyes, which only moments before had gazed at her in passion, now stared pensively toward the French doors as though he had already put her from his mind.

The muscles of his back flexed against the linen fabric of his shirt as he fastened the pearl buttons at its front and cuffs. Tucking the shirt-tail into the waist of his pants, he walked barefoot to the dressing table, raking his hand through his rumpled black hair.

She studied his reflection in the gilded mirror as he poured water from the china pitcher into the bowl and splashed it on his face. His complexion was dark, his features finely chiseled with marked intelligence; it was an aristocrat's face, though he had made no mention of his lineage. His eyes were green, fringed with long, thick lashes. A well-kept mustache drew attention to the sensual fullness of his mouth. Della's body tingled even now as she remembered the deceptive gentleness of his velvet touch.

Court walked through the doorway and out to the balcony overlooking the street. Drays, heavily laden with merchandise, nearly collided as they made their way to and from the wharves of the Vieux Carré. The street was alive with people from all walks of life: vagabonds, prostitutes, fashionably dressed men and women, and free blacks. Beautiful quadroon women, their hair hidden beneath fancy tignons, walked regally among the pedestrians with an air of hauteur. Coming from the French market, women moved briskly along the *banquette*, their shopping baskets full of fruit, vegetables, and flowers.

New Orleans reminded Court of a lady dressed in her finest evening gown. Flamboyant Spanish structures of warm peaches, blues, and pinks dominated the street. A mixture of jasmine and oleander twisted around their embellished iron balcony railings. Peering intently into the street, he wondered if Meredith could be held hostage within one of those buildings, her kidnaper watching him at that very moment.

Court's anger rekindled when he recalled the ransom note someone had slipped beneath the door of his home in Natchez. Bryce, his manservant, had found it on the floor the next morning. It demanded he deliver a certain amount of money by the indicated date, or his sister Meredith would be killed; he was to go to New Orleans to receive further instructions.

He had arrived at his townhouse a day early to make his own plans, for he had no intention of turning any money over to the kidnaper so easily. That night someone had broken into his room while he was sleeping, and had given him a severe blow to his head; then the intruder had ransacked his room until he found the ransom money.

Now Court wondered if his search for his missing sister was futile; she might be dead already and the identity of her murderer buried with her.

Beautiful, untouchable Meredith—that was what her suitors had called her. Though she was considered past marriageable age, her incredible beauty had continued to turn the heads of men. Through a friend of the family, she had been introduced to a wealthy older gentleman from New Orleans who had come to Natchez on business. He had doted on her, lavishing her with gifts appropriate for a queen. It had been obvious to Court that Meredith did not love the proud, old aristocrat, but she had played the masquerade to the hilt, knowing she could become wife to one of the richest men in New Orleans. When he proposed, she had accepted happily, marrying him soon after. He had died a year ago, leaving her with an enormous estate. But it was not until Court had arrived recently in New Orleans that he discovered the dilemma she had brought upon herself.

He learned she had been a frequent visitor to the many gaming houses and steamboat salons— not as an onlooker, but as a participant at the tables. Gambling had become an obsession with her, and she had lost everything, including her home. Evidently someone had known she was from a wealthy family and had used that knowledge.

From as far back as he could remember, Meredith had disrupted his life with her selfish actions. Her absence from their plantation in Natchez for the past few years had left him in peace. She was his father's child from a previous marriage, six years older than Court. She had made his childhood miserable, and as they had matured into young adults, the situation had only worsened. After their father's untimely death, her jealousy had destroyed any agreeable relationship that might have developed between the siblings. Being the only son, Court inherited the plantation; Meredith's legacy amounted to a sizeable fortune and an apportioned share of the income from the plantation. But she felt she had been cheated. When she married, she had requested her entire portion, and Court had complied with her wishes, purchasing her share of the interest in the plantation.

As Court ruminated about Meredith and the past, he noticed a nun in a heavy gray habit stop briefly and adjust the shopping basket on her arm. The young woman frowned as she ran her hand beneath the tight neckline, apparently un-accustomed to the weight of the fabric. She glanced over her shoulder and whipped her head from side to side, fear evident in her widened eyes. Court's gaze followed hers, but to him no one person looked any more threatening than an-other. Suddenly the nun dropped her basket of fruit and vegetables, picked up her heavy skirt, held onto her veil, and began running down the *banquette*. Court leaned over the balcony to watch her as she ran beneath it.

Pedestrians' mouths dropped open in disbelief as the nun frantically pushed them aside to clear a path.

Hearing the commotion, Della threw on her gauzy white robe and moved to the balcony. "What's happening?"

"Damnedest thing I've ever seen," he said hu-morously, still watching the figure in gray. "What in the hell does she think she's doing?" he shouted, nearly falling over the railing as the nun gathered up her skirt and leaped into an open carriage...his carriage to be exact. Grabbing the reins, she slapped them over the rump of his horse.

"Good God, she's stealing my carriage!"

The carriage lurched as the horse lunged for-ward. The wheels hit mud-filled potholes, splat-tering passersby, who soundly cursed the reckless driver. A cart of flowers, swiped by the carriage, exploded into the air, and colorful petals rained like confetti over the street.

"My God," Della uttered in amazement, "I hope she doesn't head for the market."

Court turned quickly, yanking on his waistcoat and jacket, cursing the time it took to pull on his boots. Where was Bryce? he wondered. He was supposed to be keeping an eye on the carriage.

Knowing his manservant, his eyes were probably on the pretty mulatto and quadroon women. Reaching into his pocket, Court hastily pulled out several bills and placed them in Della's hand.

She smiled. "Thank you for a very memorable day, Mr. Sinclair. I hope to see you again."

His green eyes swept over her seductive dishabille. "I don't know how long I'll be in town."

"I'm always here," she whispered, placing a chaste kiss on his lips.

Court raced down the stairs, shoving open the large double doors, searching the crowd for Bryce. He spotted him in the middle of the street, his wiry frame dodging the numerous drays and carriages as he scurried toward Court, his eyes resembling two white marbles in his mud-colored face.

"Massa Court!" He waved his hands in disbelief, his head bobbing repeatedly on his reed-thin neck as he tried to explain. "She jes', she jes'..."

"Calm down, Bryce," Court said, taking him by the elbow. "I saw it all."

Bryce nodded, clucking his tongue. "Who'd think a nun would go 'n' do sumpin' like that?"

"Did you see where she went?"

"Yassuh. Made a quick turn to the left at that blacksmithy's shop. They ain't no ways you can ketch her now."

"We'll see." Court looked around at the horses lined in front of Della's place. He thrust a wad of bills into the palm of Bryce's brown hand. "This should cover the cost of the horse should the owner return. If he's in Della's, then I should have ample time to pursue the nun."

"Massa, jes' whatcha gonta do ifen you nab her?" Bryce asked, tucking the bills into his baggy trouser pockets. "You ain't gonta have her arrested for thievery, are you, her bein' religious 'n' all?"

Court mounted the best horseflesh available and grinned deviously at Bryce. "Her religion seems to have been the furthest thing from her mind, wouldn't you say? I'll see you later . . . after I find my carriage."

Court, wheeling his mount, raced through the streets in pursuit of the young nun, wondering what other misfortunes he would encounter before his search for Meredith came to an end. The ache in his head pounded rhythmically with the staccato of the horse's hooves, which did little to cool his temper.

As he turned down the street next to the black-smith's shop, his search came to an abrupt halt. His carriage stood abandoned on one side of the road. The nun was nowhere in sight; probably she'd disappeared into one of the numerous small shops lining the street. There was no sense in attempting to find her, he thought. His horse and carriage were unharmed and what would he gain by punishing a nun?

Court tied the reins of his borrowed horse to the back of the carriage and glanced around before he stepped into it. He was completely unaware of the violet eyes peering at him through a shuttered window—eyes that watched apprehensively until the carriage was safely out of sight.

Then, moving away from the window, the watcher collapsed against the wall and wiped the perspiration from her brow with the sleeve of her habit. *"Mon Dieu,* Damien. That was too close for comfort."

Damien Baudier, *maître d'armes,* put his rapier aside and nodded his head in dismay. A tall, slim man, Damien possessed handsome, dark Creole features. His lithe movements enabled him to best the majority of his dueling opponents. He was as treacherous as he was suave. It was fortunate for his petite friend that his last student had left only minutes before her unannounced entry.

"Sit down, *ma petite.*" Damien assisted her to a chair, the only one in the sparsely furnished room. "What have you been up to today, my little *nonne?* This part of town is not a place where a young lady should take a leisurely stroll, even dressed in *nonne*'s attire."

Sighing, his visitor removed her disheveled veil, her hair falling like a black velvet cloud down her back. She looked up at him with brilliant violet eyes. "I think Pernel recognized me. If it hadn't been for the crowd, he would have surely caught me. I took the only recourse I had."

"Dare I ask what you did this time to avoid him?"

She lowered her eyes in shame. "A dastardly deed, I fear. When word gets back to the Ursuline Convent about the nun who stole a horse and carriage, someone innocent may be blamed."

Damien's eyes shot open and his laughter thundered through the room. "You actually stole a carriage?" She did not speak, offering him a strained smile instead, and he said in affectionate exasperation, "Of you, Dannie, I can believe anything."

Standing abruptly, Danielle Algernon began pacing the room, her small frame appearing lost in the habit. "I only borrowed it, and the owner has found it already. Now I have another man who would probably love to wring my neck."

Taking her by the shoulders, Damien tilted her chin. Her small rosebud mouth with its permanent pouting fullness always tempted him to kiss her, but they were only friends. At least they were according to her. "I can take care of any man who threatens you, Dannie. Just give me the word."

"Non, Damien. Though I hate and fear Rankin Pernel, he's doing his job. I can't blame him for demanding payment. It's his unsavory manner that frightens me."

He trailed a slender finger down a long black tress and wound it gently around his hand. "Have you become so accustomed to the *nonnes'* way of dressing that you would choose to follow in their footsteps?"

Danielle pursed her lips as though giving the thought consideration. "Would a nun steal, *mon ami?"* she asked with a sparkle in her eyes.

"Not the *nonnes* I have known," Damien replied, his lips twitching with amusement.

"Frankly speaking, dear Damien, I do not care for the nun's clothing...most uncomfortable on such a hot day. The only benefit is that the mosquitos cannot find their way to my skin."

He laughed. "And such pretty skin it is. I much prefer you in silks and satins."

A frown marred her brow. "There will be no silks and satins if Nicholas does not return soon and pay his debts. I can't hold off Pernel if he discovers I hide in these clothes to avoid him."

Turning from her, Damien picked up his rapier. He ran his finger lightly along the narrow blade. "A duel could be arranged if he continues to hound you. You may be assured, *ma petite,* no one will harm you."

Danielle blanched. *"S'il vous plaît,* Damien, it shall never come to that."

He ran his eyes briefly over her small frame. "Then, Dannie, you had best keep your *nonne* attire. It very well could be the only clothing you will have left to wear. Nicholas's debts could cost you everything." Seeing tears in her eyes, he added, "But I have offered you a way out of your dilemma."

"But that would be murder," she protested.

"It has happened to better men than Rankin Pernel."

She walked over to him and placed her hand affectionately on his arm. "You are my friend, Damien, and I value your friendship. I could not have you take a man's life on my behalf. Nicholas will come back and handle matters. I'm certain he's trying to find a way to pay his debts. That's why he's taking so long to return."

"And if he does not return?" Fury raged in his face. "How do you expect to pay the man, *ma amie?* By offering your pretty body to men who frequent brothels?"

Her face flushed as she clasped her hands over her ears. "Stop it, Damien. I can take no more of this talk."

He pulled her into his arms. "I'm sorry, Dannie. I spoke too hastily out of concern for you. Don't worry, I'm still keeping an ear out for any information about Nicholas. If there's any way I can help you, all you need do is ask."

Chapter 2

The silent figure sat beneath the twisting limbs of an oak, a gentle breeze rippling the flowing strands of her ebony hair. Grief filled her heart, dragging her spirit to a new low.

"*Mon Dieu,* what am I to do?" Danielle whispered despairingly. For the majority of her young life she had been alone. She had learned to accept this as a way of life, but she carried her pain like a battle-scarred warrior, deep and ever present. Painting was her one outlet for expressing her pent-up emotions.

Her father had been killed in a duel before she was born. Her *maman,* the beautiful widow Elise Algernon, had remarried when Danielle was five. Her stepfather, Nicholas Caraville, was a handsome, debonair man, who could charm a flower into bloom. He loved Elise to distraction, and their marriage had been turbulent even in the best of times. Witnessing their violent arguments and fierce love, Danielle vowed as a child that her husband would be gentle and sensitive.

Then the dreaded yellow fever had claimed her young mother. Nicholas Caraville had seemed to lose the capacity for love when he lost his wife. He lost interest in running the plantation, and in the ensuing years, had separated himself as much as possible from his stepdaughter, leaving her to the care of her mammy. His one comfort became the gaming tables.

But he had not paid his creditors for months, and they had banded together and hired Rankin Pernel to collect their money. She recalled their initial confrontation; his words were indelibly etched in her memory: If her *beau-père* did not pay his debts, drastic measures would be forthcoming. He took delight in imparting his threats, and his watery blue eyes sparkled with malice as they raked her proud carriage. Using one plan after another Danielle had managed to avoid another meeting with Pernel. She was weary from his pursuit, and he was becoming wise to her deceptions.

He was a small man with thin, mouse-brown hair. His features were common enough, except that his skin appeared stretched tightly across his face. The excess lay in wrinkled folds on his bony neck. He sported a handlebar mustache that at first sight was almost comical. One side was heavily waxed and curved upward in a definite half circle, while the other side drooped downward as though the coating of wax had melted.

His appearance was laughable, but his words had struck a deadly chord in Danielle's heart. She could only pray he had no evidence that Nicholas was missing. Only those closest to her knew of his disappearance and she aimed to keep it a secret as long as it was in her power.

The only thing she had accomplished with her latest escapade was to raise Mammy's ire when she learned of the stolen carriage.

"Lawd almighty, chile, we gonta be struck down, you hear? You a'runnin' all over town in that nun's garb, like that ain't bad enuf...no suhree," Mammy emphasized, wringing her large hands. "Then you go to stealin'. I declare, chile, I raised you up better than that. You is gonta have the law on us faster than a chicken on a June bug."

"Mammy, I told you I had little choice. Monsieur Pernel was breathing down my neck. Besides I left the coach where it could be easily found. I even saw the owner retrieve it."

"And that's anuther thin'," Mammy interrupted hastily, "You ain't got no business paradin' the streets unescorted...in nun's garb or no. You's a lady, 'n' it's 'bout time you was actin' like one."

Mammy's large brown eyes scanned the room as though Rankin Pernel would appear from thin air. "Chile, you sho' nobody seed you?" she whispered.

"Absolutely."

"Well, praise be." She sighed thankfully, clasping her hands to her generous bosom. "All's we need is to be carted off like common criminals. Chile, I jus' don't think you could stand the humiliation."

Danielle's smile vanished as she thought of her alternatives. Her only recourse was to continue the search for Nicholas. Surely someone had to know his whereabouts. People did not just disappear without a trace. Another thought troubled her, one that she had kept tucked away in her heart for fear of examining it too closely: What if he had been killed and his body dumped in one of the many swamps that abounded in the New Orleans area? Her heart ached and tears scalded her eyes at the thought of going into mourning for the man who had loved her *maman* with such fierceness.

Dragging her mind from such torturous thoughts, she let her eyes roam over her home and the overgrown weed-infested lawns. She smiled wryly at her home's ironic name:

Espérance... hope... expectation. Had it been un-
justly named? Perhaps désespoir—despair—
would have been a name closer to the truth. As
far back as she could remember, each fruitful beginning had ended disastrously. But her own
heart still burned for hope of the future and expectation of things to come.

Nestled among dipping live oaks draped with
Spanish moss, the French-raised cottage sat like a
well-worn shoe, overlooking the vast lawn and
the ever-flowing Mississippi River. The signs of
neglect were immediately visible. The walls' once
white paint was now gray and peeling. Dormers
perched like gaping eyes surveying their surroundings from the roof's gables. Some of the
dark green shutters hung askew, giving the windows an overall appearance of a weary smile.
Weeds choked the once gracious flower gardens,
and honeysuckle trailed at will over the porch
railing, its gentle fragrance drifting on the
breeze. Nonetheless, Espérance was her home.
She loved it with a passion, every creaking plank
and every window that stuck. The birds nesting
in a loosened board bothered her not one whit, as
invariably they woke her early each morning
with their careless chatter.

She, Mammy, and Tobias did all they could do
to tend to the most pressing duties of the plantation, which at one time had boasted a large complement of slaves. Now fields lay fallow with only
a handful of remaining slaves to farm the vast
acreage. She could handle the fact that her *beau-
père* had ungraciously dumped the management
of the plantation into her lap. But his leaving her
responsible for his numerous debts... that rankled.

Danielle's eyes scanned the dense foliage of the
live oak, marveling at the many birds who made

it their home. As a child she had spent many hours playing in and around the tree. She had picnicked with her dolls in its shade, never frightened by the rumors she had heard. She smiled, thinking of the gossip that still surrounded her family and home. Neighbors scoffed and whispered that they were a strange lot because they lived in a house that was haunted. Had she desired, Danielle could have told tales about her house that would have sent people scurrying from her presence in fear, vowing she was a witch who conspired with the dead.

As legend dictated, the original owner of the house, a widower, had a beautiful young daughter. He had arranged for her to marry the man whose property bordered his. She was in love with another man, and refused to go along with her father's wishes. He locked her in her room, vowing he wouldn't let her out until she agreed to marry the man he had chosen. One night her lover came for her, and as she climbed down a rope from her upstairs window, she plunged to her death. Her spirit still roamed the house and grounds, looking for the man she loved. Until she found him, the story concluded, her spirit would continue its search.

One of the first recollections Danielle had of witnessing the ghost had been when she was very young. She had been gazing out her window; a heavy fog had hung over the river. Suddenly a hazy figure rose from the fog, hovering momentarily as a mournful cry floated through the air. The sound had brought tears to Danielle's eyes. As quickly as the misty apparition had appeared, it vanished, leaving Danielle to wonder if it had been there at all. But the goose bumps and tingling up her spine had been very real.

Another incident had taken place on a stifling

hot day as she strolled through the yard trying to
find some relief from the heat. She had settled
beneath the shade of a large oak whose gnarled
limbs swayed to the ground, then arched upward.
It was rumored that this same tree had also been
a favorite place of the young girl who was now
said to be the Espérance ghost. Sitting beneath
the tree, Danielle had pondered the tragedy of the
girl torn from her lover before their union. Her
heart had gone out to them. Suddenly a cool
breeze had wafted through the limbs of the tree,
rustling the leaves softly. A scent of lavender had
tickled her nose, and she had felt a gentle touch
on her cheek. She had then glanced at the other
trees; their leaves were quiescent, whereas the
one she sat beneath moved for a minute more,
then became still once again, the scent of lavender drifting away. After that incident, Danielle
always believed the ghost had been aware that
she had felt compassion for her.

She knew the ghost meant her family no harm;
her presence was tacitly accepted. Occasionally
something got misplaced and the spirit was
blamed, which was as much as the family ever
acknowledged her existence.

Mammy's voice calling her drifted to Danielle,
interrupting her reverie. She gathered up her
skirts and hurried to the house. As she entered,
she stopped short as Mammy rushed to her side,
holding her finger over her lips and motioning
her not to say anything.

"Miss Dannie, I's sorry as I can be. That hateful
Rankin Pernel, he came marchin' in here like he
owned the place. I tole him you was busy, but
nuthin' doin', he ain't leavin' till he sees you. Sho'
enuf, he plopped hisself down in Massa Caraville's
study 'n' eyed the place like it belonged to him.
That white trash ain't seed the day he'd be ac-

cepted in polite society. Ifen he weren't holdin' you over a barrel, I'da took a broomstick to him." Her whispered words gained volume as she spoke, and by the end of her tirade, anyone within ear-shot could have heard her.

After soothing Mammy, Danielle entered the study to confront Rankin Pernel. The moment she saw him, she could tell by his scowl that he had overheard Mammy's words.

"Monsieur Pernel, Mammy said you wished to see me."

"You tell your darkie she'd better watch her mouth or she'll be the first to go when your slaves are sold to pay your stepdaddy's debts."

"You go too far, *monsieur*. You have no right to suggest such a thing."

Rising angrily from his chair, he shouted, "I have every right to suggest anything that suits me until the money is handed over to me. You'd do well to have a little caution with your tongue, Miss Algernon." He let his watery eyes roam freely over her body, and his words softened. "We could make our own arrangements for payment of the debt." Approaching her side, he trailed his hand slowly up her arm. "I might see my way clear to take care of the creditors."

When she did not reject him, he continued, his voice dropping to a whisper as he leered at her, "All you need do is be nice to me. After a while, I could set you up in a nice place. With your face and body, you could be making more money than you ever dreamed."

"When hell freezes over!" she snapped, jerking her arm away from him.

"Tsk, tsk, Danielle, is that any way for a lady to talk?" he asked, addressing her name as though they were on intimate terms. "You must learn to control your fiery temper. I happen to know that Nicholas Caraville has not been here in weeks. Looks to me like he's skipped out, leaving you holding the sack...an empty one I might add. Maybe you should consider my offer more carefully."

"Monsieur Pernel, I'd starve to death before I'd lower myself to take such a position."

"You're a bit uppity for my taste. What you need is a real man to take you down a notch or two."

With a false smile and a deceptively silky tone of voice, she asked, "And do you have anyone in mind, *monsieur?*" Before he could answer, she turned rudely and called over her shoulder, "Mammy will see you out. There's no reason for you to inconvenience yourself by making the trip out here again. I'll see that you receive your money. I believe we have disposed of any business we might have had." With her head high and her back ramrod stiff, she left the room.

"Uppity bitch," Pernel said, snarling. "You'll get yours, I can promise you that." With undue haste, he left the house.

Danielle watched as her tormentor left, wondering what his next move would be.

Smoke curled upward, embracing the crystal chandelier. Court's fingers drummed impatiently on the table in the elegantly appointed gaming room. The other players had folded their cards and were sitting in suspense, waiting for what they hoped would be the final play of the evening. Shifting restlessly in his chair, he eyed the nervous player sitting opposite him, a latecomer to the table. The stakes were high and why the man continued playing when luck was not with him was a mystery to Court.

Taking a deep draw on his cheroot, Court

leaned forward and braced his elbows on the table. Splaying his cards, he asked, "Can you beat three of a kind?"

The man's curved mustache twitched. "Either you play well, *monsieur,* or you deal well."

Court's eyes narrowed threateningly. "Are you saying I cheated?"

The tension around the table was almost tangible. The onlookers knew Court had every right to call the man out for such a serious accusation. For hours they had played cards with Sinclair and, though he won frequently, there was nothing underhanded about his playing. They watched the quiet anger suffuse his face as he awaited his opponent's response.

The stranger realized his foolish words. His eyes focused on Sinclair's hand as he clenched his empty glass. An uneasy smile replaced his sneer. "I'd be a fool to call a man a cheater when I have no proof. Evidently you misunderstood my meaning."

Court stared blatantly at the coward. "Perhaps I did," he agreed, but the tone of his voice suggested otherwise.

Sliding his chair back, he rose, leaned over, and raked in his winnings, which included a legal-looking piece of paper. Picking up the document, he scanned its contents, his interest more on the legitimacy of the deed than on the property involved. Everything appeared in order, but the man's nervousness made Court wary.

The stranger swallowed deeply, hoping the ruffled stock at his neckline hid the convulsive play of his throat.

"I think, gentlemen," Court said, facing the other men, "I shall call it an evening. I believe our debts have been settled."

Congratulating him on his winnings, the men bid him farewell and left the gaming room.

Court returned his attention to the stranger. "Do you feel no remorse in losing your home, Mr. Caraville?"

Caraville stiffened. "Of course I do," he said, shifting his eyes from Court's close scrutiny. "The property belonged to my deceased wife. Without her by my side, I no longer desire to live there. But it pains me to lose it and gain nothing in return."

"Do you have any children who won't cooperate when I take control of the plantation?"

"My wife and I had no children," he answered hastily.

Court was still not satisfied. "Are there any debts owed against the property?"

Caraville hesitated a moment before answering. "When you see the plantation, Mr. Sinclair, you'll find it in a rather run-down condition . . . not beyond reparation, mind you. To cover my debts I was forced to sell several of my slaves, and the cane fields have been neglected as a result. As you see, I'm an honest man for telling you this. It's located on the river and has its own loading docks. Look the deed over thoroughly, and I'm sure you'll realize you have won a bargain."

"All right, Caraville, but before we close this deal, I would like to have someone witness your signature."

"But . . . but . . ." he sputtered, his face reddening.

"But, being the honest man you are, I'm sure you would never try to deceive me," Court said, arching a dubious brow.

Looking around, he spied a well-dressed gentleman just rising from a chair. He walked over to him while Caraville looked on anxiously. The man willingly agreed to witness the signing of the deed. Caraville's hand shook as he wrote his name. The witness then signed his name beneath Caraville's and dated the transaction.

"You have the deed, Sinclair, all signed and legal. Since you no longer need my services, I plan to leave New Orleans tomorrow. I'm certain you will receive a warm welcome when you step over the threshold of your new home."

"For your sake, I hope we never run into one another again if all is not on the up and up. I remember faces for a long time, Mr. Caraville."

As Court watched Nicholas Caraville hurriedly walk out the door, an acute sense of déjà vu enveloped him. He had just won a sizeable plantation. So why did he feel he had actually lost?

Chapter 3

Birds sang their delight at the beautiful new morning as Danielle lay back in the cooling water.

Holding up a towel, Mammy chastised her, "Chile, you gonta shrivel up to nothin' ifen you don't get outa that tub. Mistah Damien will be here in a while, 'n' I need you to finish trying on them dresses of your mama's so's Lilly can set to work on 'em. You might gets some invites to one of them fancy balls, 'n' you needs to look like you ain't hurtin' for money." Clucking her tongue, she continued her monologue. "Ain't nobody's business that you can't afford new dresses. Why, by the time Lilly sets a bit of lace here 'n' a ribbon there, ain't nobody would know the difference. They'd probably think the dresses come all the way from Paris."

Danielle smiled tenderly at Mammy as she wrapped her in the soft towel. "What would I ever do without you, Mammy?" she asked, placing a tender kiss on her plump cheeks. "I can't possibly attend any of the balls for I have no escort."

"We'll see 'bout that," Mammy boasted. "Now come on, chile. You gots a full day ahead of you."

The dresses lay in a heap on Danielle's bed, a multitude of colors from the palest lavender to the lushest green. She had been trying them on for the past few days, and Mammy had pinned most of them for alterations. Though Danielle was as tall as her mother had been, her frame was smaller, and the gowns would have to be taken in and fresh lace applied. One of her favorites was a creamy peach gossamer silk that draped her body alluringly and rippled around her long legs. Impulsively she threw aside the wet towel and slipped the gown over her head. Pirouetting in front of the mirror, she laughed gaily at the image she presented.

Coming to an abrupt standstill, her eyes twinkling with mischief, she curtsied deeply to Mammy. "Is this the way a lady looks, Mammy?"

"Honey pie, you look jus' like an angel must look, all soft and big-eyed. Why, you'd have them gentlemen fallin' all over themselves to get a peek at you. Don't you go worryin' none. Mammy'll see that you get an escort to take you to at least one of them fancy parties."

"People are leery of getting too close to this house after sundown," Danielle commented darkly. "Do you suppose they think I'm touched? I can't believe people around here have made such a to-do over a little-bitty ghost."

Mammy swallowed rapidly. "Don't you go makin' fun of that ghost. Whether she is or she ain't, it don't make no never-mind to me. I done made me a promise a long time ago. Ifen she don't bother me, I ain't gonta bother her none. Now let's getcha fitted in the rest of the finery cause Mistah Damien will be here afore long."

Court strolled the streets of the Vieux Carré, continuing his endless search for Meredith. At the same time, he was wondering what he was going to do with the plantation he'd won the previous night. If it were as rundown as Caraville had told him, he would probably be wise to sell it. But that

decision would have to be made after he had seen
it.

He stopped as he heard a crowd of men cheer-
ing. They were standing in an alley, watching a
cock fight in progress. Moving in closer, he saw
two roosters, bloodied and nearly featherless,
stalking each other. Court had never approved of
the sport, and he moved on quickly.

Turning up another block, he made his way to
the Maspero Exchange, a long, two-story building
where businessmen met socially and discussed
current affairs. He had been here often in the past
few days, mingling with the merchants but listening covertly for any gossip that might involve
Meredith.

When he entered, there were no empty tables
and few vacant spaces at the long bar that ran the
length of the room. Weaving his way through the
throng of men, he wedged his way between two
men at the bar and ordered a tall mug of beer and
a platter of shrimp. Listening to the endless chatter, he ate and conversed periodically with the
man at his side. Suddenly his attention was di-
verted to the entrance where a tall, slim man
stood looking around the room. Court recognized
him as his friend, Jordan Phillips. He and Jordan
had studied law together at William and Mary
College, and had at one time planned to go into
practice together. Jordan was from a sea-going
family and had decided to open his own shipping
business in New Orleans, using his knowledge of
the law to get himself established. Court had returned home to Natchez to run the family plantation after his father's death. Though he had never
practiced law, he found that his studies aided in
marketing the cotton he produced and made him
more aware of pitfalls to be avoided.

Catching his friend's attention, Court motioned

him to the bar. A wide smile spread across Jordan's handsome face as he moved slowly through the crowd, shaking hands, and speaking to friends along the way.

Finally making it to the bar, he clasped Court's hand in a firm grip. "By God, it's good to see you, Court. You don't get down here as often as you used to. How long have you been here?"

Court made a space so Jordan could move in beside him. "I've been here for several days. I went by your office hoping to see you, but your clerk told me you were away. I knew Maspero's was a favorite hangout of yours so I've kept an eye out for you."

"You know me too well, my friend," he said, signaling the bartender for a drink.

They laughed and talked, catching up on happenings new and old.

"Tell me, Court," Jordan asked finally, "what has brought you to our fair city?"

"You won't believe it when I tell you."

"Sounds interesting," Jordan prompted.

"For starters, let me ask...have you seen or heard anything about Meredith?"

Jordan frowned. "No, I haven't seen her for some time."

Lowering his voice to almost a whisper, Court said, "Meredith's been kidnaped."

"Kidnaped!" Jordan nearly choked on the shrimp he had just plopped into his mouth. "But why would anyone kidnap her? I heard she had lost everything."

"True, but it was me her kidnaper approached."

"I think I need another drink," Jordan said, motioning to the bartender.

While they sipped their beer and ate, Court told him all that had transpired since his arrival, including the incident of the nun stealing his carriage.

"None of this makes sense, Court. Why would they seek to harm you when surely they knew you'd pay the money? Could it have been someone off the street who saw a wealthy man and took advantage of the situation? And for the life of me I can't figure out what part a nun would play in the scheme."

"As far as the nun's concerned, I surmise she only needed my carriage to get away in a hurry for some reason," Court said. "Like you, at first I thought I'd been the victim of a robbery, but no one has contacted me with further instructions concerning the ransom." He finished the last of his beer in one long swallow. "I think it was a setup from the very beginning. Perhaps they knew Meredith and I weren't on the best of terms and thought I'd put up a fight. Hell, I don't know."

He picked up another shrimp and continued speaking. "That isn't all that's happened to me." As he turned to get the salt, his elbow knocked over the shaker, spilling a few grains of salt. "Damn, that's all I need now." He sprinkled some salt in his hand, and then tossed it over his shoulder.

Jordan chuckled. "Still superstitious, I see."

"You know how my mammy is, Jordan. She'd walk a mile out of her way to avoid crossing the path of a black cat. After having her superstitions ingrained in me all my life, I naturally resort to her remedies. Wouldn't you after the run of luck I've had? And to top it all off, I won a plantation last night in a poker game."

Jordan's eyes shot open. "That's bad luck? Damn! I wish my luck could be so poor. Who was the owner?"

"Nicholas Caraville, do you know him?"

Jordan let out a low whistle. "This is strange. Meredith has been seen in his company quite often."

"Meredith? Are you sure?"

"I've seen them together several times. Rumor has it that he's nearly broke, and from the looks of his cane fields, there's truth to the gossip. But as to the value of the property, you've just won a bargain. That is, if your superstitious nature will let you live in a haunted house."

Court grimaced. "There's no such thing as a haunted house, and you damn well know it, Jordan."

"Yeah?" he said with a boyish grin. "You know it, and I know it, but the female ghost who roams the house and grounds...well, she hasn't begun to realize it yet." He briefly told him the history of the Espérance ghost.

Court lifted his glass, finding it empty. "Sounds like a lot of gibberish to me," he said after ordering another drink. "Talk, that's all it is. You know how slaves love ghost tales."

"No, slaves aren't the only people who supposedly have seen her and heard her mournful crying."

"So, you're saying Caraville was spooked into giving away his home."

"No, he's a poor gambler, and I suppose he thought he could try to make enough to pay his debts."

"Evidently he managed to withstand the presence of a ghost in his house. By the looks of him, I'd say he was capable of scaring away the ghost," Court said.

A perplexed expression crossed Jordan's face, but it quickly vanished. "The thing that concerns me most is what you plan to do about his dau—"

"Jordan Phillips!" A loud, boisterous voice interrupted him. Both men turned to see a robust man coming their way. Jordan made the introductions and the conversation turned to more general topics.

After waiting politely for a few minutes, Court excused himself. "Jordan, if you and Mr. Marshall will pardon me, I think I'll take a short trip up the road."

"Come by my office later and let me know how it went. I think you're in for a big surprise," Jordan said after an instant's hesitation.

"I think I can handle one more," Court said confidently, never dreaming those parting words would come back to haunt him later that afternoon.

As Danielle pulled on her britches, she saw Mammy scowling, but she ignored her and finished dressing. Lastly, she tugged on her scarred black boots, and she was ready for her fencing lesson.

Damien leaned back in the chair, a devilish smile spanning his face as Danielle entered the drawing room. "*Ma petite,* you put the sun in the shade by your radiant beauty."

"Damien, you do have a way with a flowery phrase," she teased, placing a quick kiss on his cheek. "Do you practice your glib words on me before you dazzle the young girls who flock after you?"

Placing his hand over his heart, he moaned. "You wound me deeply, *ma cherie,* with your careless chatter. Have I not told you often how your beautiful face could warm the coldest heart?"

"And you, *mon ami,* with your devil-may-care attitude and your handsome face have charms beyond your control." With a brilliant smile, she continued. "Heaven help us if your bands of restraint should ever rust. The ladies of New Orleans are not ready for the deluge of compliments that would flow from your lips."

Her innocent repartee brought a deep chuckle from her friend. *"Mon Dieu,* Dannie, do you think you might in a subtle way place a well-chosen word here and there, then you and I shall wait for the rampaging females to descend on my doorstep."

"I shall see what I can do. For the time being, would you care to go for a ride? I'm afraid Tempete will become fat and lazy if he does not get his outing. You can give me the lesson outside, if you wish." He followed her out the door and they quickly mounted their horses.

Racing side by side with him along the banks of the river, Danielle banished her troubles from her mind. She would not spoil her delight in being with her friend by dwelling on unpleasant thoughts. Slowing their mounts, they enjoyed the view of the teeming activity along the river. From their vantage point, they watched two elegant steamboats racing, their passengers at the railings shouting back and forth to each other.

Arriving at the clearing where they always had their fencing lessons, they dismounted and faced each other, their rapiers held ready. Bowing elegantly, Damien called out *en garde* and thrust smoothly. Their liquid movements made their practice look like a well-rehearsed quadrille.

"Ma petite," he said when they were through, "there is nothing else I can teach you, although I must admit I enjoy our practices immensely. The only advice I can give to you is never take your eyes from your opponent. I doubt you'll ever be placed in a position in which you'll have to defend yourself with a rapier. It's highly unlikely a gen-

tleman would call out a lady. But with your temperament, one never knows."

"I would like to lay my sword to the side of Rankin Pernel's neck." She laughed, replacing her rapier in its case. "He'd likely choke to death on his Adam's apple."

"Has he been annoying you again?" he asked, mounting his horse.

Danielle described Pernel's visit as they rode back to the house. By the time they reached the plantation, she had finished relating the story and Damien's face was suffused with anger.

"That bastard! If luck would have that I could ever encounter him, I would call him out with haste. I've never met the man, but I think I would have little trouble recognizing him from your glowing depiction. I'll set myself the pleasure of finding him, then we'll see how brave he becomes when faced by a man. I know of men like him who are only men when they can abuse those of the weaker sex. His business tactics leave much to be desired."

"Don't worry about me, Damien," she said, handing Tempete's reins to Tobias. "I can take care of myself. Nicholas will soon return and all this ugly business will be laid to rest."

"I hope you're right, *ma petite*. I'll go now, but if you should need me, send Tobias. I'll be here without delay." He looked down at her from his mount, his eyes filled with affection.

"I know, Damien."

After squeezing his hand tightly, she climbed the steps of the porch and watched until he was out of sight.

Chapter 4

The dust had barely settled when another rider approached. Thinking Damien was returning, Danielle waited on the steps. But as the rider drew nearer, she saw that it was not her friend. Recognition tugged her memory as she puzzled over the identity of the man.

He sat on his horse with ease, a light touch from his thigh commanding the steed. Suddenly she remembered; this was the man who owned the carriage she had stolen. *Mon Dieu,* had he found her out? Her mouth went dry and perspiration beaded her brow. Taking a deep breath to calm her nerves, she resolved to not give herself away by falling apart before she knew what he wanted. She would receive him graciously.

Once he was in earshot, she called *"Bonjour"* in the deepest voice she could manage and slumped her shoulders forward. Since she was already dressed in britches and a loose-fitting white shirt and her hair was tucked beneath a hat, she decided to chance trying to pass as a young man.

"And a good day to you," he answered, sliding gracefully from his mount. "Would you please run and get whoever is in charge so that I may speak with him?"

His manner was pleasant and his request ordinary under normal circumstances, but lately nothing in Danielle's life seemed normal. Even now her ears were ringing, and she was certain they were a fiery red. *Run*...the word reverberated through her brain.

Gazing into vibrant green eyes, she said evenly, "I, *Monsieur,* am in charge."

With a dubious expression and a telltale smile tugging the corner of his lips, he seemed to be sizing her up. "Well, lad," he said formally, "then it must be you with whom I should speak."

"*Monsieur,* I cannot image that we have anything to discuss. My *beau-père* is unavailable at the present time, but if you would leave your card, I will pass it on to him."

So, as he had supposed, Caraville does have a family here, Court thought irritably. Not only was the man a coward, but he was a liar as well.

He dismounted smoothly, then climbed the steps, stopping within an arm's distance of her. "I've already had the pleasure of meeting your charming stepfather." He cocked a brow questioningly. "That is, if he happens to be Nicholas Caraville."

Her eyes opened in amazement. "You've been with my *beau-père?*" Her low-pitched voice cracked.

"Is that cause for some concern? You act as though I just told you I had seen a ghost."

"No...no, it's just that I haven't seen him for a day or two," she lied. Shrugging her small shoulders, she asked, "Where did you happen to see him?"

"We sat across a card table from each other last night. A very interesting game it was, and a very profitable one for me, I might add."

"*Monsieur,* I'm sure you didn't ride all the way out here to discuss your profitable evening."

"You're right, I didn't," he answered hesitantly.

"Then, I'll have your reason for coming here, so you can be on your way."

With precise movements, he pulled a folded parchment from his pocket. Danielle's heart sank. She knew what it was before he handed it to her for her inspection. Tears sprang to her eyes. Turning quickly before he could detect the moisture, she blinked rapidly and scanned the document she held in her trembling hands. Nicholas Caraville's bold signature attested to the fact he had turned her lovely home over to Courtland Garret Sinclair.

Raising her eyes, she questioned, "And you, *monsieur,* are..."

Dragging his hat from his head, which released an abundance of ebony hair much like her own, he announced, "Court Sinclair, at your service."

"*Eh bien,* Monsieur Sinclair, it appears you are the new owner of Espérance. Do you plan to claim possession immediately, or am I to be allowed time to make arrangements?"

Her mind screamed in frustration at the cruel blow her *beau-père* had struck this time. She had no place to go, no one to turn to. What would she do?

Court's heart went out to the lad as he noticed the struggle in the young man's face. He sure is a tender-looking youth, he thought. Giving in to his conscience, he volunteered, "Lad, I don't intend to run you from your home. I'm sure we can come to some agreeable arrangement. I don't plan to be here long since I'll be returning to my own home in Natchez."

"It must be reassuring to know you will have a home to return to. I, *monsieur,* do not have that privilege."

"As I said, you're welcome to remain here. I'm

sure we can find something for you to do," he offered.

Not to be taken in by his friendliness, Danielle
stiffened her spine and at the same time tried to
hunch her shoulders. Her temper was gaining
momentum by degrees; she could barely control
her anger as she said, "I can assure you, Monsieur
Sinclair, that I do not need, nor do I desire your
offhanded charity. I am certain if you had your
way, you would have me running my tail off to do
your bidding."

Tilting his head to inspect the part of her anatomy she had referred to, he grinned in amusement. "Doesn't look to me like you could spare a
lot."

It was all Danielle could do to keep from clasping her hands over her buttocks in mortification.
Instead, she clenched her hands into tight balls
and ground her teeth together.

Court chuckled, raising his hand in supplica-
tion.

The fine hair on the back of Danielle's neck
stood up and the blood galloped through her
veins. Her mind raced with schemes. If she had
the strength, she would flatten him right where
he stood and be done with the whole mess. But on
second thought, as she viewed his masculine form
and considered his apparent strength, she quickly
changed her mind.

"*Mon Dieu,* of all the unmitigated gall. Who do
you think you are?" she stormed.

"That, young man, is not the question. Are you
going to take me up on my offer or not? My manservant will be arriving shortly with my things.
He has a tendency to become overwrought if
things are not running smoothly."

"*Excusez-moi,* Monsieur Sinclair." She took a

deep breath, an inkling of an idea blossoming in her mind. "You are an American, are you not?"

The question hung in the air for a moment.

"You're absolutely right." He smiled broadly.

"Your manner implied as much," she replied spitefully, her eyes raking his face in disgust. "More concerned for the behavior of a disgruntled servant than for a family you have just evicted. My sympathy goes out to you, I assure you." Sarcasm dripped from her voice.

"If you want to settle this matter like two gentlemen, I will oblige you. But I won't stand here and take your insults."

"Do you feel you have been insulted, *monsieur?*"

"Close, lad, awfully close."

"Then this should do it," she snapped, ripping the glove from her hand and slapping him fully across the face with it.

Surprise washed over Court's face, and his eyes sparkled with anger. "Now you've done it, lad," he said, placing a hand to his burning cheek.

"You realize the implication, do you not? I challenge you, *monsieur,* for the return of my home."

"Shall it be death, or the drawing of blood that you wish?"

"I do not desire your death...a little blood will do. The first one to draw blood owns the plantation and all it entails," she replied in a proud and haughty manner.

"Very well, but I'd like to add a little amendment to the wager. If perchance I should win, I'd like you to remain here to take care of the plantation." Using this means Court could leave the boy's pride intact, and absolve his own guilt of having to make him homeless.

"Why would I agree to such terms?" she asked, incredulously.

"If you would have a duel at all, you'll agree. After all, I own the plantation already. Why would I chance losing it, unless I have something to gain? And...as the challenged, I do have the choice of weapons, do I not...*monsieur?*" He mimicked the salutation.

The color drained from her face, and unconsciously she chewed her lower lip. "As you wish," she whispered hoarsely. "What would be your choice of weapons?"

Drawing a deep breath, he stated, "I believe that as clumsy as I am, I shall choose rapiers."

"You shall?" she questioned, pleased by his choice. She was going to win the duel!

"Only if you agree to my demands. You could do with a few lessons in manners if you're to grow into a fine gentleman."

Danielle almost sputtered. Should she lose, which she doubted, how could she continue her disguise indefinitely? She would cross that bridge when she came to it. Her deception had not been intentional. He had caught her before she had a chance to change from her fencing attire. She had used it only to gain an advantage. Now, hopefully, she would win the duel, and he would never know that he had been bested by a female. Delight bubbled through her veins at the thought.

His voice penetrated her merriment. "What is your name?"

"What?"

"Your name, lad."

"My name? Oh...Dannie Algernon."

"Well, Dannie, I can't say it's all been a pleasure. Did you have a place in mind for the duel, or do you plan to meet at the Oaks?"

The Oaks was where the majority of duels were fought, but Danielle had no wish to be a public spectacle.

"Would you be adverse to having it here at Espérance . . . say daybreak tomorrow?"

"That would be fine."

She gave him directions to the place where she and Damien had practiced earlier that day.

"Should I bring along a surgeon, or is there someone here who can take care of the wounded?"

Hunching her shoulders, she replied, "Mammy can look after the injured. She's as good as any surgeon you might bring."

"I'll take your word for it, Dannie, and bid you good day." With that remark, he mounted his horse and galloped away, leaving a billowing cloud of dust behind him.

"That devil," she fumed. "I'll show him."

As she entered the house, Mammy was waiting. Her anger had erupted into a stuttering seizure, and her big brown eyes rolled anxiously in her brown face. "You . . . you . . . sho' 'nuf done it this time, chile."

Easing her arm around Mammy, Danielle led her to the parlor and into a comfortable chair.

"Mammy, you have to understand I had no choice in the matter." With a teasing smile and in a cajoling voice, she said, "What were you doing —eavesdropping?"

"Don't you go tryin' to change the subject— that's neither here nor there. And 'sides, when I seed ya slap that glove across that man's face, my ole heart nearly stopped. I declare I turned as white as a sheet. Ifen I hadn't been propped against the wall, I'da been splattered all over the floor. Chile, you done got us in a heap o' trouble."

"Mammy, if I can win the duel, it will be one more monkey off my back. Monsieur Sinclair said he won the deed from Nicholas. If he's so close, why hasn't he shown up here? I want to send Tobias into New Orleans to search the gaming houses. Maybe he can turn up some answers. *Mon Dieu*, I'm at my wits' end." Pressing her hands to her throbbing temple, she groaned, "Why would Nicholas do something like this? I don't believe this of him."

"I know, chile, your shoulders sho' do have a heavy burden to cart around. But Lawdy mercy, what are you gonta do in the mornin'? I can't imagine whatcha had in your head to do sumpin' like that."

"Don't start, Mammy. I know what I'm doing. All I have to do is draw blood and it will be over. Damien has taught me well."

Mammy rose from her chair, wringing her hands all the while. As she left the room, she warned, "Vengeance is mine, saith de Lawd."

Chapter 5

Sleep eluded Danielle, and as she tossed and turned, Court's emerald-green eyes haunted her. Finally giving up the effort, she rose to prepare for the duel. Before dressing in her fencing attire she took a long strip of muslin and bound her breasts. She would not be able to slump her shoulders with all her thoughts trained on winning the duel. Brushing her hair until it crackled, she secured it to the top of her head, and then tugged her hat low over her brow. Gazing into the bevelled-glass mirror, she was pleased with the appearance she presented. Monsieur Sinclair would never be able to detect a trace of femininity.

At the soft knock, she was startled to see Mammy entering with a tray laden with croissants, marmalade, and a cup of steaming chocolate.

"I didn't know anyone was about this early in the morning," Danielle said.

Mammy seemed to shiver. "I didn't sleep a wink, chile. I jus' want to get this aggravatin' business over with. I figgered you didn't sleep much better than me. You need to keep up your strength ifen you is goin' through with this foolishness." Without drawing a breath, she continued, "Tobias is waitin' for you. The fog is so thick this mornin' you could cut it with a knife. Mebbe that Sinclair feller"—she rolled her eyes—"won't be able to find the place."

The stillness before dawn was eerie as Danielle slipped out of the house and mounted her horse, who had already been saddled and harnessed by Tobias, Mammy's son. She prodded Tempete through the dew-laden weeds. Tobias, guiding the creaking dray through the dense foliage, followed her until they reached the spot where the duel was to take place. An owl hooted its displeasure at the interruption as the rabbit he was eyeing scurried into the underbrush.

Dismounting, Danielle draped the reins over one of the twisting limbs of the oak, and wiped the tickling strands of Spanish moss from her face. She surveyed her surroundings as she sat down on one of the drooping boughs. She and Damien had often used this spot for her lessons over the past few years. The ground was bare and hard from repeated trampling. What would Damien say when he found out what she had done? He would probably be very displeased. But he had told her time and again that she could defeat any of his pupils.

Damien, her mentor, her confidant, was a handsome French aristocrat who had fallen on hard times. Instead of milking an existence from wealthy kin, he had set out to make it on his own. From all appearances, he had succeeded. He ran the most elite fencing academy in New Orleans, and even employed several instructors. Damien had told her how surprised and pleased he had been when Nicholas Caraville had sought him out to teach his *belle-fille* the art of fencing.

The sun raised its bright head, dissipating the lingering mist. Danielle gazed out over the lazy river, watching as a flatboat made its way toward the docks of New Orleans.

"Miss Dannie, I believes I hears hosses 'an' they is movin' fast," Tobias shouted, interrupting her musings.

Danielle jumped down from her perch. "Tobias, don't you dare call me *Miss* when Monsieur Sinclair gets here," she scolded.

"Then what would you have me call you... Massa Dannie?" he asked with a sheepish grin.

With a sparkling smile, she answered, "That will do nicely. Now don't you go getting all jittery. You'll be my second. All you have to do is hand me my rapier and stand there. It will be all over in a very short time."

"I sho' hope you know what you is doin', Miss— I mean, Massa Dannie."

The pounding horses entered the clearing. Court Sinclair slid from his mount. "Sorry I'm late."

"The thought had run across my mind that you might have chickened out."

"No way," he declared, "I'm going to see this thing through to the very end."

Danielle's tongue slid across her suddenly dry lips. *"Mon Dieu!* Let's get on with it. I have an overwhelming desire to see your eyes glazed in fear." With that, she turned, her back ramrod stiff as she exchanged whispered words with her second.

Bryce, Court's manservant, nervously untied the long, wooden box from the saddle. Carrying the box to the dray, he set it down with care, nodding his head in greeting to Tobias. He opened the box, then withdrew a gleaming rapier, its handle an artwork of intricate designs.

Court grasped the handle and with awkward strokes, slashed at the air.

Danielle grinned to herself and drew her own rapier from its resting place.

Taking their positions, they faced each other. Court measured his opponent with indifference, once again struck by the tender youth; he decided to go easy on the lad.

Danielle was also having thoughts of her own, although hers were not as kind. He probably moves like a cow, she thought with relish. A man as tall as he could never move with speed and grace. He will probably bungle his way through this. Nonetheless, she would have to admit he was a handsome man.

When he removed his coat and stood before her in form-fitting trousers that only enhanced his manliness, Danielle was momentarily stunned. Every muscle in his long legs seemed fused to the pants he wore. His white linen shirt was partially opened, showing a thick mat of crisp black hair beneath it. If she were not supposed to be a boy, she might have come close to swooning. But this was her adversary, and if she were to win, she must not forget it.

"En garde!" The words rang through the air as the opponents began their attack.

Danielle's thrust was quickly parried by his agile movements. Court's riposte was made with the minimum of movements and split-second timing. Blades clashed, the ringing sound vibrating the early morning air.

Danielle was having second thoughts. He definitely did not move like a cow...more like a stalking panther. Her rapier was becoming heavy, and her hand was tingling as she warded off one blow after another. Perspiration rolled from her temples and down her cheek, its presence irritating her. It was all she could do to keep from wiping her face. With swift determination, she cleared her mind of all thoughts except defending her honor and reclaiming her home.

Her preoccupation caused her split-second timing to falter just a fraction. In that fleeting second, she felt an acute burning sensation race up her arm. As he closed in on her, she quickly turned aside his rapid attack. She was gaining ground until she glanced at her arm. Blood...red, sticky, warm blood had stained her snowy-white shirt and covered her hand. My blood...first blood, she thought, her step faltering. She had just lost her home. Suddenly she felt lightheaded, as though she were in a tunnel, the faces and voices becoming dimmer and dimmer. Her legs felt like rubber, and then the eerie sensations ceased as a black void enshrouded her.

Court saw his opponent stumble, and with ease, caught the slumping figure in his strong arms. His brow arched upward in question as he gazed into the stark white face. He knew he had only pricked the lad. He just hadn't had it in him to harm the youth's tender flesh any more than he did.

Tobias's black face had turned a sickly gray as he knelt beside the bent figures. "Lawdy, Lawdy, Miss Dannie, I hope you ain't daid. Mammy'll skin me alive, sho' 'nuf ifen her baby is daid."

Fleetingly, Court wondered at Tobias's addressing the lad in the feminine gender, as he began loosening the buttons on the boy's shirt.

"Don't do dat," Tobias ground out, his eyes as big as saucers. "You jes' put him in that wagon, and I'll take him to Mammy."

"As you wish," Court answered, a glint of humor dancing in his eyes. Indulging the servant, he picked up his bundle with ease and climbed into the wagon.

He knew the lad was not in any great danger. He had drawn the conclusion that the sight of his own blood had been the boy's undoing. As he

shifted the weight in his arms, he knocked off the
boy's hat. Astonishment ripped across his features.

A mane of ebony hair tumbled freely over his
arm. His dark features paled as it hit him full
force what had transpired.

"Damn," he muttered through clenched teeth,
as Tobias rushed the dray helter-skelter toward
the helping hands of Mammy. He barely had time
to gather his thoughts about the charade that had
been played out for his benefit.

The flickering of her sooty eyelashes drew his
attention as he contemplated the fragile beauty of
the girl he held in his arms. Why had he not seen
through her disguise? There had been no reason
to doubt what she represented. Still, it galled him
that he had been duped so completely by her.

Her violet eyes blinked open in confusion as
she gazed up to see Court with an engaging smile
splayed across his face.

Leaning over, he tweaked her nose. "You, my
pet, were not completely honest with me."

In a soft voice, she replied, "And you, *monsieur,*
were also a bit untruthful about your skill with a
rapier."

"Touché," he returned with a flourish.

Mammy was in the yard when the dray came
creaking up the drive, Bryce following on horse-
back and leading Tempete and Court's mount.
When she saw Danielle lying in Court's arms, she
hiked up her skirt-tails and took off at a dead run
as fast as her generous bulk would allow.

"My baby's daid, I knows it," she screamed. "I
knowed they wouldn't be no good comin' from
this. Lawdy mercy, my baby."

As the cart came to a halt, Tobias and Court
tried to assure Mammy that Danielle was not
dead. With dexterity that had everyone's mouth

gaping in surprise, she left the ground in one leap, almost upending the wagon. Mammy pushed Court aside, drew Danielle to her generous bosom, and rocked to and fro, mumbling hasty prayers.

Court placed his hand on Mammy's shoulder. "Mammy, Dannie...or whatever her name is...is not dead. Unless, of course, you haven't smothered her by now." His eyes went to the death grip that Mammy held on her charge.

"Praise de Lawd," Mammy sighed, loosening her grip somewhat. Gazing down into Danielle's pale face, Mammy began upbraiding her. "What you mean lyin' back here like you is daid? You done scairt me near to death."

"Monsieur Sinclair barely pricked me. I guess I don't fence as well as I thought."

"She did fine, Mammy. I think she lost her concentration," Court offered.

"Let's get this chile in the house so I can take a look at her. I don't want no infection settin' in. I guess I owe you an apology, Mistah Sinclair. I thought you'd done gone and kilt her sho' 'nuf."

"I'd never had done that. I only allowed her to talk me into this insanity because I thought she was a he. I felt I could do no less than to take up the challenge to allow her"—he glanced at Danielle—"to defend her home."

"Them's mighty fine words, Mistah Sinclair. I'm beholdin' that the damage ain't no worst than it seems."

Mammy soon had Danielle settled in bed and her shoulder cleansed and bandaged. She chattered nonstop as she buzzed about, straightening the already immaculate room. Danielle let her mind wander to Court Sinclair.

His softly spoken words and the gentle way his eyes had caressed her were a balm for her tor-tured spirit. She had been surprised that recriminations had not flowed from him in torrents. His acceptance of her deception in such an easy manner confused her. She puzzled over the outcome.

Mammy leaned over to fluff her pillow and broke into her wandering thoughts. "Mammy, I don't plan to spend the entire day in bed. I'm fine, it's only a scratch."

With arms akimbo, Mammy eyed her charge. "Now, missy, don't you go tellin' me what you is gonta do 'n' what you ain't gonta do. You's got us in a fine kettle of fish this time. Why, that Mistah Sinclair might jus' decide to toss us out on our ears. Then where we gonna be? Chile, you has got a wild streak in you that would make the Mississippi River look like a meandering stream. Ifen you would act like the lady I brung you up to be, you could have that Mistah Sinclair eatin' outa yo' hand."

"Mammy, in spite of what you say, Monsieur Sinclair would never believe that I have any of the qualities of a lady. Turning his head would be tantamount to turning the tide. I have no such powers." Sighing deeply, she picked at the soft sheet, a forlorn look etching her delicate features. "I fear you are right about our dire predicament."

"Mistah Sinclair seems like a fair man to me."

"Did someone call my name?"

A shiny black face and a startled pale one turned in unison to the direction of the door, where Court leaned nonchalantly against the frame.

Mammy sputtered, "Why, Mistah Sinclair, you ain't 'post to be in this here room."

"As I'm sure you'll learn, Mammy, I'm not hindered by decorum. If you'll excuse us, I need to have a few words with ... Dannie."

Mammy, not pleased at all, cast Danielle a warning look and begrudgingly ambled from the room, muttering in a voice sure to be heard, "Why, I ain't never heerd of such goings-on."

Court studied Danielle, his emotions at war. He had nursed his anger, but he would not play into her hands any more than he had already. But then again, there she was, all soft and feminine, her hair spread like a billowing black cloud over the white pillows. Her cheeks were pale and her lips pink as peach blossoms in the spring. For a fleeting second, he wondered if her lips would be as sweet to taste as they looked. A sudden tightening in his loins made him curse his foolishness, and he spoke more severely than he had intended. "What's your next move?"

Cocking her brow, she questioned, "What do you mean, *monsieur?*"

"Don't play the innocent with me." His voice was harsh, causing her to wonder if she had misjudged him. Maybe his wrath was beginning to descend on her after all.

"But I play no game. I accept the guilt of posing as a boy, but I harbor no other threat to you."

"Yes, I believe I hold all the cards and, my sweet, they're stacked against you."

Danielle was taken back by his cutting reply. "I have no idea what you expect from me. If you'll give me a few minutes to gather my things, I'll be on my way," she said softly.

"Not so fast, mischief-maker. If my memory serves me right, you agreed to remain here and take care of the plantation."

Danielle sat up in bed, clutching the sheet to her breasts. "You'd hold me to that after you've learned I'm not the person you thought me to be?" she choked out.

"It matters little to me that you are not as you

appeared to be. I've learned not many people are."
He dropped down casually on the bed beside her
and she scurried to the farthest edge. "Besides,
now that I know you're a woman, how in the hell
can I just put you out of your home? By the way, is
your real name Dannie?"

"That happens to be my nickname, *monsieur*.
My name is Danielle Elise Algernon."

He smiled knowingly. "Dannie...I like that. It
suits your boyish charm."

She reddened. "Only my close friends call me
Dannie."

"All right, Miss Algernon. Look," he said, raking his hand through his hair in extreme irritation, "I don't like this arrangement any better
than you do, but there's no other alternative at
the moment. Unless, of course, you'll allow me to
find you another place to live."

"Never!" Danielle declared adamantly. "I don't
want to accept anything from you. The people of
New Orleans would think I'm your...your kept
woman. It seems that I'm forced to stay here and
do your bidding. At least you won't be residing
here." Then catching the amused grin on his face,
she asked, "You won't be staying here, will you?"

"If I'm to get the place back into operation, I'm
afraid I'll have to remain here, Miss Algernon.
There's more to running a plantation than merely
giving orders. After I get it all set up and hire an
overseer, I'll be on my way. And, I might add,
there's another good reason for my moving in
here. Eventually it will become a well-known fact
that your stepfather isn't here, and a lone woman
isn't safe living by herself, especially this far from
the city."

"What will people think? This arrangement
you speak of so lightly will have my reputation in
shreds!"

"I'm sorry, Miss Algernon, but I value your life more than I do your reputation."

"Mon Dieu," she whispered and turned her face away from him. She felt the mattress shift as he removed his weight. He closed the door behind him as he left. "You'll be sorry, Monsieur Sinclair," she vowed silently. "I don't like being backed into a corner."

Chapter 6

"Massa Court, you's all packed up 'n' ready to go."
Bryce closed the bag and shrugged his thin
shoulders. "This ain't the thang to do. Ah jes' feel
it in my bones."

Court chuckled. "You aren't going to let that
ridiculous ghost tale bother you, are you now?"

"Yassah, Ah is. Ah wouldn't be my mammy's
son ifen Ah didn't believe in haints. Anuther
thang, Ah ain't goin' to sleep under the same roof
with no female haint. That one that's alive 'n'
livin' there oughtta change your mind, too."

"What would you have me do, Bryce, throw her
out?"

"Why ain't we stayin' here? You gots your own
house."

"There's something strange going on, and I
plan to find out what it is. Besides, it's always
been her home, and if she chooses to stay, then it's
fine with me." He laughed again. "Of course, it
wasn't her choice to make. You have to admit it
isn't every day a man finds himself living with a
woman as beautiful as Danielle Algernon."

"That's anuther thang," Bryce said as they
walked out into the hall of the townhouse. "Ain't
fittin' for a man and woman to live in the same
house without jumpin' the broomstick first."

Court's good humor evaporated at this reproof.

"That has no bearing on the situation here. Marriage is the furthest thing from my mind."

The closer they came to the plantation, the more Bryce chastised Court for their new living arrangements. Court had learned a long time ago to ignore him when his scolding became unbearable.

Bryce pulled back on the reins, bringing the horse and carriage to a halt in front of the house that loomed like a shadowed specter in the moonlight. The strong summer breeze whistled eerily through the leafy oaks, causing the shutters to slam repeatedly against the house.

"Ah ain't footin' it outta this carriage, no suhree, Ah ain't. That spirit knowed we was a'comin' 'n' she done gone 'n' brung in all her friends."

The front door squeaked as it swung back on rusted hinges, and a large figure dressed in white appeared behind the yellow glow of a lantern. It moved to the edge of the porch and came down the steps, revealing another figure coming from behind, and a rifle barrel glinting in the lamplight.

"Who's out there?"

"Court Sinclair," he shouted. "Put down your rifle. We mean you no harm."

Stepping down, he walked up the path with Bryce close on his heels, and joined Mammy and Tobias on the stoop.

Mammy glared up at him, her hands placed defiantly on her broad hips. "You ain't s'post to be here till mornin', suh. The missus done gone to bed 'n' will be mighty riled at wakin' up and findin' you here. Ya'll best go back where's you got a bed to sleep in."

Didn't this woman realize he was her new

owner? Court wondered irritably. He'd have to be the one to tell her—and with consummate tact.

"Mammy," he said softly, "I know you think of me as an intruder in your home, but as long as we remember to respect each other's wishes, we should get along famously. I want you to know I mean your mistress no harm."

His comment brought a smile to Mammy's mouth.

"You'll continue to manage the house in the way you're accustomed and follow any instructions Miss Algernon gives you. I can't be here as often as I'd like, so I'm depending on you and Tobias to see that all runs smoothly when I'm here...and when I'm not."

Mammy and Tobias looked at each other and nodded approvingly.

"Now, about my presence here, if anything is bothering you, don't hesitate to speak up." He waited a moment, watching Mammy and Tobias consult each other with their questioning eyes.

Finally, with a beaming smile revealing pearly-white teeth, she asked, "Would the massa suite be fittin', Massa Sinclair?"

Court felt he had jumped one more hurdle. Mammy had called him "Massa."

Once inside, Court took a moment to gaze around the room. The foyer rose two stories, with a narrow staircase leading to the upstairs landing. The wood floor was waxed to perfection. A vase of freshly cut flowers sat on the marble shelf beneath a pier mirror. A tall case clock stood impressively on the opposite wall. The house, which appeared to be older than many of the homes in New Orleans, was not as large as his own home in Natchez, nor as grand, but it seemed warm and inviting.

"Mammy, will you show Bryce where the master suite is so he can put away my bags? Tobias, is there any brandy?"

"Massa Caraville kept his libations in his study, suh. I hopes there's some left."

Entering the study, Tobias lit a candle, went to a cabinet, and pulled out a decanter of brandy.

"I'd be grateful, Tobias, if you'd find a place for Bryce to sleep...preferably somewhere other than inside this house, if you could. He says he won't sleep where a ghost roams."

Tobias smiled, handing Court a glass of brandy. "She roams eberwhere, Massa Sinclair, but she don't hurt nobody none."

"Thank God for that," Court said beneath his breath.

"What you say, Massa Sinclair?"

"Nothing...forget it."

Stepping back, his posture rigid with the formality of a butler, Tobias said, "Anything else I can getcha, suh?"

"No, that will be all, thank you. I'll see you bright and early in the morning."

Bowing slightly and taking a few steps backward, Tobias turned and closed the door behind him.

Court moved around the room, admiring the masculine decor. Simply molded bookshelves of walnut, mellowed with age, held a multitude of books. A Chippendale secretary with a corner desk chair waited in readiness. English wing chairs in worn wine-colored leather were placed for easy conversation opposite a matching sofa near the fireplace. A threadbare Persian carpet covered the floor and harmonized with the faded wall tapestries.

Sitting down on the sofa, Court sipped his brandy, his mind wandering to Danielle. What had he gotten himself into?

He became angry when he recalled Caraville's negative response when he had asked if he had any children. Actually the man had not lied, for Danielle was not his child. But he should never have placed his stepdaughter in such a predicament. The least he could have done was find a suitable husband for her before he gambled away their home.

Then a thought struck him. Suitable? Most of the rich merchants and plantation owners sought a woman who could bring them a sizeable dowry. Danielle had nothing left to offer but her lovely face, and from his observing her in the tight britches she had worn, an alluring figure.

When she had gazed up at him after her fainting spell, he had become lost in her violet eyes, which sparkled like amethysts. Her hair reminded him of black velvet as it spilled over her shoulders. Her complexion was creamy and flawless. How he had wanted to touch that softness, trail his finger over the finely sculptured cheekbones and the small upturned nose. He remembered her barely parted lips, peach-colored, wet, and pouting.

Gulping down the rest of his drink, he cursed himself for his wayward thinking. He had to keep Meredith first in his thoughts. If only he had seen Jordan prior to the card game with Caraville and had learned of his relationship with his sister, he could have questioned the man in a casual manner.

Then another thought hit him like a bolt of lightning. Could Caraville be the man who had kidnaped and demanded a ransom for the return of his sister? If so, Caraville would have known who he was the night of the game. Jordan had told him that Caraville was near financial ruin. What purpose would he have to seek him out and intentionally lose his home? If he had not lost it to Court, then he would have lost it to his creditors. The money received from the ransom would have taken care of him for a short while, but if he were as bad a gambler as Jordan had said, then he would have lost it already.

Court prepared another brandy and sat down again. "If I had a beautiful daughter and I had lost my home, what would I do?" he mused aloud, trying to answer the puzzle. "Use my daughter to get it all back." A sickening knot lodged in his stomach. What if the ransom note had been a lure to get him to New Orleans? Could Meredith have already been killed because of what she knew? Court could have been planted in this house to become so enamored with the beautiful Danielle that he would marry her instead of evicting her. If the plan went accordingly, her husband would then have an unfortunate accident, and Mrs. Courtland Sinclair would be left with the entire estate debt-free.

He had experienced an uneasy feeling about that game from the very beginning. Was the lovely Danielle involved in the scheme? The duel could have been a cover-up to make him think she was fighting for her home when all along she was playing him for a fool. If she wanted to play a game, then he would be a willing participant. Only she would be surprised at the final outcome.

Picking up the lighted candle, he left the study, wondering in which direction he should go to find the master suite. The house was quiet except for the clock's ticking. Thinking the master suite might adjoin Danielle's room upstairs, he began his ascent. Each step creaked alarmingly until he made it to the top. There were two rooms, both with doors closed. Not remembering which one was Danielle's room, he tried the nearest door, turning the knob quietly, and entered the room.

Moonlight cast its soft glow over the large tester bed; the mosquito netting wavered from the warm breeze that drifted through the window. Still not certain he was in the right room, Court looked around for any sign of his belongings. Extinguishing the candle, he walked quietly to the bedside by the light of the moon.

When he parted the curtain, the moonbeams spilled down on a slim naked leg and partially bare thigh. His blood turned to liquid fire, racing through every inch of his body. He was powerless to look away from Danielle's loveliness. The sheer nightgown clung to her body like wet silk, dipping and shadowing along the soft curves. She shifted from her side to her back, flinging one arm to encircle her head. Her full, ripe breasts swelled against the delicate lace bodice, their peaks straining the openwork fabric. A long, thick strand of ebony hair had entwined itself around one breast. His mouth yearned to take its place.

Suppressing his desires, Court picked up the snuffed candle and crept softly to the hallway. As he closed the door, he heard her bed creak and then her soft moan of contentment.

Using the wall to guide him through the pitch-black hall, he felt his way to the next door, finding only a linen closet. Returning to the main floor, he rambled blindly until he found his room. Mammy had left a candle burning for him on the table next to the bed and had turned back the covers. He gazed about the room with a hint of surprise mingled with pleasure. Although the house was in dire need of repairs—the carpets were threadbare and the curtains had been faded by the sun long ago—it nonetheless boasted a harmonious blend of taste and elegance.

This room was dominated by a four-poster bed in the Sheraton style. The curtains and bed hangings were a rose moiré silk. Covering the floor was an Aubusson rug of warm gray. A mahogany writing desk hugged one wall. A pair of matching chairs covered in a muted blend of rose moiré and gray silk rested before a cold hearth. Rare bronze birds perched on the mantel. A dignified chest-on-chest stood against another wall, ready to store his belongings. Court shook his head. Caraville had not appeared to know the meaning of the word taste, but this room said otherwise.

After undressing, he blew out the candle and crawled between the cool sheets, drawing the mosquito netting around him. Sleep was a long time coming. As he dozed fitfully, a wisp of a thought swept across his mind and he jerked upright in bed. How was he to win the game when the odds were stacked so heavily against him?

Chapter 7

Court rose early the following morning, his senses tickled awake by the mouth-watering fragrance of baking bread. While Bryce prepared his bath, Court opened the door to the wardrobe, finding his belongings packed tightly among the previous owner's clothing.

"Have Mammy arrange for Mister Caraville's clothing to be stored elsewhere. After you've finished, have one of the servants press all my clothing."

"Yassuh, massa. The chest of drawers still got his belongin's in them, too."

"Nothing belonging to Caraville is to remain in this room."

"What 'bout this, Massa Courtland?" Bryce held up a small, hand-painted portrait from the dressing table. "Looks to be a paintin' of Miss Algernon."

Court gazed at the haunting violet eyes and black hair scooped up from the neck into a mass of curls. "Perhaps Miss Algernon would prefer to keep it in her room."

Court bathed while a servant pressed his clothing. After dressing in fawn-colored trousers and tan linen shirt, he made his way to the dining room. As he entered, he saw a young servant smooth a linen tablecloth and set a place at the head of the long table. She was dressed neatly in a gray muslin dress and madras tignon.

Raising her head, she saw him and said shyly, "Mammy is seein' to your breakfast, Massa Sinclair. I'll tell her you is here now."

"What's your name, child?"

Curtsying, she said, "Camille, suh."

Court smiled at her diffidence. "A very pretty name. I notice you've set only one place. Has Miss Algernon not yet awakened?"

"Miss Dannie done ate and gone to do some paintin'."

"Painting?" he asked curiously. "I would've thought she'd have someone like Tobias do chores such as that." However, now that he thought about it, Danielle Algernon would be capable of doing anything.

"Not that kind of paintin'. She paints purty pictures 'n' all. Most all the pictures you see 'round the house is hers."

"Where does she go when she paints, Camille? I'd like to have her show me around the plantation after breakfast."

"Most of the time, she goes down to the riverbank." Hearing Mammy call for her, she said, "'Scuse me, Massa Sinclair, but I needs to tell Mammy you is here."

Nodding his approval, he watched her depart and walked around the dining room. Though somewhat worn, the room had the same look of tasteful elegance, coupled with the same comfort that was evident throughout the rest of the house. Beneath a beautiful chandelier that adorned the center of the room, rested a Chippendale banquet table, polished to a high gloss. A block-front sideboard sported a beautiful Georgian Sheffield candelabra, leaving ample room for the placement of culinary delights.

As Mammy bustled in with plates of food, he admired the still-life paintings that graced the walls, each bearing the initials DEA. He was amazed at the talent Danielle possessed. The painting of the house was his favorite. There were no unhinged shutters and no missing slats in the porch railings. It had been painted in the spring-time, when the purple wisteria was in full bloom and the lawn lay like a lush green carpet in front of the house. Studying the fine details of the quaint setting, he firmly decided that the first thing he would undertake would be to restore the house and its surroundings to their original con-dition.

Sitting down to breakfast, he thought his own cook back home could have taken lessons from the cook at Espérance. There was nothing lacking in the meal Mammy presented to him: hot croissants served with thick molasses; a dish of fresh fruit consisting of oranges, bananas, and pineapple; riz au lait, a cereal dish prepared with rice and sea-soned with sugar, cinnamon, and vanilla; and hot Creole coffee.

As he ate his breakfast, he pondered his up-coming encounter with Danielle. More than likely, Mammy had already informed her of his late-night arrival, and she had fled the house to avoid him at the morning meal. She was a con-niving little wench, of that he was certain. She was probably sitting on the riverbank conjuring up all kinds of schemes to get him to marry her.

Telling Mammy to give his compliments to the cook, he left the house. As he strolled down the oyster-shell path, he saw her sitting on the load-ing dock with her back to him, her full lavender skirt spread around her. The sunlight glinted off the thick braid of ebony hair. She appeared fragile and vulnerable, but since he had witnessed her skill with a rapier, he knew otherwise.

Her finely-tuned ears heard his booted feet crushing the shell path. The feeling of his eyes caressing her back sent little shivers up and down her spine. When he began whistling merrily, it did nothing to calm her chaotic thoughts. All this belonged to him now, even the dock she was resting upon.

Nearing her side, he said pleasantly, "Good morning, Miss Algernon. Lovely view, isn't it?"

"It was," she answered in an icy voice.

Moving in closer, he glanced over her shoulder to see what she was sketching on the pad resting in her lap. His view was partially obscured by the creamy crescents of her breasts overflowing the bodice's low neckline. His heart pounded so loudly he was sure she could hear it.

Clearing his throat, he said, "Do you mind if I watch?"

"Do as you please."

Sitting down beside her, he stretched out his long legs, crossing them at the ankles. She ignored him. Her fingers continued to work adroitly and furiously across the pad. The sketch was in its first stages, but he could make out the lines of a steamboat.

Court gazed toward the vast waterway. Traffic was heavy going in both directions. Several steamboats, their wheels churning the muddy water, and flatboats, heavily laden with goods, were slowly making their way to New Orleans. Smaller boats sashayed back and forth in the wake of the passing steamboats.

Trying to breach her cold reserve, he said, "I've seen some of your paintings. Did you paint the one of yourself that was in my room?"

"That's not me, *monsieur*; it's my *maman*. I

painted it from memory after she died. It was a gift to my *beau-père.*"

"You're very much like her ... very beautiful." He watched her pause in her sketching. "What happened to your father?"

"He died in a duel before I was born," she said irritably. "You are full of questions, aren't you?"

"Yes, I suppose I am, Danielle. You haven't volunteered any information about yourself so I have to ask."

She tilted her head in his direction. "As I see it, *monsieur,* it's none of your business."

He smiled at her, his eyes drinking in her beauty. "Touché, my sweet."

He continued on a lighter note. "You're a very good artist. The painting of the house is my favorite."

A faint but sarcastic smile touched her lips. "I'm surprised you found any similarity in the two. Money has been scarce and we've needed the labor to tend to other things. Tobias does all he can, but most of that has been inside maintenance."

"I want to restore the outside of the house to—"

"It's yours, *monsieur,* so do anything that pleases you." She fought back tears as she gathered her skirts and started to rise. A firm yet gentle hand grasped her arm.

"Danielle, most of my friends call me Court."

Jerking her arm from his grasp, she managed to rise to her feet. Clutching her sketch pad to her heaving breasts, she staggered backward out of his reach. "You are not my friend, *monsieur.* If you were, you would return my home to me. Did you not say you have one of your own?"

Her sharp retort increased his own temper. Damn, why had he thought he could win her over with politeness? "Yes, I do, and now this one belongs to me, also. Don't you wish to see it restored to its original beauty?" Rolling to his feet, he gripped her by the shoulder and turned her brusquely toward the house. He dropped his hands and encircled her waist, pulling her small figure against his hard chest.

"Look at it, Danielle, look at what has become of your home."

Feeling her tremble, he tightened his arms around her. He glanced down at the crown of her head and caught the fresh scent of her hair.

"See those shutters with broken hinges on your upstairs windows? I'll repair those first."

"I've grown accustomed to the creaking sounds," she said defiantly.

"You have, have you? Is it going to take the whole damn house falling down to bring you to your senses? Then it will be too late."

Her firm, round breasts pressed against his arms as she breathed in deeply. "Already it's too late for me. Why should I care if it topples to the ground? It doesn't belong to me any longer."

Good acting, my sweet, he thought angrily. Are you hoping to prompt me to say it could again belong to you someday?

Danielle was struggling with her own private battle. She dropped her gaze to his arms. She had never been held this way. Why, she could feel his heartbeat synchronizing with her own. She smelled the masculine scent of his cologne and breathed in its muskiness. But he was her enemy, she reminded herself, and he was trying to take advantage of her vulnerability.

She pushed away his arms and moved out of his embrace. Turning toward him, she pierced him with her dark amethyst eyes. "You may have won my home, but you do not own me, Monsieur Sinclair."

"I never said I did, Dannie."

His eyes dropped to her breasts and his mind drifted to the night before when he had gazed down on her as she slept. He desired her, but to be taken in by her charms might be his greatest mistake.

She saw where his passionate green eyes rested. She made no effort to turn from his gaze, but countered, "Look hard, *monsieur,* for that is all you shall do. You have mistakenly offered your home to me...and I shall stay because I have no alternative. It matters little to you that I'll be the subject of conversation in every brothel and gaming house in New Orleans. People have always enjoyed gossip about Danielle Algernon, so why not add another little tidbit for them to feed upon?"

A puzzled frown etched his brow. He should have gotten back in touch with Jordan Phillips before moving out here. What had Danielle done in her past to make her the subject of idle gossip?

"Would you enlighten me concerning the rumors surrounding you, Miss Algernon?"

Stiffening her spine, she haughtily lifted her chin. "You'll have to discover that for yourself."

She turned to leave, but his voice halted her. "I'd like a tour of the plantation, if you please."

"I'll ask Tobias to show you when—"

"I don't want Tobias." He paused and ran his fingers along the length of the fabric that draped her shoulders. "I want you."

His request rang more like a proposition to her ears, and she bit her lip to keep her tongue quiet. She would not let him succeed in raising her temper again.

"*Certainement.* It should not take very long. There's not much left to see."

Espérance, as did most plantation homes, had its own smoke house, outside kitchen, stables, and slave cabins. There were few male slaves in the vicinity. Danielle told Court they were harvesting the summer vegetables. When he asked if she had an overseer to supervise the raising of the cane, she told him she had had one at one time, but he would not take orders from a woman. Nicholas had told him the cane, the land, and the slaves were all going to fall into his creditors' hands, so not to bother working any longer. The man took him at his word and he and his family had moved to another plantation. Now managing the slaves was her responsibility, and she had chosen Obediah, a slave himself, to see that her orders were carried out.

As they were heading to the house, Court saw a small room attached to the side of the main house. "What's that room?"

A rare smile touched her mouth. "It's a planting room...or at least it was at one time. Nicholas built it for my *maman,* who loved to raise flowers and plants. I used to try to keep it tended, but with so much else to do, I'm afraid I let it fall by the wayside."

She began strolling slowly toward it as though memories of the past were calling out to her. As he followed and listened to the soft, lilting tune of her voice, he noticed an undertone of deep sadness.

"*Maman* had an uncanny knowledge of how to make things grow and flourish. After my father died, it was up to her to run the plantation, and she did it well. But she was young and lonely. She met and married Nicholas Caraville when I was five years old. He was kind and showed great love for my *maman*. His only fault was that he lacked insight into the management of a plantation."

His only fault? Court thought, raising his brow in question. Surely she was not describing the man he had met. It was hard for him to imagine a woman as beautiful as the one in the portrait married to such a man.

"What about his gambling?"

"If gambling is a fault, Monsieur Sinclair," she said in defense, "then you, too, are guilty."

"Ah ... but unlike your stepfather, I know when to quit," he replied with a devilish grin.

Her mouth clamped shut. Brushing past him, she almost ran to the house. Oh, I hate him, her mind screamed. His laughter followed her long after she slammed the door behind her.

Danielle did not come out of her room until after the noon meal, and then only because of the infernal sound of a pounding hammer outside her room. Running to the window, she saw Tobias standing on a ladder, a helpless look on his face.

So, he's started on his repairs, she thought, gritting her teeth in irritation, heading downstairs and outside. She stomped around the corner of the house to witness Tobias's legs trembling noticeably as he tried to hold the shutter and fasten it to the new hinge. Below him, looking up, were Court and Bryce.

"A little to the left, Tobias."

"Yassuh," he answered shakily. Placing the hammer under his armpit so he would have both hands free, he almost lost his footing as he slipped the shutter into place.

Danielle caught her breath until he righted himself, but the hammer plunged to the ground with a dull thud.

She went hot and cold in the same instant. She sauntered up to Court, her hands clenching and unclenching in anger. "Didn't Tobias tell you he's afraid of heights? Why didn't you send your own man instead of him?"

Court spoke through gritted teeth. "Because he didn't tell me he had a fear of heights."

"Mon Dieu, what did you do, then...threaten him if he didn't do as you wished?" Looking up at Tobias, she shouted, "Come down, Tobias...now."

Court managed to cool his anger and asked Bryce, "Would you mind fixing the shutter?"

"'Course not, Massa Sinclair. Ah ain't scairt."

Tobias slowly descended the ladder, squeezing his eyes shut until he reached the bottom. His legs nearly doubled beneath him.

"Go on inside, Tobias, and have Mammy pour you a shot of whiskey," Danielle said, patting his arm affectionately.

Court's brow arched upward. "Hell, woman, no wonder your place is falling to pieces if you give your servants liquor."

"Monsieur Sinclair, Tobias is to me what Bryce is to you...not only my trusted servant, but my friend. If one shot of liquor doesn't relax his shattered nerves, then he is welcome to the whole damned bottle!"

Bryce looked from one to the other, his mouth dropping open in amazement. Never had he seen his master talked to in such a disrespectful manner. He saw Court's jaw working furiously as he fought to control his temper.

"Ah—Ah goes on up now, Massa," he stammered, warily eyeing the two of them from over his shoulder as he climbed the ladder. Once at the top, he remembered the hammer lying beneath the ladder. "Ah forgots the hammer, suh."

Shifting his stormy green eyes from Danielle's inflamed face, Court went to pick up the hammer. His fury with her still eating away at him, he unknowingly walked beneath the ladder.

Bryce came halfway down and reached for the hammer, which Court was holding up for him. "Did Ah see what Ah thinked Ah seed? Your mammy'd have a conniption fit ifen she saw you do that."

"What's that?" Court asked, puzzled.

"You ain't never walked under no ladder afore."

Court's eyebrows drew together in a noticeable frown, and a strange look washed over his countenance. "Damn, I wasn't thinking."

Seeing his superstitious nature, Danielle broke into a fit of laugher and danced merrily back and forth beneath the ladder. Her eyes sparkled with mischief as she taunted him. "*Magnifique!* Maybe if I'm fortunate, the ladder will fall on your thick, superstitious skull, and then I can reclaim my plantation."

Court puffed up with indignation. "Damn you, I'm not superstitious. That's the most ridiculous thing I've ever heard." But was it ridiculous? he asked himself as he thought of all the bad luck that had recently befallen him.

"Oh?" she asked saucily. "Then follow me beneath the ladder, *monsieur*. Prove to me you are not."

"Don't do it, massa, you done done it once. Does you wants double trouble?"

His mammy's dire predictions flooded through Court's mind, pulling at him from one direction, while Danielle's taunting words pulled him from the other. He'd be damned if he'd let her get the best of him, he vowed. He followed her with a determined thrust of his chin. "Does that prove to you I'm not a believer in superstitions?"

From high above, Bryce shouted, "Lawdy, Lawdy, let me gits down from here afore this ladder falls."

Danielle chuckled and sashayed provocatively into the house.

Chapter 8

Danielle stopped in the hallway outside the master suite. The door was open just a crack and she could hear Camille humming a tune. She must be cleaning the room, Danielle surmised, and then was startled when Bryce came out, dragging a trunk behind him.

"What on earth are you doing, Bryce?"

"Ah's cleanin' out Mistah Caraville's belongin's."

"You're what? Then you'll just have to put them all back again," she ordered.

"But Massa Sinclair says he don't have enuf room for his clothes."

She lifted her head regally. "That's his problem. When Nicholas comes home, he'll be very angry to find his things removed without his permission."

"Nicholas will not be coming home," Court's voice thundered behind her.

She turned quickly, and bumped into his towering frame.

"When are you going to realize, Danielle, that Nicholas Caraville no longer lives in this house? Even if he should return, which I doubt, he'll not live in this house with us."

"He wouldn't leave me here at your mercy," she returned heatedly.

"He's done just that, and had no scruples about

doing so. In fact, as I recall, he emphatically denied having any children."

Danielle's face fell and her eyes filled with tears.

Once again, he wondered if she were acting, yet something urged him to soften his words. "I'm sorry, Dannie, but you have been sadly duped. Please believe me when I say I have no desire to hurt you, but you need to hear the truth. Nicholas Caraville is a deceitful, uncaring man. If I could find him, I'd gladly wring his scrawny neck for putting both of us in such an embarrassing situation."

She choked back the sobs that were trapped in her throat. *"Mon Dieu,* I cannot believe he would do such a thing to me." Her voice was husky with raw emotion.

Gathering her skirts in her hands, she ran past him, nearly stumbling over the trunks in her hasty retreat.

"Wait, Danielle," he called, but she could not hear him for the pounding in her ears.

Mammy, coming from the parlor, was nearly knocked off her feet as Danielle sailed by, tears streaming down her cheeks. She followed Danielle as she bounded up the stairs and into her bedroom, where she collapsed across the bed, great choking sobs shaking her body.

Mammy sat on the edge of the bed and stroked Danielle's shuddering form. "Oh, chile, chile, what's that aggravatin' man done to you now to cause you such pain? It jus' ain't right, no suhree. I've never seed you cry like this, never in all your born days. Now don't you cry no more, sweetie. Mammy'll take care of you like she always does."

Mammy's soothing voice and the large brown hands running gently across her back served as a balm to Danielle's crushed heart. Turning over, she raked the tear-dampened strands of hair from her face and stared at the ceiling.

"Monsieur Sinclair told me that Nicholas never mentioned me to him."

"I find that hard to believe, honey-chile. That don't sound like Massa Caraville a'tall."

"I have to find him. I have to know why he did this to me, or I'll never have peace of mind."

Mammy shrugged her large shoulders in despair. "You done tried to find him 'n' ain't had no luck. What does you plan to do this time?"

Danielle rolled to her side and propped herself on her elbow. "You never told me this, but I know you're aware of the quadroon mistress Nicholas kept on Rampart Street after *maman* died."

Rolling her eyes heavenward, Mammy replied, "Yes'm, I knowed he had one, but I never knowed her name. It weren't somethin' he ever talked about."

"You must help me, Mammy. You won't approve of what I plan to do, but I can't do it alone."

She eyed her charge furtively. "I doesn't like the look in your eyes. It means trouble's comin'."

"You and I are going to the Quadroon Ball," she said emphatically. "Nicholas and his mistress might be there."

Mammy sprang up from the bed in agitation. "We ain't doin' no such thing. That ain't no place for ladies . . . 'n' 'sides, white women ain't allowed."

Danielle laughed. "I know all that, Mammy. But I've heard of white women attending in disguise. Most of them go there to catch their husbands or lovers in clandestine situations. All we need to do is dress up in clothes befitting the occasion. Don't worry so, Mammy, everything will work out perfectly."

"Oh Lawdy, Lawdy," she said, pacing frantically around the room. "What ifen one of them

Creole men takes a likin' to you? Ifen I has to talk with him to gives my permission, he'll know right off I's a fake. 'Bout the only French words I knows is *mon Dieu* 'n' *bonjour*. They don't sound too Frenchified neither. I doesn't talk like any of them fancy darkies."

"We'll make our visit short, so you won't have to speak very often. I'll teach you a few French phrases and you'll really impress them. No one will be the wiser."

"The mamas of them girls dress mighty fancy 'n' all. How does you plan to take care of that problem?"

As Danielle's eyes shifted around her room, her hands idly caressed the blue satin counterpane on her bed. Suddenly bouncing to the floor as a plan formed in her mind, she jerked the coverlet from the bed.

"Whatcha doin', chile?"

"Try this on for size, Mammy," Danielle said with a twinkle in her eyes. She began draping the shimmery satin fabric around Mammy's robust figure, placing the delicate lace edging at the hem, and then bringing a length of it up to make a shawl to go around her shoulders. She removed the matching valance from one of the windows and wrapped it around Mammy's ample waist to hold the dress in place, and then turned her toward the mirror.

Mammy groaned. "I ain't believin' it."

"Only one more thing," Danielle said, her lips pursed in thought.

Going once more to the window, she removed both tiebacks. "Sit down, Mammy, and take off your tignon."

Mammy obliged and felt Danielle's hands wrapping the fabric around her head in a tight turban. She secured it in the middle with a pearl brooch. "Now look, Mammy."

Looking in the full-length mirror, Mammy's big brown eyes swept her exquisitely draped figure from head to toe. "Yes'm, we jus' might pull it off."

A knock on the door startled them. Mammy froze, her eyes searching quickly for a place to hide. "Just a minute," Danielle called, unraveling Mammy's dress and turban with the action of a whirlwind. Haphazardly tossing the counterpane over the bed, she jumped hastily onto it.

"What 'bout the curtains?" Mammy whispered, tugging on her tignon and sitting down next to Danielle.

"If anyone asks, we're mending them," she whispered back with a sly grin. "Come in," she said throatily, replacing her smile with her former look of sadness.

Court opened the door and stood just inside the entrance. He peered intently at the small figure lying on the disheveled bed, her violet eyes still glistening from the tears she had shed. She was breathtaking. For a moment he forgot his reason for coming to her room.

"What do you want, *monsieur?* Haven't you said enough already?"

"I told you only the truth, Danielle. I'm sorry I caused you pain, but it had to be said. Now you need to pick up the pieces of your life and start anew."

"Start anew? Ha!" she said impetuously. "And how do you propose I fit these pieces back into order?"

He boldly raked his eyes over her. "Marriage would be a start."

Her heart lodged in her throat, leaving her speechless. Surely he was not asking her to marry him! Never would she accept marriage from a man who had taken everything she owned. Before she could find her voice to tell him this, he spoke.

"You're a very beautiful woman. There must be scores of men who would want you for their wife." When he thought of her possibly scheming to become his wife, he added roughly, "More often than not, a mistress is favored above a wife. I've given that considerable thought myself. After all, we do live in the same house...very convenient, wouldn't you say?"

Mammy's eyes flew open at the insult. "Massa Sinclair!"

Danielle streaked from her bed and picked up her hand mirror from the dressing table. "Leave this instant! Go home to your wife and let her warm your bed."

He walked backward to the door, his hands shielding his face. He smiled nervously as he said, "You know if you break that mirror, it's seven years bad luck."

Remembering his superstitious nature, she began stalking him, the mirror poised threateningly. "What does it matter? At least I shall have the pleasure of seeing it break against your head."

Court's hand grappled for the doorknob behind him, but before he could open it, she hurled the mirror in his direction. He reached out to grasp its handle but lost his hold on it. The mirror crashed to the floor, its glass shattering into a thousand tiny pieces.

"*Monsieur,* since you touched it last, it's you who shall have the bad luck."

Court stared down at the shattered pieces, a look of consternation on his handsome face. "My run of bad luck preceded the broken mirror," he said, glancing at her. "By the way, I'm not married. That's one misfortune I've avoided."

"Then don't expect me to satisfy your lust by becoming your mistress. Just because I'm forced to live here does not mean you have the right to invade my privacy."

"When a man and woman live together in the same house, it's damn near impossible to build walls between them."

Mammy sucked in her breath, her large eyes shifting to Danielle.

"If I desired to have you, walls and doors would not protect you from me," he went on. "You might even decide afterward to leave your door unlocked to grant me easier access."

She drew her hands into tight fists at her sides. "How dare you think I'd ever ask you into my room. You're the most arrogant man I've ever met."

He opened the door and stood just outside in case she decided to hurl another object. "No, Dannie, not arrogant, just truthful," he said with a grin and closed the door behind him. As he descended the stairs, he smiled broadly, thinking that if Danielle had had any intention of charming him into marriage, he had effectively quelled that thought.

Court walked into Jordan's office on Chartres Street later that day, and was relieved to find him behind his desk, mulling over a stack of papers.

"Court, glad to see you," he said, getting up and reaching across his desk to shake his hand.

"Business must be good. I didn't see any of your ships at the docks. I thought I might have missed you again."

Jordan chuckled and leaned back in his overstuffed chair. He lit a cheroot and propped his booted feet on the desk. "Sit down. We didn't finish our conversation the other day. I've been wondering what you thought of Espérance."

Court sat down across from him. A slow grin pulled at the corner of his mouth. "What you've been wondering, my curious friend, is not what I thought of Espérance, but its beautiful and alluring mistress, Danielle Algernon. Why the hell didn't you warn me she was there before I went out and fought a damn duel with her?"

Jordan blew out a swift stream of smoke. "A duel? Who won?" he asked, suppressing his laughter.

"I did, of course. She was damn lucky I didn't run my blade through her, but I thought she was a callow lad trying to save his home."

Jordan rolled his blue eyes. "Egad, Court, how could anyone mistake Danielle Algernon for a boy? How long has it been since you've been with a woman?"

"Dammit, she was dressed in men's clothing, britches and all," he said heatedly. "Now cut out the nonsense, I'm serious. This woman's presence has created all sorts of problems. I couldn't boot her out so I bargained with her."

"What kind of bargain?"

"She'll manage the plantation in my absence. I'll be staying there only until it becomes a working plantation again. What I want to know is what kind of woman is she? She must be around twenty years old, so why didn't some man take her as his wife years ago?"

His friend shook his head in regret. "People think she's strange. As I told you before, the house is said to be haunted. Many have witnessed the ghost of Espérance, yet her family has managed to live there all these years without incident. Some people think she has a mysterious alliance with the spirit—that she talks with her on occasion."

Court fidgeted in his chair. "Then she has no man in her life?"

"Not unless it's Damien Baudier. He goes out there quite frequently. Since she knows how to use a rapier, I'd say Baudier has been instructing her. He's the best fencing master in the city."

Court toyed with his mustache. "Enough of Danielle, have you heard anything else about Meredith or Caraville?"

"No one but you has mentioned seeing either of them in the past couple of months. I thought that maybe they'd run off together to some other city."

"Could he have kidnaped her?"

"And then lose his plantation to you?" Jordan asked, a puzzled frown etching his brow. "Why would he come back to New Orleans and take the chance that you might have prior information concerning his involvement with Meredith?"

Not having an answer for that, Court withdrew the deed and laid it on the desk. "Does this deed look legal to you? I've gone over it myself and can't find anything out of the ordinary."

Jordan perused it. "Looks like the real thing." Silent for a moment, he then said, "If he kidnaped your sister as you think, then for the life of me I cannot understand why he would dare come back here without her."

"Unless he's killed her already," Court supplied. He told Jordan he suspected Caraville planned to regain control over Espérance by using Danielle as bait.

"A bit far-fetched," Jordan said, "but at this point, I can see why you've considered it. It appears to me you have two women to beware of."

"Two?"

"Danielle . . . and the ghost of Espérance."

Court laughed. "The ghost has yet to trouble me. It's the flesh-and-blood woman I have to worry about, and believe me, I think I'd prefer the haunting lady to Danielle Algernon. She's trying her damnedest to make me think she detests me, hoping I'll make amends by marrying her. You should've seen her display of a temper tantrum when I offered her a position as my mistress. She's a superb little actress."

"What will you do if she decides to come to your bed willingly some night?" Jordan asked with a wicked gleam in his eyes. "It would be hard for any man to resist that temptation."

"I plan to enjoy every minute of it...up to a certain point."

"Well, my friend, I envy you your pleasure."

Rising, Court stuffed the deed into his coat pocket. "I've decided to stay at my townhouse for a few days. I think I need to get away from Danielle for a while and decide how I'm going to handle this situation. Also, I want to see if anything comes up concerning Meredith and Caraville."

"Great, then we can have dinner together some evening. Two bachelors out on the town, just like the old days."

"You know," Court said, "it still amazes me you've never settled down and married."

"No, I just love 'em all," he announced. On a more serious note he added, "Same reason as you, I suppose. Just never found a woman I thought I'd be happy with for the rest of my life. They all seem so artificial...no originals."

Just as Court laughed, the vision of Danielle came to mind. Now there's an original if ever there was one, he had to admit begrudgingly.

Chapter 9

Danielle lay in bed, listening for Court's return. Would he come to her room tonight to prove the futility of locked doors? she pondered worriedly. He had been in her home for only twenty-four hours and already he had made his intentions clear where she was concerned. If circumstances had been different, and Court had come to woo her in an acceptable manner, she knew she might have succumbed to his charms. Now she had to maintain her pride and dignity.

Why had her heart fluttered when he said he was not married? There seemed to be only one way she could have her home again and that would be to marry him.

"No," she said aloud, "I will never marry a man who doesn't love me." How could she even think about becoming the wife of a man who thought so little of her as to assume she would desire to be his mistress? Still, could it be any worse than what was happening to her now? Since they had first met, there had been a constant war between them. But she had to admit that he had attempted to help ease her pain in the beginning. It had been she who had accepted his generosity ungraciously. What if she changed her attitude and tempered her words?

The following day passed slowly and then another. The entire household wondered what had happened to the new master. Danielle was on pins and needles, part of her hoping he had gone back to Natchez, the other part worrying whether he had met with an accident. She was bewildered by the unfamiliar emotions that his absence stirred in her.

To take her mind off such thoughts, she began working on her attire for the Quadroon Ball. Not knowing how the women dressed for the occasion, she asked her seamstress Lilly, a French negress, her opinion on how to remake one of her mother's gowns.

The gown they decided upon was a pale amethyst satin, made in the empire style. Her mother had never worn it, saying when Nicholas purchased it for her that the scant amount of fabric was too indecent for a lady to wear, though it was the latest fashion. There was a full-length matching cape of a deeper shade of amethyst to wear over it. Danielle swore Lilly to secrecy.

As she stood before her in the revealing gown, Lilly nodded her head disapprovingly. *"Non, ma petite,* the bodice isn't right."

"Is it too low, Lilly?"

Lilly laughed and winked at her. "Not low enough, I fear. The empire waist is out of fashion. We must remake the entire dress. When I'm finished, there'll be no one who will look as magnificent as you."

Danielle frowned. "I want to be inconspicuous and not draw attention. Finding a man is not the purpose of my mission."

Lilly sighed and shook her head. "Dressed as you are now, you would turn the heads of all. Now, let me take this with me, and by tomorrow you should have it back and ready to wear."

Danielle stepped out of the gown. "Remember, not a word to anyone."

The seamstress giggled. "Only if you'll let me assist you and Mammy in your dressing when the hour arrives." As she was leaving, she stopped at the door and turned. "By the way, what is Mammy wearing?"

Danielle smiled secretively. "It's to be a surprise, although we may need your skills before her gown is finished."

Mammy and Lilly closeted themselves with Danielle in her room the night of the ball. Tobias, who was to drive them into the city, was preparing the carriage for their departure, and acting as lookout should Court come home unexpectedly. All Danielle needed was his sudden reappearance to foul her plan. She could never succeed if she had to secretly skulk out of the house.

For an hour, Danielle, who was as jittery as a young lady attending her first soiree, had soaked in the tub, a last attempt to calm her anxiety. Little good had it done, for now as she let Lilly dress her, she could feel her legs trembling beneath the sheer fabric.

"Be still," Lilly chastised. "I can't button your dress."

Mammy watched in admiration as Lilly applied the final touches to the gown. Danielle moved to the mirror and her eyes lit up like two sparkling jewels. Nothing resembled the original dress except the fabric. The bodice was cut deeper than before, barely concealing the rosy tips of her breasts.

"*Mon Dieu*, Lilly, I can't bend over one tiny bit," she exclaimed.

Lilly laughed while Mammy scowled. "You ain't gonna go like that, chile. I'll be havin' to speak French all night long tryin' to keep them men in line."

"Oh, Mammy," Lilly interrupted, "don't be such a prude. Did you ever see such loveliness? The gown is a superb fit."

"It sho' is," she grumbled. "Fits so good you can see ev'ry curve in her purty little body. I jus' hope your mama ain't lookin' down on us now and seein' what I is lettin' you do. And Massa Sinclair —Lawdy mercy, ifen he saw you like that, he'd throw me in the river for sho'.'"

Since there had not been enough fabric to increase the fullness of the skirt, Lilly had shortened the cape and used the extra fabric to create a flounce attached to the waist and draped over the hips. As Danielle turned slowly before the mirror, she heard Mammy choke and sputter.

"What is it, Mammy?" Danielle asked and looked down to where Mammy's eyes were glued. Her long silk-stockinged leg was bared from the ankle to the knee.

"Git your needle 'n' thread, Lilly, 'n' sew it up," Mammy ordered.

The two younger women exchanged bemused smiles.

Lilly said convincingly, "Now, Mammy, the dress was far too tight and showed more of her then than it does now. I had to add the split to enable Danielle to walk and dance graciously instead of having to stand in one position all night long."

"Humph!" Mammy snorted. "Women cain't even show their ankles 'n' here my chile is showin' half her leg."

"You have to understand," Lilly continued. "Quadroon women don't dress like the French ladies of the city. The truth of the matter is, they are more flamboyant in their style than the *haut monde*. Why, most of them have their evening

wear fashioned by the most expensive modiste in
New Orleans."

"Then you is goin' like that...'most near
naked?" Mammy asked in exasperation. "Ain't
nothin' I can do to change your mind?"

"Nothing, Mammy," Danielle said, smiling
broadly. "Now, it's your turn to get dressed."

Lilly was impressed with Danielle's creativity.
Though Mammy's lower lip still protruded petulantly, Lilly could see a tinge of excitement in her
round, brown eyes.

"Why, Mammy," she said enthusiastically, "you
may need someone to chaperone you. Who will
the men ask when they seek permission to court
you?"

Danielle could not see the color change in
Mammy's brown face, but it was apparent she was
blushing furiously when she lowered her eyes. "I
ain't got the time for such foolishness," she mumbled, but her eyes glanced fleetingly once more to
the mirror.

Lilly then assisted Danielle in the arrangement
of her hair. After braiding it in one long thick
plait interwoven with narrow amethyst ribbons
with tiny seed pearls, she coiled it on top of her
head, allowing several strands of wispy curls to
frame her face and the nape of her neck. As the
final touch, Danielle fastened a pearl choker
around her neck and a cluster of pearls on her
ears.

As she donned her cape, she asked Lilly to see
if Tobias was ready. Although they had waited
until dark, Danielle noticed while she boarded the
carriage that the moon was bright and full. After
they started toward the city, she cringed each
time they went around a bend in the road for fear
of seeing Court returning to the plantation. What
would he think if he should pass them, dressed

the way they were? But then, he had no right to question their actions. Should he inquire, she would say she had received an invitation to a masquerade ball. With this notion, she settled back and tried to relax.

Their journey ended on Orleans Street, where the Quadroon Ball was held. Danielle experienced a mixture of excitement and anxiety as Tobias assisted her from the carriage; he was to wait outside for their return.

They entered the two-story building with several other young ladies and their mothers. A great number of men lounged in the gaming room. Their eyes would shift intermittently from their cards to the women who were making their way upstairs to the ballroom.

When Mammy nailed herself to the floor at the entrance, Danielle took her firmly by the arm, and they ascended the curved stairway with the other party-goers. Inside the ballroom, they handed their wraps to an attendant, and found a corner to themselves, hoping they could fade into the dark paneled walls.

The dance floor was crowded as the musicians played soft, romantic music. Several men were standing on the loggia, feasting their eyes on the beautiful quadroon women, obviously talking among themselves about the one they wanted as their mistress. Occasionally, Danielle would be aware of some man's bold gaze making her uncomfortable, and she would quickly turn her head.

She had never seen so many beautiful women under one roof. Dressed in the latest Parisian fashions, the quadroon women laughed gaily, lowered their eyes demurely, and flirted openly but in a subtle way.

Mammy clutched her arm, interrupting her

musings. "Lawdy mercy, that man looks like he's comin' this way. He's been watchin' you ever since we came in."

"Let me take care of it, Mammy. Since I plan to show no interest, you needn't say a word."

A handsome Creole man approached her and smiled, showing even white teeth. Like a wolf on the prowl, she thought, pasting a smile on her face.

"May I have this dance, *mademoiselle?*"

Shyly dropping her eyes as she had seen the other women do, she replied softly, *"Je regrette, monsieur,* I am spoken for, *merci."*

"But you have only just arrived."

"Qui vrai, but my companion has not yet joined me. I'm expecting him at any moment."

He persisted. "Surely, he wouldn't care if I have just one dance with you."

Danielle nudged Mammy lightly in the ribs.

Jumping to attention, she cleared her throat. *"Au revoir, monsieur."*

Noticeably disappointed, the young man bowed and sought a new conquest for the evening.

Mammy gulped and sighed. "How'd I do?"

Danielle giggled. "Perfect. You evidently sounded authentic to him."

The men continued to come and go. Danielle had repeated the same phrase so many times she was exhausted. Mammy had become so confident in the few French phrases she had learned that Danielle had to nudge her frequently to hold her tongue. Even though it was still early in the evening, they had been successful in evading the more aggressive men and their bold proposals.

There was no sign of Nicholas, and there seemed to be no possible way to question the women present concerning the identity of his one-time mistress.

Danielle had turned to Mammy, her back to the dance floor, to discuss their plans for the remainder of the ball. She was startled to feel a gentle touch on her shoulder and a warm breath at her ear.

"*Ma petite*, you are so lovely. May I have the honor of this dance."

Danielle recognized his voice, and with a mischievous smile, turned to face him. "With my mother's permission, *monsieur*, I should love to accept your invitation."

Damien's eyes nearly popped out of his head. Clutching her by the arm, he whispered angrily, "*Mon Dieu*, Dannie, you shouldn't be here!"

She tilted her nose in the air in defiance. "And why not? I'm having a delightful time, *mon ami*."

He glared at Mammy. "How can you be so irresponsible?"

"Stop it, Damien," Danielle hissed. "Mammy had no choice but to come with me. Better this than my coming alone."

"Dance with me—*now!*" he demanded. "No wonder my friends laughed at me when I told them I would ask you to dance. You've managed to turn them away all night, but not this time, Dannie."

He whisked her onto the dance floor. He took her into his arms, and they began dancing to the soft music. His movements were precise, fluid, but she could feel the tension of his hard slim body against hers as he maneuvered her around the dance floor.

"Now, why are you here? Are times so bad that you have to look for a lover to take care of you?"

"*Non*, Damien," she said, startled by his outrageous remark. "I came here to find Nicholas or perhaps his mistress."

Tightening his arms around her, he said, "I told

you I'd keep an eye out for him. There's no need for you to continue with these foolish disguises."

"Please, *mon ami,* let me explain why it's so urgent that I find him soon. So much has happened since you left the other day."

Gazing down into her disturbed violet eyes, Damien nodded his head in concern. "I'll get us some champagne, then we'll go to the courtyard, where we will not be disturbed."

He ushered her to Mammy's side, and then left to get their drinks. Danielle was humiliated to see several of his comrades slap him on the back for his huge success. But at least they would leave her alone for the duration of the evening.

"Lawdy, I knowed we'd git caught," Mammy moaned, wringing her hands together.

"At least it's Damien. Having him with us will keep the other men at bay," Danielle said with relief.

"All's 'ceptin' one that I knows of, 'n' speakin' of the devil, there he is," Mammy said, choking on her words.

Danielle was mortified to see Court standing on the loggia, conversing with a group of men and women. He towered several inches above the others and his physique seemed overpowering in their midst. He looked extremely handsome in his tight black trousers and red evening coat. She saw a couple of quadroon women whisper to one another and knew by the direction of their eyes just who had their undivided attention. The man beside Court was only an inch or so shorter and boasted an abundance of black hair. They laughed and gazed over the dance floor, and then to the women waiting with their mothers.

Danielle quickly turned her back to them. "I have to get out of here. You stay and tell Damien to meet me in the courtyard."

"It's too late already, missy. He's headin' this way. We's in for it now."

"Non," Danielle said. "I'll keep my fan in front of my face as I walk through the crowd."

Fluttering her fan rapidly before her face, she swept hurriedly across the room, keeping her head lowered to the floor. Her heart nearly stopped when Court's red sleeve brushed her arm in passing.

She felt she would melt into the floor when he placed his hand on her shoulder. *"Mademoiselle,* are you all right?"

"Oui, merci," she said huskily, keeping her head down and waving the fan like a banner in a storm. "'Tis hot in here. I thought to get a breath of fresh air."

"Yes, it is rather warm. I'll go with you," he offered.

"Non, please ... I ..."

"It wouldn't do for a woman as beautiful as you to go into the courtyard alone." He pressed his hand to the small of her back and urged her toward the open door.

Almost to the point of fainting from fear, Danielle had difficulty making her way down the outside stairway to the courtyard. *Mon Dieu,* please don't let him recognize me, she prayed fervently.

A few couples meandered through the courtyard. Danielle swallowed deeply when she saw their overt amorous displays. Much to her dismay, the full moon in the cloudless sky was just as bright as it had been earlier.

Court could not help but notice how nervous the young woman was and wondered at her discomfort. He had caught a glimpse of her dancing from his position on the loggia. Even from that distance, he could see how beautiful she was. Why had her mother allowed her to go to the courtyard alone? She continued to avidly flutter her delicate fan in her face.

"*Mademoiselle,* the fan's unnecessary. I've seen your loveliness. You came here tonight with the intention of meeting a gentleman, so there's no need to behave so coyly."

"I'm spoken for, *monsieur,*" she replied demurely, and walked beneath the leafy boughs of a tree to hide from the moon's brightness.

"If it was the gentleman you were dancing with earlier, I saw him surrounded by a circle of beautiful women."

Oh, Damien, damn you and your female followers, she cursed silently. "I told him I'd meet him outside, *monsieur.* He cannot help being the handsome man he is. Many women find him attractive, but it is I who holds his heart." How easy it was to speak of Damien as her lover, she thought with a smile.

She leaned against the tree and folded her fan. In the shadow of its leaves, he would be unable to identify her.

"Then he's a most fortunate man, *mademoiselle.*"

He moved in closer and in the faint moonlight, he could see the generous swell of her creamy breasts. He had never wanted a quadroon mistress, but this one had managed to stir his desire. There was something vaguely familiar about her voice and carriage to which he was attracted. He became bolder with his advances.

Danielle became uneasy when he moved in much too close and braced his hands against the tree, hemming her in.

"He wouldn't like finding another man with me, *monsieur.* Perhaps you should leave before he arrives."

"Have you shared his bed, little one?"

Danielle reddened and spoke sharply. "Of course not! How dare you insult me."

Court grinned and lightly traced the contour of her lips. "Then he has no claim on you, does he?"

Her heart skipped several beats as he lowered his face to within inches of her own. The rough bark of the tree bit into her back as she pressed hard against it. She could smell the musky, male scent of him as he leaned forward and brushed his lips across her cheekbone and over to her ear.

"You are lovely," he murmured. "I think I should give your man a bit of competition."

She froze, her words of protest paralyzing in her throat. Although she feared she would draw attention to herself by warding off his advances, she was more afraid of her overwhelming desire to be kissed by him. Mammy was right; they should not have come here tonight.

His mouth hovered above hers for an instant. Unable to resist the temptation, he captured her lips in a soft, warm caress. His mustache tickled her nose, and she found she enjoyed the sensation. Her mouth quivered, and he stilled it by pressing his lips harder against her own, his tongue trying to pry her pursed lips apart. No longer capable of barring his entrance, she parted her lips and reveled in the feeling of his tongue stroking the inner recesses of her mouth.

Court stroked her bare shoulder, skimming his finger beneath the narrow ribbon of fabric. Her skin was smooth as satin. He yearned to follow the length of the ribbon downward to the soft swell of her breasts. Instead, he broke the kiss, pulling a tight rein on his own desires.

Danielle was breathless and shaken by the abrupt removal of his mouth. Her lips ached and tingled in the same instant. That he should possess her so easily caused her to question her own mind and heart. It frightened her to think she might feel something other than loathing for him. He was handsome, true, but Damien was handsome, also. Why didn't she feel this same way with him? What was there about this man that intrigued her even though he humiliated her at every turn?

"You shouldn't have kissed me, *monsieur,*" she replied softly.

"There are many things I shouldn't do, my pet."

"I need to go back inside. My *maman* will be worried if I stay away much longer. It seems my escort has been waylaid."

Court grinned devilishly. "His loss . . . my gain."

The heat rose to her face. Before she could think of a reply, she heard her name called.

"Dannie, where are you?" Damien's voice echoed through the garden.

She cringed inside. Of all times for Damien to make his appearance. She watched Court's brow furrow at the mention of her name. Dragging her by the arm into the moonlight, he stared hard into her face.

"My God, it's you. What the hell are you doing here?"

"It's none of your affair, *monsieur.*" She shot him a nasty look and shook her arm free of his grip.

Damien came upon them then, his eyes flashing dangerously. "Is he bothering you, Dannie?"

Recognizing Damien as her dancing partner, Court stepped forward and offered his hand to him. "Court Sinclair. I'm"—he cleared his throat—"a friend of Miss Algernon's."

Damien looked at her questioningly, waiting for her answer before he would consider shaking the man's hand. "Is he speaking the truth, *ma petite?*"

"I know him," she acknowledged crisply. "Monsieur Sinclair is part of the reason I'm here tonight. He's the new owner of Espérance."

"I don't understand," Damien said. "When and how did all this come about?"

"He won the plantation from Nicholas," she supplied.

Turning his attention to Court, Damien eyed him warily. "When did Nicholas return, *monsieur?*"

"He hasn't returned, Damien. That's why I'm here," she interrupted. "I was hoping to see him tonight."

Cocking a questioning brow, Damien returned his attention to Court. "Where are you staying in the meantime, *monsieur?*"

"I'm living at Espérance," Court said.

"You're living...together...in the same house?" Damien demanded, aghast.

Danielle saw his hand move to the hilt of his rapier. She knew he would think nothing of defending her honor. She did not want anyone's blood shed, even Court Sinclair's, on account of her.

"I had no choice, Damien. At least Monsieur Sinclair hasn't sent me on my way. Conditions could have been worse."

Damien grasped her by the elbow, pulling her to his side. "Then we must find a place for you to stay. I'll not have you gossiped about."

She spoke softly. "*Non*, Damien. Espérance isn't my home now...but I can remain there until I find a way out of my predicament. People will talk no matter where I go. They always do."

Court interrupted. "Danielle can remain at Espérance for as long as she desires."

"Don't you have the good grace to reside elsewhere? What manner of a man are you to place a defenseless female in such circumstances?"

"Defenseless?" Court said with a short laugh. "I'd rather wrestle with an alligator. You are aware of her skill with a rapier?"

"Oui, monsieur." He cast her a conspiring smile. "It is I who taught her. To date, she's my best pupil."

"Then you must be Damien Baudier, the noted fencing master. I've heard of you." Court wondered if there was more than just a teacher-pupil relationship between them. Did he, in truth, hold her heart? It was difficult for him to see only friendship between a man and a woman who both possessed such dynamic personalities. He had seen women fawning over Damien earlier, and he, himself, had been ready to succumb to Danielle's charms only a few moments ago.

"There's one thing that plagues me, Mr. Baudier. You accuse me of behaving in an ungentlemanly manner, yet you arrange a rendezvous with a woman who definitely should not attend the Quadroon Ball."

Seeing a blaze of fury register on Damien's face, Danielle rose to his defense. "He didn't know I was coming. You accuse him wrongly, Monsieur Sinclair. My purpose in attending was to find Nicholas and have him explain his actions. I thought if he were in the city he would more than likely come here tonight with his mistress."

"Nicholas Caraville told me he planned to leave the city, so there's no need in trying to find him," Court informed her.

"But where would he go if he has no money?" she asked, feeling her heart sinking lower and lower.

"That I don't know. Like you, I wonder the same thing," Court said cryptically, knowing if indeed Caraville were the kidnaper, the ransom money would take care of his needs.

"Why should you care?"

"I have my reasons. Now it's time you were leaving," Court declared adamantly. "Who's the woman you coerced into being your mother in this silly charade?"

"Mammy! *Mon Dieu,* I forgot all about her. She'll be beside herself with worry."

Court's eyes widened in disbelief. "Mammy? My God, how far will you go to carry out your schemes?" he shouted, then lowered his voice when he noticed a couple separate from their embrace and look in their direction. "Don't you know that all it would take for you to be discovered would be for Mammy to open her mouth just once?"

Danielle thrust her chin in the air. "Mammy did just fine, mind you. Everything would have gone as planned if you and Damien had not interfered."

"I have to agree with Monsieur Sinclair, Dannie. You must go home. If you are discovered as an interloper, there's no telling what could happen. I'll see to it myself that you arrive home safely."

"There's no need for you to go out of your way, Mr. Baudier," Court said emphatically. "I happen to live there, too, remember?"

"Oui, monsieur, I'm very well aware of that fact. You needn't remind me."

"Neither of you need escort me," Danielle said petulantly. "Tobias is waiting for Mammy and me with our carriage. We can find our own way home, *merci,* but not until the evening is over."

Court's temper flared. "You're not staying, dammit. I've never met a more headstrong woman in all my life. If I have to, I'll pick you up and carry you out. To hell with propriety."

Danielle stomped her small foot, her chest heaving with anger. "You wouldn't dare!"

"Try me," he said threateningly, slowly advancing toward her.

"Leave her be." Damien itched to pull his rapier from the sheath. "You have caused her enough problems already. She wouldn't have come here tonight were she not forced to do so by your presence in her home." Taking her gently by the arm, he said, "Come, *ma petite,* I'll follow you home." Then pivoting toward Court with the grace of a panther, he declared, "I cannot order you out of your own home, Monsieur Sinclair, but so help me if I ever hear of you trying to take advantage of her, I'll run my blade through you."

A frown etched Court's forehead. God, he thought, he was the one threatened, not Danielle. He remembered how her sweet lips had answered his kiss, the feel of her soft body pressed intimately against his own. He knew that now she would haunt his dreams and threaten his control.

Clamping down on the sensuous flow of his thoughts, he said, "Then, take her, Baudier. No woman's worth spilled blood—yours or mine."

Chapter 10

Danielle, angry as she had ever been in her life, stiffened her spine, and with unladylike movements, climbed into her carriage.

"That bastard," she fumed, jerking her twisted skirts into place.

Mammy, huffing and puffing in her finery, was boosted aboard by Tobias, her swinging arm cuffing his ear when he stumbled.

Affronted by the blow, he squawked, "Why'd you go 'n' do that for, Mammy?"

"Hush your mouth. Cain't you see that Miss Dannie has had a terrible upset?"

Holding his tongue and nursing his burning ear, Tobias guided the horses through the dimly lit streets.

Danielle stared into the darkness, pleased that she was able to convince Damien she was capable of getting home by herself. She was not in the mood for conversation with him or anyone else.

Mammy did her best to soothe the young woman's ruffled feathers. "Now, sugar pie, don't you go broodin' over that hateful scene with Massa Sinclair. I guess he had a right to fly off the handle like he did. We ain't got no business at no Quadroon Ball." She sighed. "Did you see all them fancy dresses 'n' that flashin' jewelry? Why I ain't got no more business there than I gots at the opera."

97

Danielle smiled in spite of herself. "It was something to see, wasn't it? I was surprised so many prominent men were there. All those high-society women would die if they could see their husbands flaunting their mistresses so openly." With a puzzled brow, she questioned, "Why do they do it, Mammy? Do they not love their wives?"

"Chile, I reckon sometimes the wives is jus' glad they ain't comin' to their bed no more."

"Is it so bad, Mammy...I mean...when the husband comes to his wife's bed?"

"I guess that depends on the husband, honey."

The carriage rocked along, and Mammy started to snore softly, her headdress tilting askew from her nodding head. Feeling overcome with guilt, Danielle roused her, unable to wait to apologize.

"I'm sorry I got you into all this, Mammy. *Mon Dieu,* all we went through and not only did we not see the person for whom we were looking, but we saw the one person we wanted to avoid."

Draping her large arm around Danielle's shoulder, Mammy drew her close. "That's all right, lamb. If the truth be tol' I secretly did enjoy bein' there. As long as them gentlemen didn't question me too closely, I was fine...jus' fine. Why I ain't never seed the likes in all my life. As far as Massa Nicholas goes, he's like a ghost... here, there, everywhere, but really nowhere a'tall. And I think Massa Sinclair acts so mean to you 'cause he cares 'bout you."

Mammy's innocently spoken words sent Danielle's mind whirling. On the surface it appeared she had dismissed her anger, but inside she raged like a fire out of control as she thought about Court. She would get even with him if it was the last thing she ever did, she thought as she seethed. Her mind conjured up all sorts of torture for him. In each scene that flashed before her eyes, she was the much abused maiden, wielding the shield of justice. Court was down on his knees, receiving his comeuppance.

Satisfied with her image of his seeking pardon, she let her mind drift back to his appearance at the ball. She wondered if he was seeking a mistress. She had noticed the beautiful women who sought his eye. He had seemed to accept their admiration in a manner denoting he was accustomed to such attention.

She had to concede that he was a devilishly handsome man, dressed royally in tight-fitting black pants, snowy-white silk shirt, and scarlet jacket. Her heart had skipped when he threw back his head and laughed uproariously as one of his many admirers drew his head down and whispered boldly in his ear. Danielle wondered at his easy manner and the intent politeness he displayed. Never had he shown any of these qualities toward her. But was it any wonder? she thought. From the onset, their acquaintance was fraught with anger and suspicion.

She smiled into the darkness, a plan taking shape. Even though it had been several days since Court had been at Espérance, Danielle was certain he would make an appearance sometime tonight. He would not be able to pass up the chance to reprimand her for her presence at the ball. So much the better . . . while she still had the nerve to follow through with her plan. If Court were as superstitious as his manner indicated—although he tried to hide it—then it only added credence to the idea that he would believe in ghosts. Delicious tingles coursed through her as she contemplated his reaction when he encountered the Espérance ghost face to face. He would probably turn tail and return to Natchez after restoring her property to her. If she had her way, she would have him doubting his own sanity.

When they arrived home, Danielle, buoyant with her scheme, bounded up the steps and rushed to her room. Jerking open drawers, she pulled clothes from the chest until she found what she was seeking. Hugging her find to her, she danced around the room triumphantly until she heard Mammy's lumbering gait. Quickly she stuffed the article beneath the feather ticking of her bed.

"Lawd o' mercy, chile, this room looks like a tornader done been through it," Mammy said, her eyes scanning the disheveled clothing scattered about the room.

"I'll pick it up, and you go on to bed. It's been a long day."

Shaking her head, wondering at the energy of youth, Mammy left the room.

Danielle paused at her dressing table, dabbing a hint of lavender fragrance behind her ears as she studied her reflection in the mirror. After straightening the room, she curled into a soft chair. She picked up a well-worn edition of *Godey's,* a magazine featuring the latest fashions, and flipped the pages, waiting patiently.

As Court and Bryce headed for the plantation, he had the fleeting thought that he should have stayed in his townhouse, but the large quantity of alcohol he had consumed had affected his judgment. All he wanted now was to face his nemesis and confront her with her latest deception. His drunken pride was bruised beyond repair by the vision of loveliness who had turned up so unexpectedly at the Quadroon Ball. My God, she did not have any business there, he cursed silently. But, dammit, she had been there, hanging on to that popinjay Baudier as though he were a lifeline.

His sodden mind returned again and again to the shocking image of her in that low-cut gown she had worn. For God's sake, did she want all the men ogling her? Not once in his ramblings did it occur to him to wonder why her presence at the ball bothered him so much. He would not admit that he was jealous.

Bryce looked at Court from the corner of his eye. Only a few times in his life had he seen his master so out of sorts. He had tied one on this time. Bryce chuckled to himself and shook his head in amusement.

The house stood in darkness, except for the soft light reflecting from Danielle's room. Court slammed full force into the front door, and cursed violently. Maybe he should have declined that last round of drinks, his muddled mind thought as he felt his way along in the darkness. He crashed headlong into the stair banister, his knee cracking loudly against the spindles.

"Have they rearranged the whole goddamn house in my absence?" he swore, then righted himself.

A soft light spread over the stairs, and he looked up to encounter Danielle standing at the head of the steps.

"Is something amiss, *monsieur?*"

Her softly spoken words flew all over him. "Hell no. I've only shattered my kneecap, but that doesn't concern you. I'd like to know why a light was not left burning."

"We didn't know you'd be returning. Since no one has seen you of late, how were we to know you had not decided to take up residence in town?"

He ignored the rebuke and continued his tirade. "I don't give a damn if it's a year before you lay eyes on me again! I want a light left burning in the entrance hall, by God."

"As you wish, *monsieur*." She turned rapidly, deciding she had had enough of his sharp tongue.

"Danielle." His voice slurred as he began mounting the steps. "Don't run off." Starting up the stairs, he stopped, raising his eyes to her. The light from the door behind her silhouetted her shapely form through her cotton gown. He had difficulty tearing away his gaze. He sucked in his breath sharply and stumbled back a couple of steps. "Dammit, Dannie, why did you show up there tonight? Gently bred ladies don't attend such balls."

"I told you why. I went there to search for Nicholas. I could ask you the same question, you know."

Placing one foot before the other, he attempted the stairs again, this time making progress. "It's different for a man, Dannie. For a woman, just a breath of scandal can shatter her reputation."

"Then I'm sure mine is beyond restoration. A woman doesn't live openly with a man, either."

His harsh expletive echoed through the house. "We're not living together, dammit, not like you mean." His brow arched and his lopsided smile approached a leer. "Unless, of course, this is an invitation to change our sleeping arrangements."

Not bothering to reply, she turned away in a huff. Returning to her room, she was more convinced than ever that she couldn't pass up the opportunity to rid Espérance of Court Sinclair.

Gazing after her in surprise, he mumbled, "Women," and sought his own room.

Taking the brandy decanter, he poured himself a drink. The mellow liquid went down smoothly, easing his conscience of the thought that he had contributed to the ruination of Danielle's reputation. Discarding his clothes haphazardly, he paced the room and finished his brandy. Tugging back the mosquito netting, he pulled at the bed covers and slumped naked onto the cool sheets. The room spun precariously, and he changed positions repeatedly, trying to dispel the sensation. His last coherent thoughts were of Danielle as she stood like a vision of ecstasy at the top of the stairs.

The vague outline of a wispy shadow floated before Court's bleary eyes as he tried to focus. His drink-laden mind accepted the apparition as a dream. A gossamer streamer skimmed over his chest, causing his stomach muscles to contract. The fabric continued over his stomach until it touched the border of the sheet. Court lay in limbo, wanting to move and yet afraid if he did the sensation would cease. Up and over his body, it continued, lightly trailing his expectant flesh. The streamer softly caressed his chest teasingly, like the fluttering of butterfly wings. A faint scent of lavender assailed his nostrils. A bell went off in his head . . . a dream didn't smell of lavender.

Unable to bear it a moment longer, his arm stole closer, trapping the fabric in his hand. Drawing it nearer, he closed his arms around warm, soft curves swathed in shimmering white.

An angel, his besotted mind deduced. "Come to me, my angel. Show me a glimpse of heaven," he cajoled huskily, tugging the figure down beside him.

Now, this is not going according to plan, Danielle's mind screamed as his warm lips moved over her face until they reached hers. They moved with eagerness over her softly yielding mouth, his tongue parting her lips as he sought entrance, which was hesitantly granted.

She was shocked that the fire of his kisses set

her own blood racing. Plan or no plan, her mind was swept clean of any desire to flee.

His excited lips brushed her sensitive flesh once again as they moved across her face, resting against the hollow of her neck. His warm breath teased her hair. Sweeping aside the gossamer veil, his mouth trailed over her where the fabric had only moments before enticed over him.

She was mesmerized by his touch, beyond rejecting his advances. Instead, she ran trembling fingers through his thick hair and stroked his shoulders, delighting in his urgent loveplay. She let her passion flame and burn brightly as his mouth taught her a new meaning of the word desire.

His hands cupped her swollen breasts, his mouth teasing one taut peak, tugging until she rolled her head and sighed softly. Suddenly he released it and captured the other. While he partook of that delight, his roaming hands drifted to her satiny buttocks and slim legs.

Repositioning her, he caressed her thighs. Seeking the moist softness between her legs, he stroked her, probing gently until entrance was smooth, and he explored realms never before chartered. She cried aloud and arched against him.

His mind was reeling with desire and the response of his angel. The room was dark, the moon hidden behind the shuttered window. He did not have to see her to know that she was beautiful. Her satiny skin and soft curves told him all he cared to know. He knew his passion was returned by the way she writhed against him. His experienced hand brought moans of pleasure from her. At last he drew himself over her, and with care, parted her legs.

An instant of cold reality swept over her. She pushed against him, seeking her freedom.

He felt the stiffening of her body—the rejection he could not bear. Cupping her chin, he cautioned, "Easy, angel...don't leave me."

His hand stroked her face as his whispered words soothed her fright. His warm breath danced against her sensitive flesh.

"I won't rush you, my angel. We have all the time in the world."

He stroked her, explored her, whispered words of passion that soon had her writhing beneath his experienced hand. She was hot, moist, and aching for fulfillment.

Taking her hand, he guided it to his throbbing manhood. She clasped it hesitantly, caressing it until she discovered the motion that brought a moan from him. Their mouths urgently explored, tasted, teased, and nipped.

Knowing she was ready for him, he lowered himself and entered her swiftly. Her eyes shot open in confusion. Her cry of pain was muffled as his mouth covered hers. He slowed his rhythm until her pain vanished and desire assaulted her full force. Arching against him, she urged him on. Never in her wildest dreams had she thought she was capable of such sheer unabandoned passion. The flame raged out of control, consuming them both with its urgency. Their passion flooded a chasm as deep as the ever-moving river, and overflowed its banks as though in the throes of a violent storm.

Afterward, Court rolled to his side, his arms holding her. Minutes drifted by as they lay unmoving, each savoring the experience.

"Ah, so this is heaven," he ventured.

Her voice husky with newfound delight, she whispered, *"Oui, monsieur*, it is you who have shown me a glimpse of heaven. I would see more of it..." Her mouth sought his once again.

As he once again plunged deeply, and her softness accepted the length of him, he moaned hoarsely, "I shall clip your wings and shackle you to my side for I've never found such pleasure on earth."

As he drifted deeply into sleep awhile later, the large quantity of alcohol he had consumed finally taking its toil, she crept from the room, aglow from their ardent lovemaking, her gossamer veil once more intact.

Danielle, still flushed from the recent turn of events, found sleep impossible. Every time she closed her eyes, she could see herself as she must have looked hovering over Court's bed. To say her plan had backfired would be an understatement. *Mon Dieu.* She shuddered, not believing she had acted so...so...*mon Dieu,* what would describe her behavior? she wondered. A multitude of words filled the void: promiscuous...wanton... loose...the list kept growing. The heat of her face could have warmed all of St. Louis Cathedral. She had only meant to try and scare him, not become his entertainment for the night. His superstitious nature and her desire for vengeance had sent her thoughts awhirl. She had planned to root him from her home with his own fear. Only a fool would have assumed such a plan would work, she mused.

She knew the only relief from such turbulent thoughts would be the exertion of a strenuous ride, so she dressed and headed for the stables. She walked Tempete a good distance from the house before she mounted, then nudged him into a brisk trot and felt the cool air caress her still-heated face.

She reined her horse to a halt near the river's edge and then dismounted. Solving this problem was going to take a thorough examination of her own heart. Dropping down on a bed of fir needles, she leaned against a towering pine and let her mind wander. But her treacherous thoughts insisted on again reliving the pleasure she had experienced in Court's arms. To herself she admitted she had been deeply affected by their encounter.

The sky was ablaze with the breaking of dawn, a crimson horizon stretching as far as the eye could see. In the distance a dead tree loomed like the remains of some prehistoric animal, a silent specter viewing the passage of time.

With sheer determination, Danielle plotted her course. She would bank her desire for Court until nothing remained but cold ashes. She could never let him know she had been the one in his bed... nor that she craved his touch, his lips, and his experienced body entwined with her own. Could she school her emotions so no one would know of the bubbling volcano within her? She was good at hiding her true feelings. Had she not lived her life with them suppressed and tucked away deep in her heart? Having reached that decision, she let the gentle lapping of the water soothe her and soon her head nodded in sleep.

The sun was high in the sky before her eyes flickered open. Refreshed and resigned to the path she had chosen, she whistled shrilly for Tempete. After mounting, she headed for the plantation to meet head-on whatever fate had in store for her.

The heat was sweltering as Court eased open his eyes. He would not have been surprised to see a little man perched on his brow, hammer in hand, pounding away at his head. Hoping to alleviate the ache, he closed his eyes. Shards of pain pierced his head and ran down the back of his neck.

"Damn," he groaned, clasping his head.

Right on cue, Bryce entered the room. "Good mornin', massa," he ventured daringly.

"I don't know what the hell you find so damn good about it," Court ground out, opening blood-shot green eyes.

Bryce stood beside the bed, holding out a glass of noxious-looking brew.

"You expect me to drink that?" Court asked apprehensively.

"Yassah, Massa Court. Mammy swears by it. She concocted this, wouldn't let me near her whilst she mixed it. Said it was a secret."

"Beware of secrets," Court said, but accepted the glass with trepidation. Sitting up in bed he glared at Bryce. "Don't look so pleased with yourself. And if you dare say I told you so, I'll nail your tail to the smokehouse."

"I'd never do that, Massa Court. You know that." Turning quickly before he could see him laugh— because those were to have been his next words— Bryce began picking up his master's scattered clothing.

"Don't stomp so, man," Court groaned. "Have a little sympathy for a dying man."

His shiny black face split into a wide grin. "You ain't gonta die, Massa. That heavy drinkin' you done jest telling' you what a good time you had, that's all."

Court groaned. "If my pounding head's any indication, then I must have had one helluva night." After eyeing the glass of brew for a short while, he took a deep breath and tilted the glass, draining the contents in seconds. "Ugh!" He shuddered. "Damn! If the cause doesn't get you, then the cure will."

As the words left his mouth, he broke out in a

cold sweat and trembled violently. "Oh, God, no," he wailed, leaping from the bed. Bryce had the chamber pot ready.

Lying back on the bed, weak as a kitten, Court swore vengeance on Mammy's head. But surprisingly, within minutes, he was feeling better.

"Bryce, believe it or not...I'm starving. If you would see to my bath, I'll put to good use the remainder of the day."

After Bryce left the room, Court propped his arms behind his head and contemplated Mammy's remarkable cure. Out of the clear blue, an image of shimmering white floated through his mind. He bolted upright as the dream came crashing back with clarity. His first reaction was to dismiss it, but had it been a dream? It seemed so real...soft, satiny curves, a hint of lavender, and something about an angel. Why could he remember the lovemaking so vividly and draw a blank when it came to the vision? If he could purge his mind as easily as he had his body, he would have his answers. Racking his brain did no good, and once again he cursed his foolishness for imbibing so freely.

He let his eyes roam the room. Everything was as it should be. No gossamer gown draped a chair. Then his gaze dropped to the rumpled bed clothes. His pulse raced and a chill ran up his spine. Flecks of blood stained the sheet.

"Damnation," he swore. Was it a dream after all? Were these the telltale signs of a virgin's blood? His angel? No, his better judgment ruled this as impossible. Thinking it must be his blood from injuring himself in his drunken state, he checked his arms and legs but found nothing amiss, although his left knee was a bit touchy and an angry blue.

My God, he was losing his mind, he thought. A few drops of blood and he was ready to champion the first angel he encountered, as though angels

were an everyday occurrence. He shook his head at
his foolish thoughts.

Suddenly the melodic nuance of his angel's voice
washed over him. *"Oui, monsieur,"* she had said.
Only one person he knew spoke with that distinct
flavor. "Danielle Algernon," he whispered.

The discovery puzzled him. Why? What did she
have to gain? What she had given away would have
brought a king's ransom. Had she thought to drive
him out of her home by her ghostly appearance?
Though his pride would have liked to believe his
sexual prowess had caused her surrender, suspicion
suddenly reared its ugly head, sowing doubts. Could
this have been part of her scheme? She had been a
virgin when she came to him. Was he supposed to be
overcome by guilt and offer her marriage as payment for violating her?

"No, hell no, dammit no. I won't be taken in like
some wet-nosed kid."

Rising, he lit a cheroot and gazed pensively out
the window. A spider on the sill caught his attention. Its silken web glinted in the sunlight, vibrating with the movement of its prey. In an instant,
the spider had descended on the unlucky captive,
and swathed its victim in a cocoon of deadly silk.
Would silken threads bind him as surely as the
spider had bound its victim?

Instructing Bryce to change his bed linens, he
left the room. Touring the house, he was again impressed by its simple elegance. He noticed several of
Danielle's paintings throughout. She was quite good
if he was any judge of art. Her drawings captured
the depth of her subjects—their warmth or coldness—whichever the case might be. She seemed to
have an eye for detail. Her colors were bold and
subtle at the same time. Continuing through the
house, he made note of repairs to be done and furniture to be replaced. Whether Danielle wished the

plantation restored or not, he intended to see it returned to its former glory.

Mammy's beaming face peeked around the door frame. "Mawnin', Massa Sinclair. How are you today?" Her brown eyes sparkled mischievously.

"Thanks to you, I believe I'll live. But never in all my thirty-two years have I ever tasted such a God-awful brew. What was in it, Mammy...the hair of a dog, tail of a cat, and a pinch of dried bat wings for taste?" He smiled teasingly, revealing even white teeth.

"Ah, you do go on, Massa Sinclair, but I'm mighty glad you is feelin' better," she declared.

"You don't look any worse for wear after your big night on the town."

"Sakes alive, I done tole the Lawd ifen he'd git me outta that mess, I'd git myself outta the next one."

He smiled at her words. "If I have my way, there won't be a next time...as far as Danielle is concerned," he said emphatically.

She decided she ought to give him another chance. Anybody who could tease a little couldn't be all bad. His attitude was nothing like the one of that spiteful Rankin Pernel.

"Can I git you anything, Massa Sinclair?"

"No, Mammy, I'm fine. I'm going into town later and will probably be there for several days. I'll send supplies so we can begin the repairs. Will you see to it that Danielle doesn't put up too much of a fuss?"

"She's as stubborn as a two-headed mule, 'n' proud to boot," she answered, shrugging her large shoulders.

"I can see you have your work cut out for you, Mammy, but I'm confident you have powers of persuasion to see you over the rough spots."

"Lawdy, I sho' hope so," she declared, rolling her eyes. "But, Massa Sinclair, ifen you don't mind me

sayin' so, please try to bear with Miss Dannie. She's
had a mighty hard row to hoe. She's been practi-
cally on her own for more'n half her life—'ceptin'
she's had me, of course—'n' she's powerful proud.
But when she sets her mind to sumpin', it ain't no
easy task changin' it. And beggin' your pardon,
massa, but I fear she's taken a powerful dislikin' to
you."

"I'll keep that in mind, thank you. By the way,
where is she? I haven't seen her about at all."

"Oh, that Miss Dannie. She's up with the sun
ev'ry mornin'." She cocked a brow.

He wondered if that had been a sly reprimand for
his being in bed half the day.

"She's out ridin' that ornery horse of hers. That
chile puts more stock in that hateful animal than
oughtta be right. Ain't nobody can do a thing with
that beast but her. And I'd swear that horse knows
'sactly what she's sayin' to it. Beats all I ever seed."
She huffed. "I's got work to do, Massa Sinclair. I've
lolly-gagged in here long enuf. Ifen you need me, I'll
be out back in the kitchen. I tole Maybelle I'd help
her with the menu for tonight. Ain't no rest for the
wicked." She began to hustle her generous build
from the room.

"I believe that's 'no rest for the weary,'" Court
said, stifling his laughter.

"That don't make no never mind. Wicked or
weary, I ain't gonta get no rest this day." With that,
she was gone, leaving Court laughing at her rejoinder.

He made his way to the stables, stopping in mid
stride as a sleek chestnut stallion and rider scaled a
three-rail fence. He gaped open-mouthed when the
horse and rider stopped within inches of him.

Danielle leaned from the saddle, placed a gloved
finger beneath his chin, and pressed lightly until

his mouth snapped shut. "Catching flies, *monsieur?*" she taunted, sliding down from her horse.

His anger flared. "Dammit, woman, you could've killed me."

"No such luck. Besides, I was in complete control. At no time was there any danger to anyone."

"If you choose to break your own neck, that's your business, but I'd have a care for such a beautiful horse. Should he have stumbled, both your lives would've been in jeopardy."

"Tempete doesn't stumble; he's taken that fence hundreds of times."

"There's always a first time for everything, my pet," he said carelessly, a provocative smile teasing his mouth.

Quickly, a blush warmed her cheeks. Not looking him in the eye, she snapped, "I must see to Tempete; he's had a hard run."

Court watched in amusement as she led the horse away, his eyes following her derrière as it swayed provocatively in tight-fitting pants. He must have been out of his mind to have mistaken her for a boy. Hindsight, he muttered wickedly, is better than no sight at all.

"Danielle," he called out softly.

"*Oui, monsieur.*" She turned to face him.

"What do you know of angels?"

"Angels?"

"Yes," he said with a grin.

"The only thing I know of angels, *monsieur,*" she answered without hesitation, "is that in olden times the Lord used them as messengers."

Not fooled for a minute by her response, he chuckled. "Whatever you say, my beauty." With a mock salute he excused himself.

Chapter 11

Jordan Phillips gazed across the smoke-filled room at his friend. At a glance he knew appearances were deceiving. Court Sinclair sat with an air of boredom at the table, his cards held loosely in his hand. Jordan watched the fleeting expressions of the other players as they tried not to show their apprehension as the pot increased. Perspiration beaded and rolled from one portly gentleman's forehead as he gazed once again at the hand he held. Another man tapped his cigar nervously against the already overflowing ashtray. Another clicked his false teeth in unison with the tapping of the cigar. Still the pot grew.

Court watched it all without a hint of unease marring his impassive features. At last the hand was played, and he dragged his winnings toward him. With untold relief, the other players settled back in their seats, glad the damnable nervous anticipation was over.

"It's been a pleasure, gentlemen," Court announced as he rose to his feet.

"Looks like Lady Luck has smiled favorably on you once again, my friend," Jordan declared, slapping him on the back.

"Looks that way," he agreed in amusement.

"Do you have time for a drink? I have a matter that needs brought to your attention, although you may decide Lady Luck has played you false."

When they were finally settled at their table, drinks in hand, Court arched an inquiring brow. "What is it you wanted to say?"

"Are you aware that the plantation you won has a multitude of debts against it? Several creditors holding Caraville's notes have approached me, wondering if you were taking responsibility for payment. They have hired a man by the name of Rankin Pernel to collect their money, but it seems he's left New Orleans. Since no one has seen Caraville in months, the creditors are assuming his daughter will pay his debts. It would seem Caraville lacks your skill at the gaming table."

"That bad, huh?" Court asked with indifference.

"That bad," Jordan agreed.

"I'll have a bank draft drawn up to cover the amount, but I don't want word to get out. Let them assume Danielle has taken care of it. If you can handle this with the same discretion you use to juggle your mistresses, no one will ever need know whose money has covered the debts," Court declared with a wicked smile.

Jordan laughed royally at his friend's rejoinder and promised no one would suspect a thing.

Court swore angrily at his impulsive decision to make the trip back to the plantation. He knew better than to assume Mother Nature was only testing her strength when he heard the rolling thunder and saw the jagged bolts of lightning streak across the darkened sky.

"Damn," he muttered, drawing the collar of his coat up around his neck. The rain beat down relentlessly, soaking him in a matter of minutes.

"Sorry, boy," he said, leaning over to stroke his

horse's glistening neck. "It seems your master hasn't the sense he was born with."

His horse snorted and rolled his head to the side, seeming to agree.

Bolt after bolt of lightning followed by an unusually loud drum of thunder encouraged Court to hasten his already fast pace. His mount streaked through the night in anticipation of a dry stall and an ample helping of oats. In the distance the house was silhouetted in the raging storm, a perfect setting for the superstitious tales that surrounded it and its beautiful mistress.

Neither Bryce nor Tobias greeted him when he reached the stable. Much disgruntled, he rubbed down Scoundrel himself, fed him, and headed for the house. No one met him here, either. Seeing to his own needs, he sought his room and pulled on dry clothes. The rumbling in his stomach sent him in search of Mammy. Where was everyone? he wondered as he walked to the back of the house. Only lights from the kitchen were visible as he approached. He shoved open the door.

Seated at a long wooden table were Bryce, Tobias, Mammy, and right in the middle, Danielle. A feeling of warmth and companionship emanated from the room. A low fire burned in the large fireplace, hissing momentarily when a drop of rain made its way down the chimney. Fresh baked bread filled the air with a mouth-watering aroma. Court took all this in with one glance around the room as all eyes turned with startled jerks in his direction.

Mammy jumped to her feet, smoothing her long apron in nervousness. "Can I git you sumpin', Massa Sinclair? Ifen you been trudgin' through this here downpour, I reckon you is starvin' to death. Ain't no night fit for man or beast to be traipsin' 'round in."

He wondered humorously which category he fit in.

"You come over here whilst I fix you sumpin to eat."

As he complied and sat down at the table, Mammy chattered nonstop, buzzing around, preparing his food. "Everybody else done gone to bed. We wasn't 'spectin' you back tonight."

"Mammy's been telling ghost stories, Court. Do you believe in ghosts?" Danielle asked softly.

"If the occasion warrants it, I might be tempted."

Silence filled the room until Mammy spoke up. "Now that sho' is a strange way of puttin' it. They ain't no straddlin' the fence when it comes to ghosts," she intoned, placing his food on the table. "Either you believe or you don't. Here's your dinner, massa, all good 'n' hot."

Conversation picked up once again as Bryce questioned him about his trip. Mammy sauntered back and forth, making sure Court had everything he needed, until with a great deal of patience, he asked her to resume her place at the table. After much cajoling from the others, she began her storytelling again.

Court leaned back in his chair and listened with amusement to the tale. As she became accustomed to his presence, she became bolder with her storytelling. Everyone listened attentively, leaning closer to her, not wanting to miss a word. Bryce's eyes became larger and larger, and when the lightning suddenly brightened the night and the wind whipped a moss-draped limb against the window, he bolted from his chair. Suddenly realizing he was not about to leave the presence of his companions, he sheepishly sat back down. Danielle's merry laughter rippled through the room.

* * *

Court drew on the aromatic cheroot, then exhaled slowly as he stared out the window. A new and gay side of Danielle had been unveiled to him that night as she mischievously egged Mammy on and teased Bryce unmercifully. Court's heart had swelled with pride as he noted her quick wit and easy laughter. Even now as the household slumbered, his senses were pervaded by her vivacious spirit.

A wisp of movement caught his attention and he peered intently toward the river. The rain and wind had long ceased, but now the grounds were shrouded in a thick mist that rolled from the river. His body jerked involuntarily as he saw the movement again.

"Damn," he swore as chills ran up his spine. With hurried movements, he wiped at the window. Something or someone was drawing apart from the fog, hovering momentarily, then drifting toward the oak tree. He pressed his face to the glass, watching in wonder as the apparition floated closer.

"Goddamn, how does she do that?" he swore, never questioning why he naturally assumed it was a woman. He blinked and it was gone. Had she ever been there at all, or was it his imagination? Maybe Danielle was trying to scare him off the plantation. Well, it would not work. He would go along with her masquerade for a while but not indefinitely. With undue haste, he drew on his pants and bounded as silently as he could from the room. If she were up to her shenanigans, he would catch her in the act.

Feeling his way in the dark, he eased open Danielle's door. All was quiet. A faint light fell through the window, lighting his way to her bed.

Drawing back the mosquito net, he let his eyes roam her slumbering figure.

She might be playing possum, he thought quickly and leaned forward to see if she was breathing rapidly. Her breathing was slow and even, but Court's had suddenly picked up speed. She was lying on her side in an indecently short gown, rumpled sheets haphazardly entwined around her long shapely legs. And there to his pleasure and discomfort, her little derrière was revealed seductively beneath the tangled sheet. He sucked in his breath and stepped closer, enjoying the enticing sight immensely. Seizing another idea, he decided to check her heart beat. She might be able to feign sleep and breathe normally, he reasoned, but if she had raced back to bed, her heart would be pounding. Determined to foil any plan she might have concocted, he grinned with pure wicked amusement. With slow, precise movements, he placed his hand on her rising chest.

Feels normal to me, he decided as her warm flesh seared his hand. It took all the restraint he could manage to withdraw his hand from the inviting fullness.

Her ebony hair streamed like darkness over her creamy shoulders. She was a delicate beauty, extremely captivating when she chose to be. Had the circumstances of her lonely childhood forged this beauty and hidden the spark he had glimpsed tonight? Silent suffering and solitude had strengthened and molded her. Could he intentionally cause her more pain?

As he watched the sleeping beauty, a melancholy feeling wretched his insides. She beat at his heart strings like a hummingbird. Then with anger he swore softly, determined to find a way out of this dilemma.

The only thing he could think of was to find a

suitable husband for her; then both their problems would be solved. Disregarding the unexpected knot that twisted his insides, he pursued the idea further as he treaded quietly from the room.

Before getting into bed, he took a long, sweeping glance toward the river. Nothing stirred except an occasional leaf as droplets of water rolled from one position to another.

Propping his hands behind his head, he lay in bed, pondering the idea that had seemed such a perfect solution only moments before. As sure as his name was Court Sinclair, he knew if he broached the subject to her, she would bristle and with unerring bluntness tell him what he could do with his inspiration.

He decided to reject that idea; he had to be more subtle and conniving, and better yet—come up with another solution. On that note, he drifted off to sleep, dreaming of angels and fencing opponents. Their shapes became intermingled with one another, changing forms as rapidly as an artist changes the strokes of his brush.

Early the following morning a bleary-eyed Court dragged himself from the comfort of his bed. Ordinarily this would not have caused such difficulty, but after he had witnessed the eerie vision, sleep had come in fitful spurts.

"Ghost...Danielle," he grumbled, "what the hell difference does it make?" He pulled on his trousers and donned his shirt, buttoning it as he crept out into the hallway. Looking around guardedly for any sign of life at such an early hour, he was grateful to discover blessed silence. Unbolting the front door, he opened it slowly. As it swung back, the sound of the squeaky hinge sent a shiver of apprehension up his spine. He made a mental note to remind Tobias to oil it.

Outside, he strode down to the large oak tree where he had seen the vision. Walking slowly around the tree, he searched the ground for any clue that might prove the apparition was human. He cocked his head in exasperation. "Dammit, I know I wasn't dreaming last night. I stood right there by my window and watched her."

Narrowing his eyes and chewing on his lower lip, he glanced toward the house. If the vision had been Danielle, how long would it have taken her to get from the yard to her bedroom? There was only one way to find out.

Court sprinted the distance from the tree to the house, bounded up the porch steps, shoved open the door, and slammed pell-mell into Mammy's generous bulk as she was coming outside to sweep the porch.

A whoosh of air deflated their lungs on impact. As Mammy swayed backward, Court reached to right her, but grabbed the broomstick instead just as she lost her grip on the handle. It landed with a dull thud between his eyes. Dazed, he staggered backward, turning in the nick of time to grasp the porch railing before toppling over it. The pain in his head was secondary to the one in his loins as the broom whipped its hard length between his legs and jammed into his groin. He swore heartily. Sweat broke out on his blanched face as he bent over the railing, gritting his teeth until the pain receded to an aching throb.

He took deep breaths of fresh air, the sweet fragrance of honeysuckle entwined in the railing assailing his senses. He raised his head, and peering through the vines, his gaze met a pair of eyes, black and curious. Nostrils flared and snorted as Tempete viewed him with disfavor.

Knowing who sat astride Tempete's back, Court's eyes drifted upward over the stallion's head, focusing his attention briefly on the rider's midsection. Beneath her white lawn shirt, Danielle's full breasts bobbed with the laughter she was trying to suppress.

Angry that she had witnessed his humiliation, he brought himself to his full height, the broomstick still wedged between his long legs.

"*Bonjour, monsieur,* 'tis a marvelous morning for riding, isn't it?" she asked, glancing slyly at the broom handle, a roguish smile tugging the corners of her mouth. "Is Scoundrel displeased with you, or do you prefer stick horses? Tempete and I were just on our way out for an early morning ride if you'd like to join us."

Court's tightly drawn lips turned a pasty white. Her witty remark was received in the manner in which it was intended. Gripping the broom handle, he jerked it from between his legs and pitched it to the far end of the porch. "You'd be wise to hold your damned tongue, Miss Algernon."

"*Pardon, monsieur,*" she exclaimed, clasping her hand to her chest in mock sincerity. "*Mon Dieu,* but you're in a foul mood. Didn't you sleep well?"

Mammy stood behind them in the doorway, her brown eyes casting a warning look in her charge's direction, but Danielle continued to goad him. "Could it be our ghost stories caused you to lose sleep? Stormy nights produce the perfect setting for such tales, don't you agree?"

Court glared at her, closely scrutinizing her complacent features as he remarked. "I found the evening very entertaining. True, I didn't sleep well, but it wasn't due to the presence of a ghost in my room . . . but the absence of one."

A puzzled frown etched her brow, and then suddenly disappeared. Court waited for her comment, hoping for some sign of an admission. Twirling the reins loosely around her fingers, she leaned forward and stroked Tempete's mane.

"The man's daft, *mon ami*. 'Tis he who needs a brisk ride, not us." With that, Danielle reined her horse toward the road and left him with a non-plused expression on his face.

Turning in anger, he marched past Mammy, who was still standing just inside the doorway. "For once, I have to agree with her," he murmured to himself as he passed.

"What's that?" Mammy asked.

"Nothing...forget it," he said with a wave of his hand.

Entering his room, he saw Bryce readying his bath. "Mawnin', Massa Court," he said, eyeing him curiously as Court stripped off his clothing. "Did you stay up all night?"

"What makes you think that?" he asked gruffly.

"Well, the ashtray was overflowin' 'n' Ah emptied it afore Ah went to bed, 'n' yo bed's mussed up somethin' terrible."

"I don't know how I'd ever make it through the day, Bryce, without your keen perception," Court said, stepping into the tub. He groaned as the warm water lapped against his body. He rested his head against the rim of the tub.

Seeing his pained expression, Bryc clucked his tongue knowingly. "You gots a headache agin? What you needs is anuther dose of Mammy's brew."

Court grimaced at the thought. "Where I ache, I doubt very seriously if Mammy's potion would do me one whit of good."

Misinterpreting Court's source of pain, Bryce went on to say, "I jes' bet she has a secret liniment we could rub you down with."

"Bryce?" Court glared threateningly at him from the corner of his narrowed eyes.

"Yassuh?"

"Enough."

"Yassuh," replied Bryce meekly.

Finally realizing his master was not in the best of moods, he wondered whether this was the appropriate time to bring up the vision he had seen the night before. As he was taking Court's clothing from the wardrobe, he said flippantly, "Ah ain't gonna never listen to none of them haint stories ever agin. You start seein' things 'n' then believin' them."

Court's attention immediately perked up. "What are you talking about?"

Bryce laid Court's shirt and trousers neatly over the chair. He winged a bushy brow before he spoke. "You promise you won't think Ah is teched in the haid ifen Ah tell you Ah seed that female haint last night."

"Of course not, Bryce. Tell me about it."

"Well, ain't the first time Ah seed her. Never tole nobody cause Ah wasn't quite sho' it was for real. Last night Ah was havin' a hard time sleepin' cause of them haint stories, so's Ah jus' tossed 'n' turned. Bad as Ah hated to, Ah had to go outside and relieve myself." Bryce stopped and cleared his throat. "Ah got out there in the bushes aside the house 'n' jus' happened to look toward the river. Under that big ole oak tree, Ah seed her jus' walkin' 'round 'n' 'round in that flowin' white gown...no, she warn't walkin', she was floatin' like the breeze jus' picked her up real gentle-like 'n' carried her."

His voice trembled as he recalled the incident. "Then she started floatin' toward me. Ah was so scairt, my feet wouldn't go nowhere. She kept comin' closer 'n' closer, then started makin' them scary cryin' sounds." Bryce gulped, unable to finish his story.

"Where did she go?" Court asked, taking the towel Bryce held out.

"Ah doesn't know, suh. Ah closed my eyes 'n' jus' waited for her to come 'n' git me. After a while, Ah opened them 'n' she was gone."

Court did not say anything as he got out of the tub, tossed the towel aside, and began dressing.

Bryce said with a woebegone voice, "Mebbe Ah is goin' crazy."

"You're not crazy, Bryce. Everyone around here has seen her. Evidently she's harmless or no one would remain at the plantation." He would never tell him he had seen her too, or Bryce would insist that they move back to the townhouse. Danielle was capable of many things, but floating? Hell, that was about as far-fetched as believing she could walk on water. There was indeed a ghost at Espérance, Court finally decided, but she was not the woman who apparently felt more at ease being a "ghost" in his bed rather than herself.

He sat down on the side of the bed and pulled on his boots. "I'm going to take a ride around the cane fields after breakfast."

"Ah'll have Scoundrel out front for ya."

"Thanks, Bryce."

As he rose from the bed, a dull ache shot down his legs. "On second thought, Bryce, forget the horse. Bring the wagon instead."

Several days passed without incident. The ghost did not reappear and Danielle had been just as elusive. On his daily excursions to the fields, Court would often find her in an idyllic location, sketching the scenes around her. He never bothered her, but watched her from a distance. When she returned home, she would go to her room and paint for hours on end. He sometimes wondered if she used her art as an excuse to avoid him.

He decided he had to come up with a plan to force Danielle to leave. If he returned Espérance to her, he would be defeating his own purpose. She and Nicholas Caraville would have accomplished what they had set out to do. He wouldn't tell her the debts were paid. That alone would tempt her to remain at Espérance and continue her deceitful scheme.

Another idea slowly began formulating in his mind and then developed into a full-fledged plan that might rid himself of Danielle Algernon—permanently.

Chapter 12

Court strolled casually through Jordan Phillips's library, admiring the expensive paintings and unusual art objects that Jordan had collected from the many countries he had traveled throughout the years.

"Do you ever buy paintings from unknown artists, Jordan?" he asked, noticing the embellished signatures of several renowned artists.

"Occasionally, if he shows promise. There are so many artists, but very few who have that special way with a brush."

Court finished his mint julep, then placed the glass on the table. His eyes rested on a large painting that sat against a brass easel beside the table. There was no comparison with Danielle's painting of Espérance. This was obviously a painting of Jordan's home, and he could never tell him that it lacked her eye for detail. The magnolia trees' great white flowers seemed blurred; Danielle's keen perception and adroit fingers could have brushed each white petal so realistically that one could have almost smelled the heady fragrance. And one could have seen the intricate grape cluster design of the wrought-iron stairway that curved gracefully to the upper story.

Court reached inside his jacket pocket and drew out the miniature that Danielle had painted

of her mother. "I want to show you something."
Handing it to Jordan, he asked, "What's your
opinion on the talent of this artist?"

Jordan held it beneath the soft glow of the lamp
for a better view. "This is Danielle Algernon, isn't
it? Damn, she's something to behold."

"No, it's a portrait of her mother. As you can
see, there must have been a strong resemblance
between the two of them."

Jordan continued to scrutinize the painting. "I
saw her mother only a few times before she died.
Danielle never makes an appearance at any of the
social functions—except at the Quadroon Ball, on
occasion," he added with a sheepish grin. "I remember the first time I saw Danielle. She must
have been only fourteen or so, but she was"—he
cleared his throat and grinned at Court—"very
captivating. But you know that already."

Court changed the subject abruptly. "Does this
artist have talent?"

"He definitely has potential."

"The artist was only fifteen when she painted
it," he said, watching the look of astonishment
pass over his friend's face.

"You don't say." Jordan once again glanced at
the portrait. "You said 'she.' Who is she?"

"Danielle," Court supplied. "She has several
more paintings that show how much she has matured since she painted this portrait."

Jordan opened his mouth to make a comment
about Danielle's maturity, but Court, knowing his
friend well, interrupted. "Artistic maturity, Jordan."

He chuckled. "You always could read me like a
book, Sinclair."

"Where women are concerned, you leave no
page unturned, my friend. I doubt there's a

woman in New Orleans who hasn't succumbed to your charms."

Jordan rubbed his jaw. "Oh, I've missed a few here and there. If you weren't so enamored with Danielle Algernon, I might..."

Court stiffened. "You're welcome to try any time you like. My main purpose in coming out here today is to request your assistance in getting her out of my home—and my life."

"That bad, huh?"

"Yes, that bad." Court paced the room in agitation.

Jordan raked his hand through his hair, his thoughts persisting. Was the elusive Danielle unknowingly weaving her way into Court's heart? Was that what Court feared? Jordan chuckled to himself over his friend's dilemma.

"I think I understand...at least part of it. Your home's in Natchez, so why don't you just go home and leave Danielle to run the house? Hire an overseer and buy some more slaves to tend the fields."

Court thrust his hands into his pockets. "Then she'd be alone without any protection."

"She seems to have fared well enough since Nicholas disappeared."

"Well, hell, Jordan, it's different now. She wasn't my responsibility until I won that damned plantation. Winning it has become a cross I have to bear."

"Then sell it," Jordan suggested. "You don't need the property."

He steepled his fingers and studied them closely before answering. "I would if Danielle were provided for and had a place to go. She'd never accept money from me. That's why I need to find a means for her to make her own money, and I think it lies with her artistic abilities." Leveling his eyes with Jordan's, he announced, "That's where you come in."

"What can I do?"

"You're acquainted with the art galleries here in New Orleans. I'd like to put a few of her paintings on display to judge the reaction of the public."

"Ahh..." Jordan drawled. "Now I see your plan. She sells her paintings, then has enough money to exist independently from you. But there's always the chance she won't make it. Then what?"

Court grinned slyly. "You haven't seen her current work. She'll make it."

"What if she doesn't want to show her work?"

"I'll convince her in one way or another."

"Well," Jordan said with an amused smile, "shall we drink a toast to Danielle Algernon's future fame and glory?"

Handing his empty glass to him, Court said, "I think the occasion deserves no less."

They consumed several more drinks toasting the success of the plan. With the sure knowledge that he would soon be free of Danielle's bewitchingly magnetic presence, Court felt more relaxed than he had in weeks.

Danielle brought her wagon to a halt in the dense woods surrounding the swamp. A flock of birds scattered across the dusky sky. A lone egret perched atop a rotten timber. An alligator, hearing her approach, awakened from his sleep and slid into the black water.

She sat for a moment, twisting the reins around her hand, her face betraying hurt and anger. She had just returned from New Orleans after talking with Damien. Earlier in the day, he had sent word to her that he had information regarding Nicholas. Danielle had waited until Court had departed, then dressed in her nun's attire once again. Though she had not seen or heard from Rankin Pernel in weeks, she could not chance running into him again. She wondered if Court had paid the creditors. But why should he? Her pride would not allow her to question him. Then there had been the possibility of running into Court, though she doubted he would recognize her since there were many nuns strolling the streets of the Vieux Carré.

Nom de Dieu, what was Court Sinclair's real purpose for being in New Orleans? she thought suspiciously. The shocking news that Damien had just delivered to her caused confusing thoughts to skitter around in her mind. Nicholas Caraville was last seen in Baton Rouge in the company of a woman by the name of Meredith Delanoye— Court Sinclair's sister, of all people. Damien had told her that Meredith Delanoye had lost her fortune through gambling. It galled her to think that Nicholas would give up his home for such a frivolous fortune hunter. Danielle had never thought Nicholas would be gullible enough to fall into such a cunning trap.

Was it only a coincidence that Nicholas had lost their home to Court Sinclair? Somehow, she thought not. What if Court and his sister had schemed against Nicholas? If Court were a wealthy plantation owner from Natchez, why would he want a rundown plantation outside New Orleans? Whatever their plans, she chastised herself, she had fallen into his bed without a thought of the repercussions. *Mon Dieu,* where was her brains?

The remaining rays of the sun disappeared, leaving a palette of pinks and lavender across the horizon. Retrieving the clothing she had hidden in the back of the wagon, she leaped to the ground to change into her boy's attire. Court would probably be home by now, and it would be difficult to sneak by him dressed as she was now.

Little did she know that concealed beneath the shady boughs of the trees, Court was watching her as she stepped down from the wagon. He had recognized her the moment he'd seen her sitting beside Damien at the sidewalk café. He had stood in an alley, witnessing the two with their heads together in what appeared to be serious conversation. When she had departed in her wagon, he had followed her at a distance.

Now was the perfect chance for him to tell her he knew she was the nun who had stolen his carriage.

Then he sucked in his breath. Hell, she's undressing, he cursed, but he was powerless to turn his eyes from her as she began to unfasten the multitude of tiny buttons that ran the length of her spine.

"Damn," Danielle hissed, feeling a crick in her neck from trying to reach the remaining buttons at the center of her back.

"Is that any way for a nun to talk?" a familiar voice asked laughingly. "Perhaps I can be of assistance."

Startled by his sudden appearance, she wanted to shout a stream of epithets in his face, but she knew that would give away her identity. As her eyes darted about looking for an escape route, her gaze fell upon a pit of quicksand a short distance away; at that moment she would rather have had it swallow her into its murky depths than endure Court's presence. But seeing no feasible way to avoid him, she stood her ground and waited to see what would happen next.

Her eyes widened in disbelief when she felt his

fingers undoing the buttons at her back. Fury blazed like wildfire through her veins. How dare he treat a nun in such a disrespectful manner? He's an arrogant rogue, a seducer of women, a... a... her mind went blank as she felt the heavy confining habit being eased away from her upper torso by a gentle touch.

Court bared her shoulders, his warm, rough hands stroking her skin. Her heart drummed in her ears when he lifted the back edge of her veil. Bunching her hair in his hands, he revealed the slender column of her neck, slightly chafed from the rough fabric of the collar.

"Skin as soft as a baby's bottom," he murmured, then nibbled gently on the tender skin.

His lips burned a fiery path from one shoulder to the other. Her lips parted to protest, but the words died in her throat. As every nerve ending in her slender body tingled and burned in the same instant, she became a woman experiencing the unbridled release of passion.

"Such a waste," he whispered, biting gently on the delicate shell of her ear. "Your loveliness should not be concealed by this ridiculous armor you choose to wear, but displayed in elegant gowns."

The mentioning of her disguise brought her back to reality. This man was her adversary, the man who had ruined her future. "Please release me," she pleaded, disguising her voice.

"No, my sweet. You need to know what will be lost to you—and to me—should you ever decide to take your vows seriously," he murmured teasingly.

His hands slipped through the opening of her dress and eased slowly around to the front. Damn, he swore silently, he had never planned to take his game this far. It was wrong ... very wrong, but he was lost in his desire for her.

Through the sheer fabric of her chemise, she could feel the heat emanating from his hands as they grazed her breasts. He cupped them, his thumbs leisurely stroking the rosy peaks to pebble hardness.

Danielle whimpered, wanting him to cease his torturous play, yet she ached for his touch. Leaning back, she melted against his hard chest, her head positioned beneath his chin. "You shouldn't ..." she stammered, "it's wrong for you to do this to me." She feebly attempted to push his hands away, but the heavy fabric impeded her.

"Wrong? I'm only preventing you from making a disastrous mistake. Feel how you're responding to my touch, little one." No, his conscience warned him, you're the one making a disastrous mistake. She's in your blood, admit it.

His fingers swirled around her nipples, then gently kneaded the soft fullness of her breasts. "Is this the response of a woman who has chosen chastity?"

"But you don't know me," she said breathlessly. How long could she carry on with her charade if he continued to toy with her emotions? Her resistance was ebbing, and she prayed she had the strength of mind to overcome her body's betrayal.

He laughed and reluctantly lowered his hands to her waist. "Oh, but I do know you." His grip tightened as she stiffened in his arms. "If I'm not mistaken, you're the same audacious little nun who stole my carriage. I'd hoped to run into you again."

Her stomach plummeted to her feet and she swayed in his arms. So that's why he had followed her here. He had seen her in town and followed her out here to seek revenge. Tears of rage burned behind her eyes. He had purposely sought her out to humiliate her and he had succeeded.

Wrenching from his embrace, she jerked her dress back up to her shoulders. Her stance conveyed a mixture of anger and passion as she turned to face him. She assumed the twilight shadows would obscure her true identity.

"You're mistaken, *monsieur*. How dare you assault me in such a shameless manner."

Court gazed at her boldly, his turbulent green eyes raking her from head to toe. "Shameless, you say? Perhaps you found you enjoyed my caresses, pretty nun?" At her sharp gasp, he continued, "You didn't exactly act like a nun when you ran off with my carriage. What do you think your punishment should be? Shall I turn you over to the proper authorities?"

She looked fearfully from side to side, seeking a way to escape. It would be futile to lie to him, but she needn't tell him the entire truth.

Thrusting her small chin defiantly, she said, "But I only borrowed your horse and carriage. I left it where you could find it with no problem. Now, will you let me go about my business?"

"Not yet." He took a step in her direction. "I'll make a deal with you," he said, knowing full well she would refuse. "Allow me one kiss and you can go free."

Her chest rapidly rose and fell. "That's blackmail!"

"Call it what you will," he countered, suppressing a smile.

Her heart pounded so heavily she thought it would leap from her chest. She watched him move stealthily toward her and she stepped backward. "*Non, monsieur,* I won't let you do this to me. Haven't you humiliated me enough as it is?" she pleaded.

Court towered over her. She quickly lowered her face and clenched her hands into the fabric of her skirt, biting her lower lip in trepidation. Soon it would be all over. The nun's habit had been her suit of armor, but beneath the veneer was a very vulnerable woman. He had managed to pierce her disguise and had seen her for what she was. Now he would know that the woman who melted like butter in the sun when he caressed her was the one and only Danielle Algernon.

Court, too, was sparring with his emotions. He stared down on the veiled head, his conscience still nagging him. He knew he should have stopped at the very beginning, but desire had overbalanced his better judgment. God, he wanted her more than any woman he had ever wanted in his life. But why did it have to be Danielle Algernon who caused his passion to burn out of control?

He tilted her chin, his finger tracing her full lower lip, feeling it quiver slightly from his touch. Her dark violet gaze collided with his desire-filled one, damning him for what he intended to do.

"It won't be the first time I've kissed you. Remember the night of the Quadroon Ball... Dannie?"

Just as his lips lowered to make true his threat, she backed away hastily. The ground disappeared beneath her feet. Panic surged through her as she felt the thick quicksand suck at her ankles and slowly draw her down into its dark slime. She fought the dense muck, but the heavy skirt wrapped around her legs, dragging her body downward with its weight.

"Dammit, Dannie, don't fight it, or it'll pull you under!" Court shouted. "Be still!"

"Help me, Court, please!"

Her words tore at his heart. Picking up a broken limb, he thrust it to her. "Grab it, love, and

I'll pull you out." By God, he wasn't going to let her die. If she were sucked under, he would never forgive himself for behaving like a damned rogue.

Her arm felt like lead as she tried to drag it out of the mire. Little sobs choked her when she realized the quicksand was up to her neck. The limb was so close yet her hand could not grasp it.

Court tossed away the limb and quickly picked up a longer one. Holding on to the branch of a tree for support, he leaned over the quicksand and once again thrust the limb to her. All he could see of her were two glazed eyes peering helplessly at him, and the tips of her fingers.

"Now grab it, dammit, or sink," he growled, hoping the harsh tone of his voice would raise her awareness and bring quick action. If not, he'd jump in and they'd probably both drown.

His heart leaped to his throat when he saw her hand finally grip the limb. "Hold on tight, Dannie."

Tugging slowly so she would not lose her grip, he smiled assuringly as her body emerged from the sand. Dragging her other hand free, she clutched the branch in a death hold. He increased his strength to match her own.

Danielle felt as though she were playing a game of tug of war. The quicksand seemed reluctant to give up its victim; it pulled at her body, but Court's smile gave her strength.

When she was within arm's reach, he clasped his large hands around her wrists and pulled her onto the bank. They collapsed on the ground, overcome with exhaustion. She glanced furtively at him from behind muddy strands of hair. Why had he saved her life when she was an obstacle to his scheme? Wouldn't it have been easier to let her die?

He shook his head. "Don't you think a kiss would have been less strenuous?"

Thinking of the effect his kisses had on her, she quickly changed the subject. "How long have you known I was the nun?"

"When I saw you today with Damien Baudier." A worried frown etched his brow. "Who are you hiding from, Dannie, and why?"

Danielle told him about Rankin Pernel and how he had harassed and threatened her. She explained that she wore disguises to hide from him whenever she had to go into the city. The day she had stolen Court's carriage, she had seen Pernel, and she thought he may have recognized her.

"I'm sorry I took your carriage, Court. I had to get away from him in a hurry."

"I understand," he said, smoothing a strand of hair from her eyes. "I'll make sure he never bothers you again." He would not tell her there was no reason for Pernel to threaten her again.

Danielle shivered and Court said, "We need to get you out of that wet clothing before you get sick."

She cast him a wary look. "*We* do?" she snapped.

"That was your initial plan, wasn't it?"

"Yes, but you weren't part of my plan, *monsieur*." Sitting up, she faced him angrily. "Do you know what really upsets me? All along, you knew who I was and you took advantage of me."

"How was I to know what you were going to do? When you started undressing, I...well...dammit, Dannie, even a gentleman has a few shortcomings."

"Gentleman!" she hissed, rising to her feet, her efforts hampered by the weight of her skirt.

"A gentleman's a man, Dannie, regardless of his station. All it takes is a beautiful, willing woman to bring out the animal in him."

"Willing!" she screamed out at him. "How dare you to insinuate such a thing. You...you...oh!" She shuddered. "*Mon Dieu*, I cannot think of a bad enough word to call you."

"'Fool' would be a starter," Court murmured under his breath. "Get dressed, Dannie. This time I promise I won't look."

Standing behind the wagon, she glowered at his back as she dressed. Damn him, she stormed, he won't have the last word with me. He'll wish he'd let me drown by the time I'm finished with him.

He could feel the daggers piercing his back, but didn't see her climb into the wagon. Hearing her sharp command to the horse, he turned just as the wagon jerked forward. He mounted his horse and caught up with her. When they arrived at the plantation together, Danielle halted the wagon in front of the stable and leaped to the ground.

Glaring up at Court still astride his horse, she ordered, "I should like to have a word with you after dinner."

Her commanding tone of voice irritated him. "I, too, would like a word with you, *mademoiselle* ... nun."

She pivoted and walked hurriedly toward the house. It was then that he noticed the tight-fitting breeches and her provocative derrière. He shouted out to her, "If you continue parading around in those pants, then I'll not be held accountable for my ungentlemanly conduct."

Never one to bridle her tongue, she turned around to face him and retorted saucily, "Yours are no less revealing, *monsieur*." She immediately regretted her words.

"So you've noticed," he remarked candidly.

Mortified beyond words, Danielle whirled and ran into the house, cursing herself for her foolish blunder.

Chapter 13

Court entertained himself during the evening meal by caressing Danielle with his eyes, and dropping his bold gaze to his plate when she glanced his way.

She wore a gossamer peach gown, the full skirt accentuating her tiny waist. Little did he know how much effort had been put into the remaking of her mother's clothing to create that effect. The bodice was low, and showed the gentle curve of her breasts.

The neckline teased him, the bodice seemingly decreasing each time his hungry eyes fastened on the generous swell of her creamy breasts. Since her clandestine visit to his room, he had taken great interest in her exquisite anatomy. If only he could make love to her just once more, he would make her confess to being his heaven-sent "angel." He would never forget the feel of her satiny skin pressed against his hard flesh, the lavender scent of her body, the taste of her lips, the way her breasts filled his hands as he brought her pleasure. But if he had brought her pleasure, why had she never returned to him again?

Neither had spoken during the course of the meal, each rehearsing what they intended to say to the other. When they were behind the closed doors of the study, Danielle prepared a brandy for him. He sat down on the sofa and studied her over the rim of his glass, waiting for her to speak.

His wait was short-lived.

"Why didn't you tell me Nicholas knows your sister? They've been seen together in Baton Rouge."

Court appeared unruffled by her condemning question. Taking another swig of his brandy, he said casually, "So now you know. Did your friend, Damien Baudier, happen to drop that little tidbit of information to you today?"

Tilting her chin insolently, she said, *"Oui, monsieur,* as a matter of fact he did. Now, it causes me to wonder at your true purpose for being here." With dark violet eyes, she continued, "You and your sister are responsible for Nicholas's disappearance, aren't you?" Then shaking her head in despair, she said, *"Mon Dieu,* how am I to know that you didn't steal the deed from him? Since I have heard nothing from Nicholas, could it be he's dead already . . . and I'm to be next?"

His mouth dropped open in bewilderment. Placing his glass on the table, he rose slowly and walked over to her. "Let me clear your mind of those suspicions, Miss Algernon. After the card game, I had a man witness the sign-over of the deed. If Caraville's dead, it wasn't by my hand." Her haughty attitude unnerved him. He gripped her painfully by her shoulders. "I won the plantation fair and square, and even fought a damn duel with you so you could save your pride. If I'd wanted to kill you, then that would have been the perfect time. And today, I could have let that quicksand swallow you, but I pulled you out. Are those the cold calculations of a murderer?"

"Non," she confessed, "but I'll wager you are up to no good, Court Sinclair. If Nicholas is with your sister, then somehow, I'll find him."

He dropped his hands from her shoulders and walked to the window. Running his finger down the edge of the brocade drapery, he said, "It appears to me, Danielle, that we have the same reasons for wanting to find the missing couple. You're worried your stepfather may be dead, and I wonder if my sister hasn't met with the same fate." He glanced at her from over his shoulder. "I hadn't planned to tell you this, but I may as well clear the air between us—or make it worse. The reason I came to New Orleans in the first place was because I received a ransom note from someone claiming to have kidnapped Meredith."

She clasped her hand over her mouth. "But she's with Nicholas."

"Yes, if the rumors are true," he said, narrowing his eyes at her. "The way I see it, Nicholas found out that Meredith was from a wealthy family. He needed money desperately, so he took advantage of the situation. He kidnapped Meredith, murdered her, then took off with the ransom money."

"Non," she screamed, gripping the edge of the desk for support. "Nicholas isn't a murderer."

He ignored her outburst. "He'll be back, Danielle, but Meredith will have conveniently disappeared."

"If he's guilty as you've suggested, why didn't he take the money and pay off his debts?"

"Why did he purposely gamble away his home to me?" he countered, studying her intently. "I think you know the answer to that question, Danielle."

She stared at him with fascination. "I don't know what you're accusing me of, Court," she said softly, her violet eyes searching his face for an answer.

He approached her, not knowing whether or not

to believe her. Lord, he hoped she was not mixed up in this deception. From all appearances she seemed to be innocent of his accusations. If she were guilty, then why had she not used her feminine wiles to trap him? On several occasions he had been more than willing to fall prey. She was a master at disguises. Was she also a master of deceit?

"Nicholas planned to lose that card game, Danielle. He saw, or thought he saw, a way to eventually regain Espérance free of debt."

She looked at him vacantly. "What way?"

"Through you."

Her brow furrowed. "How have you arrived at that conclusion? You could have easily forced me to leave this house ... and probably will when you ease your guilty conscience."

He chuckled, then tilted her chin, caressing the contour of her delicate but taut jaw. Even in anger, she appeared as innocent as a baby. "God, you're beautiful."

His remark brought her up short. "What does that have to do with what we're talking about?"

"Everything," he whispered and stared down at her lovely face. He wanted to kiss her and ease the doubts from his mind, but he held his desire in check. "How could any man toss out a woman as irresistible as you, Danielle? Nicholas knows the treasure he possesses. If someone gives you a precious jewel, you don't part with it. You never tire of its beauty, and you cherish it, for it never changes. And a gem you are, cut and polished to perfection."

Her heart skipped several beats. She remained silent, gazing up into his handsome face, sensing she could actually see herself through his eyes. Precious ... beautiful ... was he telling her she was special to him? Her heart ached for more of his tender words.

He defined each feature of her fine-boned face with his fingertips, as a sculptor would while creating a masterpiece. Then suddenly, a shutter closed over the gentleness in his eyes. She wondered at the change; an almost painful element had entered into their depths.

"But, Dannie, beneath the brilliance of his otherwise perfect gem does lie a flaw." He paused. "Velvet deception."

A tense hush fell in the room. Court's conviction tore at Danielle's heart. He had brought her to the top of a mountain with his beautiful words, then dropped her over the edge so uncaringly. She wondered why her eyes were dry when she was crying so inside.

With every nerve in her body twisting, she said woodenly, "I understand what you're implying, Court. But the deceit doesn't lie with me. If Nicholas is guilty of such a corrupt plan, then he has failed. With the cloud of animosity existing between us, there could never be any permanence in our relationship. That's what you're suggesting is the root to my deception, I gather?"

For some unknown reason, his heart deflated. If she had admitted her deceit, it could not have hurt him any more than he felt now.

"Then the idea of marrying me to regain your home never entered your mind?"

Danielle lowered her head and sighed. "I admit at one time such an idea did occur to me fleetingly, but it wasn't placed there by Nicholas. Though I love my home, I could never marry for the purpose of saving it."

Once again, the silence hung heavily in the

room as they tried to put their emotions into some semblance of order.

She spoke first. "Perhaps I didn't know my stepfather as well as I thought. He may have used me, but I cannot think of him as a murderer." Her eyes became misty with unshed tears. "I was never really close to him. My *maman* came first in his heart, which was as it should be. After *Maman* died, we drifted further apart." Her voice quivered as she gazed up into Court's face with sadness marring her features. "What if he couldn't endure being in my life any longer because I was a constant reminder of the love he had lost? He could have arranged this whole charade for my benefit... with my well-being uppermost in his mind."

Court thought of the man who had sat across from him at the game table that eventful evening. He was sure not a sympathetic bone existed in his loathsome body. It angered him that Danielle could be so damned naive.

His laugh was abrasive. "Yes, he certainly took care of his dead wife's little girl, didn't he? Left her with his debts, and at the mercy of anyone who might choose to harm her... Rankin Pernel being a good example. And he took the money and high-tailed it out of town." Gripping her by her arms, he lashed out at her. "You mean nothing to him, understand, nothing, just a free ticket to come back home and make our lives miserable." Shaking her, he growled, "Wake up and see him like he is, Danielle, instead of condoning the man's real reasons for using you."

Numbed by his harsh words, Danielle stared pitifully at him. "Why do you want to hurt me so much?" she finally asked, her eyes glistening with tears.

Pulling her stiff, slender body into his arms, he wanted to somehow rid her of the pain he had inflicted on her in his rage. Oh God, how good she felt against him, he thought, aching to kiss her.

"I would never intentionally hurt you, Dannie ...never. It just sickens me to see you put your trust in a man who doesn't deserve it. Life deals us some punishing blows, and though it's hard to accept them at times, we must force ourselves to overcome them." Gazing into her limpid violet eyes, he said, "I want to help you face them, little one, any way I can." His mind screamed: Open up to me, Dannie. Tell me the truth.

Her heart surged with an unrecognized emotion, and she expected it to burst at any moment. Tonight they had been on a verbal battlefield, each releasing anxieties they had harbored for weeks. One explosion set off another explosion with the force of a cannonball, and no less damaging. Court, in his own way, had called a truce, but he had not surrendered. As far as he was concerned, he was still correct in his judgment of Nicholas. Until she could prove to him otherwise, he would never change his mind. Yet, he would not have offered to help her unless he cared.

She remained in his arms, inhaling the masculine scent of him. She wondered why she felt so secure in his embrace when he had wounded her deeply with his words. The pain came from the blistering knowledge that maybe he spoke the truth. If it were indeed true, then she must either leave her home or somehow buy it back from him.

Pressing her cheek against the silken fabric of his shirt, she said, "I would never try to trap you into marriage, Court. Do you believe me?"

He looked down on the black shining crown of her head. His hand left the small of her back and moved upward to stroke the velvet tresses cascading over her shoulders. The texture, soft and satiny, seemed familiar to him as he wound it around his fingers. It felt so natural to hold her softness to him, to smell the sweet scent of her.

"I want...very much to believe you, Dannie." His voice was husky with emotion. There was an unvoiced request that lay within those words.

He cupped her chin, turning her beautiful, sweet face upward. Mirrored in her eyes was the same apprehension that flickered in his own. The rough edge of his thumb caressed the fullness of her lower lip. Unconsciously, the tip of her tongue slipped out to join his finger as she moistened her lips.

Visibly shaken by her turbulent emotions, she gathered up her courage and spoke softly, "Court, we can no longer continue living in this house together. I have a plan."

Court bristled. "I'm not moving out." Why shouldn't he move out? he wondered. He had a townhouse to stay in. Of course, she didn't know that, his conscience reminded him.

Through a haze, he heard her say, "No, I'm moving out."

He stared at her in amazement. "And where do you propose to go when you don't have enough money for your next meal?"

"Perhaps I will have...eventually."

"Oh?" he asked masterfully, mocking her with laughter-crinkled eyes. "Do you plan to sell the family jewels?"

Irritated with his mockery, she stepped out of his arms and said petulantly, "The few jewels I have were my *maman*'s and those will never be sold. But maybe my paintings will bring me my fortune, *monsieur*."

His mouth opened to protest, but he said nothing. If she had slapped him full across the face, he would have been no less surprised. He had intended to mention the sale of her art, in his own time.

"Of course, I really don't want to leave," she said with a frown.

His spirit soared.

"I could buy back my home from you later."

In a matter of minutes, Court had experienced every emotion from desire to anger, elation to depression and a multitude in between. Now his stomach was churning in such disorder, that he added sickness to the list. He mentally calculated how much she would have to net from her paintings to come up to his price. Satisfied that she could never raise that much money, he calmed himself. Why not go along with her idea? If it would make her happy and keep her at his side, he would go out of his way to assist her.

"Very well, Dannie, if this is what you want," he agreed.

She had expected him to object. Her heart deflated at his easy manner. He evidently did not believe she was capable of making it on her own. Well, she would prove to him how wrong he was to doubt her abilities.

"I have a few I've just finished. Tomorrow, I'll—"

"We'll need to arrange a public showing for you at one of the galleries in New Orleans," he interrupted, strolling around the room in a jaunty manner.

Her face wilted. "A...a showing?" She had no thought of displaying her paintings publicly. "Can't I have a private showing here at the house?"

He shook his head. "No. If you were a recognized artist, we could have it here. But the people venturing out here would be curiosity seekers, Danielle, not buyers."

"I suppose you're right," she said with a crestfallen expression.

He smiled covertly. Maybe after the first showing, she would decide to give up this idea. He could not believe he was saying this to himself after he had planned to do the very same thing for her from the beginning.

"Now," he said, clearing his throat to get her attention, "let's talk about your new studio."

"What new studio?" she asked aghast. "I have my bedroom."

"No, too dark, too confining."

Before she could voice her opinion, he went on to say, "Since the planting house is no longer in use, let's convert it into a studio for you. The glass is already there, so only a few minor changes will be necessary."

She looked strangely at him. "You would do that for me? Why?"

Because I can see you any time I desire, he thought contentedly. Instead, he said, "I want you to be happy, Danielle. Maybe we can at least be friends instead of constantly battling with each other."

Quick tears built up in her eyes. She walked over to him and placed her hand affectionately on his arm. "Thank you, Court."

"Is that all the thanks I get?" He grinned rakishly.

Danielle frowned. "What do you mean?"

His eyebrow winged upward. "A kiss, per chance?"

She returned his smile and stood on tiptoes to

give him a light kiss on his cheek. Catching the disappointment flickering across his face, she asked slyly, "Friends?"

He suppressed his disappointment with great effort. "Of course, friends, Dannie."

Chapter 14

Danielle and Tempete raced across the countryside. The wind's silken fingers lifted the hat from
her head and worked through her severely knotted hair to release a profusion of curls, which
streamed out behind her like a banner.

Jordan Phillips, known for his skill with horses
and his love of women, gazed appreciatively at
the muscular horse and striking rider. The sleek,
black horseflesh and the girl's mane of flying
ebony hair merged into the illusion that the horse
and rider were one. Cutting across the field, he
spurred his horse on until he came abreast of the
other rider.

When a shadow rocked across Tempete's neck,
Danielle was sure Court had followed her. She
turned swiftly, a lively retort on her lips. She was
startled when her glance found a different face.
Smiling hesitantly, she slowed Tempete to a
gentler pace.

Jordan, surprised at the beauty facing him,
smiled brightly and bowed from his saddle, quip-
ping, "Jordan Phillips at your service."

Danielle opened her mouth to speak, but he
went on quickly, "No, no, my beauty, let me guess.
You would be Danielle Algernon, right?"

Not unaffected by his engaging smile, Danielle
returned it and asked, "How is it you know my
name, *monsieur?*"

"You may desire to hide away out here in the country, but news has spread of your uncommon beauty. Aren't you aware of the vast number of swains who have traveled great distances to seek a glimpse and a possible introduction?"

Danielle was enjoying his banter. His manner was infectious, so it was with an unaccustomed lightheartedness that she took up the game. "I dare say, *monsieur,* you have a glib tongue and tell tall tales. If what you say is true, why haven't I seen these so-called admirers?"

His blue eyes sparkling with mischief, he admitted, "The only saving grace keeping you from being overrun by suitors is the simple fact they couldn't find your home. It was only by sheer chance that I saw you and fell immediately under your spell." His voice trailed off, but his eyes lingered on her face.

Becoming uncomfortable under his scrutiny, she asked saucily, *"Monsieur,* do I have a wart on my nose?"

"Au contraire," he said, smiling, "you have a beautiful nose. It goes so well with the rest of your face."

She laughed. "I don't know when I've had a finer compliment, Monsieur Phillips."

For the first time in his adult life, Jordan blushed. "I meant that only in the most flattering of ways. In truth, Miss Algernon, you are one of, if not the most beautiful lady I've ever met," he said with not a little reverence.

"I accept your compliment, although I fear Mammy would bemoan your use of the word, 'lady,'" she answered with a jaunty tilt of her head.

He felt a delightful wave of admiration for this spunky creature and realized with satisfaction that Court indeed had his hands full. With a touch of envy, he wished the circumstances were different, and that he was the one faced with this particular situation. "Would you mind if I joined you in your ride? I've been remiss in exercising Marco properly. He has need of a good run."

She could not refuse him, and did not want to. She was enjoying his company. And his name and face were not unknown to her. Although she had never met him, she had glimpsed him on occasion. She recognized him as the man who had been with Court at the Quadroon Ball.

Nodding her head in agreement, she took up her reins, and with smooth, graceful movements, urged Tempete across the fallow fields. Jordan darted after them, his great golden stallion eating up the distance until he and Danielle were side by side, racing into the wind. With gay laughter, she halted Tempete beneath the welcoming shade of a large chestnut tree. Leaping to the ground, she drew a canteen of water from her saddle, uncapped it, and took a long drink of cool water.

She turned to Jordan as he dismounted and offered the canteen to him. He took it from her outstretched hand, his eyes never leaving her as he raised it to his mouth and drank deeply.

His eyes were the bluest she had ever seen. They exactly matched the sky overhead. The mischievous gleam was reinforced when he winked at her audaciously.

Danielle, having never been courted, relished his outlandish charm. A dazzling smile spread across her features, and Jordan's heart skipped a beat.

"Thank you for allowing me to share your outing. I can't say when I've enjoyed myself more."

"The pleasure was twofold, then, *monsieur,* for I have enjoyed it immensely, as well."

Suddenly slapping his hand to his forehead in

chagrin, he mock berated himself. "You see, your beauty has rendered me dumfounded. My purpose in coming out here was to invite you to a party."

His words caused a frown to mar her smooth brow. She sighed deeply. "A party."

"Does the thought of a party distress you? I can assure you, my beauty, that you'll be the belle of the ball." With grim determination, he drew her hands into the warm strength of his own. "Repeatedly, I've sent you invitations through the years, but you've always declined my requests. It has puzzled me why you've always refused, so this year I decided to present your invitation in person," he finished, quite satisfied with himself.

Releasing her hands, he drew an ivory-colored parchment from his breast pocket and gave it to her, pleading, "You'll have to excuse the rumpled appearance of the invitation, but the words conveying my request are nonetheless sincere."

She quickly scanned the paper, then lifted her eyes to him. "I'm honored that you took the time to bring this to me." With apprehension evident in her eyes, she hesitated. "But, I'm afraid it's impossible for me to attend." Her mind raced, searching for a plausible excuse. She did not have the courage to tell him that besides lacking the proper clothing, the people attending would be the same people who had rejected her throughout the years.

Watching the emotions play across her features, he sensed the loneliness that had pervaded her young life. He decided she would attend the ball if he had to drag her. What Court's thoughts would be regarding his nefarious plan momentarily jarred his conscience, but brushing that worry aside, he plotted his strategy.

"Of course, I don't know your reasoning, but if I were in your position, I'd attend." Shrugging his shoulders, he went on. "Maybe it's your wish to hide away like a hermit. You'll become a vague memory to the very ones you choose to avoid. They won't care because you never gave them the chance to care."

"But I—" she stammered.

"But nothing," he said with force. "Court told me of your beautiful paintings. If you never experience life, what will you draw? Dreams that never materialized?"

"You're cruel."

"Yes, and I'm sorry. It's not a very pretty picture, is it? But it's the truth nonetheless. Painted it pretty grim, didn't I?"

"Oui," she sighed. "With astute perception, you have outlined my very existence."

Stiffening her spine and tilting her chin in defiance, she growled, "All right, enough is enough. I'll attend your ball." Wagging her fingers within inches of his face, she predicted, "Lest you forget, if you become the laughingstock of the city, don't say you weren't warned."

Smiling devilishly, he made his own predictions. "I dare say, I'll be the envy of New Orleans."

"Since your ball will launch my heretofore bleak future into the very cream of Southern society, I'll be on my best behavior not to disgrace you. If I'm to attend, I shall need an escort. Would it be in bad form if I ask to bring a guest?"

"If the guest happens to be Damien Baudier, I can safely say that he's already received his invitation."

With a questioning brow, she intoned, "I find myself wondering, *monsieur,* how you know so much about me. Has Monsieur Sinclair been filling your head with exaggerated tales of my conduct?"

"Court and I are very good friends. Our friendship goes back a long way. I'll have to admit he has mentioned you on occasion, and once spoke at great length about your artwork. You are very talented, Danielle. Court showed me a small portrait of your mother. I believe he mentioned that you had painted it from memory. Your eye for detail is like no other I have ever seen." With eagerness, he asked, "Have you ever considered a showing?"

"Not until recently had I ever thought to make money from my work. I've always painted for the pure pleasure of seeing what's in my mind take shape on canvas."

"My beauty, what a lot you have to learn. Court says you bring life to your canvas." He could see the pride in her eyes, and knew his words had found their mark. "I would like very much to see your paintings sometime."

"If you wish, *monsieur*. I only hope you're not expecting overmuch. This has been pleasant, but I must be getting back. Mammy will have Tobias searching for me. I'll see you in two weeks' time."

Cradling his hands, he gave her a lift onto Tempete's back. Quickly knotting her hair, she crammed her hat low on her head. Calling a hasty *"Au revoir"* over her shoulder, she was off at breakneck speed.

Laughing, Jordan called, "Does Tempete know only one speed ... fly? *Adieu,* my beauty," he whispered, his words lost on the breeze.

Prior to the ball, Danielle's days passed in a blur. Mammy put Lilly to the task of refurbishing another gown. Eager to help, Danielle continually sought her to offer her assistance. With soft words and gentle prodding, Lilly made it plain if she were not left alone to complete her work, there would be no gown. Between Mammy and Danielle interrupting her, she could not think about her creation.

Court had carried on with his affairs as usual, coming and going as was his wont, never mentioning the ball. Danielle had no intention of telling him she was going and threatened Mammy with dire consequences if she breathed a word of it. Damien had been ecstatic when he learned she would attend and immediately insisted he escort her. So it went . . . she and Court making their separate plans, she with a niggling touch of pain as she wondered what it would be like to share the joy of such an outing with a lover.

Court, too, was having similar thoughts. What would her reaction be if he asked her to accompany him to Jordan's party? he wondered, the hint of a smile touching his mouth. She would probably tell him in no uncertain terms what he could do with his invitation. With that thought in mind, he left the day of the party for his townhouse.

Danielle sucked in her breath as Lilly proudly held up her shimmering red satin creation, finished only hours before the party. Never had Danielle owned anything as lovely.

"*Mon Dieu*, Lilly, you have outdone yourself. If word of your skill gets out, I will be hard pressed to keep the ladies of New Orleans from our door."

Pleased with the compliment, Lilly smiled and lowered her eyes, brushing an imaginary wrinkle from the dress. "Let's get you ready, *ma petite*."

She took her in tow, and before Danielle knew it she had been bathed, dusted with fine powder, twisted and turned until she was dizzy from the flurry. Lilly even styled Danielle's hair, wielding the curling tongs with such agility that Mammy gaped in astonishment. For the finishing touch, she entwined tiny blood-red rosebuds in the soft curls. Then she and Mammy held the dress while Danielle stepped into it. The glimmering satin glided over her body, cool to the skin, startling to the eye.

The bodice was cut daringly low and embellished with glistening jet. Her creamy skin contrasted vividly with the lustrous red color. The material hugged her tiny waist, then fell freely to her satin slippers. Every movement picked up the light, giving the illusion that the fabric caressed bare skin. A brilliant ruby nestled invitingly at the base of her throat. She knew from the expression on Lilly and Mammy's faces that she looked her very best. She sent Mammy to see whether Damien had arrived.

"Miss Dannie, Mistah Baudier is choppin' at the bit," Mammy reported. "He cain't wait to see you. You can tell he is jus' tickled pink that you is goin'." Drawing a breath, she continued, "Chile, you look jus' like them roses your mama used to grow." As her eyes scanned her charge, she chuckled softly. "Lawdy, what I'd give to be a fly on the wall when you makes your appearance tonight. Now, you hurry up afore I cain't stall Mistah Baudier no more." With that, she bustled from the room, Danielle following at a slower pace.

Spying Damien staring impatiently out the window, Danielle pursed her lips, and with unladylike ability, let loose a rowdy whistle. He turned, startled, his eyes widening in pleasure as he saw her.

"Why, Damien, what a striking figure you cut, turned out in your finery," she teased.

Drawing her hand to his lips, he placed a chaste kiss on its velvety warmth. "I'm honored to have the privilege of escorting you tonight. When we make our entrance, every eye will be on you. What a delicious fuss there will be when they discover who you are," he said with a deep chuckle.

With a huff, she turned him, folding her arms before her. "If you are certain that my appearance is going to cause such a flurry," she scolded, "you will have me afraid to show my face."

Damien was quick to dispel her apprehension. *"Non,* I would not spoil your evening for anything in the world. I only meant to assure you of your loveliness. Come, we are late already."

As Damien's carriage drew up before Jordan's home, Danielle was overwhelmed by the aura of wealth it so graciously presented. The classic Greek revival mansion sat like a sentinel, its portico overlooking acres of meticulously manicured lawns. Light streamed from the many windows and a haunting melody drifted from the evening shadows. Gay laughter merged with other night sounds, bringing home to Danielle with crushing clarity that she did not belong there.

Filled with self-doubts that were foreign to her, she clenched her hands into tight fists and her mouth went dry. With a heavy heart, she turned to Damien. "I'm sorry, but I don't think I can possibly leave this carriage. Would you please have your driver take me home?" Her large violet eyes beseeched him not to tease her.

His hand lifted her chin. "Where's your spirit, Dannie? Has a specter perchance stolen through my carriage unawares and whisked my friend away, leaving this frightened creature in her stead?"

She answered with spunk. "You're right. I'm being foolish. But it frightens me terribly to face these people."

At that moment, the footman opened the carriage door. Damien descended and turned to assist

Danielle. With a deep breath, she gave him her hand. As they neared the double doors, she became subdued once more and her step faltered.

Damien, leaning close, whispered, *"Ma chérie,* you approach the festivities with all the eagerness of a gelded bull. Cheer up, you'll bewitch all who come in contact with you."

The doors opened, and Damien entered with aplomb, greeting the smiling butler with ease, urging a reluctant Danielle before him. She noted her elegant surroundings with pleasure. Black and white Italian marble floored the entrance hall. A stairway circled upward, past a three-tiered chandelier of immense proportions. Hundreds of candles shed flattering light over a magnificent foyer that was decorated with tasteful restraint.

"Good evening, my beauty."

Recognizing the voice, she turned, a warm smile lighting her features. *"Bonsoir,* Monsieur Phillips."

Jordan greeted Damien with a familiar nod, and lifting Danielle's hand, placed his warm lips to her fingers. When the proper pleasantries had been exchanged, he escorted them to the ballroom, stopping along the way to introduce her to various friends of his, names she had heard all her life, the cream of Southern society. They greeted her with friendliness, their eyes betraying their curiosity. Everyone had heard the stories that abounded about this solitary individual and the ghost that was said to occupy her home. One rotund gentleman was heard to proclaim, "She looks normal enough to me."

Had they expected her to sport horns and a pointed tail? If the truth were known, they had pictured her as frail, mousy, and fearful. Instead, they encountered a vision of loveliness as she listened quietly or answered their barrage of questions with dignity.

She noted with amusement the women flocking to Damien's side. Shooting her a questioning look, he let himself be pulled away by a petite beauty. Raising her eyes to Jordan, she thanked him for inviting her.

"The pleasure is mine, I assure you. You add charm and grace and just a touch of mystery to an otherwise commonplace event."

The ballroom was enormous, several of the same three-tiered chandeliers illuminating the room. Light dancing through the multifaceted prisms was reflected in the high gloss of the floor. Ornate plaster and wood moldings wrapped around the room, pulling its vastness together. Large potted plants dotted the room, lending warmth to an otherwise austere setting. Two sets of double doors stood open, welcoming those who wished to stroll through the gallery or view the garden.

When a lilting refrain filled the air, Jordan offered his arm to Danielle, and led her onto the floor. When he took her in his arms, she let the music fill her, matching her steps to his. Gliding across the floor as though dancing were second nature to her, she eyed the array of rainbow-colored gowns as other guests and their partners began swirling around the room.

A darkly handsome figure, resplendent in black evening dress, stood motionless in the doorway. Shock blended with anger on his features as his stormy green eyes followed every movement Danielle made. She stood out like a costly gem among artificial replicas. Indeed, he thought that she had caused a stir amidst the gathering for they all seemed impressed by her beauty. When she laughed in pleasure at some comment Jordan made, he scowled ominously, and then was amazed by his jarring anger when he overheard a spiteful gossip express her views concerning Danielle to those around her.

"You know that little tart is living openly with Court Sinclair. From the way I heard it, he moved in bag and baggage. Why no decent man would have her now."

Court's eyes flashed angrily. Clenching his jaw in disgust, he made his way to Jordan's study before he would say something that might make things worse. Mollifying his anger with strong drink was a new twist for him, but so was this rampant jealousy that raged through him. Seeing Danielle laughing and waltzing in the arms of his best friend—no matter how innocent it was—had sent his temper spiraling to new dimensions. He wanted to be the one who brought her such pleasure. After several drinks of aged brandy, he felt the rough edges of his temper mellow.

Jordan excused himself from Danielle to get them each a glass of champagne. Feeling the eyes of many of the guests upon her, she turned toward the open doors to the garden, seeking a breath of fresh air. That was when she saw him bearing down on her, his intent plain as he moved through the crowd.

"Good evening, *monsieur*," she said, barely above a whisper as she extended her hand. Court's open appraisal of her took her breath away. Clasping her slender hand in his strong one, he raised it to his mouth. At the last second, he adroitly flicked his wrist and turned over her hand to place a warm kiss on the palm, his tongue rippling across its smooth warmth.

Her eyes shot open and her blood swept through

her veins. Jerking her hand from his, she glanced around guiltily lest anyone had noticed.

"Sinful, isn't it?" he asked recklessly.

"If you mean your behavior, I have to agree."

"You won't give an inch, will you, angel?"

A blush stained her cheeks. "I don't have the slightest notion what you are implying."

"Don't you?" he whispered. "You look lovely tonight, Danielle. You put these other beauties in the shade with your vibrant loveliness."

"Thank you, Court, you're very kind. You, too, look very elegant tonight. If you're not careful, one of these beautiful girls will turn your head, and you'll be on your way to the altar before you know what happened."

Shaking his head, he vowed, "Not on your life, Dannie." Changing the subject, he inquired, "Had I known you desired to attend tonight, I would have gladly escorted you."

"I didn't realize our bargain entailed your entertaining me," she replied with a touch of sarcasm.

"To hell with the bargain, you know that's not what I meant."

"Then, *monsieur,* do you mean our bargain is null? That I no longer am to remain at Espérance?"

"Dannie, my sweet," he drawled, trailing his finger lightly over her bare collar bone, "you have a habit of turning my words to suit your purpose. I meant exactly what I said. There are no hidden meanings. Had I known you desired to attend, I would have offered my services as escort. Ah, Dannie," he sighed, "let's have a truce for the evening. No bickering, only pleasure and enjoyment of the occasion. Agreed?"

"How can I possibly refuse when you ask in such a nice way?"

As the music changed tempo and strains of a waltz filled the room, he bowed formally. "May I have the pleasure of this dance?" His eyes twinkled merrily.

"You may," she assented, taking his proffered arm.

He absorbed the warmth of her and smelled a hint of delicate perfume as he took her in his arms. They moved together across the dance floor: he, savoring the chance to hold her, she, welcoming his embrace. All too soon the music faded to an end. Court released her, then escorted her across the crowded floor.

Just as they reached a small alcove with several comfortable wing-backed chairs conveniently arranged for conversation and viewing the dancing, Jordan found them, two half-filled glasses of champagne in his grasp.

Eyeing the glasses, then Court and Danielle, he apologized good-humoredly, "They were full when I began my trek back. It's a trick to greet guests and juggle drinks at the same time."

The rest of the evening spun by in a whirl for Danielle as one eager admirer after another begged for the pleasure of a dance. She smiled until her face was tired from the effort. Her feet ached not only from dancing, but because some of her partners had been less than agile in their movements. She heard her praises sung until she doubted the validity of their words.

Begging off from a lively quadrille with a gentleman whose feet were inordinately heavy, she made a hasty retreat to the garden for some air and a minute of quiet.

Court himself had danced very little. Instead, he had deposited himself where he could view Danielle without interruption. When she moved out to the gardens, he wondered absently if she were meeting someone or only seeking fresh air. A compelling need to know prompted him to follow her.

The night air cooled her flushed face as Danielle stepped from the gallery and walked through the lush garden. Hedges of trimmed boxwood created a close intimacy with the house. The sweet scent of a profusion of roses perfumed the air. Partially lighted pathways encouraged investigation revealing one botanical delight after another, as colorful and harmonious as a rainbow settling across the sky after a spring rain. Wandering through this labyrinth, she found a secluded bench, and taking care not to wrinkle her skirts, she sank onto it with relief and eased her slippers from her tired feet. Wiggling her toes, she sighed deeply from the simple pleasure.

"Would you like me to massage them for you?" The husky timbre of Court's voice left her no doubt that he was serious.

"That won't be necessary," she answered breathlessly.

"Oh, but I insist."

Lowering himself beside her, he bent over and lifted her feet to his lap, turning her toward him as he did so. Her emotions were in a turmoil as his hands kneaded her abused feet, applying slow, precise pressure to the pad of each toe. She shivered in pleasure when he ran his supple fingers lightly, caressingly, from the ball of her foot to the heel. She could not believe the blatant tremors heaving through her body at his simple ministrations.

"I believe I'll be able to survive the rest of the evening. Thank you, Court," she said quietly, drawing her feet from his hold.

"Anytime, my pet. Have you discovered that dancing the night away is to your liking?"

Leaning closely, she whispered conspiratorily, "Only if positions were reversed and I could choose my partner."

Court laughed delightedly. "You're a rare jewel, Dannie."

"You, *monsieur*, are a very good dancing partner. I don't mean to be unkind, but some of these gentlemen would do well to consider instructions from a dancing master."

He chuckled deeply, and then suddenly a thought flashed across his mind. "Have you perchance recognized any of the gentlemen here from the Quadroon Ball?"

The color left her face. *"Mon Dieu,* I hadn't thought of that. Do you think I might have been found out?"

"I doubt anyone would make the connection. At the same time, no one would dare mention the incident without incriminating himself. Your secret's safe, Dannie. As long as you don't make a habit of attending quadroon balls."

"If I had any desire to go to another one, which I don't, I would never be able to talk Mammy into going again. That was her one and only venture as the mother of a quadroon debutante."

Subdued laughter reached their ears just as Damien and the beauty who had whisked him away earlier came into view. Seeing Danielle and Court ensconced in what appeared an intimate conversation, Damien hesitated before he approached them. "I didn't mean to abandon you, *ma petite*. Now I see my concern was useless. It would seem Monsieur Sinclair has taken it upon himself to entertain you." His words were blunt and carried a world of suspicion.

"A fine job he has done, Damien. I see you, too, are not without entertainment?" Danielle's reprimand was veiled by a smile.

After introducing his companion, Damien leaned toward her, speaking barely above a whisper. "I didn't intend to sound mean. I want this occasion to mark your introduction into society and be full of pleasant memories." Brushing his lips lightly over her cheek, he was gone.

"Even if this is the first time you have attended a social function, you seem to have gathered a regiment of males to champion your cause." Court's words were filled with sarcasm.

"What is my cause, Court?" she asked softly, her heart heavy at his implication. Did he think she had deliberately set out to attract that kind of attention?

"I'm sure that is a question which would require hours of debate. Only you could answer that, if in fact you know your own heart."

"My heart tells me to guard it well, least some smooth-talking interloper rips it from its stronghold." A solitary tear rolled down her cheek. Mortified that she might cry, she brushed at it angrily. "I must return to the ballroom, Court. There's already speculation enough about our relationship without our adding more fuel to what is already a conflagration."

Court watched the gentle sway of her hips until she was out of sight. Berating himself for his careless words, he followed her slowly. Then the vision of Nicholas Caraville nudged its way into his mind's eye. Deceiver, conniver, innocent...which category did Danielle fall under? Could anyone so bewitching exercise her sorcery until a man had no defenses left? These thoughts nagging at him, he bid Jordan good-night and sought the solace of good brandy.

Chapter 15

After bidding Damien *au revoir,* Danielle lingered in the foyer, listening intently to the tall case clock ticking a rhythmic cadence in the stillness. The lamp cast eerie shadows along the walls as she finally crept quietly to the study. Barely opening the door, she peeked inside. All she could see was a snifter and an empty decanter of brandy on the table. Court must have finished the brandy after he returned to Espérance.

Just to make certain he hadn't returned to the city, she went to the door of his room and placed her ear against it. Hearing no movement, she turned the knob and eased open the door. He lay fully clothed across the bed, his feet dangling over the edge as though he were too drunk to undress, or worse, waiting for her return. When she heard him groan and roll over, she quickly closed the door.

Once inside her room, she wondered if it might not be wise to bolt her door, but decided against it. He had once said that locked doors wouldn't keep him out. It disturbed her that he had never carried through with his threat, when she should have felt relieved that he hadn't made the effort.

Undressing, Danielle hung her clothes neatly in the chifferobe and tossed her dainty underthings into the laundry basket. Though the hour was late, she was wide awake, her mind full of the excitement of the evening. Lying naked upon her bed, she gazed out the window, and relived her wonderful evening. She had not missed Court's eyes following her as she danced; she had wondered at the coldness in his gaze when she happened to glance his way. Had he felt jealousy? She hoped that was his reason. He could have had his pick of any of the beautiful women there, yet he seemed uninterested in a casual flirtation.

She rose from the bed and walked to the window. Surely it wouldn't be as hot outside as it was in her room. Perhaps there was a breeze down by the river. She needed to walk and get a breath of fresh air until she could calm her excitement. Donning her gown, she quietly left her room.

Court's eyes shot open at the sound of the clock. "Two o'clock and all is well," he mumbled, then repositioned himself on the bed. "Or is it?" he asked uneasily.

Thinking Danielle should be home by this hour, he left his bed and ambled upstairs to her room. The first object that met his eyes when he slowly opened her door was the empty bed. The coverlet was still drawn up and the dainty lace pillows were stacked neatly at its head. Court could see no evidence that she had been there. Out of curiosity, he went to her dressing table and lifted the stopper of a perfume bottle. A lavender scent assailed his nostrils, the same fragrance his angel wore. He smiled knowingly. Another bottle contained the jasmine scent Danielle always wore. Would she come to him tonight as his angel? he wondered achingly.

She should have been home hours ago, he thought heatedly. Baudier had no business keeping her out this late. Then another thought struck him. Suppose she were not with Baudier. Bound-

ing down the stairs and out the door, he headed
for the stable to saddle Scoundrel.

Could she be with Jordan, perhaps even in his
bed? Jordan had expressed his interest in her.
Court had told him he was anxious to get her out
of his life. Had he played her right into his best
friend's arms? Entering Scoundrel's stall, he
started to lift the saddle to place it on the horse's
back, and hesitated. What the hell was he doing?
If the little vixen wanted to spend the night in
Jordan's bed, why should he care? Maybe she
would move into Jordan's house and be his mistress. That thought had a staggering effect on his
senses. Nonetheless, he firmly decided he would
not make a fool of himself by chasing after her.

The moon was half hidden behind a cloud when
he came out of the stable. He glanced toward the
river where a steamboat was making a slow journey up the Mississippi. Lights flickered from the
many portals and lively music floated across the
water.

A movement in the shadows beneath the pine
trees caught his attention. He glimpsed a streak
of white through the darkness as a figure flitted
along the bank. He sucked in his breath and
sweat beaded his brow. It must be this damnable
heat, he conjectured as the apparition disappeared. He started to turn once again to go back
to the house, but the apparition came from behind
a tree. Not an apparition, but Danielle, Court reminded himself with a rakish smile tugging the
corners of his mouth.

"By damn, she won't get away from me this
time," he resolved, planning his course of action.

Danielle stopped suddenly, her ears picking up
a foreign sound. Glancing furtively over her
shoulder, she cocked her head and listened. The
moon had gone beneath a cloud cover, and the

faint light from the steamboat had disappeared around the bend. She couldn't see through the blackness, but she knew someone or something was lurking in the shadows.

Court grinned wickedly, the bark scraping his back as he edged his way around the tree.

That small sound, ever so slight, sent Danielle vaulting toward the deep woods like a frightened rabbit. In the daylight the path would have been familiar, but in the darkness, the wild vines and undergrowth grabbed at her ankles and slapped at her face. She heard heavy footsteps behind her. She knew she was heading in the direction of the bayou, and prayed she could find a hiding place before reaching it. Fear clutched at her insides.

Court could see a blur of white, a definite advantage. He increased his stride.

A thick-roped vine snaked around her ankle and jerked her to a sudden halt. Just as she wrenched it free and turned to flee, she felt large hands grasp her hips. Losing her footing, she fell headlong into a dense mat of underbrush, pulling her captor with her and trapping herself beneath his hard, sinewy body. Court! her mind screamed as she immediately recognized her captor. Struggling, she clawed the bed of ivy, trying desperately to thrust his body away from her. She felt the hard evidence of his arousal pressed firmly against her buttocks and smothered her urge to cry out.

"Easy, angel, easy," he murmured in an achingly familiar voice, "I won't hurt you."

She ceased her struggling and lay inert beneath him. She wanted to tell him she wasn't his angel. Surely he must know who she was; couldn't he see how much she had changed since that fateful night?

"Then do what you will with me and be gone," she whispered in a disguised voice.

He lifted his weight from her. "You wound me, angel. Though I was drunk the first time, I still recall the passion between us."

He raised himself to his knees and straddled her body, securing her tightly between his muscular thighs. Beneath the thin cotton gown, she felt the burning heat of his hand as it roamed her back and slid down to caress her full buttocks.

She tried unsuccessfully to escape from his firm grasp. "Please let me go," she pleaded. "You're making a dreadful mistake, *monsieur.*"

"No, angel, not after I've waited this long to have you again."

He loosened his hold to allow her more freedom, and she rolled to her back and propped herself on her elbows. "Spirits do not make love to mortals," she insisted, hoping to thwart his plans.

Court reached out and stroked her face in the darkness. "I know of one who did."

She was certain he could feel the heat in her face. "You only imagined such a thing. You were drunk...beyond remembering anything."

Court chuckled. "I've never been so drunk that I forget everything, especially a body as warm and inviting as your own. Tonight I have complete control of my senses." Well, almost complete control, he mused. "What I want to know is just who the hell you are." Come on, Dannie, Court urged silently, give up the game.

"The ghost of Espérance. Surely you've heard of me." Danielle's chest rose and fell rapidly.

"Yes..." He cleared his throat surreptitiously. "I've heard of you. But you're a fake. Who's paying you to play this role, Nicholas Caraville?"

Her temper flared. On impulse, she slapped him across his cheek, surprised she had such luck in the darkness. "You bastard!" She immediately clasped her hand over her mouth in horror. She was behaving just as Danielle would have behaved under normal circumstances. Now she was positive that Court was aware of her identity.

Rubbing his stinging cheek, he said irritably, "You've just answered my question, angel, so you may as well confess."

"I have nothing to confess," she stated flatly.

"Nothing? Maybe not with words, but your body will tell me all I need to know."

Raw desire churned in his loins. Leaning forward, he pressed her down to the ground then covered her with his body. Her hands came up to push against his chest, but he grabbed them and pinned them behind her head.

"No, angel, you're mine to do with as I please. Those were your words if I recall correctly. You may be whomever you wish to be, it matters little to me."

As he lowered his head to capture her mouth, she turned her head aside, causing his lips to sweep hotly across her cheek. Nuzzling her hair away from her face, he nipped lightly at the tiny shell of her ear. The sweet-scented aroma of jasmine permeated his senses. "You've changed perfume, angel. I recall the lavender scent of you."

Danielle attempted to remain distant. She had thought him too drunk to remember any of their previous lovemaking. When his lips and tongue kissed and stroked the slender column of her throat, she wished she could put from her mind the sweet torment that he had created in her. She wanted him to carry her again to the height of ecstasy, but she wanted to reach it as Danielle Algernon. Her body unconsciously writhed beneath him, seeking release from her own frenzied desire.

Sensing her body slowly responding to his touch, Court withdrew one hand from her wrists. Turning her face, he captured her mouth, drawing her full lower lip into his own, and gliding his tongue over its moist softness. Tenderly he kissed her, calling her his angel, yet Danielle's name possessed his mind. He defined each portion of her face with his ravenous tongue, stroking at leisure the fine cheekbones, running it feather-lightly down the short bridge of her upturned nose.

Suddenly, she felt her body being lifted and transported to a level of sheer bliss and complete abandonment. As Danielle, she had to be aloof and unwilling, but as his ghost she could let her passions flow as freely as the river. She would continue with her charade, and he would realize she could never feel free to come to him as Danielle until all lies between them were erased. Maybe it's for my own benefit that I pretend to be his angel, she confessed silently.

"I won't resist you," she whispered huskily. "I, too, remember our passion."

Court released his tight grip on her hands and brought them to his lips. "My memory needs no refreshing, angel. I'm drunk, but not from drink. Your soft and beautiful body lying beneath me intoxicates me more than alcohol could ever do." Kissing each finger, he continued to fill her mind with his sensual words. "You're in my blood, and it runs hot with desire. Since the night I took you, I've watched for you from my window and waited for you. Why didn't you come to me the night of the storm? I saw you come up from the bank of the river, thinking my room was your destination." This should give her something to think about, he thought wickedly. Since he now believed he had really seen the ghost of Espérance, he hoped Danielle might become confused and inadvertently let her secret slip.

"You saw me?" She was perplexed. Had he actually seen the real ghost who haunted her home? She had not been out that night, so it had to have been the ghost. She decided to play upon his sensibilities. "Your bedroom is the last place I'll ever enter again, *monsieur,* since I never expected you to . . . to . . ."

"To love you to death?" Court chuckled throatily. Momentarily entertained by his choice of words, he added, "If death is that glorious, angel, then let me be a part of your heaven forever." Dammit, Dannie, Court swore silently, if this is the only way I can have you, then by God, I'll go along with your game. But the next time—and there will be a next time; I'll make certain of that —you won't get off the hook so easily.

Danielle's spirit soared to the heavens with elation. "You call me an angel, yet you deny my existence. When I didn't come to your room, why didn't you seek me out?" she asked daringly.

He turned her hand and kissed her palm. The combination of his tongue and mustache sent shivers of excitement coursing through her. He seemed to delight in taunting her.

"I would have, but you disappeared."

His finger walked lightly up the bare skin of her arm and moved across her collarbone. "You're more woman than ought to be allowed." His hand dropped to the edge of her bodice and settled on the soft swells of her breasts. He felt her heart beat rapidly beneath his hand. Daringly, he moved his thumb to stroke her nipple, feeling her respond to his touch. "Your desires deceive you, love. Were you immortal, I couldn't touch you and feel such arousal. I can remember your wine-

sweet mouth, the tightness of your velvet womanliness as I slid deeply within you."

Danielle's body turned feverish in remembrance. She brought her hand up to cover his at
her breast. "Nothing could have prepared me for
what was to come. It was...beautiful, no words
can describe such passion."

"Oh God, angel," he groaned, drawing her up
until they kneeled before each other. His hands
moved up and down her sides before settling on
her waist.

Consolingly, she lifted her hand and gently caressed his face. Oh, Court, she cried inside, if only
we could love each other in the way we should...
with trust. As her fingers touched his lips, she
gazed lovingly toward his face in the darkness.

A vision of Danielle dancing in her swirling red
gown, laughing gaily with her partners, invaded
his thoughts. He pressed her fingers to his mouth
and kissed each fingertip. Tenderly he dropped
feathery kisses across her eyelids, then trailed his
lips across her cheeks. He cupped her head, his
fingers threading their way through the abun-
dant silken hair that framed her small face, the
soft spiraling curls wrapping possessively around
his hand.

Her full-thrusted breasts with their aroused
peaks lightly grazed his chest. Night after night
he had waited for her and now she was here in his
arms. She wanted him as much as he wanted her.
He would make it a night for them both to remember.

His hands tightened in her hair as he brought
her lips to meet his own. His swift, hungry kisses
nipped and raked her mouth with an underlying
urgency. Grasping her buttocks, he drew her
womanly softness against his throbbing hardness.

Unable to bridle her tempestuous desires a second longer, she wrapped her arms around his broad shoulders, her hands joining at the nape of his neck. Her mouth opened to him, inviting the pleasure of his tongue as it entered her parted lips. She tasted the sweet brandy he had consumed earlier, and smelled the musky scent of his cologne. Flames of desire flickered through her as their tongues met and sparred, and they surrendered to the passions that swept through their bodies like wildfire.

His warm, eager hands brushed away the narrow straps on her shoulders. The bodice rested teasingly on the tips of her breasts. She waited in anticipation, wanting him to touch her with his long, skillful fingers. Grazing his fingers lightly across the swells of her breasts, Court leaned forward, his tongue following the path of his fingers. When his tongue swirled around the darkened peaks, Danielle burned inside and out, liquid heat shooting through every vein in her body.

"You taste so good...so damn good," he murmured against her breasts. Slipping the gown to her waist, his hands kneaded the creamy globes. He buried his face between their fullness, his mouth shifting from one to the other. Taking each taut bud between his hot, moist lips, he swirled his tongue around it, causing her to push her body against him and toss back her head in rapture.

"Please," she moaned beseechingly.

Court's mouth roamed up her throat, tantalizing each inch of the slender column. "Please what?" he asked with passionate humor. "Shall I cease?"

"Never stop...never."

"If it were in my power to go on forever, I'd gladly appease you...and myself. It's difficult for a man to hold back his desires for long, angel, but tonight I'm going to make every effort to delay it."

Danielle's hands traveled slowly down his chest, her fingers unfastening the buttons of his shirt. She was surprised at her boldness and paused at the last button.

He chuckled at her discomfort. "Problems, love?"

She hesitated. "I don't know what came over me to do such a thing. I—I've never undressed a man."

Sliding his hands down her satin sides, Court said huskily, "I'm honored to be the first. Don't be embarrassed, my sweet."

Danielle finally unloosened the final button, then shyly slipped the shirt from his shoulders. Teasingly, she stroked his chest, her fingers tugging and entwining in the crisp, matted hair. Her hand brushed across his nipples. She was surprised to feel them grow as taut as her own. How would it feel to touch him there with her lips? she wondered. Would he feel the same pleasure that she did? Unabashed in the dark, she lowered her head and flicked her wet, agile tongue over the erect nipples.

He sucked in his breath, the muscles in his stomach drawing tight. "God, Da—angel." He bit his tongue to keep from saying her name. "No more...woman...for a while...please."

She withdrew her mouth, bringing her hand up to trace the contour of his lips. "Didn't I please you?"

His soft laughter wavered. "Overly much. But if I'm to go on...forever...too much of a good thing will defeat my intentions."

Spreading his shirt down on the ground, he gently pressed Danielle back to lie upon it. He removed her gown from beneath her, and then finished undressing himself, boots first landing with a thud, and next, the rustling sound of his trousers as he jerked them from his long legs.

The sky with its expansion of gray cloud cover denied them the light of the moon and stars. But the forest was alive with summer night sounds: the cadence of katydids, a whippoorwill's soothing song, the thrash of small creatures scampering through the dense undergrowth.

Court knelt beside her, and took one small foot in his hand. Instantly, Danielle remembered his gentle massage of her tired feet at the ball. But this time, he touched each toe with his lips, kissing and nibbling, sending a rush of shivers up her legs. Roaming his hand sensuously up the long length of her slender leg, he marveled at the texture of it, satiny, yet with a firmness that belied its softness. He felt her muscles contract as his hand caressed her thighs and the curve of her hip.

"You're so lovely, my angel," he whispered hoarsely, continuing his sensual journey by palming the narrow indentation of her waist, his thumbs resting in the hollows of her rib cage.

Her eyes closed in ecstasy, her mind conscious only of his hands moving lightly over her abdomen.

Lying down beside her, Court stroked the smooth underside of her breast. "Were I a blind sculptor, I could mold your image to perfection. After tonight, there'll be no part of your loveliness left undiscovered."

He leaned over her and gathered a swollen breast, circling the taut nipple with his tongue. A shudder coursed through her body, lodging deep within her.

"I'll unearth those emotions that come solely with complete fulfillment. That, my love, is what will bring you back to me time and time again."

But not as an angel, Dannie, he warned her mutely.

Danielle, though aching for satisfaction, could not help but reply crisply, *"Mon Dieu,* but you are vain, *monsieur.* There must be countless men on this earth who know how to please a woman."

He chuckled. "I'm certain there are, love, but I'm going to be the only one who'll ever please you."

He drowned out any further protest by capturing her soft mouth possessively, petitioning her to deny his arrogant words. Lying half across her, he unleashed the passions that swept through him like a riptide. His mouth was wet and feverish, his tongue demanding and determined as it plunged heatedly into the cavern of her mouth. And she welcomed its savage entrance, felt its alluring presence stimulating every pore of her being.

He wanted to possess her, kiss and touch her everywhere in the same instant. Never would she want another man, he thought insolently. He would invade her dreams at night, consume her every waking hour with thoughts of their impassioned loveplay. Her needs would be so great that she would throw away her disguise and come to him as Danielle, his enticing spirit. No longer would she steal away from him when he approached her; she would come to him willingly, longingly.

With his long leg covering her own, Danielle could feel the torrid arousal of his manhood pulsating against her soft thigh, a glorious reminder of what was to come. He taunted her slowly, leaving her kiss-swollen lips to progress downward, devouring her breasts as though they were ripe, succulent fruits bequeathed solely to him to satisfy his ravenous appetite. The white heat of his mouth seared her flesh, gliding over her quivering belly, his tongue pausing to define fleeting circles inside and around her navel.

Her fingers tangled in his ebony hair as she clutched him to her, her other hand grasping his muscular shoulder. When his hand slipped between her thighs, her fingers bit into his flesh. Involuntarily, she closed her thighs tightly against his hand.

"Open to me, angel," he whispered urgently, his breath warm on her abdomen. "I want you...all of you."

Feeling her legs relax, he spread her thighs and moved his body between them. Lovingly, he brushed his hand over her soft triangle, pulling gently at the wispy curls.

He heard her breathing quicken as she moaned, "Touch me."

Complying to her wishes, he dipped a finger into the moist, velvet channel of her womanhood and moved it hungrily within her. His thumb fondled the small nodule, erect with arousing passion, and her body undulated against his hand.

The throbbing magnified as his adroit fingers wreaked havoc on her senses. Every emotion that surged through her, manifested itself in the center of her desire. When she felt him withdraw his hand and pause in his skillful ministrations, she felt a moment of despair. Until, with a mixture of shock and pleasure, she felt his warm breath and mustache caress her inner thigh. Surely, he would not ...*non,* he could not...but he was!

Grabbing a handful of his hair, she pulled at him. *"Non, monsieur,* you cannot."

Raising his head, he countered, "But, yes, my love. I said I would know all of you."

He grasped her hips and brought her up to meet the lambent heat of his mouth. Her mind rebelled at this outrageous foreplay, but her body responded wantonly, bursting inside as she arched and writhed against his mouth while waves of ecstasy surged through every vein of her body. When she felt she could not endure the tumultuous stirrings a moment longer, he ceased his rapturous torment.

Stroking the smooth flesh of her inner thigh, he said huskily, "Now, my love, we will soar together."

Lifting her hips, the tip of his swollen maleness lingered tauntingly at the entrance of her trembling femininity. She arched her hips, urging him to carry her over the brink of her swirling desires. He answered her appeal and plunged deeply, feeling her soft womanliness tightly enwrap him. His slow, methodical movements enticed her hips to undulate of their own volition. His momentum increased, his resplendent length stroking her tender walls, creating a series of heated spasms that raced through her like an all-consuming inferno.

Each movement within her satin sheath brought Court further to the edge of his restraint. When he felt her contractions mingle spontaneously with his own pulsating hardness, the hot seed of his passion spilled within her. He collapsed against her soft body, exhausted and replete.

After several moments, Danielle traced her fingertips over his sweat-laden back, feeling the muscles ripple and then grow taut. Court lifted his weight from her in response, brushed the damp tendrils from her face, and kissed her tenderly.

"I must go now, my love," she sighed reluctantly. Her words of endearment came so easily to her lips. He was her love, yet there still existed barriers between them... Nicholas and Meredith.

He shifted his body so he lay partially across her. "Am I your love, angel, or will you leave me and never return again?"

Her heart twisted at her precarious dilemma. "You have a special place in my heart, but there can be no place for you in my life. We must—"

He pressed his finger against her lips. "I don't believe that, angel. If it were so, fate wouldn't have brought us together again this night. Rather than frighten me away from this house, you have drawn me to it. Do you think for an instant that I could ever walk away from the haunting memories of your passionate loveliness?"

"Please don't do this to me," she cried softly. "I, too, will have beautiful memories. Perhaps they will have to last me an eternity."

As she tried to get up, he clasped her firmly by the arm. "You may go, angel, but rest assured, I'll find you again."

Handing her nightgown to her, he helped her to her feet, watching her shapely silhouette as she dressed. Resting his hands on her shoulders, he bent down and kissed her softly. "Sleep well, my love. May the memory of our night of love haunt your dreams and bring you back to me."

Choking back the sobs that caught in her throat, Danielle managed to reply in a trembling voice, "Please don't follow me, *monsieur.*"

Court chuckled. "Why would it matter, love? I thought ghosts could disappear with the blinking of an eye."

"If I were capable of performing such a miraculous feat," she sighed sorrowfully, "don't you think I would have vanished into thin air instead of running into the woods to escape you?"

He trailed a bold finger along the edge of her bodice, then dipped inside the cup to her breast. "Not unless you wanted to be caught and seduced."

His touch seared her flesh. She placed her hand in his, feeling the pounding of their hearts through the pulse of their hands. She wanted him to make love to her again and again, wanted to wake up beside him. To think that tonight would be their last night together unless she came to him in the darkness weighed heavily on her heart. But she could never chance such a rendezvous again.

"You didn't seduce me," she finally whispered. "You . . . you loved me." She brought his hand to her cheek for a brief moment. Turning from him quickly, she vanished down the path. The white glimmer of her gown faded into the night, but left an everlasting image in Court's mind and a burning imprint on his heart.

He stood silently in the woods, oblivious of the night sounds around him. "Dannie," he lamented aloud, clenching his fists in anguish. Then he touched his tongue to his palm, tasting the salty tears from her cheek, which further tormented his aching heart.

Chapter 16

By the time Danielle reached the security of her room, she had cried a waterfall of tears. Frantically, she removed her gown and hid it in her chifferobe. Fearing that Court had checked her room before he had come out and caught her unawares, she removed the ballgown from the chifferobe and placed it neatly over a chair. Next, she strewed her dainty petticoats and pantaloons in disarray around the room. Should he come to check on her again, he would think she had arrived home during the time of his assignation with his angel.

Going quickly to her dressing table with the intention of brushing the twigs from her tangled hair, she caught a glimpse of her face in the mirror. She moved in closer to the lamplight, her eyes widening in shock as small red welts appeared on her face and neck. She had to restrain herself from clawing at them to relieve the itchiness.

"Nom de Dieu," she whispered as a giant welt grew over her lip, distorting the whole lower portion of her face. Another one rose on an eyelid, the swelling closing her eye to a mere slit.

There was a light rapping on her door. She was so engrossed in the study of her face, that she carelessly answered, "Come in."

The door creaked open. "Oh, Mammy, what am I to—" her words suspended in midair when she saw Court lingering against the doorjamb, viewing her nakedness with great interest.

She thrust her arms over her breasts and ran to retrieve her robe. "Get out of my room, *monsieur,*" she spat, keeping her back to him. Flinging her robe around her nudity, she wondered if he had seen her face.

"You said, come in," he said mockingly, his eyes taking in the clothing scattered about the room.

"I thought you were Mammy," she said over her shoulder. "I believe I asked you to leave."

Court moved on into the room, ignoring her request. "Are you just now coming home, Danielle, or have you been out for an evening stroll?"

Goosebumps rose on her flesh at his insinuation. "'Tis none of your business, *monsieur.* You're not my guardian."

Picking up one of her petticoats, he tossed it over the chair with her ballgown. "According to all the gossip I overheard tonight at the ball, I'm your lover."

She heard the floor creaking behind her. Wrapping his arms intimately around her waist, he brushed the hair from her ear and whispered, "May I be your lover, Dannie? Shall we add truth to the rumors?"

"Please go away," she wailed. "You shouldn't be in my room. What if Mammy should find you here?"

Court turned her in his arms; she quickly dropped her face to hide her ugliness. Her eyes focused on his bare, hairy chest. Damn him for not buttoning his shirt before coming in here, she swore, remembering how the crinkled mat of hair had teased her breasts. He tried to lift her chin to meet his eyes, but it was like prying open a reluctant oyster shell.

"Why are you afraid to look at me, Dannie? Does it embarrass you that I saw you unclothed?"

She tried to push away from him, but he pulled her tightly against him. "Yes, you embarrassed me," she said, gritting her teeth. "I'm not in the habit of displaying my nakedness, *monsieur.*"

"Do you reveal your beauty only in darkness, angel?" he countered.

She was well aware that he was baiting her. "I don't understand what you're implying."

Would he think she was his angel if he saw her ugly, distorted face? Maybe the grotesque welts would be her lifesaver. Thrusting up her face, she watched his handsome features transfer from desire to shock.

"Shall I extinguish the lamplight, *monsieur?* Surely you would prefer the darkness over this," she snapped.

"My God, Dannie, what happened to you?" he asked aghast.

Moving out of his arms, she turned her distorted features away from him. "It must have been the strawberry tart I ate at the ball. I've had this happen before, but never quite this extreme."

"When did this happen?"

Danielle shuddered convincingly. "I doubt that it started at the ball or Damien would have surely mentioned it. Of course, he couldn't see me well when he brought me home." She did not want to lie outright, but a little twist to the story might convince him she could not be his angel. "The itching began in the carriage. It was when I first entered my room that I noticed the welts. For an hour I've been debating on whether or not to awaken Mammy."

"An hour?" He ran his tongue over his dry lips. She was lying. Only by a sheer stroke of luck had these welts appeared so soon after their lovemaking. He knew he had just spent that memorable hour with her.

He looked wretchedly uncomfortable and she smiled secretively. Should he check with Jordan concerning her departure time, it would coincide with her story. Whether or not he completely believed her did not matter; at least for the moment she might have him doubting his own sanity.

"Would you mind waking Mammy before you retire? I need some relief from this insufferable itching."

He walked to the door. "Of course. Will I see you at breakfast?"

She laughed. "Are you certain you want to see me? I won't be a pleasant sight to view the first thing in the morning. Besides, I doubt I'll be up in time for breakfast since it is nearly that hour already."

"Your temporary deformity won't faze me in the least, angel. I know what you look like without the swelling." Opening the door, he said over his shoulder, "I'll send Mammy on up to tend to your needs."

As he closed the door to her room, Court thought, if only I had someone to tend to mine.

The following day passed with Danielle remaining in her room. The ugly swelling on her face had diminished to flat red patches, still unsightly, but at least the itching had subsided. Camille brought her meals to her, while Mammy bustled in and out, applying salve every hour on the hour.

Mammy's cooling balm had helped soothe Danielle's burning skin, but it could not relieve the frustration of her predicament. She was actually jealous of the ghost she had created. Court's infamous angel had captured his heart and she was left to wallow in her own agony. How could she compete with herself? she wondered miserably. If she discontinued her role as the ghost, she would never again experience the rapture of his love-making. She could not go to him as Danielle for fear that her love for him would destroy her in the end. As long as he suspected she and Nicholas were scheming to trap him, what hope did she have of winning his love?

With a good excuse to avoid him for the day, she sorted through her sketches, choosing those she wanted to work on for her future showing. Was she talented enough to display her art to the public? she wondered, critically examining each of the paintings. Jordan had told her how Court had praised her talents, and had shown him the miniature she had painted of her mother. That alone gave her a feeling of accomplishment. Court had openly admired her paintings, but she had never expected him to concur so readily to her idea of selling them. When he suggested a studio for her to work in, she had been doubly amazed. He seemed to want to be rid of her by giving her a chance to make the money to buy back her home. A pain dwelled in her heart at that nagging suspicion.

Throughout the day, she could hear the tapping of a hammer and fought the urge to go downstairs to see the progress being made on the studio. Court wanted her to wait until it was finished. Since the walls of glass were there already, the alterations consisted mainly of laying a cyprus floor. She recalled her *maman*'s happiness when the planting room had been completed. It had been difficult to obtain that much glass at one time, so it had arrived in several shipments. The project had taken nearly a year to complete, but

Nicholas had managed to have it finished it by her birthday.

On the morning of the second day, Danielle knew she would have to go downstairs and join Court for breakfast. There were no more angry welts marring her complexion. After taking a leisurely bath, she donned her chemise, pantaloons, and petticoats, and carefully selected a pale yellow morning gown. The bodice, which was overlaid with delicate lace, embraced her throat, and the sleeves ended at her wrists with a ruffle of matching lace. She pivoted before the cheval mirror, and the skirt twirled around her small ankles, the layers of petticoats screening the soft curves of her hips and long, slender legs.

Brushing her hair until it gleamed, she wound it in a soft knot atop her head, ignoring the stray wispy tendrils that framed her face. Pleased with her innocent appearance, she took a deep breath and made her way to the dining room.

Would she be strong enough to face Court in a demure manner when the chaotic thoughts of his exquisite lovemaking constantly occupied her mind? How could she look at his mouth without recalling its heated exploration of her body? What unsettled her even more was that she did not know if she had convinced him she was not the ghost, and he would be remembering those same things. She flushed as she paused briefly in the arched entrance.

If she had only known how deeply affected his thoughts were as he watched her enter the dining room, she would have bolted from the room. He gazed at her peculiarly, his green eyes seemingly to pierce her soul. There was a grim set to his mouth, which drew the flesh tightly over his jawbone. Straightening her back, she gathered the courage to face him.

"Bonjour," she said lightly, seeing his eyes snap to attention.

"Good morning," he answered in forced politeness. Rising from his chair at the head of the table, he assisted her into the seat to his left. Sitting back down, he rang the small bell to summon Camille to serve them.

Conversation lagged. Danielle looked curiously at him, twisting the napkin in her lap. She started to say something about his unusual behavior when Camille entered the room with a large silver tray balanced precariously in one hand, a steaming pot of coffee in the other.

"It's mighty nice to see you up 'n' about, Miss Dannie," Camille said, setting the tray on the table. Placing a bowl of fresh fruit and pastries before them, she continued, "You looks awfully purty this mawnin' to have suffered so . . . don't you think, Massah Sinclair?"

He regarded Danielle intently from behind hooded eyes. "Yes, she does," he said in a dull monotone.

"Why, you can't even see those bad ole spots no more, can you, Massa Sinclair?"

She saw his teeth grind together. "No, you can't."

Camille went through the ritual of preparing café au lait by pouring hot coffee and boiling milk into the cups simultaneously. She said casually, "I betcha Massa Sinclair is glad you is here to join him. This big ole table gets mighty lonely with jus' one person, don't it, Massa Sinclair?"

"I haven't found it so disturbing." He eyed Camille threateningly, but she was too busy to notice. His words never reached her ears.

Danielle saw the fury blazing in his countenance as Camille's prattle continued. Finally, she stepped back from the table, a modest smile on her face. "Will that be all, Massah Sinclair?"

"That is all, Camille," he growled.

She frowned in puzzlement, noticing for the first time his rising anger. Turning, she swiftly left the room to warn Mammy of their master's unnatural behavior.

He stabbed the fork into a chunk of pineapple. Danielle wondered fleetingly if in his mind, she were the target. He should be ecstatic and overflowing with joy since his assignation with his angel. Unless he somehow had proof that she had duped him.

The rich pastry did nothing to ease the butterflies in her stomach. His continued silence was unbearable. She lay her fork aside and drummed up enough courage to approach him.

"Court, are you angry with me?" she asked him in desperation.

His brow winged upward. He looked her in the eye for the first time since she had sat down. "Should I be angry with you?"

"I . . . don't think so," Danielle stammered. "You —you seem angry with someone."

Laying his napkin aside, he propped his elbows on the table. "I haven't been sleeping well for the past couple of nights. You wouldn't by any chance know the reason why, would you?"

"No, why should I?"

He gave her a smug smile. His eyes drifted over her fastidious bodice then back to her face. "Surely you aren't that naive, Dannie. You're the cause of my sleepless nights."

Burning heat rose in her face. The high collar constricted her throat, threatening to choke her. Sliding back her chair, she said waspishly, "Then you have my deepest sympathy, *monsieur*."

After an angry Danielle left the room, Court

remained at the table, contemplating her complex nature. He wondered how much longer he could postpone the inevitable. He was almost to the point of not caring whether or not she ever admitted her disguise.

Midafternoon, after her scene with Court, Danielle came downstairs. Mammy was polishing the table in the foyer.

"Where is Court?" she asked, peering uneasily into the open door of his room.

"He tole me he had to go to the auction, 'n' didn't know when he'd be back," Mammy said, sticking the dusting cloth in the pocket of her apron.

Danielle knew the auction Mammy was referring to, the slave auction in New Orleans. Court had finally decided to keep the fields in sugar cane rather than to convert them to cotton.

Clasping her arm, Mammy pulled her to a quiet corner in the foyer. Conspiringly, she whispered, "Miss Dannie, I think I knows sumpin' 'bout Massa Sinclair that you needs to know."

Danielle rolled her eyes in exasperation. "I certainly hope so. He was such a beast this morning. For a moment I thought he was going to devour Camille and me for breakfast."

"Well, I don't want you to think I make a habit of eavesdroppin', but I was passin' by his room this mawnin' when sumpin' he said to Bryce 'bout nailed me to the floor." Mammy hesitated, taking a deep gulp of air.

"Mammy, don't keep me in suspense. This isn't one of your ghost tales, is it?"

"Chile, I wisht it was. I heard Bryce say sumpin' to Massa Sinclair 'bout moving to his townhouse in the city."

Danielle's stomach lurched. "Townhouse?"

"Ifen he has a townhouse, then why is he stayin' here, puttin' my chile's reputation on the line? 'Course, it's his house 'en all, but—"

"Never mind, Mammy," Danielle said, squeezing her eyes against the hurt. Slowly her anger overcame the pain. Just you wait, Court Sinclair, she vowed. You will pay for the humiliation you have dealt me.

"What you gonna do, chile?" Seeing the anger on her face, Mammy said, "Now, don't you go doin' sumpin' that you ought not."

Before her charge could reply, the sound of carriage wheels in the distance caught her attention. Going quickly to the window, she saw a polished black coach pulled by two matching white steeds make its way toward the front of her home. As it neared, she saw a gold emblazoned crest on the door.

"Oh, Mammy," she said breathlessly, "who could be coming here in such a fine carriage?"

Mammy was speechless, but only for a second. "You might have a suitor comin' to call on you, chile. One of them fancy men who was at the ball the other night."

Glancing disapprovingly at her morning dress, Danielle moaned, "I'm not suitably dressed for callers."

"You looks purty, chile. Don't worry none."

"That's the problem, I look like a child."

When the carriage halted in front of the house, Danielle peeked through the window, watching as the footman opened the carriage door. Jordan Phillips, elegantly dressed in black trousers and black coat, stepped down. Behind him, another man came into view whom she did not recognize. He was tall and slim, and wore buff-colored trousers and a dark green jacket. Standing beside Jordan, he gazed at his surroundings.

"Mon Dieu," Danielle gasped. "Mammy, please take the gentlemen into the study and serve them some refreshments while I make myself presentable. Jordan Phillips is a good friend of Court's, but I don't recognize the other man."

Without a backward glance she scurried up the stairs and into her room. A caller, she thought bemused, perhaps her very first suitor.

Chapter 17

Searching through her wardrobe, Danielle pulled out a deep rose daygown, knowing it was one of Court's favorites for he never failed to compliment her when she wore it. She eased the gown over her head. Delicate lace bordered the low-sweeping neckline; the sleeves were full and sheer, ending with a band of lace at her wrist. The skirt was narrow, draping her hips alluringly and flowing gracefully to the floor. She worked feverishly on her hair, tucking the unruly wisps into place.

Deciding this was all the time she could spare on her toilette without appearing rude to her guests, she left her room to join them in the study.

Both men turned as she entered the room, their eyes lighting admiringly on the enchanting woman before them. Each time Jordan encountered her, he had to remind himself that his good friend had prior claim. No matter how many times Court denied that fact, it was obvious that she had found a place in his heart.

Stepping forward, Jordan took her gently by the hand, leading her toward the man he wished to introduce to her.

"Danielle, I'm sorry if we have inconvenienced you," he said, smiling down at her with his warm blue eyes. "Mister Bernard, I'd like to introduce you to Miss Danielle Algernon, the beautiful mistress of Espérance. Danielle, Julian Bernard, a friend and business acquaintance."

"Monsieur Bernard," she said smilingly, assessing his patrician features. She placed her hand into his own. "It's a pleasure to meet you."

His dark brown eyes, the color of aged brandy, caressed her face as he said, "My pleasure, Miss Algernon." He lifted her hand graciously to his lips, barely grazing its surface.

Raising his head, he said, "Jordan tells me you are an artist?"

She glanced at Jordan, then back to his friend. "I enjoy painting, but whether one could deem me an artist, I don't know."

He smiled, showing even white teeth. "If the paintings I have viewed since entering your lovely home are examples of your work, an artist then you are, my dear."

Danielle flushed. "Why—why thank you, Monsieur Bernard."

Jordan intervened. "Julian has an art gallery in New Orleans, Danielle. I hope you don't feel that I have imposed by taking the liberty of showing him your paintings."

"*Non,* of course not," she said hastily, "but you've never seen my work, except for the miniature of my *maman.* You could have brought embarrassment to yourself, Jordan."

"True, but Court should be given some credit, Danielle. If you could ever take a tour of his magnificent home, you'd immediately see he has the credentials to recognize a gifted artist."

As he continued to praise his friend's home and art collection, Danielle thought of her previous suspicions and how wrong she was to have thought Court a wastrel. His clothing and manner had always denoted a man of wealth, yet she had felt it was a front to cover up his schemes.

She had surmised that he looked toward Espérance as a business venture to increase his wealth,
and his sister, Meredith, had teamed with him to
bring about Danielle's ruin. Now to learn he had a
beautiful home as well as a townhouse, she had to
change her attitude about him. Still, it bothered
her that he had never mentioned his townhouse.
What else was he hiding from her?

"Is Mister Sinclair in?" Julian Bernard asked,
breaking through the haze in her mind.

"I'm truly sorry, but Monsieur Sinclair is in the
city. Perhaps he will return before you leave." Noticing a tray of bite-sized delicacies and a pitcher
of lemonade on the low marble-topped table, she
said, "I see Mammy has provided us with refreshments. If you would prefer a stronger drink, I can
summon Tobias."

"Thank you," Bernard said, "but that will be
unnecessary."

"No, lemonade will be fine," Jordan assured
her. "We are mixing business with pleasure this
afternoon, Danielle."

"Business?" she asked, her eyes shifting from
one to the other.

"Shall we sit down, Miss Algernon?" Bernard
asked, motioning to the sofa. "I think you and I
should discuss the marketing of your art. That is,
if you're interested."

Surprise washed over her features. She sat
down on the sofa with Julian Bernard while Jordan took a chair nearby. Their conversation became serious and she wished Court were there to
guide her. Had he known they were coming and
left her alone to make her own decisions?

"I'm very impressed with your talent and would
like to give you the opportunity to profit from
your endeavors, Miss Algernon," Bernard said. "If

you wish, we could have a private showing and introduce you to—

"*Monsieur,* if," Danielle interrupted nervously, "if we could handle it discreetly, I might consider your generous offer."

"How discreetly?" Bernard asked, arching a questioning brow.

Jordan rose from his chair and came around to stand behind the sofa and place his hands on her shoulder. "Though Danielle would never admit it, Julian, she's a trifle shy. Perhaps after her first showing, she'll become more familiar with the routine of things. Would it be possible to display her art informally so she wouldn't have to make an appearance?"

Bernard rubbed his jaw, giving his suggestion consideration. "I don't know why not. But if anyone is interested in her paintings, they'll undoubtedly want to know something about the artist."

She smiled demurely. "I'd rather handle it in that way, *monsieur.* If someone does express an interest, then feel free to supply them with any information you deem necessary." She wondered if anyone would consider buying her work once they found out the name of the artist. That was a chance she would just have to take.

"Very well," he said, "then the next matter we should discuss is money. You've worked many hours on your beautiful creations. Do you have any idea of what price you would like to place on your paintings?"

"You're more familiar in that area than I. How does one place a value on hours of love?"

"You're a true artist," Bernard said warmly. "Perhaps I can aid you in making the decision."

She listened attentively as he explained at length how an artist and dealer complement each other. He would receive a certain percentage of each painting he sold. As her popularity grew, so would the value of her paintings. When he offered a satisfactory proposition, she accepted, grateful for Jordan's discreet squeeze on her shoulder. She did not know how she could have managed without his support.

At the conclusion of their discussion, Jordan saw the sparkle in her violet eyes, and the coquettish curve of her mouth. He felt honored to witness this moment of her sublime happiness.

No one was aware of the towering figure standing beneath the arch of the doorway. Court's eyes lingered on the unfamiliar blond man who, in his judgment, was sitting too close to Danielle. He did not remember having seen the gentleman at Jordan's home on the night of the ball, but there had been so many people attending, he could have missed him. Now that Danielle had made her formal entrance into society, would he have to fend off a stream of foppish suitors on his doorstep?

Her merry laughter echoed through the room as the gentleman evidently made a witty remark. Court chose that particular moment to make his presence known. All heads turned in his direction as he leisurely strolled into the parlor.

She almost choked on her bubbling laughter when she glanced up and saw his cynical green eyes boring into her.

"I leave your side for only a few hours and it takes two men to entertain you?"

If his remark were intended to sound humorous, it was ruined by the cutting edge in his voice.

Noticing the streak of jealousy running just beneath the surface of Court's words, Jordan said astutely, "There may be some question as to who's doing the entertaining. The truth is . . . Miss Algernon is such a delightful and charming hostess, you may find Mr. Bernard and me frequent visitors to your home."

At the mention of the other man's name, Court transferred his attention to him. With forced politeness, he said, "Court Sinclair," and offered his hand.

Julian rose from the sofa and clasped his hand. "Julian Bernard," he said with a hint of uneasiness, wondering what he had done to deserve the other man's scowl.

After the introductions, Bernard took his place once again beside Danielle on the sofa. Court glowered and seated himself in the wingback chair across from them. Jordan, amused by his open display of jealousy, purposely added more fuel to the fire by sitting down on the other side of Danielle.

"Please excuse my rudeness," Court apologized without warmth. "Had Miss Algernon informed me earlier we were to receive callers, I would have been here to greet you."

She bristled. "It's not necessary for you to be here when I entertain callers, *monsieur*. I'm perfectly capable of performing the role of hostess when you're absent." She smiled falsely, and squaring her shoulders, added, "They came to see me—not you."

With a cocksure, vexing grin, Jordan supplied, "Danielle has agreed to allow Mr. Bernard to display her paintings in his gallery."

Court was caught unprepared and cursed himself for behaving like a blundering fool. He could see Jordan was in his element, absolutely reveling in Court's misconception. It had been several weeks since he had talked with Jordan concerning the sale of Danielle's paintings. As each day had passed without his approaching him on the subject, he had hoped that he had forgotten the favor he had asked of him. He had decided that even if Danielle was able to make a name for herself, she would never earn enough money to buy back her home; he'd make damn sure of it. But with a substantial income, she might give up the idea and leave Espérance, never to return. Wasn't that the whole purpose of his scheme? He wanted her to be successful, yet now, when he thought he might lose her if she gained monetary security with her talent, he was left with a hollow feeling. He wished he had never told Jordan his plans.

Masking his riotous emotions, Court said, "I thought perhaps you'd forgotten the favor I asked of you, Jordan."

"No," he replied. "Julian's been out of town. I just happened to run into him at Maspero's. He had the afternoon free, so we decided to ride out here."

"When do you plan to display Danielle's paintings, Mr. Bernard?" Court asked as he took a small tart from the tray of food.

"Miss Algernon said I could take several back with me today. I should have these ready for the public to view in a day or so."

Rising from the sofa, she said, "If you gentlemen will excuse me, I'll gather up my paintings."

"There are several you have displayed around the house I'd like to show," Bernard said. "Would you be willing to sell the painting of Espérance?"

Before she could reply, Court stressed firmly, "That one is not for sale."

Though she had had no intention of selling that particular painting, his intrusion irritated her. "I can paint another one just like it."

Looking up at her angry face, he said, "Consider that one sold, Miss Algernon. I just bought it."

Her mouth dropped open in surprise. "Do—do you want it that much, Court?"

A slow smile tugged the corners of his mouth. "I've told you all along it's my favorite."

Happiness mounted within her heart. "Then consider it my gift to you in appreciation for aiding me in my cause."

Where he should have felt gratitude, he only had a sense of remorse. In aiding her in her cause, as she had so appropriately called it, he was pushing her farther and farther away from him. At one time he had thought if he could get her out of his sight, he could get her out of his mind. That was before she insinuated her way into that soft, vulnerable place in his heart.

"That's very kind of you," he said, shifting his eyes from her, lest she see the painful evidence of his feelings lurking in his eyes.

Their evening meal was a quiet affair. Jordan and Mr. Bernard had been invited to dine with them, but declined due to previous plans. To celebrate Danielle's new venture, Maybelle had prepared a feast. Candlelight flickered over the table laden with crayfish bisque, oysters, and a medley of summer vegetables. A bottle of vintage white wine complemented the meal.

Court was still not in a pleasant mood, Danielle noted as she eyed him from over the rim of her wineglass. He had been cranky since breakfast. She had hoped when she presented him with her painting that it would lighten his mood.

His bad temper had not affected his appetite. Danielle had dallied with her food, rearranging it several times on her plate. If only he would smile, she thought in aggravation. He is so devastatingly handsome when he teases me or loses his

temper. Even anger would be better than his ac-
cursed silence.

What would his attitude be if she told him she
was his angel? She cringed at the thought. If anything would force him to move to his townhouse,
that little tidbit of information would. He would
be furious with her if he knew she had played him
for a fool. It was his own fault, she decided firmly.
If he had stayed in the townhouse where he belonged, he would never have bedded his angel.
And she would never have experienced the most
exquisite pleasure in her life. That thought
abated some of the anger she was feeling. It would
not hurt so much if she did not love him.

She stole another glance at him. Their eyes met
and clashed. His jaw was twitching nervously beneath his tanned skin, and his brows drew together in a frown. His eyes disturbed her. They
were as threatening as a gathering storm.

Court was angry, not so much with Danielle as
he was with himself. She had appeared so at ease
when in the presence of Jordan and Julian Bernard. He had noticed her same carefree manner
the night of Jordan's ball. Her violet eyes, dripping with innocence, and her graceful, regal cool-
ness seemed to draw men to her as a bee to honey.
Why could he not successfully draw her to him?
She admitted she enjoyed his kisses, yet she
wanted to be friends. Just how many men friends
does a woman need, he thought irately. Damien
Baudier was her friend. Jordan was her friend,
but he doubted Jordan preferred it that way. Now
she had added another damned friend, Julian
Bernard. He was a charmer in every sense of the
word—smooth and fast talking.

He finally spoke, his tone brusque and imper-
sonal. "Did you enjoy your day?"

She gave an involuntary start, surprised he

had actually said something. "Yes, I had a wonderful day." Happiness lit her face. "Can you believe I'm actually on my way to becoming an artist?"

He looked at her sharply. "You have been an artist all along, Danielle. What's your opinion of the gentleman who plans to make you a success?"

She answered without hesitation. "He seems to be very knowledgeable in the world of art. But, if Jordan hadn't been at my side, I doubt I could have come to such a quick decision."

"Your quick decision wasn't reached because Bernard appears to be a great catch?"

She angrily tossed her napkin on the table. "And what if that was my purpose, Court? Why shouldn't I try to make a new life for myself? Julian Bernard is handsome, wealthy, and a gentleman." She had never considered him as anything but a business partner, but Court had once again managed to provoke her temper. "You have no right to approve or disapprove any man who comes to visit me at this house. If it bothers you so much for me to have callers, then why don't you..." She couldn't finish her statement.

"Why don't I what?" he asked with a sour look.

Jumping up from her chair, she glared at him, provoked. "Why don't you move into your townhouse?"

His tongue rolled in his cheek. "I wondered how long it would be before you found out. Was it Baudier or Jordan who enlightened you?"

Not wanting to implicate Mammy, she said, piqued, "It's none of your business who told me. The point is, Court, you could have stayed there rather than here. Why didn't you?"

"Why should I? I do own this house now, Danielle. You seem to forget that quite frequently."

"But do you plan to make Espérance your permanent residence?"

Sliding back his chair, Court rose and came around to her side. He spoke to her quietly. "I thought you intended to buy it back from me one day."

"I have a feeling that no matter how much money I make from my paintings, you'll always keep it out of my reach." Leaving his side, she paced the room. Suddenly she whirled around to face him, burying her fist in the folds of her skirts. "Money may not buy back my home, Court, but it will help buy my freedom."

Court recoiled as though she had slapped him. For a moment he stood watching her as his own thoughts came back to haunt him. The worst fear he had harbored had just been voiced. The only way he could force her to stay at Espérance would be to marry her—and that he could not do until the barriers were removed between them. But he no longer could deny his love for her. He had fought that emotion from the first time-stilled moment he laid eyes on her, that precarious moment after their duel when her hat fell off and black velvet tresses spilled over her shoulders. And her eyes—those damnable killing violet eyes with their wild, untameable gleam—had captivated his heart the moment they fluttered open and gazed innocently into his own.

With a sense of defeat, he walked over and placed his hands on her shoulders. "Soon I'll give you a chance to sample that taste of freedom. I've been corresponding with my mother, and I've just learned there are matters that need my attention."

Danielle looked at him curiously. "You've never mentioned your mother. I—I assumed..."

"That my sister was my only family?" He

smiled and tilted her chin, caressing the contour of her jaw. "There's so much you don't know about me, little one, but you've never asked."

"May I ask?"

"I may bore you."

All her anger evaporated at his soft-spoken words. "There's nothing about you that bores me, Court," she said, feeling a rush of blood flow to her face.

He laughed lightly and her spirit lifted at the joyous sound. He poured them both another glass of wine, and they sat back down at the table. There existed no animosity between them. They shared a rare moment of peace, each with an overpowering sense they had crossed one more obstacle in their path to contentment.

Chapter 18

The buzzing of a mosquito startled Danielle from sleep. Slapping out at the aggravating insect, she mumbled angrily, "I'll not be your breakfast this day. I've had enough welts to last for some time. No mosquitos and no more strawberry tarts." With a vengeance, she rid the world of the pest.

Dropping back on her pillows, she planned her day. A smile streaked across her face as she remembered her studio. At last it was completed, a bright, inviting, sun-washed room. An additional treat had been the arrival of new furniture. Unknown to her, Court had ordered it for the exclusive purpose of furnishing her studio. When she had thanked him, he had only shrugged and told her she could not very well enjoy her time in a bare studio.

There was a Sheridan sofa covered in a warm green fabric and matching chairs covered in a complementary green. Should she become tired or simply want to lie down and watch the flowing of the river, there was a plump chaise in vivid yellows and greens. The overall effect was refreshing and inviting. Her heart swelled with joy that Court had gone to such great trouble for her.

Fed by buoyant hope, she bounded from the bed. With the vitality of youth she stretched her lithe frame. Drawing her arms high over her head, the short gown rising by degrees, she swung

down and touched her fingertips to the carpeted
floor. Her agile movements pulled her gown up,
exposing her tight little bottom perched in midair.
This was the sight that met Mammy's eyes as she
entered the room. She jerked the door shut, in
case someone passing by might see her charge in
such a questionable position.

"Lawdy mercy, chile, you's gonna pull everthin'
that you got loose. You straighten up here so's I
can check to see ifen your parts is still in the right
places," she said with a hug.

With unabashed pleasure, Danielle righted
herself and hugged Mammy tightly. "Isn't it a glorious day, Mammy? *Mon Dieu,* I can't wait to get
downstairs."

Mammy smiled indulgently. "That sho' is a fine
place Massa Sinclair done fixed up for you. How
'bout ifen we get you dressed so's you can git on
down there? I'll bring your breakfast out there to
you."

"Oh, Mammy, you spoil me terribly, but I do
want to get down there soon. I thought I could
work while the light is just right."

Mammy loved seeing her in such an exuberant
mood. She helped her charge get dressed, then
followed her downstairs to prepare breakfast.

Unimpeded light greeted Danielle as she entered her studio. Some of the glass had been carefully framed, and hinges anchored for opening
and closing. Several now stood open. Gentle
breezes wafted from the river and cooled the
room.

The previous spring, she had spent hours painstakingly making numerous sketches of a Carolina
parakeet. As she had viewed the dainty bird, it
sickened her to think people actually killed the
enchanting creature for its colorful feathers.

She had become enthralled with the little creature, and had drawn dozens of sketches of her friend after she had trained him to accept her presence.

One day, her worst fear was finally realized when her friend never returned. She had been saddened by the loss and vowed to do a painting of the clever little bird one day. She had her sketches and hopefully she could bring him back to life on her canvas. She was now ready to attempt it.

She tacked a width of linen fabric over a wooden frame. Then she put several coats of a paintlike substance called ground on the canvas to make it easier to apply paint and increase the paint's brightness. It also helped to avoid cracking. If her paintings were to be shown publicly, she wanted to take every precaution. With this thought foremost in her mind, she picked up her sketches, and with a discerning eye, went over each.

Taking up her palette, she mixed her paint, and then brushed sure, strong lines on the canvas. In a matter of moments, her concentration was enmeshed in her work. Years of loneliness and apprehension melted away as she filled her canvas. Thoughts of Nicholas Caraville, debts, and Court did not intrude on her creativity. She painted what she saw, drawing from a well that overflowed with ideas. She felt euphoric when she stepped back and viewed the canvas. Giddy with pleasure, she turned from side to side, viewing her work from every angle. Laughing, she held out her arm, thumb up, and with one eye squeezed shut, she repeated her inspection.

She felt drained when she finally collapsed on the chaise. She rubbed her tired eyes, exhausted to the point of napping. She jumped when she heard Mammy's voice.

"Why, chile, how purty. Ifen I didn't know better, I'd think that bird done flew in the window 'n' landed on that canvas. I jus' don't know how you do it...make 'em so real, I mean." She shook her head in wonder as she gazed at the lifelike portrait.

Perched on the limb of pine was a Carolina parakeet, its talons clutching the branch. He had a beautiful yellow head, which shaded to a rich orange around the bill, and eyes that seemed to follow every movement. The plump little body was adorned in brilliant green feathers, his sweeping tail feathers adding grace and allure. His head was perched at such an angle, leaving the viewer with the impression that the parakeet was proudly showing off his wardrobe.

After they shared an unusually enjoyable dinner, Court asked Danielle to see her work. She cast Mammy a look, noting with a frown that she knew Mammy had been talking to him.

"You're welcome to view the painting, but let me warn you, it's not completed."

They left the table and strolled outside to the studio, neither speaking to the other. Spellbound, Court stopped upon seeing the canvas, admiration apparent in his features. "Audubon would be impressed, Dannie."

Her reaction to that comment was pure astonishment. "Do you truly think so? I could think of no greater compliment than to have another artist find favor with my meager attempts."

"Meager, Dannie?" he questioned. "I think not. You breathe life into your subjects. Every time I view one of your paintings, it's as though I clearly see something I've only glimpsed before. You bring it to my attention by your compelling art. You impart life to your work."

Cupping her chin, he stroked her cheek with his thumb. "When I look at you, I see beauty, courage, loneliness, determination, and a real zest for life."

Pulling from his touch, she turned to the windows. She wanted to scream out in rage: Look at me then! Look deeply. Are you so blind you can't see your angel lurking just beneath the surface? A whippoorwill calling out to its mate in the darkness seemed to mock her torment as a kaleidoscope of images flashed through her mind: lovers entwined on Mother Nature's bed beneath lofty branches, each rendering pleasure to the other... freely.

Changing her train of thought, she faced him. "Did you know I met James Audubon? Several times in fact. When I was younger I rambled at will through the bayou, carrying a rag-tag satchel containing my sketching materials and lunch. At that time I was only trying my wings, so to speak. But I had heard of the man who explored the marshes, seeking birds in their natural settings. I wasn't frightened when I happened to see him one day because I knew he was the man I had heard about. With all the grace of a charging elephant, I approached him."

Court laughed and urged her to continue.

"Truthfully, he was quite put out by my intrusion. As it happened, I sent the bird he was sketching into flight. When I asked him if I might see his drawing, his anger eased somewhat. It wasn't long before we were in deep discussion about the merits of painting birds in their natural habitat. He consented to share my lunch without hesitation. As we talked, he told me of the setbacks he had endured in his effort to do his painting. At every turn, he met hardship and was forced to commission portraits for his very existence. When his spirits had been at a very low ebb, he did not think of himself as an artist at all, but wholly as a naturalist. He encouraged my attempts at drawing and gave me pointers. As you probably know, he's a firm believer in using plants, trees, and flowers for the idyllic setting of his drawings. Unless, of course, the bird is in flight."

"Sounds as though he made quite an impression on you, Dannie."

"He did," she answered quietly. "I've never attempted to attain wealth from my work. It's always brought me peace and unrestricted pleasure. Now I discover it could help me to achieve what I covet most."

Her words rankled, and Court, with a dark scowl, growled, "Of course, that's owning a clear deed to Espérance. You'd go to any lengths to gain back the plantation, wouldn't you?" he demanded, a vision of gossamer haunting his memory.

"Anything in my power," she answered smoothly.

"You don't have any hidden supernatural powers, do you?" he questioned curiously.

"If I did, I assure you, *monsieur,* I would never have lost control of Espérance in the first place."

Court wanted to shake her until her teeth rattled whenever she put up her haughty facade. Instead he replied in the same unaffected manner, "I see your point, my sweet. Let's talk of other things. I find I grow weary of beating the same dead horse. You should be pleased to learn my absence will be sooner than I expected."

"Have you at last decided to take up residence at your townhouse?"

"Would that displease you, little one?"

"On the contrary, it would ease my position enormously. Maybe someday I could live down the fact that I shared my home with a rogue such as yourself."

"It's not my desire to make you unhappy, but our living arrangements will remain the same. I'll only be gone a few weeks. I've left my interests in capable hands, but there are things needing my attention."

Danielle smiled up at him mockingly. "I'm sure the belles of Natchez have worn their carpets bare puzzling over your absence."

"You overrate my prowess, I fear." A devilish smile teased the corners of his mouth, giving untruth to his claim. "I've yet to find any particular lady I rate above all others."

Strange flames sparked in Danielle's heart, and for an instant she wished his words were true. What about spiritual beings? she wanted to ask. Her courage left her before she could utter the words. Her lips formed a perfect circle, poised for speech, but she was left floundering for something to say. Nonplused, she rapidly made her retreat. *"Bonsoir, monsieur."*

"Good night, Dannie, sleep well. I'll probably be gone when you get up in the morning. Try to stay out of mischief while I'm gone."

"I'm not a child, *monsieur.*"

That, my love, has been brought to my attention with undeniable clarity, Court thought. As he watched the graceful sway of her skirts, a bolt of desire shot through him.

A feeling of unease settled over Danielle. Was it Court's absence, of her unacknowledged fear that her work might suffer from public ridicule? She was thankful her paintings would be discreetly displayed in Monsieur Bernard's collection. Private showings were common for a man of his artistic range. She felt confident he would handle the situation with finesse should anyone be interested in her work.

She worked nonstop on the painting, her untouched lunch long since grown cold. Mammy would fuss because she had not eaten, claiming Danielle was already too thin.

After a while, Danielle lay her brush aside and flexed her tired fingers, then she massaged her taut shoulders. She was pleased with the results. A couple of more hours would see the painting finished. Her mind rushed ahead to the subject of her next painting. The river had always been one of her favorite subjects. It should have been named "Woman," for it changes as rapidly as a woman changes her mind, from a gentle flow leisurely lapping its banks, to a raging tempest of unbelievable force.

Absorbed in her work, she did not notice the long shadow until it fell across her canvas. Thinking Mammy had returned, she quickly assured her, "I wasn't hungry, Mammy. I'll eat later."

When no response was forthcoming, she glanced over her shoulder, and the color drained from her face. Rankin Pernel's sinister eyes impaled her and his thin lips drew back from yellowed teeth to curl into a lewd grin.

"Well, I see he's set you up nicely." His eyes skirted around the room, taking in every detail. "There's been a lot of changes since my last visit," he commented, shifting his eyes to her. He insolently raked his gaze over her gown, lingering on her breasts, sliding down to her paint-stained apron.

Gaining control, she muttered, "You!"

"Yes, have you missed me?" He sneered with the assurance of a predator confident of his victim. Moving in for the kill, he stepped closer. In what he imagined was a silky voice, he added,

"Had I realized you were so eager to share your charms, I would've pressed my suit."

"You're evil and vile, Monsieur Pernel. Not only do you live off the misfortunes of others, you seek to dig your claws in deeper, searching for blood when there's none left. I'd advise you to take yourself as fast and as far as you can before Court returns."

"Perhaps, Danielle, you presume you're dealing with a fool. Let me assure you that you're not. I haven't made my plans in haste. I watched Court Sinclair board a steamboat bound for Natchez. I know, too, that your darkie isn't here. It's just you and me." With growing confidence, he lifted his hand and stroked the smooth skin of her cheek.

Repelled by his clammy touch and frightened to learn what his "plans" were, Danielle slapped away his hand. "Get out," she shouted.

"Have you forgotten about the debts? You've had ample time to collect the monies Caraville owed."

His announcement threw her off-guard. "You're lying. Court must have paid the debts."

Shaking his head, he said indulgently, "Well, well, looks like Sinclair didn't set you up as well as you thought."

"But—but I figured Court had paid them since you haven't been around in so long."

"Miss Algernon, the men of New Orleans who hired me to collect Caraville's debts aren't my only clients. I'm a very busy man," he bragged.

"Well, I can pay the debts if you'll only give me a little longer. Soon I'll have my own income."

Pernel looked at her doubtfully.

She hurried on, "It could be that Nicholas has already received the money, and you'll be hearing from him any day."

He lifted a tempting curl and twisted it around

his finger, drawing her closer. "No, Dannie," he cooed, "you've had ample time. I'm afraid unless you can pay, it's the Cabildo for you. The only way out, I see, is for you to take me up on my offer. My proposition is still open, only the value of the merchandise has depreciated since you've been spreading your legs for Sinclair."

Oh, how she hated this man, she thought, her mind churning.

Clamping his hand on her shoulder, he pulled her harshly into his arms. She struggled desperately, but to no avail. As she opened her mouth to scream, his head lowered, and he covered her trembling lips with his plunging tongue, violating her tender flesh. She pushed frantically at his narrow chest, nausea threatening her stomach. Releasing her from his revolting kiss, he wrapped his hand around her chin, his reptilian eyes skirting over her face.

"You can count on a very intimate relationship between us," he stated with confidence. "Only next time, I expect a little more response."

Danielle uttered not a sound, only looked at him with disgust. Suddenly she pursed her lips, spitting straight into his abhorrent face.

Jerking from her, he swiped hastily at his face. "Bitch, damn cold-blooded bitch," he swore, wiping away the spittle.

She hurried around the easel, placing it between them. He lunged forward, slapping the easel aside. Momentarily shocked, she watched as her painting went hurtling across the room, landing with a dull thud against a chair leg. Her cries lodged in her throat as she viewed the senseless destruction. That was Pernel's fatal mistake. She may have been able to take his physical abuse, but not this—all the hours she had spent on the painting...wasted. The little parakeet would not be destroyed again without retribution. Anger overriding her fear, she faced her attacker, bloodlust in her eyes.

Pernel was too overcome by his own overweaning desires to note the change in her. Dragging her to him, he once more covered her mouth with his. Sick with his pawing, she waited. His breathing was becoming heavier and his mouth bolder. As his tongue slid again across her teeth, she clamped down as hard as she could until she tasted his blood.

Violently, he yanked his mouth from her. A glimpse of his blood flowing freely was all she saw before his fist cracked against the side of her jaw and his vicious curses rent the air. She saw stars and stumbled to her knees. Before she could right herself, he struck her again. His every movement sent his blood splattering around the room. Pacing herself, she dodged his blows until she could stand.

Just as she gained an upright position, his flying hand grabbed the front of her dress and ripped it to the waist, revealing her creamy smooth breasts. Pernel's watery eyes sparkled and his curses colored the air as he used her torn bodice like a lifeline to pull her to him. His cruel fingers pinched her breasts, his fondling, rough and degrading. Blood dripped from his chin as he told her in the most repulsive way what he was going to do to her. Grasping her hand, he forced it to the bulge in his pants.

I'll die before I submit to him, she vowed in desperation. He is mad, completely mad. Fear enveloped her like a mist for she saw no escape. He drew her close and rubbed his swollen manhood against her. She suffered the degradation in silence, searching for some weapon to use against him. Within arm's reach lay the scissors she had used to cut the linen for her canvas. Leaning into Pernel, she eased her arm around his shoulder.

Thinking she was enjoying his loveplay, he

ground out hoarsely, "You like it, don't you? Well, don't get in a hurry, I'm going to—"

Turning his head slightly, he caught just a glimpse of the scissors rushing through the air by a hand bent on vengeance. He shoved her from his grasp just as the deadly weapon found its target and marked it well.

From that point on, it seemed to Danielle everything happened in slow motion. Pernel stumbled and his body slammed full length into the window glass, sending sparkling prisms showering into the air. At the last slow second, Pernel shifted his body to the side, and jagged shards of glass enbedded themselves in his clothes. The scissors caught and hung momentarily on a jutting fragment, then fell unencumbered onto a bed of glass.

Danielle stood for several minutes, blocking out everything, except that her beautiful room was no longer beautiful. The sparkling glass that had admitted precious sunlight was shattered. The peaceful joy of this room had been destroyed. A solitary tear glistened, clinging to her lash, then rolled gradually down her face. Fear settled heavily on her heart as she realized the room's destruction was the least of her worries.

What had she done? Taking stock of her disheveled state, she picked up the tail of her apron and swiped at the blood...Pernel's blood. The sight churned her stomach. Making her way carefully through the broken glass, she leaned down by his side. He lay sprawled at an odd angle. She could see the damage the scissors had done; his blood seeped from the puncture. Had she not been in a state of shock, she could not have viewed the mangled body with such indifference. Pieces of broken glass had shredded his clothing, leaving gaping wounds in the flesh. Across his pale face was a particularly vicious gash slanting over the brow and across his eye to his ear. His eye had the peculiar appearance of being open. It was not.

The reality of the carnage permeated her numbed mind. A frightened whimper escaped her bloodless lips, and she scooted away from the sight. Covering her face with trembling hands, she sobbed quietly. What repercussions would fall at her door? she wondered. She could not bear the disgrace. People would naturally assume she had killed him because he had tried to collect the money Nicholas owed. Fed by her fear, she covered her chest with her torn bodice and stumbled back to the house. Upstairs in her room, she pinned her dress shut in several places, not caring how shabby she looked. Her mind was more preoccupied with the sorts of punishments that might be meted out to her for her crime.

Dragging out a worn carpetbag, she stuffed her boy's clothes inside. In a last quick trip to her studio, she gathered her paints and sketch pad. She would not leave them behind; they were the only things left truly belonging to her. She left her *maman*'s jewelry behind, their value sufficient for the care of Mammy and Tobias.

Avoiding the kitchen area, Danielle headed for the protection of the woods. She could not risk taking Tempete with her because she did not know how arduous her journey might be. He was too precious for her to endanger him. Fate must have had a change of heart for just as she reached the cover of trees, the sight of a tethered horse stopped her short.

"Pernel's horse," she whispered.

Securing her carpetbag to the saddle, she mounted the horse. "Come on, boy. It's a long way to Baton Rouge," she urged with a gentle nudge.

Chapter 19

Mammy ambled toward the house, the last robust notes of "Rock of Ages" on her lips. A satisfied smile wreathed on her face. All was well in her world. Miss Dannie seemed to have reached an understanding with her new master, and they didn't argue as much anymore. All she had to do was watch him watch Danielle to know that she had wormed her way into his heart. She wasn't blind, Mammy thought with a laugh. She noticed, too, how much effort her lamb took with her appearance when Court Sinclair was around. They weren't fooling anybody but themselves. Maybe it wouldn't be too much longer till they realized what Mammy already knew. Taking a deep breath, she let loose another lively hymn, "There's a happy land—"

Camille darted toward Mammy crying hysterically, motioning wildly with her hands. Mammy enfolded her in her arms and cooed gently, "Sh... sh... nothin' can be as bad as all that. Calm down, chile, Mammy's here."

Camille's garbled words were intermingled with deep heaving shudders.

"Chile, Mammy can't understand a word you is sayin'. Now calm down 'n' tell me what got you in such a state."

"Miss... Miss... D—Dan..."

"What that you say? What 'bout Miss Dannie?"

Unable to stop the shuddering, she took Mammy's arm and led her in the direction of Danielle's studio. Rounding the end of the house, Mammy stopped stone cold. Her eyes flashed across the destruction. All was quiet, even the birds ceased their chatter as Mammy began to weep with heartbroken sadness.

"Where's my baby?" she whispered.

"That's just it, Mammy, there ain't no sign of Miss Dannie . . . no where. I done been through the house a'callin' for her. I jus' knows sumpin' terrible has happened to her."

"Shut your mouth," Mammy stormed, startling Camille. Viewing the ravaged scene once more, she noted the blood stains on the grass. Entering the room, she walked carefully around the broken glass, with Camille right behind her. Spying Danielle's painting tilted precariously against a chair leg, she knew that indeed something terrible had befallen her baby. In a forlorn voice, she announced, "I gots to sit down."

"Looky here, Mammy," Camille shouted, reaching for the blood-stained scissors.

"No!" Mammy bellowed. "No, don't tech a thing. We gots to find Massa Court."

"But, Mammy, he's gone to Natchez. How you gonna get word to him ifen you can't find him?"

"Mistah Phillips can help. He'll know where Massa Court lives. Now, I want you to go and fetch Tobias for me."

By late afternoon, Mammy had sent Tobias into town for Jordan Phillips, and had gathered together every soul on the plantation. Dividing them into groups of four, she had sent them out with stern orders to search everywhere for Miss Dannie. "She could be layin' somewheres a'bleedin' to death. Ya'll better not come back without her."

It was a crushing blow when word was brought to Mammy that Tempete was in his stall. "Miss Dannie always takes that horse with her. What happened to her?" she wailed. "Has some no-account sneaked in while Miss Dannie was alone 'n' carted her away?" It was obvious something terrible had happened; somebody had been hurt. From the looks of the blood splattered everywhere, someone had been hurt bad.

A cloud of dust in the distance caught Mammy's attention. She shot from her seat and rushed to meet the oncoming rider. "Praise the Lawd, I sho' am glad to see you."

Court looked at her strangely. "I'm sure I would be on my way to Natchez at this very moment, but one of the ship's boilers gave out and we had to return to shore."

"Well, I for one don't know nuthin' 'bout boilers, but I thank the Lawd that you is back. Somethin' terrible has happened."

Court suddenly felt as though a great hand was squeezing his heart. "Where is Danielle?"

Mammy's great dark eyes stared at him mutely for a moment. How was she going to tell him? The words finally came. She had faith he would find her baby.

She was right behind him as he entered the studio. "I wouldn't let nobody tech a thing. This is the way I found it."

Court viewed the destruction without a word, vowing vengeance on the head of whoever was responsible for Danielle's disappearance.

Dawn of the third day since her disappearance saw Court astride Scoundrel, picking his way through a wooded area with dense undergrowth that might have provided shelter for Danielle. When his search proved futile, he returned to the house, defeat etching his face. Once more he was met by Mammy. One look told him she was fired up about something.

"Massa Court, I want you to come with me. Maybelle done got her grandson in the kitchen. That little dickens, he done tol' us pretty as you please that he needs to see you. His mama 'bout wrung his ear off for keepin' his mouth shut this long." She huffed, never breaking her stride as she led him to the kitchen.

A small, wiry youth sat before Court.

"You wanted to see me?" Court asked gently.

"Yassuh," the boy said nervously. He swallowed loudly and looked to his grandmother for support.

"Go on, Jackson, tell Massa Sinclair what you seed," she encouraged.

"Well, the day Miss Dannie disappeared the sun was shinin' bright 'n' my mouth was waterin' for some crawfish pie. Ah headed for the bayou and was down on all fours diggin' for this fat crawfish. That rascal could dig faster than anythin' Ah ever seed." His voice trailed off as though he were once again plotting against the crawfish.

"And?" Court asked with impatience.

"Yassuh, like Ah said, Ah was diggin' when Ah heard somethin' crashin' through the weeds. Ah hunkered down real low so's Ah wouldn't be seen. Ah didn't know what it was 'n' Ah was scairt. Then this hoss breaks through the clearin'. Now this hoss has been rode hard cause they was white foam clingin' to his mouth. The man that was ridin' him was grumblin' 'n' fussin'. Then alluva sudden he done smiled 'n' pushed his hoss on. It weren't no happy smile neither. It scairt me near to death, so's Ah laid down flat as Ah could git, smack dab in that water. Mah mama whupped my tail when Ah come back cause Ah gots my clothes all wet and muddy."

"Why didn't you come forward with this information sooner?"

Rolling his big eyes, he divulged, "Ah was scairt. Ah done had one whuppin' 'n' Ah wasn't hankerin' for anuther. You ain't mad at me, are you, Massa Sinclair?"

"No, I'm not mad, but next time you see anything out of the ordinary you come tell me or Mammy, understand?"

"Yassuh," he said, lowering his face in shame.

"Jackson, what did this man look like?" Court asked.

"Ugly," he said with a shiver. "He was skinny. His eyes was sorta shifty...ifen you knows what Ah mean."

Court nodded.

"Oh, yeah," Jackson said hurriedly, "he was sportin' a funny mustache...a handlebar, Ah think, 'ceptin' one side looked like it sorta wilted."

Mammy knew distinctly who the man was. "Pernel," she whispered.

Court looked at her in confusion. "What?"

"They ain't no doubt about it. Sounds jus' like that no-account Rankin Pernel. He's always been a'prowlin' 'round here, aggravatin' my little lamb over them bills her stepdaddy done run up all over town."

"You're sure, Mammy?" he demanded, perspiration suddenly beading his brow.

"Yassah, as I'm sure as anythin'. Why that loathsome creature was here jus' a few days afore you showed up as new owner of Espérance. He just sat hisself down in Massa Caraville's study like he owned the place, 'n' ordered me to go get Miss Dannie. And Lawdy, Lawdy, you oughta heard all the bad things he said to her. I done tol'

Miss Dannie I'd a'took the broomstick to him ifen he weren't holdin' her over a barrel. He upset her sumpin' terrible that day. He left madder than a wet hen."

"My God," Court stormed, jumping to his feet. Pacing the room, he ran his hand through his hair, stopping periodically to shake his head in wonderment at his own stupidity.

"What done got hold of you, Massa Court?" Mammy asked, concerned.

Trying to mask his discovery, he shook his head wearily. "I'm just glad at last to know the man's identity. Now I have something to go on."

His thoughts were a caldron of torment. If what Mammy said was true, then he had been the one living a lie, not Danielle. She was innocent of his accusations. Passing himself off as Nicholas Caraville, Rankin Pernel had lost the deed to Espérance. What a fool he'd been, he thought. Oh, God, what had his stupidity cost Dannie?

Dropping back into his seat at the table, he stared quietly into space. The muscle in his cheek worked furiously as he contemplated Pernel's downfall. Knowing the identity of Danielle's assailant answered a great many questions. Still, another one haunted him: One of them or maybe both had sustained injuries; had Dannie's been fatal? He would do anything in his power to have the assurance that she was well. He mourned her loss with a grief that overwhelmed him.

Tempete snorted his displeasure when Court mounted him. Since he had not been ridden since Danielle's disappearance, Court thought he needed the exercise. "I mean you no harm, big fellow. I only wish to find Danielle." At his mistress's name, Tempete settled down, accepting the man's weight.

As he headed in the direction of the bayou, Court's memory swept back to the last time he had been there—his encounter with the little nun. He admired the ingenuity of her various escapades. It would have been easy for her to accept the hand fate had dealt her. But instead Danielle had faced her problems with a forthright determination unequaled in any female he had ever known, never using feminine wiles to gain what she desired most. Instead she had set about to see the problem through with any means she could devise. Conjuring up her image, he recalled soft curves tempting the hand, graceful moves teasing the eyes, gentle words pleasing the ear.

The sharp stinging lash of a tree limb brought Court out of his preoccupation, cursing. Forcing his attention on his surroundings, he became aware of the dense undergrowth. Vines wove their way at random through the trees, sometimes creating an arch as they reached from one tree to another. Fragrant flowers blended with the smell of damp earth. Tempete neared the marshy banks of the water, and he guided the horse around mammoth cypress trees. The quagmire sucked at Tempete's hoofs as they made their way arduously along the bank. To the right lay the pit of quicksand that had almost claimed Danielle.

Court's mind recoiled in anger when he thought of how he had saved her from the quicksand only so she could be subjected to the evilness of Rankin Pernel. Would it have made any difference had Danielle known she was debt-free? Probably not, he thought. Pernel would have used another means to threaten her. His whole body tensed at the thought.

He massaged the taut muscles of his neck, letting his head fall forward, rolling it around his shoulders like a pivot. Just as the tightness was easing, he glimpsed a length of white fabric dangling in the foliage. His stomach muscles coiled into a knot of dread. Dismounting, he rounded the pit of quicksand and jerked the fabric free from a bramble bush. A large lump formed in his throat, making swallowing difficult. He knew what it was he held in his trembling hands. How many times had he seen Danielle with the paint-splattered apron cinched tightly around her waist? Though this was only a fragment of it, the blood stains mingled with the paint smears spoke volumes about her disappearance. Court stared at the innocent-looking pool of quicksand. Had that hellhole claimed his beloved after all?

All was quiet in the darkened house. Court tossed and turned, seeking the oblivion of sleep to give him a short reprieve from his torturous thoughts. He heard the clock strike three. Dragging himself from the bed, he shrugged on his robe. Lighting a candle, he made his way through the darkness to Danielle's room. Placing the candle on her night stand, he sank down onto her bed.

Everything in the room spoke of her presence. His eye was caught by dozens of her sketches and several paintings propped neatly in one corner. He sat studying the stack for several minutes.

At last, giving in to his curiosity, he pushed himself from the bed. Easing down on the floor, he picked up several of the drawings. A smile tugged at his mouth as he looked at the sketches. There was one of Mammy with arms akimbo as though she were listing Danielle's misdemeanors. Another of Tobias in pursuit of a chicken. Danielle had titled this one, "Sunday's Dinner." He chuckled as he flipped through the drawings of familiar faces going about daily chores, unaware their likenesses were being put to paper.

His hand paused in midair. His own image stared back at him. He had to admit it pleased him that Danielle had taken the time to sketch him. After all, his behavior had left a lot to be desired. It was becoming increasingly clear that he had been a fool to set himself up as her judge, jury, and executioner.

Moving on, he was astonished to discover drawing after drawing of himself. There was one of him astride Scoundrel and another as he strode across the fields, his shirt hanging loosely from his fingers. He could almost feel the heat as he recalled the day she must have drawn it. It had been damnably hot. He had not been aware that anyone had seen him. If she had bothered to follow him, he concluded, she would have caught him in the altogether as he cooled himself off in a wet-weather spring.

Reminiscing did little to ease his torment. Flipping through the remaining sketches, he felt a cold chill suddenly run up his spine. The hand holding the sketch began to tremble. Before his eyes was his ghost. A gossamer gown of shimmering white floated about an alluring figure whose face evoked softness, the violet eyes filled with love. Court's likeness was in the foreground; he was hunkered down on a bed of ivy, Danielle hovering behind him, her arms outstretched as she reached to touch him. His eyes widened as he examined the drawing. How many times had he relived this very scene?

He cursed his damnable pride a thousand times over. If the love filling her eyes were true, then his deepest yearning was manifested in this drawing.

It seemed he and Danielle each had shared an

abundance of pride. A sad smile pulled at his lips as he thought of the scripture his own mammy had cautioned him with repeatedly: "Be not wise in your own conceits."

The truth of the words slammed full force into his thoughts. He had never been wise in his dealings with Danielle. The proud Court Sinclair had lost what he desired most, never understanding it had belonged to him all along.

But for him it was too late. Now that he was free to admit he loved Danielle, he was alone and mourning her loss. What a cruel hand fate had dealt him in this game of hearts.

Chapter 20

A smudge-faced youth sat on a crate at the end of the gangway, watching passengers disembark from an elegant steamboat at the harbor in Baton Rouge. Then he hastily picked up his sketch pad and made quick, precise strokes beginning a likeness of a young couple as they made their descent.

"A portrait of you and your beautiful lady, *monsieur?*" he asked as they sauntered past him.

Waving his hand in dismissal, the man answered, "Not today, sonny, we haven't the time."

"Haven't the time...haven't the time," he mimicked, his mouth forming a defiant moue.

No wonder they pass me by, he thought disgruntled. After a week without a bath and clothing that looked as though it belonged in the rag bag, he probably smelled worse than the dead fish that floated against the edge of the pilings.

His keen senses picked up the aroma of over-ripe fruit, and his growling stomach rivaled the clattering of cart wheels behind him. He gazed down at his food sack; it was as empty as his stomach. Frustrated with his misfortunes, he kicked away the sack. Resting his elbows on his knees, his chin cupped in his hands, he stared up at the crewmen on the steamboat as they hustled back and forth, mopping the decks and unloading cargo.

A distinguished older gentleman, dressed in a

navy uniform and white shirt, paced the deck, shouting orders to the crew. He paused and removed his hat to wipe his brow. The sun glinted down on his silver hair, and the warm breeze brushed it from his sun-weathered face. Leaning against the railing, his eyes scanned the harbor.

Without a thought, the youth picked up his pad and began sketching the captain of the steamboat.

As he became aware of someone watching him, Capt. David Winthrop dropped his gaze to the boardwalk. There he is again, he thought, nodding his head sympathetically. For the past week as he came and went, Capt. Winthrop had noticed the young, shabbily dressed artist sitting on the dock. He had not missed the disappointment on the lad's face when people shrugged him aside. He descended the gangway, his eyes focused on the slumped back of the youth.

A shadow fell across the boy's sketch pad, and Danielle raised her head to meet a pair of warm, gray eyes. Embarrassed, she quickly tilted the pad from his view.

Capt. Winthrop was startled by a pair of violet eyes fringed with long, sweeping lashes. Where the rivulets of perspiration had cut a path down the dirt-covered face, he could see a creamy complexion. The lad was not safe on the streets alone, the captain thought uneasily.

"Mind if I take a look?" he asked affably.

"Oui, capitaine, I would," Danielle countered, then realizing she was rude, she added softly, "I'm not finished yet."

He smiled. "I understand. My name's David Winthrop. What's yours?"

"It's...uh...Dannie."

"Well, nice to meet you, Dannie. Can I sit a spell with you?"

"Suit yourself."

"Business has been kind of slow this week, hasn't it?"

"Whose?" she asked irritably. "Mine or yours?"

"Mine couldn't be better."

"Do you own that boat?"

"You betcha," he answered proudly, giving the steamboat a sweeping glance of admiration. "Call her the *Lucky Lady*. Beautiful, isn't she?"

She gazed at the steamboat with its glistening white paint. "You take very good care of her."

Cocking his head at her, he grinned broadly. "Well, it's not an easy task, mind you. Just like a woman, you gotta spend money on her if you plan to keep her. She has about as bad a temper, too. If she don't want to go anywhere, she don't go."

Danielle laughed. "Are you pulling out again today?"

"If she's willing, I am. We're heading for New Orleans tonight."

At the mentioning of her home city, Danielle quickly lowered her eyes in painful remembrance. Putting the final touches on her sketch, she asked, "Would you like to see my drawing now?"

"Are you finished already?"

"It's only a quick sketch, *Capitaine*."

She turned the drawing in his direction. He nodded his head, smiling broadly, and said, "Onery-looking cuss, isn't he? Say, you're pretty good for such a young feller. How old are you anyway?"

"Eighteen," she lied, hoping it was a believable age for a boy who would look like her.

"Eighteen." He sighed wistfully. "Got any family?"

"Not...not really."

"So you're kind of on your own, huh?"

Danielle stiffened her spine. "I've always been pretty much on my own."

"Would you like a job on my boat?"

His question caught her off-guard. "Are you serious, *Capitaine?*"

"Of course I am, Dannie. I'm always needing an extra hand or two. The pay isn't tremendous, but you'll get a free bed and meals."

Just the mention of food was all she needed to make up her mind. "When can I start?" she asked with a smile.

"How's about right now?"

"What would you like for me to do first, *Capitaine?*"

"First, why don't you go get your belongings, and I'll show you where you'll be sleeping."

She gazed at him disparagingly. "You're looking at them, all wrapped up in one dirty bundle."

"Then the first thing we'll have to do is get you a change of clothing."

Before thinking, she asked, "May I have a bath?"

The captain eyed her strangely. He cleared his throat. "I don't deny you probably need one, but..." Seeing the lad's crestfallen expression, he added with a smile, "There's a tub in your sleeping quarters."

He thought he heard the lad's stomach growl. "When was the last time you had a decent meal?"

"A couple of weeks ago," she answered quickly. If it had not been for the numerous orchards and vegetable gardens she had raided on her trip to Baton Rouge, she would have starved. After she had arrived, she had sold Pernel's horse. With the scant amount of money she had received, she had managed to find a cheap room.

"Let's see if Kelly, our cook, can round up something for you to eat."

After Danielle had eaten, Capt. Winthrop introduced her to the crew and showed her about the boat. The gentlemen's staterooms were lavishly appointed with red silk curtains and matching bed hangings. Expensive carpets, sofas, and plump chairs were provided for each berth.

The ladies' quarters were below deck. White curtains fringed with lace adorned the numerous portholes and plump sofas, chairs, and cheval mirrors were placed throughout the long room.

The salon was the most impressive room on the boat. Ornate gaming tables were placed invitingly around the room; brass chandeliers with numerous candles hung over each table, and thick carpeting muffled distracting footsteps. At one end of the room was a large stage with a calliope, which provided entertainment when a live band was not available.

When the captain showed her the crews' sleeping quarters, Danielle felt the heat rise from the tip of her toes to the top of her head. How could she sleep in a roomful of men? What would she do when they started to undress and bathe? Worst of all, how could she protest without giving away her identity? *Nom de Dieu,* what had she gotten herself into this time? she wondered frantically.

Her eyes lingered on the large tub in the corner of the room, in complete sight of everyone. The wonderful thought of a relaxing bath was hastily dismissed from her mind.

Night came and the steamboat began its journey downriver to New Orleans. The crew retired to their quarters, a reluctant Danielle lagging in behind them. Their raucous laughter and bawdy language defiled her ears, but she uneasily laughed with them, nonetheless. She sank down on the bed that Capt. Winthrop had assigned to her, her heart slamming against the walls of her chest. She turned her head to the wall as the men began undressing. She drew the lightweight blanket over her so they couldn't see that she was fully dressed. She heard water being poured into the tub.

"Hey, shrimp," one of the men said, nudging her shoulder. "The captain said you wanted a bath. It's ready and waitin' for you."

"I ... I think I'll skip it tonight—if you don't mind."

"Well, I do mind," he said sarcastically. "I didn't tote them buckets of hot water in here for nuthin'."

"Please feel free to use it yourself, *monsieur*," she retaliated.

"You hear that, fellers? We got us a fancy-pants, French-speakin' dandy. Whatsa matter, Frenchy, you afraid we'll see that skinny little ass of yours?"

Danielle moved closer to the wall.

Suddenly she was hoisted from her bed and slung her over his shoulder. Humiliated, she beat at his back with her fists.

"Fights just like a woman, don't he," he said, laughing boisterously as he walked across the room.

"You big oaf, put me down."

"I'll put you down, all right."

No sooner had he said it than Danielle felt herself being tossed into the tub of warm water. She clamped her hand over her hat to keep it in place, thankful the room was nearly dark because her loose-fitting clothes were clinging to her body. Everyone laughed at her humiliation. Rather than scamper out of the tub in a frenzy, she lay in its depths, savoring the warmth of the water as it lapped against her.

Knowing they expected her to lash out at them in anger, she said surprisingly, "Do you have any soap? While I'm in here, I may as well do my laundry, too."

She looked up at the man staring down at her. He was grinning from ear to ear. "Glad to see you got spunk, Frenchy." He tossed a bar of soap into the tub and walked to his bed.

It was then she noticed he was as naked as the day he was born. Red-faced, she grabbed the soap and scrubbed at her clothing as though she were cleansing away her sins. She remained in the tub until the water had turned cold, when she heard the rhythmic snoring of the men, she eased quietly from the tub. She took her only change of clothes and the blanket from her bed, and crept from the room to an alcove to dress. Then she climbed back into bed.

Sleep would not come. She longed for her thick down mattress, the chorus of the katydids, and the familiar song of the mockingbirds. Mammy, her dear sweet Mammy, was forever lost to her, but the memory of her loving care would follow her the rest of her life.

After several weeks of working on the *Lucky Lady*, Danielle became ghastly ill in the mornings. One could always find her small figure slumped over the railing, retching and heaving. Her malady was diagnosed as sea sickness, but she knew the truth—Court's angel was pregnant with his child. She laughed and cried hysterically at her appalling predicament. How could she support her child after it was born? There was only one solution—leave the country and go to France. Perhaps there, she could start her life over. But that would require money for passage that she didn't have. Her meager earnings from her work aboard the steamboat would never be enough. Then again, in a few more weeks, the crew would wonder how Frenchy had managed to put on so much weight in such a short time. She didn't know what she would do when they discovered she was a woman. Perhaps she could sell some paintings to raise money for passage. But if her artwork was recognized, she could be traced to Capt. Winthrop's boat, then taken back to New Orleans and imprisoned for the murder of Rankin Pernel. It was a chance she would have to take.

Pernel had been the winner. His death had put the finish to whatever happiness she might have had. Perhaps she and Court might have one day settled their differences, and he might have come to love her as she loved him. Instead, he would have returned to Espérance by now and discovered the woman he had lived with and fought with was a murderess.

Damn you, Pernel, she swore vengefully, wondering what she had done in her life to deserve such hardship.

She had accepted the drudgery of her tasks as though they were commonplace. She ignored her chafed hands and confided to no one how her body ached continually from the back-breaking chore of mopping the decks. She had learned to accept the teasing from the crewmen, and she joked with them from time to time. No one knew she slept in her clothes because she made an effort to be the first one in bed at night and the first one up in the morning.

She found time to bathe privately. Whenever they docked in a city, the men would leave the boat after completing their chores, and she used this time to take care of her needs.

In her spare time, which was seldom, she finally completed a painting of the *Lucky Lady* as a gift for the captain. Surprised, delighted, and full of admiration, he immediately displayed it in his quarters. But there never seemed enough hours left in the day for her to paint anything else.

It was a particularly bad day. Danielle's spirit was low; she was hot and tired, her miseries apparent by the constant frown on her face. Capt. Winthrop had asked her to whitewash a portion of the above deck, a task she dreaded. Painting pictures was her joy, not walls and floors, she thought irritably.

Placing a bucket of paint on the deck, she began working on the outside walls of the gentlemen's staterooms. Glancing down, she saw passengers boarding, and heard their laughter and hearty farewells. Laying her paintbrush aside, she placed a sign at the end of the companionway, which read CAUTION—WET PAINT.

Picking up her brush again, she continued her task. One man caught her attention. He was potbellied and dressed gaudily. She noticed his hands, each finger sporting a wealth of gold and gems, as he conversed boisterously with another gentleman. She cringed when his black sleeve raked across the wet white wall.

The man glanced down at his sleeve, then scowled at her, the veins throbbing in his temple. He stomped her way.

"Look at what you've done!" he growled, shoving his white sleeve in her face. "It'll take your year's wages to pay for this."

Danielle stiffened her back and faced him defiantly. Clenching the paintbrush in anger, she said, "There's a caution sign posted, *monsieur*. Everyone else seems to have read it."

"I'm not everyone else!"

"Mon Dieu, but that's certainly a blessing," she could not help but reply.

Grabbing her by the collar of her shirt, he jerked her to within inches of his malevolent face. "I'll have you fired, you little son of a bitch."

"Then let's make it worth your while," Danielle said and slapped him across the face with the wet paintbrush. Stepping back quickly, she surveyed her handiwork with a satisfied smirk on her face. The paint had not only whitewashed his face, but rained over his entire black silk suiting. Paint dripped from his eyelashes and thick mustache. One large drop ran down the wide bridge of his bulbous nose and clung to the edge like a giant white wart.

Big Ed, one of Danielle's fellow crewmen, stood at the top of the steps, watching the whole scene. He never expected what followed or he would have stepped in immediately to prevent it. The irate passenger slammed his beefy fist into Dannie's jaw, sending her hurling toward the railing and plunging over it head-first. Rage boiled within Big Ed and he burst forth, thoughts of revenge for his little friend uppermost in his mind.

The passenger stood motionless, his mouth dropping open in fear as he saw the giant man advancing toward him like an enraged bull. With a ferocious growl, Big Ed lifted the man and clamped his huge arms around the man's middle, squeezing the life from him. He heard the frantic shouts on the lower deck as he increased the strength of his arms to match the pain in his heart.

Had Big Ed not heard the faint call for help, the passenger would have been dead in another instant. Instead, Big Ed tossed his burden callously aside, never seeing the unconscious man slide down the wall.

Danielle gripped the iron post of the railing, her

feet dangling in the air. She expected to die at any moment, and joining her in death would be her child. She felt her fingers slipping from their hold. Fear surged through her. As blackness enveloped her senses, she prayed she would feel no pain.

There was pain. In a state of shock, she thought she was dead. How could she be feeling such pain after death? Her head felt like it had been trampled on by a herd of wild horses. She was completely unaware that Big Ed had grasped her wrists the second she had lost her hold on the railing.

Hearing Capt. Winthrop's voice roar in outrage, Danielle opened her eyes, the bright colors of the awning above her blurring. I'm alive, she thought in a daze, then closed her eyes.

She was jolted back to awareness by someone's large hands shaking her. Her eyes fluttered open to see Big Ed staring worriedly into her face. Lightly slapping her cheek, he said, "You're all right, Frenchy."

Danielle smiled faintly and groaned.

Big Ed gazed into her violet eyes, eyes that did not belong on a boy's face. "I almost didn't reach you in time."

Capt. Winthrop knelt down beside them. His face was red with anger. "That bastard won't hurt you again, lad. So help me God if I ever lay eyes on him again, I'll kill him. He was fortunate Ed didn't finish him off for me. I had him and his bags dragged off the ship." He frowned as he saw Danielle's bruised face. "I'll go find Doc. Dannie's jawbone may be broken."

Saliva built up in her throat and she gulped. "I don't need a doctor."

"That swelling needs tending to," he protested.

"Frenchy, you took quite a beating when I pulled you over the railing. Doc's got a powerfully good liniment to ease your aches and pains," Big Ed added as he rubbed Danielle's shoulder.

"Non," Danielle objected and raised herself to a sitting position, shaking her head to clear it. "He can take care of my jaw . . . but nothing else."

Big Ed grinned, knowing Frenchy always slept in his clothes and bathed when the others were gone. He could not keep from teasing him. "Don't be so modest, Frenchy, we're all grown men. You don't have nothing we don't all have . . . 'cept maybe on a smaller scale."

She turned beet-red. Big Ed played upon her misery. "You're still a growing boy; we all realize that. What you need's a woman to make a man out of you."

"Mon Dieu," she said petulantly, trying to cover her embarrassment. "I'll grow up in my own time and I don't need your help doing it."

Capt. Winthrop laughed uproariously. "Carry him downstairs, Ed."

All the way to sick bay, Danielle's mind worked furiously on how to get herself out of this new dilemma. Ed opened the door to the small room where the sick were taken care of and lay her on the cot. She immediately jumped up, but feeling light-headed, she braced the back of her legs against the bed for support. Big Ed rummaged around in a cabinet and brought out a jar.

"Might as well get started. No telling when Doc'll get here. Now, get out of those clothes and remove that damn silly hat."

"Non," she stated defiantly. "You leave and I'll take care of my own doctoring."

He nodded his head impatiently. "Just how're you going to rub down your backside?"

"It isn't my backside that took the beating."

"Damn," he swore beneath his breath, "I'd hoped I wouldn't have to do this."

Her face paled as he towered over her, his intentions evident on his face. "Do—do what?"

"Strip you myself," he said adamantly and reached for the front of her blousy shirt.

"Wait!" Danielle's eyes sparkled with tears as she jerked the cap from her head. The wealth of ebony hair cascaded over her shoulders.

"Well, I'll be damned," he said, fingering a long tress. "I wondered why every time I looked into your eyes they bothered me so damned much."

She lowered her gaze. "I—I guess I should pack up my things." Then in exasperation, she stomped her small foot. *"Nom de Dieu,* I can't seem to do anything right."

Taking her hat from her clenched hands, Big Ed pulled it over her head and tucked her hair beneath it. "You're wrong, Frenchy. You've carried more than your fair share of the load, being the pint-sized squirt that you are. Now, as soon as Doc gets here and checks your jaw, there's a paint job that needs finishing."

"But—but—" Danielle stammered.

"But nothing," he charged. "I don't know why you're here and I won't ask you for an explanation. The only reason a woman would ever dress like a man and work like one as well would be out of desperation."

Smiling impishly up at him, she said, "Now that you know I'm a woman, I suppose I'll have to make other sleeping arrangements."

Big Ed chuckled. "I think that would be wise. You're fortunate the men haven't caught the scent of a woman in their midst already. If even one long black strand of your hair escaped your hat, I couldn't vouch for your safety. I'll speak to Capt. Winthrop and see what I can do for you."

"You won't tell him who I am?"

Tweaking her nose, he said, "Your secret's safe with me."

That night, Danielle found herself in a small room near the captain's quarters. How Big Ed had arranged private facilities for her, she would never know. Capt. Winthrop also had changed her duties. She would now help out in the salon and clean the staterooms after the passengers departed, working on deck only when absolutely necessary.

"Hey, Frenchy," a voice shouted from across the vast salon, "the table in the corner needs a new deck of cards."

Danielle placed a tray of empty glasses on the bar. Picking up a new deck of cards, she veered through the tightly packed crowd toward the table of gamblers.

She placed the deck of cards on the table. "May I get you—" Her words died in her throat as she stared at the man with the patch over his eye.

"It's about time," he said belligerently and raked the deck toward him. He raised his ugly face and Danielle turned a sickly gray. *Non,* it can't be, she thought in stunned amazement as she gazed into Rankin Pernel's watery-blue eye. A long jagged scar, puckered and red, split his eyebrow, then disappeared beneath the patch, reappearing on his cheek. His hands were scarred, the end of his little finger missing.

Her stomach rolling with fear, she turned and walked hastily through the crowded room and out to the deck. Leaning against the railing, she took deep breaths of the fresh air and tried to calm the rapid pounding of her heart. Pernel's alive! she thought with relief. I'm not a murderess. I can go home to Espérance...to Mammy...to Court. Court ...*Mon Dieu,* how can I go home to him now, pregnant with his child?

She gazed at the starlit sky, grappling with her thoughts. She was amazed Pernel had not recognized her even in her male attire. Pacing the deck, she listened to the revelry in the salon. She needed a few more moments of fresh air, then she had to get back to work. Now that she knew Pernel was alive, she wondered what Court and Mammy thought had become of her. How devastated and confused the whole household must have been, not understanding her mysterious disappearance; no body in sight, and the only clues a room of shattered glass and pools of blood. Whose blood? they would wonder. If she had been in her right mind after the tragic incident, she would have left a note explaining her ordeal. She must go home, if for no other reason than to let them know she was alive.

After that, if Court did not want her to remain at Espérance, she would make other arrangements. Perhaps Monsieur Bernard had sold some of her paintings and that would enable her to start her life over again. She not only had her own life to think of now, but that of her unborn child.

As she headed back to the entrance of the salon, Pernel and the woman who had been sitting next to him came out through the doorway. Danielle quickly stepped into an alcove to avoid running into them.

"They didn't see me, dammit," he cursed loudly.

"With many more careless tricks like that last one, they will, you fool," she countered.

"Well, miss high 'n' mighty, where would you be today if I hadn't pulled a few tricks along the way? You could take a few lessons from me yourself."

They moved to the railing and Danielle had difficulty hearing their conversation over the noise in the background.

"Keep your voice down, Rankin," she hissed. "Do you want to get us thrown off the boat for certain?

Lose a few hands occasionally. And regarding your previous remark on where I would be today without your help, I have managed quite well so far without you."

"Yeah, well, don't get any bright ideas...like thinking about tossing me overboard like you did your husband," Pernel said viciously. "Don't think I wouldn't report you in a minute if you ever try to double-cross me."

The woman laughed harshly. "You can't blackmail me, Pernel, we both know that. I know enough about your debauchery to hang you right beside me."

Danielle, hearing everything, wondered about the woman's identity. Whoever she was, she had evidently murdered her husband.

While in the salon, Danielle had only glimpsed the mysterious woman. She had the impression of black hair streaked with silver and a widow's peak, but her attention had been riveted to Pernel, her shock blocking out everything else. She waited in the darkened alcove until the couple re-entered the salon.

Later that night, Danielle could not sleep, her rambling thoughts giving her no rest. She decided she would check the passenger list first thing the following morning, and find out the identity of Pernel's partner in crime.

The next morning when they docked in Memphis, Danielle saw Big Ed forcibly dragging Rankin Pernel down the gangway, the woman angrily following close behind them. Afterward, when Danielle asked their names, Big Ed said, "Mr. and Mrs. Rankin Pernel. Quite a pair, weren't they? Captain prides himself on running honest tables. Those two would've had it otherwise."

Chapter 21

Court leaned against the railing of the shifting boat, his mood as unsettled as the water lapping against the hull of the ship. He was consumed with finding Rankin Pernel. He would not rest until he learned the truth about Danielle's attack. And he would kill him on the spot if he doubted one word of Pernel's confession.

He had hired men to search every quarter of New Orleans. Jordan had promised him that Pernel would not set foot in the city without his being aware of it within minutes. Confident of his friend's assurance, Court had set out to search every port between New Orleans and Natchez, his final destination. His effort had gained him no clues. It was as though Pernel had vanished into thin air, just as Meredith had appeared to do. Learning that Capt. Winthrop was due in port, Court had remained in Baton Rouge in order to book passage on the *Lucky Lady*.

Court was thinner and his stormy green eyes glittered with determination. His body craved sleep, but his mind never rested. Continually he sorted through the fragments of information he had gleaned about Pernel. Nothing he knew completed the puzzle. Pernel had nothing to gain by viciously taking Danielle's life. Could his desire for her have pushed him beyond reasonable thought? Defeated by his own conclusions, Court accepted the invitation brought by one of the crewmen to join the captain for a drink.

Walking through the corridor, his attention was caught by the cabin boy. His derrière was perched in midair as he gathered the spilled contents of a tray. Before Court could offer his help, the boy straightened and hurried away. Court's stomach knotted. He was not in the habit of speculating on the buttocks of everyone he encountered, but something seemed so familiar.

As he and Capt. Winthrop stood outside the captain's quarters talking, Court again spied the back of the cabin boy as he struggled to coil a rope.

Capt. Winthrop noticed the direction of Court's gaze. "That's Frenchy," he said proudly.

"A little on the delicate side, isn't he?"

"Yeah, I guess you could say that, but he makes up for what he lacks in strength with stamina."

They watched the boy hoist a coil of rope almost as big as himself over his shoulder. Staggering under its weight, he made it to a chest and deposited his burden. When the boy reached up and massaged his abused shoulder, a light went on in Court's mind. How many times had he viewed Danielle doing the same thing after hours of painting?

Shaking his head to clear the memory, he missed the departure of Frenchy. Capt. Winthrop put Court's preoccupation down to tiredness.

Seated in the captain's quarters a few hours later, Court took a long pull of the aged brandy. He and the captain had been in deep discussion of Jordan Phillips's outlandish exploits. When Capt. Winthrop finally had to go in search of another bottle of brandy, Court studied his surroundings.

It was not a large room, but every inch was utilized. Dark wood framed a comfortable-looking bed, its matching chest resting nearby. A large desk scattered with nautical paraphernalia sat conveniently at one end of the room. Complementing the desk were comfortable chairs, in one of which Court now slumped. As his eyes drifted around the room, he noted a painting of the captain's steamboat. Nice work, he thought with a glance. Dismissing the thought, he continued his study of the room.

His eyes shifted direction so rapidly it took him a moment to focus. His heart surged to his throat and he bounded from his chair. He would recognize the subtle tones and bold lines of that artist anywhere. No work he had ever viewed had the distinct flavor of Danielle's paintings. In the lower right-hand corner saw his proof. Blending with the churning river were the initials, D.E.A.

His heart stopped as another thought leaped to the forefront. Was this an old painting? How long had the captain had it? Court had never noticed it before, and he had spent hours in this room in the past. Lifting the painting from its hanger, he inspected the wall behind it. Had it been there for a long period the wood underneath would have been noticeably darker. But the wall was the same mellow blend overall. There was nothing to indicate the painting had hung there for any length of time.

Just then, Capt. Winthrop returned to the room. "Ah, so you've noticed my pride and joy."

"Yes, it's beautiful. I haven't seen it before, have I?" Court waited with bated breath.

"I guess not, since I've only had it for a few weeks."

Court's heart tripped over several beats.

"Remember Frenchy, the lad we saw wrestling with the ropes?"

Court nodded.

"Well, I picked him up a few months ago on the docks at Baton Rouge." The captain reached for a pouch of tobacco from the desk. It took him several minutes to get the tobacco tamped and his pipe drawing to suit him. Court waited. Gesturing with the pipe in his hand, the captain continued, "He was trying to make some money by drawing pictures of people disembarking from the different boats. Wasn't doing much good. I offered him a job and three meals a day with a place to sleep. We struck a bargain."

The word, bargain, struck a chord in Court's memory, a bittersweet recollection.

"It wasn't long afterward that Frenchy presented me with this painting." The captain finished his story and looked at Court. "Are you all right, Court? You look a little green around the gills."

"No, I'm fine," he assured him. Not desiring to rush from the room like a madman, he changed his tactics. "David, I believe you're right. I haven't been sleeping well lately. Maybe I'll retire for a while."

"You do that, Court. We can't have you feeling poorly. You'll miss all the fun." Capt. Winthrop chuckled, bidding him to be on his way.

Court was itching to search for Frenchy, but with quiet determination, he reined in his emotions. With the appearance of a curious passenger, he scoured the boat. Not a sign of Frenchy. He began the search again. No luck. With flagging spirits, he gave up and sought the comfort of his own room. Entering his suite, he stopped stone cold.

Meeting his hungry stare were dark britches snuggled tightly across a trim little bottom. Frenchy was bending over in front of the dressing table. Court's breath whistled through clenched teeth.

Danielle, hearing the sound, lifted her head. She peered into the mirror before her, meeting Court's eyes head on, her violet eyes blinking in disbelief. Her blood rushed to the tip of her toes, and she swayed precariously toward the glass.

Court grabbed her and bundled her in his arms in a matter of seconds. "Dannie," he ground out hoarsely.

She sobbed quietly, letting her fingers trace the beloved features of his handsome face. "Pinch me, Court," she whispered. "No, don't," she added quickly. "If I'm dreaming I don't want to wake up."

"You're not dreaming, love, nor am I," he assured her as his hungry mouth closed over hers. Desperation bound their embrace as their lips sought what they had mourned and believed lost to them. Eagerly, their mouths searched to renew and their hands explored to reclaim each feature.

When their lips finally parted, Court groaned hoarsely, "Angel, my angel." His warm breath mingled with hers. Cupping her chin, he searched her luminous eyes. She was hypnotized by the force of his questioning green gaze and the warm finger that played across her cheek. "Why, Dannie?" he asked softly.

"It's a long, confusing story, Court," she replied weakly. Shamed by her longing for him, she lowered her eyes.

Lifting her chin, he implored in a voice thick with emotion, "No, sweet, don't turn from me. I've dreamed of this moment for a long time. Come, let me hold you a little longer. We have no need to rush."

Danielle moved eagerly into his embrace. They stood motionless for several minutes, savoring the feel of each other. Then he pulled her to the bed. He lay across the foot, his arm propped beneath his head. She sat cross-legged in the middle. They were close enough to reach out and touch as her story unfolded.

She told him of Pernel's attack and how she had wielded the scissors to gain her release. Then she related Pernel's horrendous fall through the glass.

"I thought he was dead; that I had killed him. I fled the scene, hoping I could find Nicholas and he would help me. I knew the authorities would arrest me for Pernel's murder. They would have thought I killed him because I couldn't pay him the money he came to collect," she recounted breathlessly.

Court's heart felt as though cold water had been dashed upon it. Should he tell her the debts had been paid weeks before? If he did, would she turn from him in anger, destroying this fragile balance they had achieved. No, his mind urged, wait until her trust is stronger.

"Court," she said, interrupting his thoughts, "I'm free. Pernel's not dead. I saw him. I'll grant he looks so different that I almost didn't recognize him. He has a terrible scar on his face and wears a black patch to conceal his eye. And he was accompanied by a woman."

He nodded. "When the destruction of your studio was discovered," he said, "there was no body. Pernel must have been only dazed because there was no sign of him...or of you." He told her of the search and of Mammy's grief and his own. Drawing her close, he ground out hoarsely, "I thought you were dead."

Tears sparkled in her eyes. "I thought I was dead to you also."

Drawing back from her, he teased, "I see you've donned your britches once more. You've made a marked impression on the captain. He doesn't know of your disguise, I presume."

"No." She smiled sheepishly. "I've had the devil's own time getting away with it." She told him of her run-in with the passenger and how Big Ed had befriended her after learning her identity.

"Speaking of identities..." he said warningly. "You realize your game has run its course."

"Please, Court, try to understand. After I found out you were so superstitious, I decided to use the ghost to my advantage. But there really is a ghost at Espérance."

He chuckled, recalling the first appearance of Dannie as the ghost.

She stiffened her back. "It would have worked if you hadn't decided to take matters into your own hands."

He laughed outright.

Court could not keep his hands off her. He had immediately tossed her cap aside, and as they talked, he trailed his hand up her arm, and wrapped it in her flowing hair.

He lowered her head, capturing her lips. His mouth was teasing, urgent, as hot desire shot through him. With agile fingers, he loosened the buttons of her shirt, releasing her creamy mounds for his unrestricted pleasure. He drew her closer until they were both on their knees in the middle of the bed. Her shirt hung loosely from her shoulders as his mouth feasted on the inviting fullness of her breasts. Lowering his head, he swirled his tongue around one aroused bud. Cupping the other in his hand, his thumb stroked until she was moaning out loud. Her own fingers quickly released the buttons of his shirt, and she ran them over his chest, stopping only when they reached his turgid peaks. Adroitly, she played with them while her mouth trailed across his shoulder to the hollow of his neck.

Raising his head, he gazed hungrily into her smoldering eyes. "God, I need you next to me," he ground out. "I need you to surround me.... Let me feel you."

"I need you, too," she whispered.

With a hoarse groan, his mouth took hers, his tongue whipping over her lips. Capturing her lower lip, he tugged gently. With an utterance of overwhelming desire, his tongue plunged into the warm softness of her mouth. His hands mocked hers as they roamed over her back and down to her slim buttocks. Her body trembled in anticipation as his hand slid and began unfastening the buttons of her britches. When he slipped his hand inside her pants, her fervent passion escalated as he stroked her womanly softness. She moaned and pressed against the hand bringing her such pleasure.

Touching him, feeling the throbbing heat of him foremost in her desire-filled mind, she accepted her own boldness without a qualm. Easing her hand to the waist of his pants, she teased him subtly. Her exploring fingers soon had the buttons undone. Free from the binding fabric, his throbbing manhood greeted her, and she used the knowledge she had been taught with a skill that had Court warning her of the consequences.

Drawing back from her, his eyes devoured her. Her hair tumbled wildly around her face. Resting on her knees with the shirt hanging freely from her shoulders, and her boy's britches gapped open to reveal a hint of her womanly curls, she had as devastating an effect on his senses as if she had been completely naked.

She was no less affected by the sight of him. His sun-browned body quivered beneath her touch as she leaned forward and circled his taut nipples with her wet tongue.

"God," he growled. Sinking his face into her mane of hair, he eased her down on the bed. Rising to his feet he tugged off his boots and discarded his clothes. Danielle watched him in rapture. Taking his time, he pulled off her boots, and slowly slid her britches down her hips.

As every inch was unveiled, he rained greedy kisses over the satiny length of her, his tongue leaving her writhing in passion as it trailed across her. Tossing her clothes aside, he lifted her feet and nibbled at the pads of her toes, before sliding his mouth up the inside of her leg.

"Mon Dieu," she moaned, pulling at his ebony hair. "Stop, Court, stop. . . ."

Lifting his mouth, he smiled wickedly. His voice raw with emotion, he asked, "Are you sure, love?"

"I need you now," she cried softly.

"In time, Dannie."

His words rocked her and the blood racing through her veins gathered speed. She arched against him, encouraging his ardent exploration. Lifting her hips, he repositioned her, his voyage leading him to her warm velvet softness. Danielle thought she was dying, when suddenly she was gripped with pleasure so intense, it left her panting in fulfillment.

Reaching out to him, she kissed him deeply. Mimicking his loveplay, she worked her own magic. She ran her hands over his body, and then her mouth took free rein and followed suit. Gaining confidence in this newfound delight, her tongue explored every hollow. Court was soon moaning his pleasure, growling for release.

"You're no angel, you're a sorceress. Thank

God, I'm the one you've chosen to cast your spell on."

Gripping her shoulders, he turned her until she was staring up at him, rapture etching her gaze. Their bodies surged together, craving what only their joining could fulfill. He entered her swiftly, her wet channel drawing him still deeper. They arched together, their lips meeting, murmuring words of love and passion.

"Oh, God, Dannie," he cried, exploding inside her.

Danielle's release was simultaneous and no less violent. Contented, they held each other. Court's breath teased the wayward curls that lay in disarray over the pillow. He nibbled at the column of her throat.

"Court?"

"Yes, love?"

"Are you disappointed that your angel is no more?"

"Ah...that's where you're mistaken. Didn't I tell you once that I would clip your wings to keep you by my side?"

She nodded.

"What's this?" he questioned tenderly as he stroked the gentle swell of her stomach.

"Would you be terribly upset if I told you I was going to have a baby...your baby, Court?"

"Might I ask if you were disappointed with your discovery?"

"Disappointed—no, but frightened—yes, considering my situation."

A dark shadow passed over his face. Rearing up, he asked, "What were you going to do about the baby, if you hadn't seen Pernel?"

"I was on my way home, Court. I knew when I saw Pernel that it was safe for me to return."

"You still haven't answered my question."

"All right," she sighed. "I had thought to save my money until I had enough to book passage to France. Honest to God, Court, I really didn't know what I was going to do. I had no set plan. I was frightened."

Closing his arms around her, he comforted her. "It would seem that fate was on our side."

"What do you mean?"

"The painting in the captain's quarters...I saw it and knew you were alive. I searched every corner of this boat for you. I'd almost given up when I came into this room. And there you were...."

"Capt. Winthrop had asked me to deliver a bottle of brandy to this suite with his compliments. I was so busy I almost forgot. What if I had missed you?"

"Not a chance, love. After I saw the painting I knew my dream had been restored." Cupping her face, he whispered, "Do you think a band of gold could hold you earthbound?" He drowned in the violet depths of her eyes, his heart hammering wildly in his chest. "Dannie, will you marry me, let me take care of you and our baby?"

Her breath caught in her throat. She had never dreamed she would hear that question from Court. Tears gathered in her eyes and rolled down her cheeks. Catching them with his tongue, he murmured, "I hope these are happy tears."

She could never tell him her tears were mixed with happiness and sorrow. She wanted him to have a different reason for marrying her—for love, not obligation. But she had time on her side. She put her black thoughts from her mind and hugged him tightly. "Yes, I'm happy...and yes, I will marry you."

"I'll have no sprite in my bed," he vowed. "I knew you and the ghost were one and the same, yet no matter what I did, you wouldn't come to me as Danielle...my real angel. You'll never know the frustration I endured yearning for your return."

Quirking a brow, she questioned, "Don't you think I've taken long enough to deliver your bottle of brandy? You'll cost me my job, Court."

"That was my intention, my pet."

Leaving the ship in Baton Rouge, they boarded another that would take them to Natchez. Standing at the railing as the boat plunged through the muddy water, Danielle's nerves faltered. She dreaded meeting Court's mother.

He stood with his arm around her waist. Tightening his hold, he whispered, "Don't worry. You think for one instant my mother isn't going to accept you, the future mother of her grandchildren? That's been her heart's desire for more years than I care to count."

"Mon Dieu, I hope you're right."

"I am."

They fell silent, each enjoying the passing scenery. Suddenly Danielle giggled. "Have you noticed the stares we've been receiving? We must be making quite an impression. Have you forgotten I'm dressed as a boy?"

"If anyone should question why I'm standing here with my arms around you, I'll tell them I'm protecting you from leaping overboard."

"Do you think they'll believe you?" she asked impishly.

"Not for a minute," he answered, pulling her more tightly against him.

She snuggled close. "If I live to be a hundred, I'll never forget the look on Capt. Winthrop's face when you told him we were getting married."

"It did take him aback, didn't it?"

But he had congratulated them, broken out a new bottle of brandy, and proceeded to get rip-roaring drunk.

With the pain of a hangover still marching through his head the next day, Capt. David Winthrop had nevertheless outdone himself arranging for a quiet marriage ceremony. His quarters were appropriately decorated with candles and flowers adorning every available surface. No one had questioned his resourcefulness, and all were humbled by the miracle transformation.

Once again Lady Luck had smiled with favor on the couple. Captain Winthrop discovered a preacher and his family were aboard. Brother James, as he requested they call him, agreed with pleasure to perform the ceremony. His eagerness quickly turned to skepticism as he was introduced to the couple. With a jaundiced eye, he viewed the girl attired in boy's clothing. Capt. Winthrop stepped in and quickly corrected the impression. He soon had Brother James shaking his head in despair as the tale unfolded.

Danielle had been enroute to meet Mr. Sinclair when she was set upon by thieves. Her trunks had been stolen and her maid killed. Her own clothes had been damaged beyond repair when she barely escaped, hiding in the woods and underbrush even as the thieves searched for her.

During the telling of this blatant lie, Capt. Winthrop had not blinked an eye, believing the end justified the means.

After the ceremony, they had toasted the couple. Big Ed had shaken Court's hand and hugged Danielle tightly, a glistening sheen sparkling in his eyes.

Then they were alone, an elaborate feast spread before them.

Chapter 22

Time passed at a snail's pace as Danielle and Court made their way to Shadowbrook. She gazed out the carriage window in awe at the beautiful plantation homes dotting the countryside, nestled within fields of cotton and stately trees. Her anxiety mounted whenever she thought of her first meeting with Court's mother, Elizabeth Sinclair. At least she would be properly dressed instead of clad in men's clothing.

When they had docked at Natchez, Court had taken her immediately to a dressmaker in town, hoping she could help them out on a moment's notice. He told the woman they had met with a castastrophe enroute to Natchez without elaborating on any details. Remarkably, a young woman of similar build to Danielle was so heartbroken when she was spurned by her fiancé, that she couldn't bear to see the clothing she had so painstakingly ordered. Danielle tried on all the clothing, and only minor alterations were required. Court bought the entire trousseau, which consisted of sheer gowns, delicate chemises, lacy pantalets, and matching accessories. Danielle had never owned such beautiful things, and her heart had swelled with joy. The dressmaker promised to have the clothing ready for them early the next day. Court had then taken Danielle to a cobbler and a millinery shop to complete her wardrobe.

That night they had taken a room at an inn. Danielle, so full of love for her husband, yet apprehensive to declare that deep-felt emotion, had presented Court with a most precious gift, the generous, tender offering of herself.

The carriage rounded a bend. "If you'll look toward that rise," Court said, pointing out the window, "you'll see my home through that clump of trees."

All that was visible was the upper portion of the house. White paint peeked teasingly through the lofty, verdant branches, revealing massive chimneys standing like sentries atop the roof. They passed through an impressive black iron gate and journeyed up the shadowed lane lined with tall boxwoods and live oaks. Beyond the trees, Danielle could see the beginning of the cotton fields that stretched for miles. She was astounded by the vast acreage surrounding her.

The carriage circled around a courtyard erupting with brilliant fall flowers, and came to a halt. After Court assisted her from the carriage and paid the driver, she stood in a trance, gazing up the numerous stone steps that led to the wide verandah of the galleried brick mansion. A lush, broad lawn, shaded by twin chestnut trees on either side of the walk, swept down the hillside. Skirting the steps were camellias, their large red blossoms contrasting vividly with the white brick background of the mansion. Massive ionic stone columns rose two stories, and a wooden balcony overlooked the magnificent landscape.

Their gaze swept upward to the verandah. Danielle saw an attractive woman staring down at them in puzzlement. Elizabeth Sinclair's tall stature and regal bearing were in perfect union with the majestic home. She was completely silver-haired, and her clothing was stylish, yet unpretentious. She studied Danielle curiously, a hint of a smile touching her lips.

"Good morning, Mother," Court said, leading Danielle up the steps. "Danielle, this is my mother, Elizabeth Sinclair. And dearest Mother, this is my wife, Danielle Algernon...Sinclair."

Elizabeth's eyes sparkled like a sixteen-candled chandelier. Taking Danielle's hand in her own, she kissed her affectionately on the cheek. "Welcome to Shadowbrook, my dear."

"Thank you, Madame Sinclair."

"Please call me Elizabeth, Danielle. Let's go inside and have refreshments. Birdie will be delighted with the news."

Pausing at the door, Court asked, "Mother, did Bryce make it all right from Espérance?"

"Yes," she said, "he's been here several weeks, but he made no mention of your marriage."

"No, I swore him to secrecy. I wanted to surprise you," he said teasingly.

As they entered the home, sunlight spilled into the foyer from tall stained-glass windows in the well of the sweeping staircase. Danielle's glance rested on the impressive handpainted mural of Shadowbrook, which covered the wall. The foyer was immense, boasting a floor of gray marble, and a crystal teardrop chandelier suspended from the high ceiling. An assortment of chairs, tables, and mirrors lined the walls. Tall arched doorways, rich with walnut carvings, led to the other rooms of the house.

"Court, dear, find Bryce and have your belongings brought in. I'm sure Danielle would like to bathe and change after she has had some light refreshment."

"Yes, I think I'll do just that." Court was anxious to relate to Bryce the details of their sudden marriage in case he should hear it secondhand and inadvertently expose their secret.

After Court departed, Elizabeth took Danielle into an oval drawing room. Tall bay windows encompassed the walls. Atop the mantel of a beautiful fireplace inlaid with marble were delicate Meissen and Chelsea figurines.

"Please make yourself comfortable, Danielle, while I summon Birdie," Elizabeth said as she left the room.

She settled herself on the Hepplewhite sofa. A few minutes later Court entered.

Noticing his mother's absence, he said quietly, "I had to forewarn Bryce before he let the cat out of the bag."

He joined her on the sofa and stretched out his long legs, crossing them at the ankles.

"What are you going to tell her about our marriage?"

He draped his arm behind her and peered at her from the corner of his eye, a vexing smile tugging the corner of his mouth. "Don't worry about a thing, love, I'll handle it."

His hand crept beneath her hair and gently massaged the nape of her neck. It was small gestures like this that made Danielle's heart blossom with love for him.

Elizabeth and a slim black woman entered the room. Danielle could see at once that Birdie must be Bryce's mother. They both possessed the same tall, wiry frame.

Birdie placed a tray of hot tea and petits four on the table before them. Elizabeth introduced the two of them, then added conspiringly, "If there's anything you ever want to know about your husband, Danielle, just ask Birdie. She's taken care of him since the day he was born."

"Yes'm, I sure have," she said, smiling joyously and bending over to pour out the tea.

"May I ask how you and Danielle met?" Elizabeth asked, watching them curiously as Birdie politely excused herself from the room.

"No, of course not," her son answered, gently squeezing Danielle's hand reassuringly. "I suppose I should begin with how I came to acquire Espérance."

He briefly summarized their relationship, omitting the ghost entirely and Danielle's escape from Pernel. From his fanciful detailing of events, he had his mother believing they had fallen in love at the onset and married shortly thereafter.

Danielle waited nervously for him to announce the impending birth of their child. When he finally imparted the news, she looked shyly toward her mother-in-law, waiting for her reaction.

Tears of happiness flooded Elizabeth's eyes. "Today is the happiest day of my life. Not only have I acquired a lovely daughter-in-law, but news of a beloved grandchild as well."

Danielle sat in silence. No words could express the profound emotions in her heart. This should have been the happiest moment of her life, too, but she knew Court had only married her because of the child. She prayed Elizabeth would never find out.

Elizabeth herself was consumed with sentimental thoughts...thoughts of her deceased husband, Garrett Sinclair. It had been ten years since his death, and though time had dimmed her pain, it had not diminished her love for him or the loneliness his absence had created. Had their love not been strong, it could have never survived during those strained years of raising Court and Meredith. The only arguments she and Garrett had ever had were caused by the rift between the two children. She had tried not to show partiality since Meredith was not her child, but Meredith's temper and fierce jealousy had her siding with Court from the day he was born.

She shuddered inside when she recalled the traumatic scene she had witnessed in the nursery a week after Court was born. She had come into the room and caught the six-year-old Meredith in the process of smothering the infant, her hand clasped over his mouth and nose. She had shoved Meredith aside to find her child's cherub face turning blue, his little body, lifeless. Her screams had brought Birdie in an instant; together they revived Court.

After the crisis, she and Garrett had talked for hours with Meredith, trying to convince her of their love for her and at the same moment reprimanding her for her monstrous action. She had never told Court what his sister had tried to do to him.

She sometimes wondered if Garrett might not be alive today if it weren't for his disappointment in his daughter, for he had blamed himself for her conduct and her jealousy of Court. It was difficult for her to feel any remorse over Meredith's disappearance. She had tried and failed in her upbringing of Garrett's child. If Meredith had been murdered, as her son believed, she had probably brought it on herself.

Court, too, was in deep thought. He knew Danielle wasn't being completely open. Somehow, he had to gain Danielle's trust. He loved her regardless of her stepfather's involvement with his sister. He could not, would not believe Danielle was involved with the kidnapping. But until she confided in him, his hands were tied. He also understood her intense desire to keep her home. But if he told her the card game had been a sham, that

Espérance still belonged to her family free of debt, he might lose her. He now hoped the child she carried would help bind her to him. It was ironic that at one time he would have thought the child part of Danielle's deception. How had their lives become so wrought with deceit? he wondered in despair.

"Court," Elizabeth said suddenly, "you haven't mentioned Meredith."

"That's because I've failed to learn anything about her, Mother. I still don't know if she's dead or alive."

"But none of this makes any sense," she declared. "You'd think that by now we'd have heard something."

"I won't discontinue my search until I solve the mystery," he assured her.

Danielle sensed what Court was thinking, but she was sure Nicholas had nothing to do with Meredith's disappearance. If only he would return and clear up this mess. But then Court would probably have him imprisoned for Meredith's murder. How long could they pretend to be happily married in Elizabeth's presence when too many suspicions blocked their road to happiness?

"Danielle, would you like to go upstairs and have a nice, leisurely bath and rest awhile?"

"*Oui*, Elizabeth. That sounds marvelous." Then smiling at Court, she said, "Maybe afterward, you'll show me Shadowbrook?"

"It would be my pleasure, love," he replied, brushing his lips lightly across her own.

Elizabeth led her upstairs to Court's room. "Here we are, dear."

"Thank you, Elizabeth."

Danielle looked around her with interest. Subtle hues of blues and grays were the color scheme throughout the room. Large double doors with blue silk draperies opened to a balcony; a Grecian couch was placed to its side. The tester bed was adorned with a gray-striped coverlet with matching bed hangings.

With an engaging smile, Danielle said, "It's lovely, Elizabeth."

"If you'd like to add a touch of femininity, I'm sure Court wouldn't mind."

"Oh, *non*, Elizabeth, it's really not necessary."

Danielle moved to the open doors. A warm breeze caressed her face. Beyond, she could see the Mississippi River, and once again she thought of Espérance.

"Just relax and enjoy yourself. As you can see, the tub is ready and waiting." A huge brass tub stood in one corner of the room. Someone had already filled it with hot water for the steam still rose from its surface.

After Elizabeth left the room, Danielle quickly removed her clothing and eased into the warm, scented bath to enjoy a few minutes of blissful quiet. Everything she needed had been placed on a small brass rack near the tub. A pail of fresh water had been provided to rinse the soap from her hair. But for several minutes, Danielle just closed her eyes and rested her head against the rim of the tub.

Now she had two homes, Shadowbrook and Espérance. She could be happy living in either house if only Court could come to love her. Surely he must love me a little, she mused, remembering the tender moments they had shared. Maybe he would love her if she bore him a son to carry on the Sinclair name, she thought while stroking her abdomen. But every time she had these comforting thoughts, she wondered at his purpose for keeping Espérance from her in the very beginning. Though Espérance now partially belonged to her since she was married to him, he could still sell it, or do anything with it that pleased him. From what she had seen of this magnificent estate, she knew he had never needed Espérance.

Dipping her hair beneath the water, she washed it thoroughly, then poured the clean water over it. She rose from the tub, dried herself with a large linen towel, and donned a sheer dressing gown. Sitting down at the dressing table, she picked up a brush and ran it through her tangled mass of hair. Afterward, she lay down on the bed and quickly fell asleep.

A shrill whistle awakened her. She walked outside on the balcony and saw below her a huge Great Dane lumbering across the lawn toward Court. Amused, she watched them play for several minutes, then dressed quickly, eager to have Court show her the grounds.

Court's hand paused in midair, the game he was playing with Rolfe forgotten as he gazed hypnotically in Danielle's direction as she strode toward him. Her apple-green gown flowed like sea foam around her supple body; the breeze from the river whipped her black curls about her face.

Rolfe, not understanding his master's sudden disinterest, nudged him to continue the game. Instinctively, Court tossed the ball, his eyes never leaving Danielle. Rolfe took off to retrieve the ball as it rolled beneath the dense shrubbery.

"How do I look, *monsieur?*" she asked coyly, twirling around for his inspection.

His Adam's apple lodged in his throat as his eyes fastened on the snug bodice. "If you'll walk down to the garden with me, I'll show you."

Her eyes shifted to the big dog that was halfway into the bush trying to get his ball. "What about him?"

"Rolfe?" Court grinned. "He won't come out of there until he finds his ball. He has a very determined nature . . . like his master."

Clasping his hand in hers, she said, *"Mon Dieu,* but you have such wicked thoughts."

"Only when I think of you." He squeezed her hand and led her down the terraced hillside to the thick foliage below.

Late afternoon shadows fell across the pebble path. Alongside the moss-carpeted bank, a shallow brook wound its way through the woods. In the distance the sound of splashing water could be heard. When they came into a clearing, Danielle's breath was taken away at the sheer beauty of it all. A small waterfall cascaded down a steep slope through a thicket of reeds and trees. Purple wisteria draped an arched wooden bridge that spanned the brook. On the opposite bank was a small gazebo made of cypress, its color and texture blending into the natural setting.

They strolled over the bridge, halting midway to gaze at the clear pool formed by the waterfall. Ferns with thick fronds lined the bank and a school of goldfish swam beneath the crystalline surface.

"Now you know why we named our plantation Shadowbrook."

"I don't remember ever having seen anything more beautiful, Court. It's like a dream world. If only I had my painting tools with me, I'd sketch it now."

Turning a thick tress around his hand, he said softly, "It will always be here, love. Every season Mother Nature will provided a special treat for you to paint."

"When I do, I shall give the paintings to your mother in gratitude for her kindness. I never expected her to accept me into your family so quickly. Most mothers would collapse with the news we just delivered to her."

He slipped his arm around her waist and led her across the bridge to the gazebo. "She likes you, Dannie. You're not a whimpering, spoiled woman, but a woman with spirit and courage. The two of you are very much alike in that aspect."

Once inside the gazebo, Court pulled her into his arms and kissed her, his tongue stroking the soft recesses of her mouth. "I've waited to do this all afternoon. Rest assured, that's not all I want to do." His fingers trailed up her arm to her shoulder, then skimmed lightly along the edge of her bodice. Resting his hand on its soft fullness, his finger slid within the narrow cleavage. He could feel the rapid pulse of her heart as he reached inside to stroke the hard, rosy peaks hidden beneath.

"Aren't you comfortable, love?" he asked, bending down and sliding his wet tongue along the ripe swell of her breasts.

Danielle's soft laughter rippled out. "Not as uncomfortable as you are, I would think, *monsieur*."

While his mouth continued its delicious exploration of her throat and breasts, she felt his hands unloosening the tiny buttons at her back. "Damn," he muttered against her velvet skin, "how did you ever get into this dress anyway?"

"Court, what if someone should seek us out?" she asked as she felt the last button give way.

"No one will bother us," he said, sliding the bodice down to her waist. He gazed hungrily at he milky-white breasts, their dark tips erect with passion. Pushing the fabric farther down on her hips, he caressed the gentle swell of her abdomen. He thought of how her body had changed since he had first taken her. "To think it was my seed that created this tiny miracle within you."

She placed her hand over his. *"Oui,* but a miracle that was easily created, my love."

Removing his coat, he spread it out on the wooden bench. As he scooped her up in his arms, her gown slid to the floor. After lowering her to the bench, he discarded his clothing.

The setting sun's rays spilled through the latticework framing, casting its checkered pattern across their naked bodies as they loved uninhibitedly. Their quiet cries of ecstasy soared, terminating in a brilliant cadenza.

She lay beside his hard, damp body, her head resting peacefully against his shoulder. Contented, she gazed upward at the blanket of ivy that trailed at will through the trellis, and listened to Nature's ballad, a continuous love song in her Garden of Eden. Yes, love, she sighed wistfully.

Their moment of quiet reprieve was suddenly interrupted by the loud thumping of heavy feet galloping across the wooden bridge. Danielle shrieked, the blood surging to her face.

"You said no one would come here." Lowering her head over his chest, she said, "There's no time to dress. *Mon Dieu,* I shall die of embarrassment."

Something round and slimy dropped across her bare buttocks and rolled between them, nestling against her stomach. She jumped in sheer fright. Another object, wet and soft, ran in rapid succession up her body. She froze, her eyes wide, her fingers biting into Court's arm. Raising her head, she was puzzled to see him laughing.

"What . . . ?"

"Look behind you, Dannie," he managed to say.

Frowning, she cautiously glanced over her shoulder. There was Rolfe, Court's Great Dane, towering over her. He was panting from his laborious journey, and his long pink tongue dangled from his huge mouth.

Court reached down between them and retrieved the ball. "It didn't take as long as I had hoped for ...but long enough," he said, winking rakishly.

Rolfe came to attention and barked, waiting for Court to throw the ball once again. Court raised up and tossed the ball through the entrance of the gazebo; it bounced several times then landed in the pool. Rolfe ran after it, but came to a standstill at the edge of the pool, watching the ball bob up and down beneath the waterfall.

"Why doesn't he go in after it?" Danielle asked.

"He doesn't like to get his feet wet. He'll wait until it drifts to the bank and then snatch it up."

"That could be quite awhile," she said, snuggling up to her husband.

"Yes, I know," he answered slyly, pulling her down on top of him.

Chapter 23

Accustomed to rising early, Danielle awoke the moment the sun filtered through a narrow opening in the curtains. Pushing aside the mosquito netting, she rose from the bed and padded across the thick carpet. After hastily donning her dressing gown, she walked outside to the balcony and stretched like a contented cat, lifting her face to the sun, relishing its warmth.

The familiar fragrant smoke from a cheroot drifted her way, and she turned around to see Court, fully dressed, standing a few feet from her. He leaned casually against the railing, his green eyes sweeping her dishevelment from head to toe.

The gentle morning breeze molded her dressing gown to her slim legs, outlining the shadow of her womanhood beneath the sheer fabric. This, coupled with the hint of her darkened peaks pressing against the lace bodice, had a pronounced effect on his already mounting passion.

"It's a beautiful morning, isn't it?" she asked huskily.

With a crooked grin, he replied, "Very."

She swept up the mass of ebony hair from her neck, then let it fall at will. "Aren't you going to kiss me good-morning, my husband?"

"If you're willing to reap the consequences," he replied, crossing the few feet that separated them.

"I'll take that chance, *monsieur*. After all, you do have work to do."

Closing her eyes, she puckered her lips, waiting for the touch of his mouth. His warm, soft lips grazed her cheek and teased the corner of her mouth, then moved down the slender white column of her neck. Her eyes shot open when she felt his hand slip beneath her lace bodice and bare her breasts. His hot lips pulled gently at one nipple, his tongue flicking the bud to aroused hardness.

"Court!" she gasped, feeling spasms begin low in her abdomen. She watched as he placed heated kisses over the creamy surface of her breasts.

Raising his head, he saw her violet eyes smoldering with desire. "You didn't say, love, where I should kiss you good-morning."

Jerking her gown to cover her breasts, she said in a teasing reprimand, *"Mon Dieu!* Do you wish for the whole world to view your amorous display?"

He drew her into his arms, and cupping her buttocks, pulled her slender body tightly against him. She could feel the bulge of his swollen manhood pressing against her thigh. "See, love, it's already too late. Now I have to go downstairs and make a real spectacle of myself. My senses I can mask, but my body speaks for itself."

That evening, as Danielle dressed for dinner, she thought she heard voices coming from the drawing room adjoining the master suite. Barely opening the door, she peeked inside and saw Court seated at his desk, rummaging through some papers. No one was with him so she entered.

"May I come in?" she asked. "I thought I heard voices."

He looked up and smiled. "I just finished going over a few things with my overseer."

Danielle had only caught a quick glimpse of the upstairs drawing room the previous day. Her eyes drifted around the large room. A monumental bookcase of mahogany, elaborately inlaid with satinwood and ivory, encompassed one wall. Several chairs covered with grospoint were intimately arranged around a Hepplewhite sofa. There was a collection of paintings spanning one wall.

It took several seconds to recognize her own paintings since they were so eloquently framed. Time stood still, but her heart beat an erratic pace. Above the fireplace mantel was her unfinished painting of the Carolina parakeet.

Court, seeing where her eyes rested, moved to her side, placing his hands on her shoulders.

Tears threatened to spill over the rim of her eyes. "I thought it was destroyed when Pernel—"

"No," he interrupted, "as you can see, it's only slightly damaged, nothing that can't be repaired. I knew how special this particular painting was to you. I hope you'll finish it someday."

Turning in his arms, she looked up at him with misty eyes. "Of course I will, Court. But these other paintings were the ones Julian Bernard exhibited in his gallery." She looked up at him in askance.

"I bought them immediately after you disappeared," he answered softly. "All the paintings were shipped here along with my instructions for displaying them."

"Could he not sell them?" she asked as an expression of failure etched her smooth features.

Court smiled. "I'm sure he could have had he been given the time."

"I feel honored that you think so much of my work, Court, but you must have spent quite a large sum of money."

Staring down into her violet eyes, he wanted to

tell her that one can't place a price on memories; he thought he'd lost her, and memories were all he had left. But rather than open his heart to her, he answered, "I wanted them, Dannie." To help mask his true feelings, he broke his gaze and walked to the window that overlooked the gardens.

Danielle watched him for a moment, sensing he wanted to say more. But he said nothing, and finally, to fill the unbearable silence, she spoke.

"Court, you haven't mentioned when we plan to return to Espérance?"

Turning toward her, he asked, "Would you mind remaining here until the child is born? Of course, we can go back for a visit before that time. Right now, Shadowbrook needs my attention. The overseer I hired to run Espérance is doing a fine job."

She smiled wistfully. "I know."

"How would you know?" he asked curiously.

"Every time the steamboat passed Espérance, I stood at the railing, watching the activity at the dock and in the fields. My heart died a little each time for I wanted so much to be a part of it all." Then a thought occurred to her. *"Mon Dieu,* I miss Mammy."

"I do, too. So much, in fact, that I've sent a message for her to come stay with us. Jordan will be bringing her on his boat when he comes for the festivities."

Her face lit up with excitement. She ran to him and threw her arms around him, kissing him, tears sparkling in her eyes. "Thank you, Court. You don't know what happiness this news bring me."

He grinned down at her. "I think I do, love."

Cocking her head, she frowned and asked, "What festivities are you talking about?"

"Mother informed me earlier that she wants to introduce you to our neighbors by having a lawn party."

"When is she planning to have this great affair?"

"In two weeks. That will give Jordan ample time to travel up here with Mammy."

A worried frown etched her brow. "How do you feel about this party, Court? Your friends are going to ask all kinds of questions."

He tweaked her nose. "Don't worry, love, I can handle any question that will arise. Mother hasn't given a party such as this since Meredith married. If it'll make her happy, then we can oblige her this one time."

For the next two weeks, there was not a quiet place in the house. Elizabeth seemed to be everywhere in the same instant. The kitchen servants worked from dawn until dusk, preparing the foods for the gala event. Not only did the interior of the house sparkle from the industrious activities taking place, but the vast lawn and gardens were immaculately groomed.

One afternoon as Danielle was sitting near the riverbank, her art supplies spread out around her, she heard the blast of a horn coming from a distant steamboat. Hope welled inside her as it veered in the direction of Shadowbrook. Hurrying to the house, she put away her supplies and summoned Bryce to drive her to the loading dock. When she arrived there, Court was ordering his men to move several of the flatboats out of the way to make room for Jordan's magnificent steamboat.

Jordan waved down at them, a beaming Mammy at his side. Gathering up her skirts, Danielle ran across the dock. She waited silently, watching Mammy's slow descent down the gangway with Jordan at her elbow to lend additional support.

When Mammy's feet touched the dock, she shuddered. Never raising her head, she mumbled, "Praise the Lawd."

Tears streamed down Danielle's cheek when she heard her familiar voice. Reaching out, she lifted her chin and gazed lovingly into her round, dark brown eyes.

"My chile," Mammy cried softly, "my chile." Her arms wrapped around Danielle, pulling her against the soft cushioning of her ample breasts. Then she pushed her from her, her eyes sweeping her from head to toe. "Ifen I didn't know better, I'd think I was seein' a ghost ... 'n' a married one at that. I knows what happened to you, but I wants to hear it from you in detail, chile."

Kissing her on her cheek, Danielle said, "There's so much to tell you, Mammy, but not now. Let's go back to the house and get you settled in."

"Just a minute," Jordan interrupted, "there's someone else who wanted to join the celebration."

Hesitating midway down the gangway was Damien Baudier, a look of uncertainty on his handsome countenance. Danielle's face changed from surprise to sheer happiness.

"Damien, I'm so glad you have come. Now I have all my friends here."

Court was stunned by her heartfelt words. Were these her only friends in life, numbering less than the fingers on one hand?

"Welcome to Shadowbrook, Damien," he said sincerely.

Noting the warmth with which he was received, Damien cast them a winning smile, showing even white teeth against his dark features. *"Merci,"* he said, joining them and pressing a soft kiss to the back of Danielle's hand.

"Mon Dieu, Damien," she declared, "I'm so happy Jordan thought to include you."

"You're wrong, Danielle," Jordan said. "Court asked that I issue Damien the invitation."

She smiled at her husband, her eyes undeniably filled with love. *"Merci, monsieur . . .* for everything."

Bryce put everyone's belongings into the carriage and took his place on the bench. As they traveled the short distance to the house, she and Court told their friends about discovering each other on the steamboat and then being married en route to Natchez.

When they arrived at the house, Mammy's chatter stopped as she gazed in bewilderment at the immense structure. She nodded her head and patted Danielle's hand. "I believes my lamb's gonna be jus' fine . . . jus' fine."

Although Danielle had sent a note to Mammy when she and Court had first docked in Natchez, she spent the remainder of the afternoon explaining in detail all that had occurred since the day she had fled Espérance. She expected a severe reprimanding when she told her of the impending birth, urging her not to breathe a word about their marriage date. She was afraid such information would bring embarrassment to Elizabeth. Court planned to ask Jordan and Damien to keep silent also.

Instead of chastising her, Mammy said gleefully, "My baby's gonna have a baby. I knowed all along you and Massa Sinclair was right for each other. One of these days we gonna have bunches of little Sinclairs for ole Mammy to take care of, yassuhree."

A nightmare jolted Danielle awake bright and early on the morning of the social event. Court was still asleep, his black hair tousled boyishly about his handsome face. Resting her head against his shoulder, she recalled the subject of her dream—Rankin Pernel. When she returned to Espérance as Court's wife, Pernel might be there, just waiting, with vengeance uppermost in his mind. She should feel secure knowing she had Court's protection, but he could not protect her every hour of the day. Pernel was a sly, devious man. Since his plans had once been foiled, the thorn of hate would have sunk deeper into his twisted mind.

Suddenly needing the security of his arms, she kissed Court softly on his lips. "Hold me," she moaned as trepidation mounted within her.

Though still drugged by sleep, he noted the unnamed fear in her eyes. "You needn't ask, love," he said, drawing her into his arms.

Passion leaped within them as volatile as a dying ember nourished by the wind. Neither heard the light rap on the door. Bryce stood outside the door, waiting for permission to enter. Mammy joined him with a breakfast tray in her hand.

"He ain't answerin'," Bryce said in aggravation. "It's past time for him to rise 'n' shine."

"Don't you think that's for him to decide, not you? Now git yourself away from there." Mammy grinned knowingly and ambled to the head of the stairs, waiting for Bryce to follow. Turning, she saw him rap once again on the door. "Is you deaf, boy? 'Cause, ifen you ain't, youse gonna be when Massa Sinclair jerks open that door and boxes your ears!"

"Time to get up, sleepy head," Court announced several hours later, nibbling at Danielle's ear. "We've only a couple of hours left before our guests begin arriving."

She groaned and stretched lazily as he rose from the bed. There was a loud knock at their bedroom door. Danielle hastily donned her dressing gown while Court drew on his pants, calling out, "Just a minute."

When he opened the door and saw Jordan, a feeling of apprehension swept through him.

"I'm sorry to disturb you, Court, but a message just arrived from Espérance. You're needed there without delay."

"Has something happened?'

Danielle could tell by the tone of his voice that something was wrong. Joining him, she questioned, "What is it?"

"Danielle," Court said, pulling her close to his side, "Jordan says Tobias needs us back at Espérance. A steamboat captain delivered the message on his way upriver."

"Nom de Dieu, did he say nothing else?"

Jordan looked at Court with a frown. "He said Tobias told him that something terrible has happened there."

"Is—is it Nicholas?" she asked hesitantly.

"He didn't say. I'm sorry but that's all the information I have."

"Court, we must leave at once," she said, tears blistering her eyes.

"Can you and Mammy be ready within the hour? Jordan has offered to take us."

"Oui, of course. But the party—"

"Don't worry, love," Court said, drawing her into his arms. "Mother will understand."

Elizabeth and her servant helped Danielle pack her trunks while Mammy paced the room, the sudden turn of events weighing heavily on her mind.

"I jus' don't understand," she mumbled. "Tobias would never send for us ifen it wasn't sumpin' real bad."

Danielle placed her hat atop her head and positioned it. "If only he'd given us more information. For all we know, Espérance could have burned to the ground." With a trembling smile, she placed her hand on Mammy's shoulder. "At least you're here with me, so I know it's not you I should worry about."

Elizabeth closed the lid of the trunk. "Everything's ready, Danielle."

"I'm so sorry I've ruined your party."

Drawing Danielle into her arms, she whispered, "Shh, no apologies are necessary, dear. We can have a party anytime." Releasing her, she smiled sweetly. "Whatever awaits you, my dear, you are fortunate to have a loving husband at your side to comfort you. He loves you very much, Danielle."

Flustered by her words, Danielle admitted, "I ... love him, too. When I think of all the work he has done at Espérance, and then imagine what might have happened..."

"Now, now," Elizabeth said. "You may be worrying about nothing. Just remember, my dear, that no matter what has happened at Espérance, you'll always have Shadowbrook awaiting your return."

"Thank you, Elizabeth," she said softly, tears filling her eyes.

After kissing her mother-in-law lightly on her cheek, Danielle took Mammy's arm, and they made their way down the winding stairway.

Chapter 24

"I may never set foot on another boat again," Danielle vowed as Court helped her disembark.

"Them's my feelin's 'sactly," Mammy chimed in, staying close behind.

"Isn't she beautiful?" Danielle exclaimed, her attention riveted on Espérance.

Sunlight played over the fresh paint, and the newly repaired shutters framed the sparkling glass of the windows. Her home stood proud and inviting among a profusion of flowers that contrasted colorfully with the manicured lawn.

Relief raced through Danielle. From her position on the landing, everything appeared in order. She could see workers going about their daily chores, halting their work long enough to see who was getting off the steamboat. Neither Camille nor Tobias were in sight. What was going on? she wondered uneasily.

Leaning close, Court reassured her. "Don't worry, love, we'll soon know the reason behind the message. Espérance seems intact."

She smiled up at him, her love radiant in her eyes.

"Be careful, pet, you're treading on very dangerous ground."

"What can you mean?" she murmured.

Staring down at her, Court was struck once again by her beauty. The clothes he had purchased for her only added the finishing touch. This day she wore a confection of silk in pale blue set off with delicate white lace trim. Pearl buttons hugged her wrists and traveled from her breasts to the high collar of her gown. A straw hat shaded her flawless skin. Her hands were encased in lace gloves, one of which she tenderly drew across Court's cheek.

Hard-pressed to keep from taking her into his arms in front of the crew, Court hurried her along the shell path, threatening dire repercussions if she kept tantalizing him. Danielle laughed gaily.

A subdued Camille met them at the door, congratulating them quietly on their marriage, assuring Danielle she was happy to have her home.

Court opened his mouth to ask about the message. "Camille, what..." His words trailed off as he saw the frightened look glinting in her eyes and the slight shake of her head. Changing his tactics, he declared, "Camille, it surely is good to be back at Espérance. How is everything?"

Mammy was not so subtle. Shoving her way inside, she blurted out, "Camille, what's come over you? Cat got your tongue? I ain't never seen you when the words didn't spill outta your mouth like a street-corner preacher whats got the callin'."

The rustling of petticoats drew everyone's attention.

"Well, I do declare if Court Sinclair hasn't decided to grace us with his presence."

Shocked, Danielle edged closer to Court as a tall, familiar figure attired completely in black moved toward them, her hair pulled severely into a bun at the nape of her neck. She might have been considered beautiful were it not for the cold eyes shrouded with hatred.

"I must thank you, Court, for all the repairs you've done." She arched her brow. "I'm told you are responsible. I never dreamed this place could be any more than the rundown shamble it was before you restored it. Surprising what a little paint will do. Gives it a homey effect, don't you agree?"

Danielle's blood was traveling through her veins at an alarming speed. "Who are you?" she stormed out. "What are you doing in my home?"

"Court, darling, have you forgotten the manners our 'dear' mother ingrained in us?" Extending her hand to Danielle, she announced, "I'm Meredith Caraville... Court's sister."

As the words registered, Danielle felt her stomach knot. "But you are—" She bit her tongue.

Misunderstanding, Meredith finished the sentence. "Nicholas's wife... or I should say, his widow." She lowered her eyes, letting sadness wash over her features.

"*Non*... you can't be," Danielle cried.

"Oh, but I am. Poor Nicholas fell overboard as we journeyed here to tell you our good news. I'm afraid his dear body was never found. So begging your pardon... Espérance now belongs to me."

Danielle paled. Court shifted nervously. "Of course, you have the marriage document to prove your claim?" he asked.

"Of course, darling." She turned to Danielle. "I'm aware that congratulations are in order. I hope you and Court will be very happy."

"We intend to be," he assured her, resting his hand on the nape of Danielle's neck. He could feel the tenseness and knew what she must be thinking of him at that very moment.

Meredith did not miss the gesture. With a forced smile, she asked, turning for Court's inspection, "How do you like me in widow's weeds?"

Ignoring her, he turned to Danielle. "Would you

like to rest awhile, love?" His fingers never slowed their gentle massage of her taut muscles.

Stiffening visibly, she snapped, *"Non,* Court, I'm eager to see Tempete."

Placing a chaste kiss to her cheek, he agreed, "All right, love, but no riding, promise?"

Danielle glared up at him, her eyes cold and darkened with suspicion. "I'm not an invalid, Court. Women have babies every day."

Meredith's gasp was audible, drawing their attention back to her. Her face was a mixture of curious emotions. "Since we are imparting good news, I, too, have more news of my own. I'm going to have a baby, also."

Danielle clenched her fists. She hurriedly excused herself, and headed out toward the stables. Her heart ached for Nicholas, and at the same time, her mind churned with Meredith's news. If Meredith owned the plantation, and not Court, then she and Court's whole time together had been a lie—a vicious lie that had been invented to take her home from her. How could she ever forgive him this transgression?

As her heart wept, her mind rushed ahead. Court's sister was the same woman who had been with Rankin Pernel on the boat. Had the conversation she overheard been about Nicholas? Tormented thoughts crashed over her with the force of a wave. Meredith was a murderess, and Danielle had no evidence. She would have to keep silent until she discovered a way to prove Meredith had killed Nicholas, she firmly decided.

But what could she do about Court? She was now his wife and carrying his child. Tears of anger and hurt flowed from her eyes as she thought of how her heart had deceived her.

* * *

Tobias was leaving the stable as she approached. When he did not see her, she called out to him. He turned with a jerk, fear apparent on his features.

"What's wrong, Tobias?"

He lowered his head and shuffled his feet. "Ah's jes' checkin' on Tempete, Miss Dannie."

"Is something the matter with him?"

"Wal...he ain't none too happy, but since you done come back, Ah figgers things will be gettin' better." He smiled proudly.

"I'm glad to be back, Tobias."

As she started into the stables, he rushed ahead of her. "Missy, this ain't none of my doin'. Ah done tried to tell the new mistress that Tempete wouldn't take to bein' tied."

As he spoke, she noticed him rub at a wicked mark across his cheek. "Tobias, what are you talking about? You're not making a bit of sense."

Her eyes came to rest on her beloved horse. His eyes rolled wildly as he reared his head, trying to break the restraints that hindered his movement. *"Mon Dieu,"* she cried out, rushing to him. "Bring me a knife. Why in God's name is Tempete bound like a wild animal?"

Tobias handed her a knife from the workbench. Anger filled her as she slashed at the ropes. She swore vengeance on the person responsible for this cruel treatment of her spirited horse. Angry sobs caught in her throat and she feared she would smother from her overriding fury. She knew her anger was frightening Tempete, so she sought to control herself. Resting her head on the horse's neck, she cooed softly, seeking to calm him as well as herself. After a while, she unlatched the gate of his stall.

"Come on, big boy, what you need is sunshine and

exercise." With her face turned to Tempete, she did not see the large black man blocking the door until she plowed headlong into him. "What?"

"Ah got orders sayin' that hoss ain't to be moved."

With disgust coloring each word, Danielle spat, "I don't know who would treat an animal in such a degrading manner. Furthermore, I don't know on whose orders you are acting, but let me assure you, this is my horse. No one is to lay a hand on him unless they have my permission. Now move out of my way or I will go over you. Move!" she shouted.

Taken back by her words, the big black man did as she commanded. Tobias smiled with glee.

Leaning on the fence, she watched Tempete as he raced across the meadow. Returning to her, he whinnied and swung his head as though telling her what had transpired in her absence. Rearing on his hind legs, he pawed the air, and then lunged once more to the ground, taking off in a dead run. His black coat gleamed in the sun as he reveled in his restored freedom.

Beside her, Tobias whispered, "Tempete ain't the only one glad to have you back."

Studying his face, she asked, "What's the mark on your cheek? Tempete is sporting the same mark on his coat."

"Ah ain't one to carry tales, Miss Dannie."

"I know that, Tobias. Now out with it."

"Wal...it seems that new Mistress Caraville is awful fond of the ridin' whip. She marches through the house smackin' that thing against her hand. Ifen she comes over sumpin' that don't suit her, she lets loose with the whip. Ah reckon we's all felt the bite of that thing. 'Ceptin' that black of hers. The seem to see eye to eye on ever'thin'."

Overcome with rage, Danielle stormed toward the house. Once again she felt something was wrong. Then it hit her. Silence. There were no voices raised in song, no children's laughter ringing through a melee of games. She slammed the door behind her with a resounding whack.

Meredith and Court turned as she whirled into the room, astonishment apparent on both their faces at her unladylike entry. Spying the notorious quirt on a small table Danielle grabbed it. "Do you see this?" she asked, pointing the riding whip at Meredith.

Meredith nodded; Court looked on puzzled.

Raising a bent leg, Danielle broke the quirt over her knee, snapping it into two pieces. Meredith almost came out of her chair.

"You are never to mistreat the people or the animals of Espérance again. Do you understand?" Danielle stormed. Her eyes swung toward Court, daring him to open his mouth, and then back to Meredith who did not seem at all troubled by her anger. "You would be wise to heed my warning. These people are dear to me. They've never experienced harsh treatment."

"That could be the reason you don't get an honest day's work out of them," Meredith interposed. "From my point of view, your slaves are petted—overfed and underworked."

"No one asked you for your point of view. One more thing," Danielle snapped, "keep your big black out of my way."

Court opened his mouth to speak, but Meredith interrupted. "I'm afraid, my dear, you're living under a vast misconception. Espérance is mine. If I choose, I can do anything I please with these people. In fact, if I desire to do so, I can sell Espérance and all the blacks on the place." She lifted her chin defiantly. "It would be wise for you to heed *my* warning. Don't presume to tell me what I may or may not do as far as this plantation is concerned. Espérance belongs to me...I am judge, jury, and executioner here—not you."

Danielle stood ramrod straight, her words slicing through the air. "How can you suggest such a thing? These people are human beings. We've always cared for them, and kept their families together. Only someone as vicious as you would do otherwise." Turning sharply on her heels, she marched out of the room.

Meredith turned to her half brother. "I can see you've got your hands full. Does she have these temper tantrums often?"

"This is something you'll never understand, Meredith," Court answered contemptuously. "Danielle loves very deeply. Anything that would encroach on the well-being of her loved ones naturally distresses her."

As the days passed, Danielle noticed the strained behavior of the servants. Everyone seemed to be walking on eggshells. Her fury was so great she did not want to be left alone with Court. At night in their chamber, she hugged her corner of the bed, her icy reserve daring him to touch her.

No one was more surprised than Court to find his sister at Espérance. But from the way Danielle scorned him, he knew she would never believe him if he told her about the deed. She would only think he was trying to cleanse away his own guilt by throwing all the blame on his sister.

Meredith had shown Court the marriage document, and he had immediately checked the validity of the certificate; it was as legal and binding as his own vows. Their hands were tied; Meredith owned Espérance lock, stock, and barrel. Court knew his half sister well enough to realize that she would hold on to anything she thought he desired, just to spite him.

When he had questioned her about the ransom note, she had denied any knowledge of it. With veiled innuendos, she implied that Nicholas could have been responsible, as he had always been short on funds. She asked Court if he thought she might be in danger, and he assured her that whoever had been responsible for the ransom note had come into enough money to take care of his needs for some time to come. Unless, he added with a raised brow, that person had a weakness for the gaming table. Meredith had shrugged off his insinuations and changed the subject.

Court, however, was a good judge of character, and Meredith did not fool him for a minute. He could not put his finger on it, but his gut instinct told him that she had been up to her neck in the demand for the ransom money. He knew Danielle would not be taken in by his sister. His own mammy had always warned him to be leery of anyone, as she had put it, "who talked outta both sides of their mouth."

Since she had arrived at Espérance, Mammy had filled Danielle's ears with gossip about Meredith's transgressions. According to Camille, Meredith had marched into the house proclaiming herself the owner shortly after Mammy had departed for Espérance. She assured everyone she would tolerate no laziness or back talk. She did not care how things had been run up to this point; they would now be done as she wished. Jude, her manservant, would dispense any punishment he saw fit with her blessing.

Danielle had never seen Mammy as upset as she was when she related Meredith's plan to have Tobias and Camille beaten over an incident which had happened before they had returned from Shadowbrook.

"Ain't no cause to have them whipped. They

didn't do nuthin' wrong. They ain't never been treated like that. They do the work what needs to be done." Mammy shook her head in disbelief mumbling, "They ain't no cause. I been thinkin' that woman is jus' mean ... plumb through. That woman got a chip on her shoulder what's gonna cause trouble." Then puffing up, she continued, "That's anuther thing. That big black of hers—Jude, she calls him—he's watchin' like he's jus' waitin' for somebody to step outta line. Lawdy mercy, ifen he ever whips Tobias—"

"Don't fret, Mammy, there will be no whippings a Espérance," Danielle assured her.

"I hope you's right, chile," she said, sighing.

Since their arrival Court had questioned Meredith repeatedly about signing the papers for Mammy and Tobias over to him, but she would not hear of it. Because of this, Danielle and Court remained at Espérance. Danielle would not leave Mammy in the cruel hands of his sister.

Danielle watched as Court disappeared into the distance. He had numerous business appointments in New Orleans that would take the better part of the day. Grateful to have some time alone, she scooped up her sketching materials and headed for the riverbank. Curling beneath the arms of an ageless magnolia, she began sketching the refurbished Espérance.

As was her habit of late, she felt in need of a nap. She seemed to require more sleep lately. The rapid changes taking place in her body made her aware, as nothing else could have, of the tiny life she and Court had created. Resting her head against the tree, she drifted off into a light nap.

Camille's screaming woke Danielle with a jerk. Jumping to her feet, she rushed to meet the distraught girl.

"Mon Dieu, Camille, what is it? Has something happened to Court?"

The girl only shook her head. Grabbing her shoulders, Danielle shook her. "Now, calm down and tell me what's wrong."

"I's sorry, Miss Dannie, but I jes' knows the blame is gonna fall right on my head. I ain't done nuthin, I swear."

"Just a minute, Camille, blamed for what?"

Drawing a deep, shuddering breath, she said shakily, "Massa Court's sister left the house to go ridin'. She weren't gone no time 'til Jude comes totin' her back in his arms. She's sobbin' 'n' moanin' 'bout her baby. I reckon they ain't gonna be no baby from the way she's carryin' on. That Jude, he marched right in 'n' took the missus to her room. Wouldn't let nobody touch her."

"Nom de Dieu, Mammy is better qualified to see to her needs than Jude, especially if she has lost the baby. Do you know what brought this on?"

"I's not rightly sure. I heard sumpin' 'bout the horse throwin' her, or she fell; it's one or the other. Couldn't make much sense outta her caterwaulin'."

"Camille," Danielle said sharply.

"I's sorry, Miss Dannie, but you mark my word, she'll find some way to lay the blame on me or Tobias. I jes' know she will."

Danielle rushed into the house, where she was met with silence. Making her way to Court's former room, she tapped lightly on the door. Jude cracked the door, peeking out as though Danielle were a nuisance.

"Jude, is there anything I can do?"

"No," he growled. "Ah'll take care of the missus."

"I'll send Tobias for the doctor."

"No!" Opening the door just wide enough for him to get through it, he grasped Danielle's shoulder.

"No doctor. Ah'll tend to the missus, you hear?" Jude turned abruptly and closed the door in her face.

Danielle was so shocked by his rough handling of her that she stood several seconds staring at the closed portal. Her anger gaining ground, she shoved through the door and walked determinedly to Meredith's bedside. Jude started toward her as though he would remove her forcibly, but she did not miss the slight shake of Meredith's head. Jude changed his course and ambled to the window.

Resolutely, Danielle approached Meredith. "I'm so sorry about the baby. Is there anything I can do?"

"Haven't you done enough already?" Danielle was taken aback at the coldness of her voice.

"What do you mean?"

"The girth on my saddle had been tampered with. It was cut almost completely through. As I was riding, it snapped, throwing me from the horse. The fall ripped my baby from me." With a cruel stare, she added, "I'll never forgive you, Danielle."

"Whatever you may think, I had nothing to do with your accident. I truly cannot believe anyone here would intentionally cause you harm."

"Believe what you will, but I have the proof. Court should be interested in my discovery."

"*Mon Dieu*, I'm sure I don't have the slightest idea what you're implying. Court will be as upset as I am about your unfortunate accident."

Meredith's eyes shot daggers at her. "You don't fool me for a second, Mrs. Sinclair. You would go to any length to keep Espérance."

Danielle paled. "I'll not stand here and endure your outrageous claims. If you need anything, let Mammy know." She turned with dignity and headed for the door.

"How fortunate for you that you still carry the Sinclair heir."

Meredith's malicious words brought quick tears to Danielle's eyes. Her back stiffened as she left the room.

Entering the peacefulness of her own room, she paced the floor, trying to figure out Meredith's scheme.

If she succeeded in widening the breach between Court and her, the repercussions could do irreparable damage. Weren't they having enough problems without Meredith interfering?

Mammy hustled into the room, shaking her head. "I knowed that aggravatin' woman done upset you. Don't you pay no nevermind to that spiteful she-cat. Ifen she could arrange for you 'n' the Massa to commence to arguin' and fightin', she'd be as pleased as a kitten what's full of clotted milk."

Danielle inwardly groaned. Of course Mammy was aware of the dissension between Court and her. With a raised brow, she asked, "Mammy, were you eavesdropping?"

Thrusting out her ample bosom, she claimed, "I was only standin' ready in case you needed me. I seed the way that Jude was treatin' you. I was ready to make him a necktie outta my broom. Before I knowed it, you went into her room."

As soon as Court returned from the city, he was ushered into Meredith's room. Danielle dreaded facing Court after he had spoken to Meredith and heard her accusations. She stayed in her room, mulling the question of what Meredith's real intention was, and whether Court would believe her. She was so deep in thought she did not hear the door open. Suddenly feeling another presence, she whipped around. Court leaned against the door frame, eyeing Danielle with a hungry look.

"Dannie, love, don't think even for an instant that I believe Meredith's accusations."

"I—I don't know what to believe anymore, Court," she said turning her back to him.

"Then let me explain."

"How, when you were caught in a lie?" she snapped. "Please leave me alone."

Infuriated with her, he exploded, "Dammit, we can't continue like this, Dannie!"

"You should have thought of that a long time ago."

She heard the door slam behind her. Disillusioned and heartbroken, she wiped the tears from her eyes and lay down on the bed. Court was right. They couldn't continue to live like this, but how, *Mon Dieu*, just how could they live any other way?

Once again, Camille's urgent plea awakened Danielle. "Miss Dannie, Miss Dannie, I gots to tell you sumpin'," she whispered.

"What is it, Camille."

"I was leavin' the kitchen when I seed Jude cartin' away a whole armful of bed linens."

"Bed linens?" Danielle's eyes grew larger as she listened.

"That ain't all I seed. He had the ridin' habit that Caraville woman was wearin' when she left this morning. I followed him. You know what he done with them things?"

Danielle shook her head.

"He burned them. I thought maybe it was 'cause she lost the baby 'n' all. That maybe they needed to be laundered. But the way he was fannin' them over the fire, I could see pretty good that they weren't ruined. Why do you think she'd have him do sumpin' like that?"

"My thoughts exactly, Camille. If the sheets had

been stained beyond cleaning, they could have been used for one thing or another. On the other hand, what if there were no stains? This way we only have her word that she was ever carrying a baby."

Camille's mouth dropped open. "That's right. Lord a'mercy, what's you think they're up to?"

Chapter 25

Meredith prolonged her convalescence as long as possible, making everyone miserable. Her angry voice carried through the house at the slightest misdeed, imagined or otherwise.

One afternoon, piercing screams rent the air, stilling every hand and turning every head.

"*Mon Dieu*, what is it now?" Danielle whispered to Mammy.

"They ain't no tellin', chile. I jus' hope she ain't swangin' that ridin' whip she's so fond of."

Cautiously, they approached Meredith's room and knocked gently on the door. Suddenly it was jerked open and slammed back against the wall.

"Come in!" Meredith shouted.

Hesitantly, they stepped across the threshold. She was angrily pacing the floor. Stopping before Danielle, she ground out, "Your little trick won't work."

"I'm afraid I don't understand what you're referring to."

"The ghost bit," Meredith snapped, "as if you didn't know. I've heard the wailing cries in the dead of night, saw the curtains shimmering when there was no breeze, smelled a hint of lavender encircling my room when no one was there. How you arranged these things is beyond me, but I will not be scared away from Espérance by the likes of you. I thought I would let it pass because I did not want to even give you the satisfaction of acknowledging your game."

Danielle protested. "But I didn't—"

"Don't lie." Meredith shook her finger. "You've gone too far this time." Jerking a bright red dressing gown from her closet, she thrust it in Danielle's face. "The deliberate destruction of my clothing and tampering with my toiletries is a wicked child's game. I won't stand for it."

Danielle and Mammy glanced at each other knowingly as Meredith continued her tirade.

"I'll see that Court replaces this garment," Meredith said, hurling the gown at Danielle. "Look at it!" The fabric had been split from bodice to hem. There was no way the gown could be mended because of the jagged tear.

"I know everyone has heard of the ghost that roams Espérance in search of her lover. I'll tell you what I believe. I think it's a scheme you've concocted to hang on to your precious home. Let me assure you I will not fall for the theatrics. You won't scare me from my newly acquired home." Her lips formed the semblance of a smile. "I do not believe in ghosts."

As Danielle and Mammy filed from the room, Mammy was wishing every pestilence she had ever heard of to descend on the head of Court's sister—immediately. Danielle's thoughts were of a gentler vein. She hugged the newfound knowledge to her with glee; the ghost of Espérance objected to Meredith Caraville's presence, also.

As the days passed, Espérance turned into a house of fearful dread. No one knew when something would send Meredith into a rage again. The occupants tread quietly and talked in whispers. This in itself caused her temper to flare. She accused them of plotting against her. When Court was home things ran smoother, but he had business to take care of that took him from the plantation more than he liked.

At every turn Meredith belittled Danielle. She destroyed the pleasure Danielle took in her studio. When Danielle could stand the intrusions no longer, she would spend the day on the riverbank.

Jude was always watching. She rarely saw him, but she could always feel his malevolent gaze. He made Danielle uncomfortable, particularly after Mammy told her of his attitude toward the other blacks.

"He sets hisself apart from us like he was better. He don't know it, but I ain't gots no use for him nohow. The way he's always creepin' 'round spyin' on everbody like we's gonna do sumpin' wrong. Ifen I gets half a chance, I'll tell him so."

Julian Bernard was delighted to learn that Court and Danielle were again in residence at Espérance. At the first opportunity he came calling, eager to find out if she was still painting. With a beaming smile he gave her her share of the profits from the first sale of her work.

"But Court . . ." she protested to him, knowing her husband had bought the paintings.

Shaking his head, Court silenced her. "You've earned it, love. It was your work." Leaning close, he whispered, "Can I help it if I have such good taste?"

Not wanting Bernard to sense the friction between them, Danielle accepted the money graciously.

During the course of his visit, Julian persuaded Danielle to let him take some of her new paintings on consignment.

Meredith dripped with kindness. "Our little Dannie is just a storehouse of surprises. Who would ever have dreamed that she was so talented with a brush?"

From the onset it was evident that Julian was not interested in Meredith. He only had eyes for Danielle's new work. Assuring Court and Danielle that he would send for the paintings, he took his leave, but not before Meredith wangled a promise from him that he would return for a small dinner party she was planning. Court and Danielle exchanged surprised glances.

On the day of the dinner party, an unexpected storm whipped the branches of the trees, and a cold rain pounded the earth. Meredith stomped through the house, venting her childish anger on anyone in her path. She vowed the only reason it had rained was to spoil her party.

Exasperated with her tantrum, Court cautioned, "Don't overestimate your worth, Meredith. The good Lord would not deliberately send a storm to spoil your fun. He was probably as surprised by your announcement as we were."

Ignoring him, she hurried to her room, remaining there until her dinner guests arrived. Her reappearance was startling. Her gown was as black as night, plunging into a deep vee in the front. As she turned for their inspection, she revealed the same detail in the back of her dress.

Jordan appeared, resplendent in cloud-gray evening wear. Danielle did not miss the coveted glances with which Meredith graced him. Julian Bernard could not seem to praise Danielle's latest work enough. He predicted her art would grace the walls of some of the most beautiful homes in New Orleans, and possibly be displayed in art galleries for generations to come. She was quite astonished by his prophecy.

Surprisingly, the evening was quite a success. Court and Danielle played the role of the happy couple, neither wanting their guests to witness their discord. Danielle reveled in the rapport between them, even though it was a pretense. This is the way it should be, she thought with yearning.

It did not take Meredith long to divert her attention from a disinterested Julian to Jordan. From all appearances, Jordan was captivated by Meredith. Only occasionally would a frown crease his forehead, and this seemed to happen only when she made a disparaging reference about Danielle. His quick defense of Danielle brought a strange light to Meredith's eyes.

It irritated Danielle beyond belief that Meredith could be so pleasant and accommodating to the guests, then treat her own family with such disdain.

Court was never far from his wife's side, and he paid only scant attention to conversation buzzing around him. Perhaps Meredith's dinner party wasn't such a bad idea after all, he mused. At least Danielle could not avoid him. She actually seemed to be enjoying herself.

"Court," Jordan repeated for the second time, "I'll agree the scenery you seem so bent on devouring is breathtaking, but I thought you might be interested in investigating some property I understand will be on the market in a short time."

With a devilish grin, Court removed his gaze from his lovely wife. "What makes you think I might be interested?"

"From what I've discovered, it is prime bottomland, and the price will be right," Jordan assured him. "You don't have anything to lose but possibly a day of your time. If you're free tomorrow, we could check it out before word spreads that it's being offered for sale."

When their plans were finalized, Meredith once

again directed the course of the conversation until their guests departed. Afterward, she declared the evening a success and flounced toward her room.

Her parting shot destroyed Danielle's hard-won self-confidence. "You'd just as well dispose of your gowns and plan to have new ones made. After the baby is born, you'll probably spread like the limbs of an oak. You'll never be able to squeeze back into your clothes."

The following day Court went to meet Jordan. Everyone at Espérance was about his or her chores when a bloodcurdling scream split the air. Dropping what they were doing, everyone raced in the direction of the shriek. The sight that met Danielle stopped her cold. Meredith's arm was swinging through the air, her hand landing with a resounding whack on Mammy's face. Mammy didn't move, not even to lift her hand to the burning welt. Her big eyes sparkled with tears, and perspiration beaded her wide forehead.

Danielle rushed to her, throwing herself into Mammy's arms. Sobbing frantically, she cried out, "*Non,* you'll not treat Mammy like this."

Smoothing Danielle's hair, Mammy offered quietly, "Sh...sh...don't you be frettin' over Mammy. It's gonna be all right. You just put yo' mind on that baby you is carryin'."

Rough hands jerked Danielle from her embrace. For a split second, hatred flashed in Mammy's eyes.

"What do you mean going against me to side with her? It's no wonder your home was in a shambles. You've only encouraged disobedience with your lax discipline."

"And you're always overly eager to dole out punishment for the slightest infraction," Danielle retorted.

"This isn't slight by any means," Meredith snapped. "Did you stop to wonder why she was being punished?"

At that second, Tobias came bounding down the hall, his eyes swinging from one to the other as he quickly assessed the situation. Ever-watchful Jude stepped out to halt him. Danielle could see his powerful fingers biting into Tobias's arm. She also noted the corded muscles of Tobias's neck and his clenched hands.

"Take a look," Meredith demanded, plucking an object from the pocket of her dressing gown. She hurled it to the floor.

Danielle leaned over and gingerly picked up a small wax doll, a replica of Meredith, even to the silver streaks in her black hair. The doll was dressed in a riding habit identical to the one she had been wearing the day of her accident. Plunged into the stomach of the doll was a wicked-looking needle. Unconsciously Danielle's hands went to her own stomach.

"Do you understand what this implies?" Meredith asked, loathing dripping from her words.

Suddenly her accusation hit Danielle full force. "You can't think Mammy did this."

"There's no doubt in my mind. She's the only one who has access to any room in this house. She has gone too far. If it were her intention to frighten me away, she's failed miserably. I will not stand for the practicing of voodoo. With her knowledge of potions and balms, suppose I'm fortunate that I wasn't poisoned." She nodded slightly to Jude, and he moved steadily toward Mammy.

Danielle tossed the doll away carelessly and moved to Mammy's side.

Again Meredith grabbed her.

Piercing her with an angry stare, Danielle warned, "Don't touch me."

Meredith dropped her hands immediately. "As you wish, Mrs. Sinclair," she said with a vicious sneer.

Jude roughly pushed Mammy ahead of him.

"What are you planning to do to Mammy?"

A satisfied gleam filled her eyes. "A good whipping should straighten her out." With that she turned and followed Jude.

Tobias was powerless to interfere. It could mean instant death if he went against the new mistress. Apprehension dogging their steps, they sadly trooped after Meredith. Camille could be heard sobbing from somewhere in the house.

They stepped into the yard to see Jude securing Mammy's hands above her head. Knotting the rope, he tossed it over a limb of the tree. A lethal whip lay coiled on the ground, ready for use. Danielle looked puzzled. How had these things gotten there? Had this been planned? Everything pointed at that. Jude had not had time to gather them. What sense was there in all this?

Mammy's bonds had been tightened until her feet barely touched the ground. Camille had been sent to gather the house servants and field hands. When everyone had assembled on the lawn, their eyes staring in disbelief at Mammy, Meredith stood before them, slapping her new riding crop repeatedly against her hand.

As every eye turned in her direction, Meredith elaborated the reason for the punishment. Gasps rippled through the crowd. She went on to explain that as new mistress of Espérance, she would not tolerate disobedience in any form. The practice of voodoo was forbidden. The servants looked at each other questioningly.

The crack of the whip split the air. Several

times Jude sent the lash ripping out, seeking a target. Finally he turned to Mammy and raised his arm. Danielle could not bear it. This was the one person who had loved her unconditionally since her birth, who had stood beside her regardless of the circumstances. She would not stand there and see the spirit crushed from her by this trash. Bolting forward, she covered her body with her own. The trembling shield broke Mammy's composure. Tears streamed down her face.

Jude callously dragged Danielle from Mammy. No sooner had he released her than she flew into him and plowed her head into his stomach. He was unprepared for her attack, and the wind was knocked from him. Before he could catch his breath, her sharp nails raked his face and down his naked chest. And all the while, her flying feet pounded his shins.

Regaining his composure, he drew back and knocked her to the ground. Mammy screamed hysterically and pandemonium broke loose as the blacks rushed forward to help their beloved Danielle.

The loud report of a pistol stopped everyone in their tracks. Fear momentarily flashed across Jude's face, but before anyone noticed, his usual sneer was back in place.

Anger clear in his voice, Court bellowed, "What the hell is the meaning of this?" As the crowd parted, he received the shock of his life. Danielle was lying on the ground, moaning softly at Mammy's feet.

Hurriedly dismounting, he rushed to her side, easing her into his arms. He whispered, "My God, what's going on here?"

"Help Mammy," she pleaded, tears streaming down her cheeks.

Bryce had already dismounted and was slicing

through the bonds that secured Mammy, mumbling prayers all the while. Mammy scurried to Danielle's side the minute she was free.

"Lawdy, Lawdy, I knowed my baby was quick to rile, but I never dreamed she'd go up against the likes of that hateful Jude. Ifen he's hurt her, I reckon he might as well make plans to meet his Maker. Are you all right, lamb?" she questioned as Court helped Danielle to her feet.

"Mammy, if you'll see that Danielle lies down for a while, I'll get to the bottom of this."

Heaving her breasts, she assured him, "I'll take care of her, don't you worry 'bout that. Massa Court, I wants you and Miss Dannie to know I didn't have nuthin' to do with that infernal voodoo doll. I don't practice no voodoo. I figger the good Lord gonna take care of things in his own good time without no help from old Mammy."

"I'm sure I'll understand more fully what you're saying when I've heard the entire story. But let me assure you that your word is as good as gold." After placing a tender kiss on Danielle's lips, he secured a promise from her that she would lie down.

Turning to the towering black, he was not surprised to see Meredith apparently coaching Jude for the forthcoming inquisition. Court's eyes were cold and hard as he viewed the couple. "Follow me," he commanded harshly, and without looking to see if they followed, he led the way to the study.

Once there, Meredith proceeded to make herself comfortable. Court stood before the windows trying to mask his intense dislike for his half sister.

Jude lingered by the door, waiting for the ax to fall. Despite what the Missus had told him about her brother, he couldn't help but feel an inkling of respect for the man. Sometimes, he just didn't understand these white folks, especially the hatred the missus had for her own blood kin. Whatever ...his loyalty had to remain with the missus. Hadn't she saved him when his former master would have cut off his thumbs for stealing? He'd always done whatever she asked, even though his stomach had turned over at some of her demands. The pain she seemed to inflict with such joy had become second nature to him from necessity. He knew that she would only keep him as long as he remained useful. If possible, he would see that she continued to require his services.

Meredith's voice dripped with contempt when she broke the silence. "I declare, Court, I don't know why you're so upset. What happened to Danielle was an accident. She brought it on herself by interfering and creating a scene that will be long remembered."

Swearing violently, he said, Meredith, is it so hard for you to understand that she was trying to protect a loved one? Mammy is more than a servant to her."

"Humph," she snorted. "She's a cantankerous old woman who doesn't know her place. I assume she's already filled your head with her innocence concerning the voodoo doll that happened to be sharing my bed when I woke today."

"She had nothing to do with the doll."

Meredith jumped to her feet. "Well, by God, someone placed that thing in my room. What about my saddle? I guess you deny that anyone at Espérance was responsible for cutting the cinch. Dammit, Court, someone here wants to get rid of me." Sneering at him, she added, "We all know who would benefit by my departure."

"You go too far, Meredith."

"No, Court, you're the one behaving like a horse with blinders. You only see straight ahead. Danielle has you so besotted, you've lost your sense of perception. Unless a firm hand is wielded here at Espérance, I might just as well shutter the doors and turn the slaves loose."

"What puzzles me is your decision to have Mammy whipped when you were only speculating about her guilt. It's as though by punishing Mammy, you sought to hurt Danielle."

"That's a lie," she stormed.

"I think not," he maintained.

"You don't know what you're talking about. Mammy put that doll in my room."

Court eyed Meredith with disgust. "For what is only an assumption, you ordered a beloved servant whipped."

"Beloved to whom, Court? She means nothing to me."

"Meredith, you goddamn better hope your sins never catch up to you, because you'll never be able to bear the consequences."

The coldness of his voice startled her. She did not have a chance to reply, for he had turned on his heel. Eyeing Jude, he warned, "Keep away from my wife. If ever I hear so much as a hint that you've had any contact with her, I'll cut out your heart."

Chapter 26

His concern for Danielle hastened his steps to their bedroom. Easing the door open, he peeked inside. Danielle appeared to be dozing. Mammy sat beside the bed, worry playing across her face. Her expression brightened as he approached the bed.

"I believe Miss Dannie is gonna be fine. The only thing what's botherin' me is that she was complainin' 'bout her stomach. Said it felt like it was full of knots, 'n' the lower part of her back was achin' jus' a bit. Now that sounds to me like that baby's tryin' to tell us sumpin'. Ifen we could manage it, I think Miss Dannie should stay in bed for a day or two. Now I'll be the first to admit that them's mighty big orders"—she rolled her eyes—"but that baby is growin' and I figger them pains is his way tellin' us he ain't none too pleased with being shook around like he was today."

"I'll see that she stays in bed," Court volunteered. His words held a hollow ring. "I'm sure you have things to do, Mammy. I'll sit with her."

She was out the door, planning a nourishing meal for Danielle before the door closed behind her. He laughed, shaking his head in wonder at her devotion. He dragged a chair to the side of the bed and made himself comfortable. Noting her

pale color, he vowed Danielle would not set foot
from her bed until Mammy pronounced her fit.

Her nap was short-lived, bits of the conversation she had overheard between Meredith and
Pernel pervaded her dreams. Bolting upright in
the bed, she searched wildly for Court's comforting presence.

Pulling him to her, she sobbed, "Court, I've
kept something from you. I've had no peace carrying the knowledge inside me."

"Shh," he murmured soothingly. "It's all right.
Whatever it is we can work it out."

"I'm sorry. I—I thought you and Meredith were
plotting against me, but I was wrong—so very
wrong," she confessed tearfully. "You've always
been there to protect me, but I was too blind to
realize it until today. I can only cleanse my conscience of this weighty burden and let you mea-
sure the truth of it."

Without further hesitation, she told him of
Meredith being the woman with Rankin Pernel
and of the conversation she had overheard about
her killing her husband. She had had no idea that
Pernel's friend and Court's sister were one and
the same until seeing her at Espérance.

Court's heart leaped knowing that at last Danielle trusted him. He was quick to assure her that
although he had had no knowledge of Meredith's
horrendous crime, he would not doubt for a minute that she was capable of murder. He shared
with Danielle some of the details of his childhood
with his spiteful older sister.

"Court," Danielle wondered, "if you all loved
Meredith, why didn't she love you in return?"

"Who's to know, pet? Nowhere is it written that
when you love, you'll be loved in return. I can
only assume that she resented the love our father
bestowed on my mother and me. Meredith only

understands a possessive, smothering love, not a sharing, growing one."

Tears glistened in Danielle's eyes. "Is it the love we have for Mammy that causes Meredith to lash out at her? I'm worried she'll take vengeance on her or Tobias after what I did today."

"Though she cares nothing for Mammy and Tobias, I've already told her she's not to lay a hand on them. It's her connection with Pernel that worries me. She'll use him to gain what she covets most."

"And what would that be?" Danielle asked.

"Money," he replied coldly.

As she digested his words, he studied her intently, trying to decide if the time was right to clear the air of the mistrust between them.

His hand roamed to the nape of her neck, his fingers lost in the wealth of her hair. Cradling her head, he began quietly. "Dannie, love, I know your mind must be in a turmoil over what to believe, and what not to believe, but first, I want you to know that I'm convinced you are innocent of my accusations. As I've learned the truth, I can't help but admire the way you handled yourself. I can only presume what I might have done if someone had placed at my doorstep the burdens that have been cast on yours."

At his hesitation, Danielle said, "What I don't understand, Court, is how you came to possess the deed to Espérance when Nicholas still owned it? Did you ... steal it?"

"No, my love," he said, drawing his hand to the side of her face. "That's where the deceit began."

She cocked her brow in question.

"To my knowledge I've never met Nicholas," he supplied. "Rankin Pernel passed himself off as your stepfather. He carried the deed to Espérance, and I won it from him, thinking all along that he

was Nicholas Caraville. I had no reason to doubt
he was someone else...although I did question
the legality of the deed."

"But how did he gain possession of the deed?"

"He must have stolen it from the desk when he
was left alone in the study."

"Mon Dieu!" she cried out. She recalled the day
he was left alone there; Mammy had left him
there, then gone to find her to announce his unexpected arrival. "We have both been deceived!"

A gleam sparkled in his eyes. "You realize, of
course, that I never legally owned Espérance. It
belonged to you all along. When Meredith announced she was Caraville's widow and owned the
plantation, I knew I'd made a grave error by not
telling you sooner. Everything backfired on me at
once. I couldn't blame you for not trusting me."

"But the debts..."

"I paid them as soon as I was aware of them.
When I think of all the pain I've caused you...
believe me, my love, my silence on that score has
haunted me unmercifully."

"But why, *why* didn't you tell me?"

"In the beginning, I thought it would fit into
the scheme I was sure you and Nicholas were
plotting against me. It wasn't until after you disappeared, that I discovered Pernel was the impos-
tor."

"You should have told me on the boat," she
chided through trembling lips.

"Oh, God, Dannie, I messed up again. I had my
heart where my head should have been. I was
afraid you'd leave me again if you found out. With
that armor of pride you wear, love, I couldn't take
that chance. Marrying you was my only hope of
keeping you at my side until I could gain your
love and trust."

Wrapping her arms around him, she brushed

his lips with hers, whispering softly, "You have my love in spite of everything that has happened. Even with all the deceit between us, I have always craved your love."

Her words were like an elixir to him. As he absorbed their meaning, his heart overflowed with hope. Just as his lips touched hers, he whispered hoarsely, "I love you, Dannie, my angel."

His declaration opened the floodgates of her heart, and she surrendered her soul, proclaiming her love freely.

Thank God, she's mine at last, Court thought. No ghost, no angel, no make-believe...only my beloved Dannie.

They had finally overcome the barriers of pride and distrust. Their love was a shroud, protecting them from the evil intentions of those around them. The desire burning in their hearts lighted their path to fulfillment. Snuggled securely in his arms, she slept peacefully.

Upon waking, she stretched her lithe body, unaware that his eyes were transfixed on the fullness of her breasts as they pressed against the fine lawn fabric of her dressing gown. Lowering his head, he captured one taut bud; his tongue played a melody of its own, creating within her a chaotic rhythm to his music.

Groaning hoarsely, he buried his face in her disheveled hair. "God, woman, you drive my better judgment right out the window."

"What do you mean?" she asked, rolling from his embrace.

Placing a gentle kiss on her pert little nose, he considered his words carefully. "Mammy told me of the pains you were having. It might be best if we abstain fulfilling our desire until we are sure you're in no danger."

"But Court—"

A warm finger sliding deliciously over her lips cut her argument short. "No buts, my pet. It's only for a few days. I would never do anything to jeopardize your health or the baby's. I truly need your help if I'm to outwit my body."

Her puzzled frown drew a chuckle from him. "Let me warn you, my little temptress, although my mind is agreeable to 'no,' my body is screaming 'yes.' As you see, I appear to be calm and level-headed. Don't be fooled, for my insides are having one hell of a battle. Do you realize how long it has been since we've made love?"

Danielle laughed and tumbled on top of him, agreeing to do what she could to see that he made it through the next few days. Their only point of disagreement was her acceptance of remaining in bed. Court promised he would entertain her.

At first opportunity, Court approached Tobias and asked him to join him as he checked the cane fields. When he was certain they were far enough away from the house not to be overheard or seen, he stopped.

Turning to Tobias, he cautioned, "I need your help with Danielle."

The black nodded his head, wondering at his odd request. "Ah'll do what Ah can. You know that, Massa."

"This is to be between us; no one's to suspect a thing."

"Ah understand."

Court removed a small pistol from inside his coat. Tobias's eyes widened, and his mouth dropped open as he stared at the gun in astonishment. "You—you wants that Ah shoot Miss Dannie?"

"Good God, no, I want you to protect her," Court explained. "I realize it's against the law for you to be armed, but she must be protected during my absence. Do you know how to use this thing should the need arise?"

"Ah ain't rightly sure, but Ah can learn."

Tobias's interest in the weapon spurred Court to teach him the rudiments of firearms. Before long, he was handling the gun comfortably enough to see his way through a difficult situation.

Court cautioned him to keep a close eye on Jude and not to hesitate to use the weapon should he attempt to harm Danielle. But at all costs, he had to keep the gun hidden. This understanding secured between them, they returned to Espérance.

Mammy met them in the yard. "I thought I heard gun shots. Ya'll didn't notice anybody snoopin' 'round, did you?"

"I guess what you heard was me. Tobias and I almost ran headlong into the path of a cottonmouth."

"Humph," she snorted, "it sho' took you enuf shots to kill it." She turned and went back to the house.

Court eyed her with respect. Mammy was nobody's fool. If she suspected what was going on, she would never breathe a word of it. Satisfied, he pursed his lips and began whistling strains of one of Mammy's favorite hymns.

Danielle had fidgeted from one side of the bed to the other, bored beyond belief when Court's duties took him from her side. He entertained her with ribald tales of his youth. Their laughter rang through the house, bringing smiles to all who had heard them, except one.

Mammy had stuck her head into the room on more than one occasion, threatening Court if he

was teaching her little lamb unladylike things.
This had brought ripples of laughter from the couple as they emphatically denied her accusations.
Hours passed as they made plans for their future.
He assured her that she would never be bothered
by Jude again. He promised to secure the papers
for Mammy and Tobias—even if he had to steal
them. As soon as he was able to complete this
transaction, they would return to Shadowbrook.

Thankful to be outside once again, Danielle
breathed deeply of the sweet-smelling air, treading softly among the fragrant rose bushes, admiring Tobias's handiwork. A smile tugged her lips
as she noticed the conspicuous absence of weeds.
They were plucked from the garden as soon as
they peeked through the soil. Never had Espérance looked better.

Court joined her in the garden, pleased that
Mammy had pronounced her fit. They strolled
down the path, comparing the difference between
now and when he had first seen the plantation.

His lips teasing the smooth column of her neck,
he whispered, "Come, love, I believe I heard
Mammy say something about preparing your
bath."

She went gladly.

Sinking down into the steaming water, she
closed her eyes, letting the warm water ease the
tightness of her muscles. Court leaned over, placing a tender kiss on her soft lips. Her eyes remained closed as she wrapped wet arms around
him. Welcoming the thrust of his tongue, her lips
opened of their own accord. His hand cupped her
chin, his fingers traversing the contour of her jaw.
With his arm trapped between them, he could feel
the wet fullness of her breast as she strained
against him. Removing his mouth, he continued
his exploration of her lips with his fingers. She

caught it between her teeth and drew it into her eager mouth. The gentle sucking motion was Court's undoing.

"Oh, God," he groaned hoarsely, sinking to his knees. Plunging his hand beneath the water, he sought her womanly softness, caressing with unscrupulous strokes until she moaned in surrender.

"Would you care to join me in my bath, *monsieur?*" she purred.

He cocked a wicked brow. "I thought you'd never ask."

Hurriedly dropping his clothes to the floor, he eased his tall frame behind her, causing the water to slosh dangerously close to the rim. She giggled, thinking of the picture they must make, and wiggled her derrière closer against him.

His hands glided around her until he filled them with her swollen breasts. His warm breath teased the column of her neck as he moved his lips over her sweet-smelling flesh. His tongue wove its own spell as it snaked out to taste her. She dipped her hand beneath the surface of the water and clasped his throbbing manhood. His longing heightened her own spiraling need. As he shifted her slippery body for easier access, his lips mocked the motions of his hands. Taking matters into her own hands, she slid onto his lap. Slowly, she eased down, his male hardness finding the home it sought, sinking deeply into the honey softness of her wet chamber.

Their moans mingled as they strove to satisfy the insatiable craving they had for each other. She twisted her head, and their lips met. Their passion grew until they were united by blinding release.

Court, nibbling on her neck, vowed, "God, woman, when it comes to making love, you are the lovemaker."

Scooping the dripping cloth from the tub, he soaped it liberally. Applying soothing strokes, he proceeded to bathe every inch of her. She, in turn, treated him with her own delightful ablutions, which had Court vowing to keep her in bed for a week. She teased him unmercifully with her antics, bringing sensual predictions from his kiss-swollen mouth.

Bracing her hands on his hairy legs, she stood up in the tub. Placing her hands on her hips, much the same as was Mammy's habit, she turned to Court with mischief sparkling in her eyes. "Why, Massa Court, what you mean layin' round in that tub in broad daylight? They's work to do. It's gonna take me the better part of the day to clean up this mess." Shaking her head in Mammy's fashion, she continued. "They ain't no rest for the wicked, no suhree."

Laughter bubbled up from his chest. He enjoyed her play immensely, and the delicious view of her body was wreaking havoc on his soaring desire. It was becoming difficult for him to concentrate on what she was saying. Stepping from the tub, she bent over to pick up a linen towel, and his heart almost leaped from his chest.

"Damn," he growled, leaving the tub to draw his alluring wife into his wet embrace.

Unless it was absolutely unavoidable, Danielle stayed away from Meredith, whose tongue remained as sharp as a razor, leaving its victim waiting for the show of blood. Meal times were the worst. No longer did Meredith temper her words in Court's presence. She made it plain they were unwelcome guests. Court stood his ground. With every hint and sly insinuation she delivered, he retaliated with an offer for Mammy and

Tobias's papers. Meredith would stubbornly refuse.

One evening, sitting at the table waiting for Camille to serve the dessert, Court winked boldly at Danielle. Meredith did not miss the gesture. Suddenly she began berating Camille for her slowness. This only caused the young girl to become frightened. With a trembling hand, she poured too much rich cream over Meredith's peach cobbler. The cream overflowed the dish and was rapidly absorbed by the delicate tatted tablecloth.

Meredith stormed from her seat, slapping Camille viciously across her face. "You stupid bitch. How thankful I'll be to be rid of the lot of you. You've been coddled till you are useless."

"Non," Danielle shouted, protecting her from any further abuse.

Court, too, had sprung to his feet, disgusted at Meredith's actions. "Damn you, Meredith! I curse the fact the same blood runs in our veins! Our father would be ashamed of you!"

Danielle had led the fearful Camille to the outside kitchen, doing her best to reassure the girl that Court's sister was mistaken about her usefulness.

Re-entering the dining room, she heard Court's infuriated shout. "You had no right to strike the girl."

"I had every right, dear brother," Meredith contradicted. "In case it has conveniently slipped your mind, I'll refresh your memory. I own Espérance, not you or your dainty wife." She lifted a brow in Danielle's direction. "It's mine to do with as I please. Since we happen to be on your favorite subject, Espérance, I have some news you should find interesting." She paused, a sneer curling her

lips as she raised her glass. "I am selling Espérance. I already have a buyer."

Her news sent a cold chill through their bodies.

"By whose authority?" a voice bellowed from
the doorway.

Chapter 27

The sound of shattering glass echoed through the dining room as the wineglass Meredith had held slipped through her fingers and crashed against her plate. Tiny fragments of crystal sprayed the table, while deep red wine blended with the rich cream already staining the cloth.

All eyes shifted to the arched entrance. Court, his head cocked at an angle, stared curiously at the stranger with a question posed in his eyes. Danielle's mouth gaped open, her expression a combination of surprise and happiness. Meredith completely lost control, her lack of composure visible in her features: Her face paled, her blood-red lips thinned, one corner of her cheek twitched uncontrollably, and her eyes widened and dilated, becoming as black as a gathering storm.

Nicholas Caraville leaned casually against the door frame, arms crossed in front of him. He was fashionably dressed in tan trousers and a deep green coat. Still as handsome as ever, Danielle thought with admiration. His hair, once coal-black, was sprinkled with gray. A stray lock fell over his forehead, partially concealing a small scar on his temple. He was not as tall as Court, but he was solidly built, which belied the slimness of his frame.

Nicholas's eyes hardened, piercing like daggers into the woman who had put him through hell. He pushed away from the door and walked to the end of the long table. Leaning forward, he splayed his hands on the surface of the table, scrutinizing Meredith as she sat in stunned silence at the opposite end. "Why, dear wife, the silent tongue? Could it be that a ghost has risen from a watery grave and come back to reap vengeance on its murderer?"

Hearing no response from her, he moved around the table, positioning himself behind her chair. His fingers trailed over her bare shoulder and up the stiff column of her neck until both hands spanned her throat. She shivered, her hands gripping the edge of the table. "Feel my touch, Meredith, and know these hands are those of a living man, capable of crushing the life out of you."

"Don't...please," Meredith said chokingly. "It —it was an...accident."

Removing his hands from her throat, Nicholas walked away from her in disgust. "An accident," he said with a shake of his head. "Before I cancel out that perverted lie, I think in all politeness I should introduce myself to our guest, who no doubt thinks I'm deranged." Extending his hand to Court, he said, "Nicholas Caraville, the real owner of Espérance."

Court took his hand. "Court Sinclair, Mister Caraville. Your reference to me as being a guest is a trifle misleading." He smiled at Danielle. "In your absence, I married your stepdaughter."

With surprise washing over his face, Nicholas looked down at her upturned face. "It would seem, *ma petite*, that much has happened since my"—he paused, glancing at Meredith—"disappearance."

"*Oui*, Nicholas," Danielle answered softly. "So many questions have now been answered." Peering intently at Meredith, she asked, "Were you aware that Meredith carried your child up until a few weeks ago?" Shaking her head sadly, she clucked her tongue. "Poor Meredith."

"If you were with child, Meredith, then it wasn't mine," Nicholas said adamantly. "For three months or more, I've been working my way back from St. Louis to New Orleans. Even before that time, you avoided me like I had a disease."

Meredith slid back her chair and stood up, avoiding his threatening eyes. "I'll go pack my things."

"Sit down!" he commanded. "You'll not leave this room until I'm finished with you. Do you think I plan to let you go scot-free after what you've done to me? If I choose to do so, I can have you put in prison for the remainder of your life."

She gasped and quickly sat down. Tears sprung to her eyes. "Nicholas, let me explain," she pleaded. "I love you."

"No!" he shouted, slamming his fist on the table, nearly upsetting the crystal wineglasses. The flickering candles cast eerie shadows across his handsome, angry face. "You're not capable of such an emotion. God," he groaned desolately, lowering and shaking his head, "if I had only known that in the very beginning."

Suddenly his agonized eyes gazed at Danielle beseechingly. "Believe me, Danielle, when I say that the only woman I've ever truly loved was your mother. Why I thought this wretched woman could take her place, I'll never understand. Elise's death left a painful emptiness in my heart; I was consumed with self-pity."

A single, crystalline tear rolled down Danielle's cheek. She placed her hand tenderly on her step-father's arm. "I understand, Nicholas. You need not say more."

The touch of her hand, her reassuring words,

warmed his heart. He did not feel he deserved her kindness. Could he, after all these years, make up for his past? Would she believe him when he told her he had not intended to leave her in such dire straits?

"You say you understand, *ma petite,* and I believe you. Yet, you must wonder why you never heard from me after I left Espérance."

Danielle's attention focused angrily toward Meredith. *"Oui,* I did wonder—until now. I'm certain she had something to do with all this. After all, a woman who has murder in her heart must possess no conscience."

"Meredith," Nicholas said, "tell Danielle what happened to all the letters I wrote to her explaining my absence, and about the money I had collected while gambling to clear Espérance from its debts."

Meredith looked at Danielle with contempt. "The letters I destroyed, the money I kept. Why shouldn't I have had the money, Nicholas *dear?* I am your wife and Danielle is not even your daughter."

Ignoring her outrage, he said, "My first letter explained my intentions, Danielle. Espérance was not a home to me after Elise died. I had hoped to lose the aching memory of her by giving the plantation to you, its rightful owner. Fortunately, I had a winning streak and eventually made enough money to cover all my debts. Little did I know that the money I gave to Meredith to send to you never reached your hands... nor the letters which were included with each payment."

Court, who had remained silent for most of the conversation, intervened. "Nicholas, what I'm about to say doesn't discredit the information you've just delivered. I, too, have reason to doubt your wife's credibility. Were you aware that Meredith is my half sister?"

The shock registering on Nicholas's face was answer enough. *"Non . . .* I did not."

"Let me assure you she's not worthy of the Sinclair name," Court said disgustedly.

"Damn you," Meredith swore, rising so quickly the chair fell backward. "All my life I've been second place. My own father cast me aside like a worn shoe to coddle you. I hated you before you even came into this world." She tossed back her head haughtily. "While Elizabeth carried you and grew like a cow, my father fawned over her, pampered her, and patted her huge belly, saying, 'We shall have a son, my love, I just know we will.' I stood in the background, listening and watching it all." Baring her teeth, she hissed, "Yes, I hated you and I hated Elizabeth and I hated my own father!"

The room fell silent as Court weighed her words. She had not seen nor felt the love and attention his parents had tried to give her for the fierce jealousy she harbored. "Then you're to be pitied, Meredith," he said softly, "for your jealousy was unwarranted. There are no words I can say to convince you otherwise. Your malignant hatred has filled every chamber of your heart."

Nicholas rose and picked up her chair, repositioning it behind her. When she did not make the move to sit down, he placed his hands on her shoulders and pulled her back into it. "You're not free to leave yet, Meredith."

Court pushed aside his dessert plate and crossed his arm on the table. When Nicholas took his chair again, Court said to Meredith, "I asked you once before about the ransom note. Now I want the truth."

"Ransom note?" Nicholas asked, frowning.

"Yes." Court narrowed his eyes at Meredith. "That's how I came to be in New Orleans in the first place." His face softened as he smiled lovingly at Danielle. "Of course, had I not received that note, I never would have met Danielle. As it was, I almost met my maker. Now, as I think back, I believe I know what happened without hearing Meredith's denial. You may correct me if I'm wrong, Meredith. You were out of money, so you pretended to have been kidnaped. Once I arrived with the ransom money, Jude slipped into the townhouse, struck me while I was sleeping, and took off with the money. Am I right?"

Before she could answer, Nicholas said, "That money, coupled with the money intended for Danielle, made quite a stake. We were suddenly living like royalty. We took a boat to Baton Rouge, traveling first class, then we gambled our way up the Mississippi to St. Louis. She told me all along she was doing well at the gaming tables. She lost every dime she took from you, just like she lost the Delanoye fortune. *Mon Dieu*, what a fool I've been," he groaned, lowering his head into his hands.

When he finally lifted his head, he spat out furiously, "You had it all planned from the beginning of our relationship, didn't you, Meredith? You knew I owned valuable river property. If I were dead, you would inherit it all. You planned to gamble Espérance away, and then find another fool to keep you in luxury."

"Danielle," he said tenderly, turning in her direction, "had I not come back today, Meredith would have wrested Espérance away from you... legally."

Court chuckled. "It would seem the deed to Espérance has come full circle. At one time even I held it, though not legitimately." Seeing the bemused expression on Nicholas's face, he said, "The irony of it all is that I thought I won the deed from you in a card game." Court went on to tell Nicholas about Rankin Pernel's deceit. As he recounted the story, he scrutinized Meredith's countenance carefully, wondering if she had been in on that earlier scheme also. He and Danielle had decided to keep their knowledge of Meredith and Pernel's relationship to themselves until they had some idea what the vicious pair was planning.

When Court finished, Nicholas turned to her. "You said my near death was an accident. True, I had imbibed very freely the night I was pushed" —he stressed the word, seeing the fear suffuse Meredith's face—"struck first, then pushed over the railing of the steamboat. If I recall correctly, I had earlier found one of my letters to Danielle partially burned in the wastebasket. We had an argument and I left for the salon. Several card games and numerous drinks later, I started back to our room to pack my things, planning to take the next boat back to New Orleans when we arrived at the next port. You and Jude were outside the salon, waiting for me to come out. As the three of us stood by the railing, I told you my plans to somehow free myself from our farcical marriage." He took a deep breath before continuing. "The next thing I recollect was Jude's large fist plowing into my face and your hushed words, 'Throw him overboard, Jude. No one's watching.'"

"Mon Dieu," Danielle gasped, pressing the back of her hand tightly against her mouth.

Nicholas left his chair and jerked Meredith up by the arm, his fingers biting into her flesh. "The only thing you hadn't banked on, my vile and scheming wife, was my survival. I was dazed when I hit the water and the paddle wheel of the boat came within an inch of striking me. Fortunately, just as I was almost pulled under by the wake, a log bumped against my head. I grabbed it and passed out. When I woke up, I found myself near the riverbank, still clinging to it."

Meredith's mouth trembled. Danielle could see her teeth biting into her lip.

"You should have emptied my pockets, Meredith. At least I wasn't left totally destitute. I gambled my way back to Espérance."

Meredith tried to pry his hands from her arm, but he increased his strength. "Let me go, you bastard," she hissed.

"Oh, I'll let you go, Meredith, but it will be to a place of my own choosing."

She paled. "You wouldn't dare send your own wife to rot in prison, would you? Then everyone would know what a pompous fool you were for falling into such trickery."

"No," he said derisively, "in prison you would have a bed and food. You belong in the streets, begging for your next meal, seeking a place in an alley among other derelicts for your rest. No man will look at you for your beauty will fade as the skin falls from your bones from hunger. That, my wife, will be your hell to live. But my name will not be yours, nor do I ever want to hear you speak it. I can easily obtain a divorce from you now. Who could blame a man for wanting freedom from a wife who planned his eulogy before they said their marriage vows?"

Thrusting her from him, he shrugged his shoulders in dismissal. "Now, Meredith, you may pack your things and get out. I'll offer you one last thing—a ride into New Orleans."

Meredith looked from Nicholas to Court, her eyes filled with tears. Danielle wondered whether they were the first true tears Meredith had ever shed, or if they were false, like everything else about her.

"Surely, Court, you, my own brother, won't allow Nicholas to treat me this way."

Court stared at her in utter astonishment. "What would you have me do, Meredith? Offer you your old room back at Shadowbrook? I will never let you set foot in that house again."

Meredith's murderous eyes glowered at each of them. "You will regret this day—all of you," she said stonily, then left the room to gather her belongings.

Breathing a sigh of relief, Nicholas sat down once again at the table. "Do you think I might have a bite to eat? Suddenly I feel famished."

"Of course," Danielle said, rising from her chair. Stopping by him, she placed her hand on his shoulder and smiled down at him. "Welcome home, Nicholas. I'll see that Maybelle prepares a plate for you."

As she opened the door, Mammy and Camille leaped back, each smiling broadly. Closing the door behind her, Danielle asked with a sly wink, "Is there anything that happens at Espérance that you two don't know about?"

"We was jes' happenin' by, Miss Dannie, 'n' heard all the ruckus," Camille said apologetically.

"Is Massa Caraville here for good this time, chile?" Mammy asked, wringing her hands excitedly.

"He hasn't said what his intentions are as yet. I certainly wish he would consider it. Oh, I do hope Maybelle hasn't put away all the food."

"Don't worry, chile," Mammy said, patting her on the arm. "I done tole Maybelle to fix him up sumpin'."

As Danielle re-entered the dining room, she heard the front door slam. Presently the sound of the carriage carrying Meredith and Jude from Espérance died away in the distance.

"I fear we haven't heard the last from her," she said apprehensively. "I pity poor Tobias's having to sit next to Jude and listen to Meredith's tirade all the way to New Orleans."

Court chuckled. "He was whistling a happy tune as he escorted them out."

When Nicholas had finished dining, they retired with him to the study, bringing him up to date on the happenings at Espérance. Danielle told him that Court had converted the planting room to a studio for her, and that he had also encouraged her to display her art in Julian Bernard's gallery.

"You've come a long way since you painted the portrait of your mother. It's a shame I never arranged lessons for you." He smiled sadly. "There are many things I failed to do for you."

Danielle handed him a snifter of brandy. To lift his spirit, she said humorously, "You did arrange fencing lessons for me. If it weren't for a split-second distraction, I might have won back the deed to Espérance and sent Court on his merry way."

Court laughed. "And all would have been for naught, for it was never mine to win or lose in the first place."

"But where would we be now had fate not played us against each other?" she asked.

Nicholas's mind was not on their lighthearted banter. "Court, I must thank you for restoring Espérance. I almost didn't recognize it when I got off the boat. It may take me a few years, but I plan to repay you every dime you've put into it, and that includes the debts you paid off for me."

"You need never repay me," Court insisted, swirling the amber liquid around in his snifter. "Having Danielle as my wife is my reward."

Her heart beat wildly at his tender words. She watched the play of emotions on Nicholas's face.

"I'm grateful, not only for your generosity, but for the happiness you have brought to Danielle." His voice wavered slightly, and he took a long pull on the brandy.

Danielle thought that since the tension of the evening had finally ceased, she would relate the good news. "Nicholas, I do hope you can tolerate another bit of news."

Court, knowing what she intended to bring up, smiled proudly.

"Only if it doesn't concern Meredith. I've had my fill of her," he said with a sigh.

She smiled. "Court and I are going to have a baby."

Happiness radiated from Nicholas's face. "Then I'm to be a grandfather. I mean, well, I can be, if it is all right with the two of you."

She hugged him to her, tears glistening in her eyes.

"Maybe this is my chance to make up for my lack of attention to you all these years, Danielle."

She smiled tenderly. "I believe you'll make a fine grandfather."

"Then shall we retire on that happy note?" he asked, placing his empty glass on the table.

After they bid good-night to one another and departed for their rooms, a thought suddenly occurred to Court as he reached the top of the stairs. "All Nicholas's belongings were removed from his room, remember?"

"*Mon Dieu,* it's too late now to do anything about it. We can tell him Meredith had them removed when she took his room. He'll be none the wiser." She couldn't resist one more dig at the woman who had caused so much grief to her and her loved ones.

"I'd better tell him now," Court said, leaning

down to kiss her. "Go on to bed and I'll be up in a minute."

She was in bed, when he finally came into their room. Thinking she was asleep, he stripped and slipped quietly between the sheets. Leaning over, he kissed her softly parted mouth, and brushed his lips over her eyelashes.

She smiled dreamily and asked, "Did he believe you?"

"Yes, no problem. I told him Tobias would bring in his things in the morning."

"You were gone for quite some time. What else did you talk about?"

Laughing lightly, he settled down beside her. "Oh, a surprise or two, but wouldn't you rather talk about it tomorrow? I thought you were asleep, love."

"I'm too excited to sleep," she answered, rolling over and nestling against his warmth.

"Excited?" he asked rakishly, slipping his hand beneath her gown.

She giggled and trapped his wandering hand with her own. "You'll not go another inch, *monsieur,* until you tell me this surprise you've mentioned so casually."

"It appears I'm being blackmailed." He lightly squeezed her thigh. "Very well, then. Mammy and Tobias are returning to Shadowbrook with us."

Danielle bolted straight up, coming to rest on her knees beside him. She asked excitedly, "Do you mean permanently?"

"Yes, love. Nicholas made the generous offer before I even had a chance to bring up the matter."

"But—but who'll take over the household duties?"

"I suggested Camille. She's young, but she seems responsible. Nicholas knows the rest of the blacks better than I do, so I'm sure he won't have difficulty choosing one to take over Tobias's chores."

She leaned down and kissed him thoroughly. "This has been a day of surprises, hasn't it?"

He laughed uneasily. "Indeed it has. I'm afraid we're due a few more surprises in the near future— some rather unpleasant ones."

Court could see the silhouette of her body against the backdrop of moonlight. He saw her slowly nod her head before she spoke. "You mean Meredith, don't you?"

"You've lived with her and know how conniving she is. She's too shrewd to become a street hag. No, I'd say that right this moment she is sleeping in luxury beneath silken sheets."

Her eyes narrowed. "But where?"

"Evidently she has access to the townhouse or how would Jude have entered and taken the ransom money."

"Can you force her to leave?"

"I could, Danielle, but it could work to our advantage if we let her remain there."

She lay down once again, her head resting on Court's shoulder. "I noticed you didn't mention my seeing Meredith and Pernel together. Shouldn't we tell Nicholas?"

"No, love, not yet. First I want to make certain my suspicions are justified. Since there's no reason for me to return to the townhouse, and Meredith knows this, she'll feel free to come and go as she pleases . . . and have whomever she wants as visitors."

A devious smile pulled at one corner of Danielle's mouth. "And we shall keep a constant surveillance on her, am I correct?"

"Damien lives not too far from the townhouse; Jordan has his business nearby, also. I'm certain they won't mind doing a little spy work for us."

An icy chill ran up her spine. "Meredith and Pernel could be plotting their revenge right this very minute."

Hearing the slight quiver in her voice, he drew her closer to his side. "Yes, Dannie, and we have to stay one step ahead of them so they will not succeed. Before we return to Shadowbrook, I'll tell Nicholas our suspicions so he will know to be on guard. Right now, I think it would be wise if we keep our knowledge secret. I noticed he has a hot temper and could unintentionally thwart our plans."

"When are we returning home?"

"Soon, my love, soon," he whispered softly, her casual reference to Shadowbrook as home swelling his heart with joy.

Chapter 28

Court surprised Danielle with his announcement that they would be Jordan's house guests for several days. He did not tell Danielle the real reason behind their visit: He thought she would be safer there than Espérance. He also had made an appointment for Danielle with a well-known dressmaker during their coming visit, since she would soon be in need of dresses that would accommodate her growing condition.

Espérance once again returned to its old vitality. Mammy's voice could be heard raised in song as she went about her chores, and Nicholas began going to the fields early in the morning. Court brought him up to date on the renovations, going over Espérance's books with him, explaining the various accounts that Nicholas was unfamiliar with. The only time Nicholas went into New Orleans was when he had business; the gaming houses were no longer an enticement. The void that had driven him there in the beginning was now filled with dedication to Espérance.

Court had received word from Jordan that Meredith had indeed set herself up in his townhouse and was receiving nocturnal visits. The identity of her visitor had yet to be discovered, but Jordan was watching carefully. Court had already drawn his own conclusions concerning the visitor, and acting accordingly by secretly tightening the security of Espérance. He was sick to death of his persistent fear that once again Danielle might be lost to him.

Yawning, Mammy shifted on the plush seat of the carriage and discreetly eyed Danielle as they made their way to Jordan's home. Nodding her head, she let drowsiness claim her, dreaming of all the little Sinclair babies who would need a loving mammy.

Danielle and Court spent a pleasant evening with Jordan. After dinner, the men relaxed with their brandy and she enjoyed a small glass of sherry while they made their plans for the following day. Court and Jordan had business to take care of, and Danielle's appointment with the dressmaker was scheduled during the morning. Afterward with Tobias acting as their escort, she and Mammy planned to shop until it was time to meet Court. They were slated to go to the opera in the evening.

The next morning passed in a flurry for Danielle as she met with the dressmaker, then afterward explored one shop after another, Mammy's, Tobias's and her arms overloaded with her discoveries.

The day suddenly became cloudy and the distant roll of thunder rumbled across the horizon. Tobias arranged the packages neatly in the back while Mammy urged him to hurry.

"I, for one, don't hanker gettin' soaked ifen them clouds take a notion to split open," Mammy commanded.

"Ah'll be through in a minute. You wants Ah should pile all these packages here so's they get crumpled? Then you be givin' me 'what for' cause they is smashed," Tobias grumbled.

"I'm just going across the street, Tobias," Danielle said suddenly. "I saw a lovely little hat shop. You can catch up with us when you are finished."

Mumbling to himself, Tobias placed the last parcel neatly beside the others and rushed after her and Mammy. To his dismay they were nowhere in sight. Fear churning his insides, he opened the door to the hat shop. The little bell above the door tinkled loudly. Embarrassed beyond belief, he stuck his head inside, scanning the shop for his mistress. To his relief Mammy hurried toward him.

"What's done got into you, Tobias? You looks like you seed a ghost. Now, you wait outside. We'll be right out. You ain't gots no business in here," she chided.

Relief flooding him, Tobias positioned himself for the wait. Eyeing the shoppers he berated himself for being foolish. No one would dare harm Miss Dannie, least not in broad daylight. Secure that he had been overreacting, he let his eyes drift shut. He didn't stir until he heard Mammy's voice mingling with his dreams.

"Serve 'em right ifen we jus' left him," she snorted.

"Ah wasn't asleep, Ah was jes' resting my eyes," Tobias informed them, as he set out behind them. This was a new experience for him. Miss Dannie had never had the means to shop before. If she needed anything, she would usually send him. She sho' seems to git a kick outta shoppin', he thought. And Mammy is jes' as bad. He dropped back a ways, but he still had his eye on Miss Dannie, not taking any chances.

In a blink, Danielle and Mammy disappeared from sight. Rushing headlong up the *banquette*, he turned into an alley.

"Lawd, God Almighty," he prayed. Right there,

mean as a snake, was Jude towering over Miss
Dannie.

She was shaking her head furiously. *"Non,* if
Meredith would like to see me, she knows where
she can find me."

"She tole me to fetch you," Jude bellowed.

He grabbed her arm. Mammy was speechless;
she did not know what to do. Should she leave her
mistress and seek help, or try to talk some sense
into him. She could not believe he would actually
force Danielle to go with him. Finding her voice,
she said, "You no-account darkie. Take your
hands off 'n Miss Dannie."

Before she knew what happened, Mammy was
staring at the glistening edge of a knife.

"What's you gonna do with that?" she asked,
drawing back from the knife.

"Jude's gonna cut out your tongue ifen you
don't shut up," he said with a sneer, easing the
blade within inches of her face.

Mammy's mouth clamped shut.

Danielle struggled to break free of Jude's grasp.
Her foot found its mark and gained her temporary
freedom. Before she could flee, she was shoved
roughly against a wall. She could feel shards of
wood piercing her back as his wicked blade
pinned her to the wall.

"The missus tole Jude to bring you to her anyway Ah can."

"I'll go with you," she relented.

Standing close behind her, Jude shoved her in
the direction of the street. But before anyone
knew what was happening, a large mass of muscle and bone plunged into their midst.

"Run, Miss Dannie!" the interloper charged.

Danielle and Mammy needed no urging. They
bolted from the melee as passersby gaped in astonishment, wondering what madness had over-

taken the lady and her black companion who were dashing down the *banquette* toward Jordan's office.

Jordan and Court were just leaving when Danielle fell breathlessly into her husband's arms. Mammy slowed her bounding footsteps just in time to keep from plowing a confused Jordan through the door. Catching her breath, Mammy detailed what had happened.

"That no 'count Jude done tried to force Miss Dannie to go with him. He was sportin' a knife what he was swingin' 'round, threatnin' us with."

"Where's Tobias?" Court asked.

"Lawd a'mercy, we done left him with the whole mess. He jumped in and said run, 'n' that's 'sactly what we done."

"Where are they?" Jordan asked.

The foursome rushed back along the *banquette*. Court's thoughts were black as he vowed to kill Jude. Entering the alley, they saw Tobias sitting astride the unconscious form of the big black man.

"Are you all right, Tobias?" Court shouted.

Bobbing his wiry head up and down, Tobias clucked his tongue. "Yas suhree, Massa, Ah'm fine. That knife don't cut no black meat."

"What about the gun, Tobias?"

Danielle looked on in puzzlement. "What gun?"

"I'll explain later," Court said, returning his attention to Tobias.

"Massa, Ah got so all-fired mad when Ah seed that ugly nigger touch Miss Dannie, Ah plumb forgot 'bout that gun. It's in my pocket. You wants it?"

Court shook his head in astonishment. "No, you keep it, Tobias. You might find a good use for it sometime—for cracking nuts or something," he added wryly.

Mammy gently cuffed Tobias's ear. "Alls I's concerned with is that this aggravatin' mess is done with. I don't believe my heart can stand much more excitement." Turning to Danielle, she asked, "Are you all right, sweetie pie?"

"I'm fine now," she answered, edging closer to Court.

Jordan saw them safely to his home while Court informed the authorities of the mishap. Tobias had been beside himself with fear when they discovered Jude was dead. Jude's powerful bull neck had been unable to withstand Tobias's crushing blows, which had snapped it like a twig in a gale wind. No action would be taken against Tobias when Court explained that he had been protecting his mistress.

Court let himself into the townhouse with his own key. The place was a shambles, clothes strewn on every available surface.

"Meredith," he called out.

Silence. As he searched for her, he noticed the same unkempt appearance throughout the house. On closer inspection, he discovered missing paintings and objects of art that were very valuable. It was obvious that Meredith had sold them to feed her gaming habit. From the state of the townhouse, she had taken little care of it—other than to purge it of its valuable contents. The knowledge that she had disposed of his lovingly collected possessions sent him into a fury. She could never pay enough to fully satisfy his need for retaliation.

The front door slammed, accompanied by angry expletives announcing that Meredith had arrived.

"What are you doing here?" she snapped.

"I believe it's my right to be here. I do own the place."

"That's not what I mean and you know it. Are you spying on me?" she accused.

"Should I be?" he asked coldly.

Ignoring his question, she retorted, "Once again, you have it all. You have an uncanny ability to always land on your feet regardless of the situation."

"As I see it, you've benefitted from my wealth. If you'd been in control of Shadowbrook, I'm sure it would have fallen to your creditors just as your own home did."

"I know you didn't come here to rehash my past, Court."

"No, I came to inform you that Jude is dead."

"Dead? But how?" she asked, shrieking in shock.

"He was manhandling Danielle, trying to force her to accompany him. Tobias defended her. Jude's knife was little defense against Tobias's angry blows."

In control of herself once more, Meredith lifted her chin haughtily. "And has Tobias been punished?"

"For what? He took his life in his hands when he faced Jude. He should be commended for his bravery."

She turned in a huff. "Have it your way, Court. You usually do."

"Meredith, why did you want to see Danielle?"

Her forced laughter filled the room. "I had hoped to convince her to help me patch the breach between us. Brotherly love, sisterly love...that sort of thing," she tossed out lightly.

"You'll have to do better than that, Meredith. Regardless of what you think, I'm no fool."

"Will that be all Court? I find this conversation is beginning to bore me."

"If you'll tell me where you sold my belongings,

I will try to recover them," Court said angrily. "And if I may add, if this townhouse had not belonged to our father, you would not find room and board here. I'll caution you only one more time, Meredith. Stay out of my way, or I'll toss you out of here."

Danielle Algernon Sinclair set a new style that evening at the opera, when she appeared dressed in a startling creation. Her gown of silk warp and worsted wool was a vibrant sea green. A wide neckline revealed her creamy flesh. Curved tucks in the bodice added an alluring fullness to her already ample breasts. Bishop sleeves, pleated tightly at the shoulders and full below, encased her slender arms. Her ear lobes sparkled with emerald and diamond chips; a wide gem-encrusted choker hugged her throat.

As they joined the queue entering the opera house, Danielle leaned close to Court and whispered, "Have I sprouted horns? I have this strange sensation I am being stared at."

He laughed. "Horns, my love?" With a bold wink, he added, "Maybe you've earned your angel's wings. Are they uncomfortable?"

"Angel's wings? Hmmm... only if they begin here," she answered placing her hand over her abdomen. "I do feel a slight flutter occasionally, other times a definite movement. Do you truly think I've earned my wings?" she teased.

His eyes followed her hand. His look became soft and liquid as he raised his gaze to her face. "I love you," he whispered.

The distinct clearing of a throat behind them caught their attention. Court quickly apologized for the delay and moved with Danielle into the theater. Their seats were in the dress circle. This was divided into stalls, each containing four seats. A curtain was drawn beside them, where other seats were situated for those in mourning.

After they were seated, Danielle, with discreet eyes, explored her surroundings. Then she leaned to Court, whispering, "I have decided you are the most handsome man here this evening."

He threw back his head and chuckled. "Ogling the men, are you, my pet?"

"Discreetly," she reminded him. Danielle appraised Court's handsome figure once again. His dress coat and pants were a deep gray, his shirt a snowy-white silk, and his cravat had just a hint of fullness. The cuffs of his shirt peeked just beneath the sleeve of his jacket, revealing diamond links matching his shirt studs. White kid gloves lay in readiness beside his white top hat.

As the curtain rose, Jordan and a lovely companion rushed to join them, and introductions were made hastily.

Danielle became absorbed in the performance and scarcely blinked an eye. During the intermission, Court and Jordan excused themselves to get refreshments while Danielle and Suzette Cheve, Jordan's companion, talked about the performance. From the corner of her eye, Danielle noticed the drawn curtains of the loge waver. She felt a premonition of danger for she knew no one was occupying the seats. In an instant the curtains parted and her nightmare took form and approached her.

Suzette saw the fear wash over Danielle's face and turned her head to find the source. She gasped and fell silent.

"I'm amazed that you're not flanked by protectors. I've been trying to catch you alone for weeks."

"I'm not alone, *monsieur.*"

"This will have to do," he replied coldly. "I

thought you might be interested in seeing your handiwork."

"I can assure you, Monsieur Pernel, you have nothing I desire to see."

"Whether you desire it or not, you shall see."

He jerked off the patch with a quick flick of his wrist, revealing an ugly, jagged scar that ran across his brow and ended in his hairline. A sightless eye rolled randomly in the socket, looking even larger with the absence of the eyelid. The scar was puckered, drawing the shape into an odd position.

"I'm terribly sorry for your misfortune, but you brought it on yourself." Her voice shook.

As though he had not heard her, he continued. "Shards of glass still work free from the scar." He idly ran his finger over the protrusion. "I suppose that's why it can't heal properly."

Suddenly noting that members of the audience were returning to their boxes, he repositioned the patch over his eye. With a blatant sneer, he cautioned, "Just don't get too comfortable, little lady, our business isn't completed yet."

Before she could respond, he was gone, the rippling of the curtains the only evidence of his departure.

"*Mon Dieu,* will it never end?" she cried.

Court comforted her when he returned, trying to control the rage that ripped through him. The pleasure of the outing had been ruined for her. The thought that Pernel could strike again tormented her.

As the curtains rose for the second act. Court spoke quietly with Jordan, and, assuring Danielle he would return shortly, he left silently.

Once out of the theater, he quickened his pace until he reached the older wing of the building that contained the Orleans Ballroom. Entering the room, he scanned the crowd. In a moment, he spotted his quarry, who had not taken pains to hide. As though the light would reveal his sins, Pernel had scurried to the darkest table to cheat unwary players. Court bided his time until Pernel had accumulated substantial winnings.

Approaching him from behind, he grabbed Pernel by the nape of the neck and lifted him from his chair. Kicking the chair aside, he shook him, watching with the other players as hidden cards fluttered to the floor. Pernel squealed like a rat and craned his neck to identify his assailant. He paled when he saw Court.

Court hurled him aside and peered angrily into his good eye. "You damn fool. You must place little value on your life. I won't stand idle and watch you destroy my wife."

"I—I don't know what you're t-talking about," Pernel stuttered, stalling for time. If he could only reach the derringer in his coat pocket, he would see Court Sinclair dead. Easing his hand cautiously to the pocket he wrapped his fingers around the cold metal. Not bothering to remove the gun, he positioned it in the direction of Court's chest. A vile expletive spewed from Pernel's mouth as he squeezed the trigger.

Court's foot slammed into the cloaked hand, causing the shot to go astray. Pernel's scream blended with the shouts of the spectators as they sought cover. Pain ripped up Pernel's arm. He tried to jerk his hand free of his pocket, but the force of Court's blow had wedged the gun to his crushed finger. Hammering blows riddled Pernel's senses and he sank helplessly to the floor. Court glared down at the sniveling figure.

Pernel rolled his battered head from side to side, cradling his rapidly swelling hand. "You broke my damn hand," he whined.

"Take heed, Pernel, if you want to stay alive, don't cross my path or my wife's again." Disgust evident in his features, Court turned on his heel, abandoning the attack.

Damien Baudier stepped into his path, announcing, "It has been my greatest wish to see that vermin brought to heel."

"My sincere hope is that this will deter him from tormenting Danielle at every turn," Court noted with a frown.

Damien smiled without humor. "If this didn't do the trick, your only recourse is Pernel's death."

Court nodded in agreement. If it weren't necessary to discover what Meredith and Pernel were plotting, he knew he would have killed him right then and there.

Torrential rains fell on New Orleans, filling the potholes to overflowing. Only those who had good reason attempted to travel the muddy streets.

Meredith paced back and forth within the rooms of the townhouse, bored and restless, her temper as volatile as the storm taking place outside. Stopping by a table, she reached for another piece of chocolate, and finding the box empty, cursed it and hurled it into the fireplace. She cursed Jude for dying and not being there to build a fire that would remove the cold, damp chill from the room. Damn him for being so ignorant, she swore, tugging her wrap tightly around her shoulders. She had always depended on him to run her errands and now there was no food left in the house. Her back hurt continuously from bringing in water for her bath, heating it, and then carrying it upstairs to the tub.

A knock on the door startled her. She peeked out the window through the sheets of rain to identify her visitor. She scowled and cursed again.

"I've told you not to come here in the daylight,"

she whispered angrily through the crack in the door.

Pushing his way in, Rankin Pernel gripped Meredith harshly by the arm and slammed the door with his foot. Rainwater dripped from his clothing and pooled around him. He pulled a gun from inside his coat, expecting Jude to come to the protection of his mistress. "Your big black had better stay where he is if he nows what's good for him."

"Jude?" she asked with a sharp laugh. "You don't have to worry about him." Seeing his bandaged hand and bruises on his already misshapen face, she asked, "What happened to you? You look like you were run over by a carriage."

Pernel thrust his gun back into his coat pocket. "That damn brother of yours is what happened to me. Last night I saw the happy couple going into the theater and managed to sneak up to her box while he stepped out at intermission." A look of madness passed over his features. "I wanted to show the little bitch what she did to me—and I did manage to do that. He found me later in the gaming house and beat the bloody hell out of me. He'll pay for this . . . later.

"You stupid bastard," Meredith shouted. "You were supposed to stay out of sight until everything was over, and off you go for a night at the opera."

"Dammit, I'm tired of hiding in the dark like some night creature," Pernel countered, glaring at her through the battered slit that was all that was left of his good eye.

"That was a stupid mistake, Pernel. Up until now Court has had no reason to link the two of us together. Now he must know you are the one who was passing himself off as Nicholas. He's not stupid by any means. If he sees you here, he'll know we're up to something. See my point, Rankin, darling?"

He frowned at her. "Well, at least he won't know to look for you here."

Turning from him, she walked into the small parlor. "Oh, but he has found that out already. He knew all along I wouldn't end up in the streets as Nicholas predicted. Why not use his townhouse?"

"He has someone spying on us?" he asked nervously.

"He came here, you idiot!" she exclaimed, whirling around to face him. "You asked about Jude? Well, Court came here to tell me one of Danielle's servants killed him."

"But why would he do that?"

"Because he was protecting his mistress from Jude. Oh, you might as well know," she said in exasperation. "When I discovered she and Court were in town, I had Jude follow her. His orders were to bring her to me if he could get her alone. My excuse for wanting to see her was to make amends between Court and me."

Pernel laughed. "And you call me stupid."

She flinched. "I was hoping to divert Court's attention from me by being agreeable. As it turned out, I lost a damned good servant."

"Did you tell Court this...I mean, about being agreeable and all?"

"Yes," she answered angrily.

"I gather he didn't believe you."

"No, after all that has happened, I didn't really expect him to, but I had to try."

Pernel did not press the issue. After they had their revenge and Meredith married him as she had promised, things would be different.

She noticed the sudden strange expression cross his face and felt uneasy. He had always repulsed her. But, now she needed him...later she would not.

Leaning in close to him, she reached up and

traced the length of the jagged scar. "We do have a common bond, Rankin, don't we? One that can make us very, very rich if we stick together."

"Then why are we waiting? The Sinclairs will surely be leaving Espérance now that your beloved Nicholas is home again." He clasped his hand around her wrist to halt her exploration of his face. "I wish I'd been there to take care of Nicholas in the beginning. Then there'd be one less thing we'd have to worry about."

"Let's forget what would have been, darling," she said smoothly, "and determine what will be."

Chapter 29

"Whew—ee!" Maybelle exclaimed, wiping the perspiration from her brow with the corner of her apron. She continued stirring the contents of the huge black pot, adding a sprinkle of this and a tad of that to its already appetizing contents.

Camille entered the cookhouse and sniffed the spicy aroma. "Is the jambalaya 'bout ready?"

"Almost," Maybelle said, putting the lid back on the pot. "Ifen it tastes as hot as the steam risin' from it, Massa Caraville may decide to hire hisself a new cook."

Camille giggled. "Why, Massa Caraville won't do no such thing. You has been 'round here longer'n him."

Maybelle pulled the bread out of the oven. "I reckon you's right. I sho' am gonna miss Mammy though. Won't be the same 'round here without her."

Seeing tears streaming down Maybelle's cheeks, Camille said tenderly, "Why, Maybelle, I ain't never seed you cryin' like that afore."

The cook straightened up immediately and wiped at the tears with the back of her hand. "I ain't cryin'... much. It's all the spices 'n' the heat what's in this room," she insisted.

"Ifen it's gonna be a minute afore it's ready, why don't you take a break and git some fresh air whilst I finish gittin' the table all ready?"

"I believes I will, chile," she said, following her outside.

Maybelle settled her robust frame in the rocking chair in the yard next to the cookhouse and Camille went on inside to tend to her chores. As Maybelle rocked, she mumbled, "I ain't gonna cry, no suhree. Mammy's gonna be happy where she's goin', so's I oughta be happy, too." She laughed through her tears. "Maybe that jambalaya will get me fired and Massa Sinclair will take me 'long too."

"Maybelle," a quiet voice called to her.

She cocked her head and listened, and then decided she had only imagined it.

"Maybelle, come here," the voice called to her.

The rocking chair halted as she peered all around her. "Now, who could that be callin' me? Could be that grandson of mine. I wonder what he's gotten hisself into this time." Rising from her chair, she left the cookhouse to find Jackson.

The full moon, partially obscured by moving gray clouds and towering pines, cast slanted shadows across the cookhouse and on the lone figure moving stealthily between the trees. No one heard the approaching footsteps except the small creatures, who scurried from the path of the intruder. The enticing scent of the jambalaya wafted through the cookhouse's open back door. Before entering, the figure peered inside, and then slipped in quietly. Pulling out a vial of belladonna from inside his black cloak, he opened it and lifted the lid of the simmering pot. He poured the contents over the jambalaya and hastily stirred it to blend the poison with the herbs. Hearing Maybelle's step approach the cookhouse, the figure quickly put the lid back on the pot and made his escape out the back door, disappearing into the dark woods.

"That's the strangest thing," Maybelle mused as she entered the cookhouse. "I woulda swore somebody was callin' me. Must be the heat gittin' to me," she decided, shrugging the matter aside.

Lifting the lid once again, she picked up the ladle, and spooned the jambalaya into the serving dish. Taking a long wooden spoon, she scraped the bottom of the pot to sample her favorite food.

As she opened her mouth, Camille's high-pitched voice startled her. The spoon dropped and clattered on the floor.

"Won't do no good to taste it now, Maybelle. They's all in the dinin' room waitin' for your specialty."

"You's right," Maybelle said, picking up the spoon and hastily sweeping up the rice from the floor. "It would jes' please me to death ifen they all comes back for seconds."

Fog swirled on the back of the still water. Heavy rains had swelled the river, forcing the excess to flood the bayous. The hooting of an owl startled the darkly clad pair.

"You're sure it was only an owl?" Pernel questioned.

"If it were my brother, I assure you he wouldn't take cover in the shadows."

"You're right," he agreed. "I've no desire to meet him face to face again," he added, stroking his bandaged hand.

"After tonight we needn't worry about that happening. Then . . . everything will be all mine," Meredith vowed.

"*Ours,*" Pernel reminded her in a cold voice.

"Oh, yes, ours," she amended quickly.

"I know you've planned this to the letter, but I can't help but wonder what your plans are for Court's mother."

Her cold voice chilled him. "She will be like putty in my hands when I take over Shadowbrook. She'll have no one left but me, the loving stepchild. Not only will Shadowbrook be mine, but Espérance as well. How do you think she will react?"

Pernel's evil chortle permeated the stillness. "I see what you mean. How long should we wait before going to the house?"

She rubbed her hands together in glee. "It won't be long now."

Around them, the undergrowth shook as though pushed aside, and the night creatures became silent in expectation. Neither Meredith or Pernel took note of this.

Meredith forced herself to move slowly to the tied horses. Draped around the saddle horn was a satchel. An empty vial was moved quickly aside as she dug deeply into the bag and removed a gun. Everything was going exactly as planned. The outcome would see her set for life without a blemish to taint the wealthy Meredith Caraville.

According to Rankin's ramblings, Court had threatened him with death should they ever meet again. That stupid fool had unknowingly set himself up to take the blame. When Rankin turned up dead everyone would think Court had killed him. It was of little concern because he would be dead, also . . . but she did not want to leave any room for speculation. She had protected herself at every turn.

She stepped close to Rankin as though to show affection. When he opened his arms she slammed the cold metal of the barrel against his chest. Disbelief washed over his distorted features.

"You've played your part well, Rankin . . . thank you." She squeezed the trigger.

Pernel gasped as the shot sent his body reeling backward.

Meredith threw back her head and laughed madly. It was time...time to return to Espérance and take possession of what should have been hers all along.

Melancholy cries filled the bayou, snapping Meredith to attention. "My God, what now?" she groaned, searching through the darkness for the source of the wailing. Seeing nothing, she dismissed the cries as her imagination and hastened to her horse. Suddenly the scent of lavender surrounded her. She began to run, but the scent became stronger and the sorrowful weeping grew louder. She fell and became tangled in brier. Heedless of the thorns tearing at her face and hands, she scrambled to her feet and scanned the darkness.

The moon now cast a bright light, creating a profusion of shadows that took form in Meredith's mind. "It's mine!" she shouted. "The money belongs to me!"

She turned in a circle, screaming hysterically, "It's mine!"

A fragrant breeze lifted strands of her disheveled hair. The shimmering of a gossamer veil caught her attention. "No!" she shouted once more. "No!" She backed away cautiously. It came closer. Cold air surrounded her as the glimmering veil wavered before her, taking shape.

She could hardly breathe as she viewed the transformation. Fear gripped and squeezed her heart as she continued to back away. The figure had long black hair that flowed almost to the ground. Her skin was palest ivory and the eyes were a strange golden color. Meredith shuddered. At that instant, she tripped over Pernel's body. Losing her balance, she fell head first into the murky water. Struggling to the surface, she gasped for air. The water seemed to suck at her flailing limbs.

When she could shake her tangled hair from her eyes, she lifted her face. "Oh, God, no," she sobbed. Hovering before her was the apparition. The beauty shrouded in the veil had transformed into a gray skull with gaping black holes where the eyes should have been. The mouth was a travesty of a lingering smile, the nose, a dark cavity. Madness claimed Meredith and the specter evaporated into the mist. The quicksand, disguised by the flooded bayou, sucked greedily until Meredith rested quietly in its arms.

Peace settled over the marshy land. Once more the bayou jargon returned: the trill of the whippoorwill as it called to its mate, the cadence of the crickets, and an ornery screech owl shouting "who" to no one in particular.

"I'll take the jambalaya first, then come back for the bread," Camille said as she picked up the steaming serving dish.

Pushing the door open with her foot, she headed for the dining room, humming a lively tune, its rhythmic tempo synchronized with the jaunty swing of her hips. Without warning, a furry creature darted across her path as she stepped forward. It became trapped within the folds of her skirt as her legs involuntarily scissored it. She lost her balance, which sent the dish sailing into the air, her screams vying with those of her small captive. Righting herself, she stared in bewilderment when a sleek black cat wiggled free and scrambled off into the night, its hair raised stiffly on its back and tail.

Tears pooled in her eyes and her lips trembled as she gazed down at the fluffy white rice with all its delicious meats and herbs scattering the path. The only thing remaining intact was the silver serving dish.

Maybelle, hearing the commotion, hurried outside. Her mouth dropped open as she gazed down at the jambalaya she had so painstakingly prepared. "Lawdy, Lawdy, Camille, what has you gone and done?"

Between choking sobs, she said softly, "It weren't my fault, Maybelle, honest it weren't. All of a sudden this black cat comes from outta nowhere smack dab in front of me."

"I ain't seen no black mousers 'round here in a long time."

Camille picked up the serving dish. Clucking her tongue and shaking her head, she said sorrowfully, "Black cat...bad luck...no dinner."

In the dining room, the soft glow from the chandelier spilled across the lawn. Inside could be heard the occupants' jubilant laughter and their lively conversation indicating they were not overly disturbed by the loss of their dinner.

Outside, a mysterious black cat sat atop a wagon wheel, backdropped by the full, luminous moon. As she unpretentiously groomed her glistening coat, she frequently raised her head and gazed toward the house with satisfaction glittering in her slanted, golden eyes.

of Espérance. It started me wondering again about the deaths of Meredith and Pernel."

"Do you want to tell me about your dream?" she asked.

Absently running his fingers over his mustache, he thought for a moment before he spoke. "This is going to sound crazy, but I've always thought the ghost of Espérance had something to do with our well-being."

Danielle considered this, then asked, "Why?"

"The empty vial of poison, the black cat tripping Camille—think about it, love."

"Do you really think..."

"I do," he answered. "Never again will I think of a black cat as being bad luck."

"Mon Dieu," she said, breathing deeply.

"I've never had cause to question the existence of ghosts one way or the other until..."

"I understand," she admitted.

"You know, when a ghost roams the earth, it's to set right whatever's causing its discontent, so it may enter the other side in peace. Supposedly," he added as though he were not completely comfortable with the idea, "the ghost of Espérance was searching for her lost lover. Until she found him she could have no peace."

"That's the story as far as I know it," Danielle concurred.

Court smiled. "In my dream we were back at Espérance. It was late at night and I couldn't sleep. I was standing at the window staring out over the river. Suddenly a fog billowed in from the river, swirling from tree to tree until it sank to the ground and spread its tentacles as though it were resting. I only blinked my eyes and the mist evaporated. A joyous cry filled the silence. I began searching frantically for the source. Just then a cloud covered the moon; I couldn't see anything.

When it moved away, I searched again. Almost out of sight was the ghost of Espérance. . . ."

"And?" she persisted.

"She wasn't alone."

"Her lover must have come back for her after all this time," Danielle exclaimed.

"Only in my dream."

"I would like to think they are finally together. Court?" she questioned, "would you have come for me?"

"Never doubt it for a minute, my pet." His hands began their familiar journey. As his mouth explored her neck and ear, he whispered, "I'd be draped in so many damn chains you'd hear me before you ever saw me."

"Chains?" she questioned.

He teased her lips. "To bind you to my side, so you could never leave me again."

She sighed with satisfaction as his mouth closed over hers.